Book 1: Interloper

"If you could see into the hearts of others, could you dare to look away?"

"If you possessed everything you could ever want, would you ever be satisfied with what you have?"

Jaiden Winters

Edited by R.J.T.

TABLE OF CONTENTS

Chapter 1

Those Who Are Blessed

She is blessed. That's what her life is. Either from the heavens above or from the goddess of luck herself. No matter what it is that she wanted in life, all she had to do was say the word, and it was hers. Who knew the reason why? Perhaps it is due to the natural beauty she obtained from her mother, her wealth, thanks to her father's world-renowned business, or the fame and social status she obtained on the internet. Freya Young thought it was a combination of all those things. After all, who wouldn't love her? She is perfect.

Freya held her head high and beckoned to her butler that was nearby.

"Herald, would you fetch me my favorite drink?" She asked

"Yes, Lady Freya. Right away." Herald politely replied.

Herald quickly scurried off at the sound of her command. It was getting late, and she had school in the morning so she usually sent one of her servants to fetch her a glass of warm milk heated at a perfect 65 degrees. Any colder and she would complain to her father, and any warmer Freya would risk damaging her tongue. Of course, perfection needed to match perfection, so Herald quickly returned and did not disappoint. As she took a sip of the beverage, the warmth hit the back of her throat putting Freya at ease.

"Very good, Herald. Go fetch the head maid of the house and have her prepare my bed chambers, as well as a bath." Freya ordered

"As you wish, Milady," Herald said with a bow.

Herald made haste with the order, elegantly rushing out the door. Meanwhile, Freya sat in her comfy red chair next to a fireplace, drinking her warm milk and reading a good book she pulled from a shelf from her family's library. She couldn't be bothered to read it, however. It wasn't that she didn't enjoy reading, it was merely the fact that she could only read something for an hour or so before she got bored of it and needed a break. Freya was the one who had her father install this library in her family's mansion. He had it done simply because she asked for it, like most things. After a few minutes, Freya left the book on the nightstand, substituting it for her phone. She knew her maid would clean up the glass and book later. Freya made sure not to reply to any of her friends. She did this so they would want her attention even more. After reading her now-opened texts, Freya began to scroll through social media.

"I wonder what I'll find on here," Freya said with a mischievous tone. She spent the next hour, looking at her classmates' posts, commenting on them, either being fake with some, or outright bullying others. Only to post a "Just joking!" on the ones she disliked, but only after all her fans ravaged whomever she pointed them at. Her fans were like a loaded gun and all she had to do was point them in the direction of a person's life she wanted to make miserable that day. She never felt bad about it either. She often thought things like *"They deserved it."* or *"Now they'll think twice next time."* the girls she would do this to would "fly too close to the sun", starting to climb up the ladder of popularity merely by being around Freya. There was one girl however that Freya felt as though she could tolerate, or even call a true friend. It was her childhood friend Destiny.

Destiny was the closest thing to a childhood friend that Freya had, If childhood friends were forced to spend time together because their parents were business partners. Freya's father came up with the ideas and provided the funds for their company Slowsoft, while Destiny's father was the one to develop the company's projects. Slowsoft was a world-renowned software development Company with many subsidiary branches. They had the means to quite literally make or buy out any company, idea, or patent they set their minds to. It was a 98:2 ratio of ownership. Freya's father owned the rights to the majority of the company. Still, her father considered his partner a good friend and often invited him over for dinner bringing Destiny along with him.

Despite their differences in wealth Freya and Destiny got along well growing up. At first, Freya thought of Destiny as a nuisance, who couldn't act seriously even if her life depended on it. However, over time her opinion of Destiny changed. The reason is that she never asked Freya for

3

anything. Even though she wasn't poor by any standard, she didn't have the power to ask for whatever she wanted. Everyone always wanted something from Freya. So when someone came along that just wanted to be friends with Freya and nothing more, it shook her world slightly.

Freya heard a beeping sound from her phone. She had received a text from Destiny.

Destiny: Hey! Are you excited for school tomorrow? I hear there is a new transfer student. Supposedly he's pretty cute.

Freya stared blankly at the message sent by Destiny. It was odd to get a transfer student after spring break as most people who joined that late would fall behind from the start. She honestly didn't care too much, she had her fair share of boys she dated in her first year of high school. She was more of a heartbreaker than anyone she knew. Dating just to entertain the thought in their head, only to crush their heart once they got too comfortable. Boys were like books to her. It's not her fault they became boring so quickly. It didn't help that they were not worthy of her beauty, fame, or status.

Freya: He's probably another idiot who's more trouble than he's worth.

She replied. Freya thought this about most boys her age, so to get back at them for wasting her time she would just break their hearts.

Destiny: Isn't that your opinion on all guys? If I were you I would at least be careful. Rumor has it that he's a delinquent who got kicked out of middle school. Break his heart and he might break your legs. Haha!

A chuckle escaped Freya's mouth, as she took Destiny's warning to heart. It wouldn't be the first time someone would have snapped at her. She did have an insane amount of crazed fanboys who would threaten or stalk her from time to time. However, she didn't fret over it, since one of her father's subsidiaries was a private security company. This was just the normal outcome of being famous. Everyone would want her. Freya messaged back some laughter and a quick goodbye as her head maid, Elise arrived through the doors.

"Your bath and room are ready for you milady." Elise bowed and gestured towards the door. "Is there anything else you need before bed Lady Freya?"

Freya shook her head no, and got up, putting her phone in her pocket. After waiting for Elise to leave, Freya walked out into the hallway making her way toward her freshly prepared bath. It was dark with only the moonlight from the windows lighting the hall. Several doors down she could see a light peak through a door crack. She knew exactly what room that was. It was her father's office. Freya was told never to go into that room while her father was working. He was a busy man who ran a multibillion-dollar corporation, so he couldn't be distracted or he would fall behind in his schedule. Freya crept up to the door peeking her eye through the crack. She saw her father working on several laptops at once, with a phone on his shoulder. He was on a business call.

Freya frowned as her father looked exhausted, but quickly felt a sense of pride as he was a sort of role model for her.

"You really can do anything you set your mind to," Freya muttered as she turned away quietly, making sure she didn't interrupt her father at work. Freya headed toward the bathroom which was a short walk away.

She stopped and looked through a hallway window staring up at the sky. Her gaze was met by the full moon when a thought came into her head. Freya couldn't remember the last time she had spent a day with her father. On her birthdays he would visit for an hour before going back to work. Most of their conversations happened at the dinner table, as her father always made sure he had a meal with his family if he was home of course. It was enough for Freya, and she knew if he could, he would make more time for her. After a minute passed, Freya snapped back into reality and continued walking towards her room. Another two minutes passed and she arrived.

Freya took a bath and got ready for bed. She sat down on her queen-size mattress placed in the center of her room and began to brush her hair. A thought occurred in her head. She wondered how long it would take for the new transfer student to be head over heels in love with her. So far, every guy she ever met instantly fell head over heels in love with her, so he shouldn't be an exception. She bet that because of his background as a delinquent, he would make a perfect school bodyguard. In the end, It didn't matter too much to her how it all turned out, as she would get her way regardless.

Freya looked around her large room and saw the many things she had been given, and felt as though something was missing. Perhaps she had forgotten or misplaced something. Unable to figure it out, she shrugged it off, lay in her bed, and fell asleep shortly after.

The next morning arrived and Freya was awakened by her personal handmaid. It was 5:30 AM. The school gates did not close until 7:30 AM. So, with plenty of time to spare, Freya got up. Freya's handmaid assisted her with a multitude of things. She would get her school uniform ready and even do her makeup for her. However, Freya didn't let anyone touch her luscious red locks of hair as she had some pride of course. This was a normal routine for her. Freya's maids helped with everything, whether that be getting outfits that Freya had personally picked out prepared for her, or cleaning the messes she made. They would even tutor her, not that it was necessary. Freya was one of the top three students in her school. She would spend most of her day after school studying to live up to her father's expectations. She tried her best to not just be a perfect student, but a perfect daughter that her dad could be proud of. After about thirty minutes of prep time, Freya was presentable enough to go downstairs and have breakfast with her family.

Freya lived upstairs in their large mansion. They had a built-in elevator she would use in the morning so she wouldn't build up any sweat on their large spiral staircase. She used the elevator and went down to the base floor, then she went to their family dining room. Awaiting her in the room where her family's large table stretched across the regal floor, was her mother Marine, and her head maid Elise standing at her side. Marine was gorgeous, nearly as pretty as Freya herself, but not quite. She had red auburn hair with luscious red lips and a blue hue to her eyes. Freya and her mother got along well as they would often chat about all the things that would happen in Freya's life during the week. It was almost as if her mother was living vicariously through her, re-experiencing her youth.

"Hello dear, you look absolutely lovely this morning. How is your homework going?" Marine asked.

"Good, I just finished it last night. Will Father be joining us this morning?" She asked as she took a seat across from her mother.

"I'm afraid not. He left late last night on a flight. He had another meeting to attend overseas." Freya was a little disappointed but didn't let her face show it. This was usually how most mornings turned out. Her father usually could only make it to dinner, so Freya foresaw this outcome as it was the norm.

"I see. Mother, isn't it a little early to be drinking wine? Don't you have a fashion meeting this morning?" Freya mentioned, as her mother was taking a sip of wine out of a crystal-cut glass.

"Well, whatever do you mean?" Marine choked on her words. This didn't happen too frequently, but whenever Freya's father was out of the house, she would occasionally open a bottle of wine, indulging in alcohol early in the morning. "This is how I get through long days. Be sure not to take after your mother dear. Also, have you thought about what you wanted for your upcoming birthday? Your father was asking. I told him you were going to have a party. He planned on stopping by." Freya has had a birthday party every year since she began attending Gilford Academy. Her mother suggested it would be a good idea to boost her popularity. So, they rented out the high-class restaurant Fiore Gemello. A five-star Italian restaurant, and only invited people she wanted to show off to. With one exception of course.

"A party would be fine, Mother. Elise, have someone send an invitation to Destiny. I would like her to be there." Freya answered.

"Very well, Lady Freya." Elise leaned forward with a bow. Freya waited until her Mother took another sip of her wine and asked a question she had on her mind for some time.

"Mother, what would you think if I brought a boy over to our house?" Marine spit out her drink from the shock of the question. It wasn't uncommon for Freya to have a new boyfriend each week, but she never introduced them to her family as she broke up soon after they got together.

"What has brought this up? I thought you found the boys at your school unworthy?" Marine replied after wiping the wine off her lips.

"I do. They are all a bunch of sheep drawn to their shepherd. It would probably kill them if they thought for themselves. I was just curious about your thoughts on the matter. However, supposedly a new transfer student is starting at our school as of today. Destiny said he was pretty cute from what she had heard. I was thinking about making him my new dog. Though, I hear he's a bad boy." Freya said jokingly.

"You know, your father was a bit of a bad boy too back in our youth. I'll hire a personal guard to be on watch, just in case, and have him conduct a background check on this boy. Although, this transfer student shouldn't be too rough around the edges. Gilford High School isn't exactly an easy school to get into. However, I suppose he could just be another charity case." Marine said with a laugh.

"Very Well. Having some protection nearby wouldn't hurt." Freya agreed. Marine was technically right about it. They wouldn't take in just anybody. Gilford High School was a prestigious private school with an acceptance rate of only thirty percent. To get in, you needed exceptional grades or a lot of money. Since Freya had never heard of this boy, she assumed he must be fairly smart, as the majority of other families got in because of their wealth. She knew most of the family names of the boys at her school, as they lived in the area nearby. In her opinion, most of them were outright idiots who shouldn't be allowed to breathe the same air as her.

"You're right, I must keep my little angel safe. Elise, have Officer Templeton be assigned to the high school for today. He should be off duty today. Have him keep an eye on the new student as well as conduct an extensive background check." Marine commanded while looking towards Elise.

"As you wish, Lady Prismarine (Priss-Mah-Reen)." Elise bowed once again and then rang a bell. Immediately after the chime was made, four maids entered the dining room and took Elise's place. Freya and Marine finished up the gossip as it was beginning to get late and Marine had to leave soon. They both finished their breakfast, said their goodbyes, and then went their separate ways for the day. It was 6:20 AM. Freya had some downtime to spend. So, Freya used the rest of her morning free time streaming a video of her for her followers to enjoy. She would entertain them with stories of grandeur and wealth. Showing off how nice of a home she had. In just a few years Freya had amassed over two million followers on several social media sites she used. Her growth of popularity had yet to slow down. After thirty minutes passed, Freya said her goodbyes to her fans and walked toward her front door. Before she left home, she was given a pre-made lunch by one of her maids. It was slotted into the pink and black custom-made leather backpack she had. Freya often switched out what she wore to what was trending at the time. Right now that trend is cat backpacks and pink ribbons.

"You look absolutely wonderful this morning Lady Freya." said the maid that gave Freya her lunch. This maid's name was Lily. Lily had platinum blonde silk-like hair that appeared almost white at first glance. She had a black and white French maid uniform on and was around the same age as Freya. Lily was a high schooler like Freya, though for whatever reason she worked for her family as her handmaid since Freya was eight years old. Lily was usually the one to clean up after Freya whenever she made a mess. She was also the one who helped Freya get ready in the morning. Although Freya didn't know it, Lily's opinion of her was ill-willed. She often secretly wished for misfortune to fall upon Freya for leaving messes behind everywhere she went. Despite all her hard work, Lily never got a break.

"Thank you, Lily," Freya replied. Though Lily was stating the obvious. Freya was gorgeous. She was often included in many of her mother's fashion shoots. Her mother liked to bring her along as people would tell Marine that the two looked like sisters. It was untrue, however. Though she had her mother's auburn hair and aquamarine blue eyes, as well as her slender figure. She had one thing her mother did not. Youth. She thought of herself as a future bride that men would only dream of. Men from her father's neighboring rival companies would often suggest marriage to unionize their businesses between the companies' children. Most thought it a great idea, as her beauty might boost company ratings. However, Freya's father always declined as he did not see any man fit for his daughter. He would then sever any ties with those companies for having the audacity to ask such a thing.

Lily bowed as Freya stepped outside. Parked on the side of the road waiting for her was Herald. He was in a white limousine, with blue-tinted windows. Herald was Freya's designated driver, who took her to school daily. Once Herald saw Freya exit the mansion, he stepped out of the vehicle, took Freya's backpack, and opened the back door for her. Freya got inside and sat down on a cooled black leather seat and strapped her safety belt on. Meanwhile, Herald took her bag and placed it in the trunk of the vehicle. He then proceeded into the driver's seat and began his daily route toward Gilford High School. Freya's home was approximately twenty minutes from the school. During the ride, she would play on her phone without a care in the world. Everything was going smoothly until the sound of rubber tires clashing with the concrete road, accompanied by the honking of car horns was heard up ahead at a stop light. Herald stomped on his brakes causing Freya to jerk forward only to be caught on her safety belt, making her phone fly out of her hand.

"Hey! Are you crazy? Get off the road maniac!" An angry driver a few cars ahead of them, up by the crosswalk screamed. Freya picked up her phone off the floor and dusted it off. Afterward, she looked up at all the commotion only to see a boy on the ground. He was laying down at the end of the sidewalk by the stoplight pole.

"He is pretty bruised up," she thought. He had curly black hair and wore glasses, though it looked like his glasses may have broken from the predicament. What surprised her was what the boy was wearing. It was the Gilford High School uniform. Their school had the boys wear a black dress shirt, red ascot, and white undershirt, accompanied by black and white checkered pants, a black leather belt, and black dress shoes. The girls wore a black cardigan, red bow, white undershirt, and a black skirt, with black flats for dress shoes.

Freya was surprised again after seeing what the boy was holding in his arms. It was a cat. A kitten to be exact as the animal barely looked six months old. The boy got up and dusted himself off, while holding on to the cat in one arm, and then began to check if the feline had any injuries.

"Are you okay Lady Freya?" Herald questioned with concern, as he rolled down the window that separated the two.

"Yes, I am quite all right. Thank you." Freya answered without glancing at Herald, as she was too busy captivated by the boy. The boy politely bowed towards the angry driver, apologizing profusely numerous times. The driver seemed less upset after he saw what the boy was holding. He scolded the boy and then continued, trying not to hold traffic. Once traffic began to move, Herald joined in and continued to drive Freya to school. When the limousine passed the boy, he turned and looked at it. Freya knew he couldn't see her, as their windows were made with a reflective tint, somewhat like a one-way mirror or sunglasses. However the boy must have seen himself in the mirror, as he looked upset he dirtied his school uniform and broke his glasses. That pout quickly switched to a smile as he held the uninjured cat he rescued up in the air. At that point, Freya lost sight of the boy. She couldn't help but think about him during the rest of the ride up. She wondered if he was the new transfer student that started at her school today, as she didn't recognize him. She hoped that if he was, the two would share the same classes, so she could make him her new boyfriend. She couldn't possibly understand why he would risk his life for some stray, but she admired his bravery and hoped to meet him. If he would risk his life for a cat, she could only imagine the undying loyalty someone like him would devote to her.

Some time passed and Freya arrived at Gilford Academy. It was a private school that had different buildings depending on what grade you were in. Since Freya was in tenth grade, she went to Gilford High School. The building's color was a bright white, that almost glistened with the reflection of the morning sun. Herald parked the limousine, opened the trunk of the vehicle, retrieved Freya's bags, and then opened the door for her. After she got out he handed Freya her bag and wished her a good day taking off shortly after. Students were flowing into the school's entrance, but many of them stopped in awe of Freya and her luxurious ride. She pretended not to notice, flipped her hair, and began walking past the gate guard. It was Officer Templeton, the police officer that her mother requested to be on guard duty today. Templeton was part of a police department but also helped Freya's father as a private investigator. He often was requested to guard Freya in many events, due to him being overprotective. When the two met eyes, Freya nodded, and Templeton nodded back.

"Be Careful today Ms. Freya. I conducted a background check on the new transfer student. His name is Reighley Summers (Ray-Lee Sum-Mers) and he has a criminal record for assault. Just say the word and I'll have the kid thrown in the slammer." Templeton said, giving Freya a thumbs up.

"He shouldn't be anything I can't handle," Freya replied jokingly while making sure to keep a mental note of the boy's name. "Reighley, huh?" she whispered curiously. With all eyes on her, Freya began to walk into school, only to be interrupted by a voice behind her that she recognized. She looked back with a smile. Waving at her with a cheery demeanor, was Destiny. Freya stopped and waited for her friend to catch up with her before the two continued into the school together.

"You had a pretty nice livestream this morning, those boys were all over you," Destiny mentioned.

"Thanks, It helps that you moderate it. I wouldn't be able to handle all the creeps by myself." Freya replied. Destiny watched Freya's live streams and managed her websites. Even though she could have hired a professional to do that, Freya didn't mind. Destiny enjoyed that sort of thing. Plus, it was Freya's idea to let her help. It was her way of saying thanks for being her friend for all these years.

"Make sure you keep your eyes peeled. He's here. I can smell it." Destiny squinted her eyes and glanced around the halls, sniffing the air.

"What are you talking about?" Freya decided to play dumb, she knew that Destiny was talking about Reighley, but decided not to interrupt her little game.

"It smells like a criminal." Destiny boasted. "My crime sniffer never lies."

"Crime sniffer?" Freya couldn't help but laugh. "I better be sure not to commit any crimes near you then, I don't think I could avoid your sleuthing skills." The two laughed and carried onward to their class.

Freya asked her father to make arrangements so Destiny and she would have the same classes together. Since Freya's father was a heavy financial supporter of the school, they said yes. The two walked and talked more while heading to class. Freya told Destiny all about the boy she saw and the cat he saved. Shortly after the two arrived at room 2-B. They started their day with a History class. While walking through the halls Freya felt many gazes on her as she passed. That feeling didn't change when she arrived in her classroom either. When she walked inside she felt eyes lock onto her, as people began to whisper things about her. She gracefully walked towards her desk, batting an eye at the boys that stared at her. Infatuated was the word she would use to describe their reaction. Once she sat down, Destiny joined her as her desk was right in front of Freya's. The two pulled out their history books and prepared for the start of class.

8:00 AM came quickly and all the students in the classroom rushed towards their seats when the school bell rang. Everyone took their seats, but there was one empty desk remaining. It was just left of Freya, by the window. She saw it and couldn't help but hope it was Reighley's new desk. Freya's thoughts were shortened as the class history teacher Mr. Rugborn walked in through the door. He walked in towards his podium and pulled out a piece of white chalk.

"Good morning class." He greeted as he began to write a name on the blackboard behind him. "I'm sure some of you are aware, but we have a new transfer student coming to join our school starting today." He finished writing and turned to reveal the name Reighley Summers on the board. Freya's heart began to race as the entire class was filled with excitement and chatter until interrupted by Mr. Rugborn. "Settle down class. Let's make sure to welcome Mr. Summers to our class. Reighley, you may come in now." At his command, the door opened, and through came a boy in a tattered school uniform. "Come introduce yourself." Mr. Rugborn leaned in and whispered something into Reighley's ear, and was only given a nod in response.

"Hello, I am Reighley Summers. Thanks for having me." Reighley bowed politely.

"Your desk is over there in the far back over by Ms. Young." Mr. Rugborn pointed toward the desk right next to Freya. After a brief pause, Reighley walked over to his new desk and sat down. The classroom began to whisper about his appearance, some wondered why his clothes were so dirty, while others made jokes about being careful not to anger him. Freya however, couldn't keep her eyes off him. As he walked over to his desk, finally their eyes met and she couldn't have been happier by the outcome. Once any man would take a single look into her eyes, they would be lost to her charms. She had him right where she wanted him. It was perfect, she thought. There was no way he couldn't fall for her now. All she had to do was have him bask in her beauty and he would be wrapped around her finger. Freya heard a girl to the right of her mention that he was cute looking and quickly gave the girl a death glare, squashing any hope the girl may have. She also noticed that Reighley was starting to get envious stares at him, just for being lucky enough to sit by her. She waved over at the boys to cool their daggers for eyes and was successful. When class began, Freya began to take notes from class making sure not to miss anything. However, whenever the opportunity arose, she would look over at Reighley. He didn't look back a single time after their first initial glance, but that didn't matter to her. He must have been nervous after all, having the prettiest girl in school give him attention out of nowhere would make anyone freak out.

Time flew by for Freya, and before she knew it, history class was over and Mr. Rugborn left the classroom for the next teacher to switch with him. After the bell rang, many of the students got up and rushed over toward Freya and Reighley, surrounding the two.

"Do you two know each other?" a student asked.

"Yeah! Freya was looking at you the entire time during class!" said another.

"No… I've never met her before. I'm actually new to the area, so I don't know just about anyone here." Reighley perked up to the accusations with a quick response. Freya couldn't help but smile at him.

"Say, Reighley was it? I am Freya Young." She pretended that she didn't already know his name and leaned toward him on her desk, giving him a mischievous look.

"How about I give you a tour of the school grounds once our classes are over? It would be just the two of us." The crowd gasped. Her plan was simple. She would spend the rest of the day with Reighley, and after she finished showing him around she would ask him out.

"Thanks, but no," Reighley responded. "I should be fine on my own." Some gasps from the crowd turned into shouts, as a small uproar began from his response. It was loud enough that some people began crowding in from other classes. Freya was shocked but didn't give up right then and there. She thought that he must not want to bother a beauty like herself. So, Freya decided to be a bit more bold and upfront with what she wanted.

"Well, aren't you shy? How about you come over to my private library and I help you get caught up with all the subjects you're behind on?" She was asking him out in front of the entire class, and then some. Several girls behind Freya became lightheaded after her offer, and many of the guys were filled with a passionate rage of envy. They wished they were in his shoes. Several people at the school would kill for some alone time with her. It was an offer of a lifetime.

"I'll have to pass. Sorry." Reighley turned her down politely. There was an awkward silence, and Freya was dumbfounded. No one had ever told her no. Not a day in her life passed that she didn't get exactly what she wanted, so it didn't make any sense. How could he turn her down when she was the perfect woman? Freya turned a bright red from sheer embarrassment and stood up from her desk.

"I must need my ears checked because it sounded like you turned down my offer," Freya spoke in an upset tone. She proceeded to walk over to Reighley's desk just a few steps away. "I would like to make you my boyfriend." She guessed she must not have been clear enough. With her face still red as a tomato, Freya leaned over, placing her hand on his desk. "So, what do you say?"

"I'm good, thanks. Besides, I don't even know you and something tells me that if I did say yes, you would just dump me the week after." The crowd looked displeased by the answer.

Freya's whole world turned upside down all at once. Her head began to spin. Not only did he turn her down three times in a row, but he also saw right through her plan and her intentions. Completely out of options, Freya stormed out of the classroom after grabbing Destiny by the hand.

"This isn't over!" She said, Dragging her friend out of her desk, she slammed the glass door behind her and stomped away.

Chapter 2

Those Who Are Cursed

He was cursed. Things always seemed to end up stacked against him. Though, there wasn't anything he could do about it. As far back as Reighley could remember he could always tell people's true intentions. He could see their true colors, quite literally in fact. Whenever Reighley looked another person in the eyes, a color would drown out everything else to some degree. The color represented what type of person lay behind those eyes. If it was a lighter color, then generally that person was genuine or some other type of positive trait. However, if the color the person had was darker, then that person was not worth his time by a long shot.

"How is everyone I've met so far in this school so malicious?" He couldn't believe it. Every pair of eyes he had met so far had yet to be a bright color. It's not like it was too rare for him to see. Plenty of people he knew back in his hometown were bright. His mother, and his younger sister for example, not to mention all the animals he's seen. Reighley tended to trust animals more than people because he could read them like a book. If they were vicious and wished to eat him, they would be a bright red. If they were kind, they would have a gentle sky blue. However, when a person's color was red, that could mean several things. Dark red usually meant the person had some sort of aggression. While a light red meant more of a desire or passion. So when he saw a rabid dog with a bright red at least he knew what he was in for. All animals had bright colors, as their intentions are pure. People on the other hand were a wild card.

He ended up calling the color around the people he saw, an aura. When he was growing up he didn't understand exactly what the colors meant until he was in middle school. During that time he also learned that the aura's color wasn't set in stone either. The hue could change with time. From light to dark or vice versa. The more people he met, the better grasp he had on who they were from just a look. At this point, he could get a general estimation of how someone might be, but not the specifics. The downside to this was that he couldn't turn this ability off.

When Reighley walked into Gilford High School, he thought about the problem at hand. The cat he rescued, and his dirty uniform. It all started this morning when Reighley woke up at 6:00 AM. His younger sister Isabelle would wake him up if he missed his alarm.

"Hey! Time to wake up. You'll miss breakfast at this point." Reighley was awakened by a splash of cold water hitting his face, as Isabelle poured a small amount of water on him from a cup. "If I hear you say 'five more minutes again.' I'll bring an entire bucket up next time." It's our first day at school." Reighley looked up with annoyance at his sister, but quickly cooled his temper as he was the one who asked her to wake him up, by whatever means necessary.

"Okay, okay, I get it. Sheesh!" Reighley sat up on his twin-size mattress and wiped his face with his hands. "Did you have to pour water on me?" he asked.

"Yes, yes I did. I tried waking you up plenty of times. I've been trying since 5:30 AM." Isabelle retorted.

"Well... Fair enough." Reighley stretched his arms and yawned and looked over at his sister. She was already ready for school. He felt kind of bad since that meant she was up long before him, to get ready in time. He made a mental note that he owed her one, and then proceeded to kick her out of his room. "Thanks. Now get out, please. I have to get ready now."

Isabelle was fairly short, being only 5 '1, and had black curly hair up in twin ponytails, with bangs that reached down to her eyebrows. She was two years younger than him, only thirteen years old. She would probably end up joining his school next year, as she was starting classes at Gilford Middle School today. Reighley thought of his sister as someone he needed to protect. He was constantly looking after her since he knew she couldn't always handle things by herself ever since their dad left the picture. His sister had a light blue aura around her, and to Reighley, he would want to keep it that way, as it meant she hadn't changed since they were little. Light blue auras around someone would tell Reighley that the person he was looking at was genuinely kind, gentle, or calm.

He didn't know too many people of that color, so that's why he swore to protect his sister if needed.

Reighley spent fifteen minutes getting ready; from brushing his teeth to his hair and then eventually changing out of his pajamas into his school uniform. After he finished, he looked into his mirror in the bathroom, and couldn't help but dislike the school uniform. It was too flashy for him. He preferred to wear all black if he could, but the checkered pants were just too much for him to take seriously. He decided it was worth it, however, as this school was his ticket out of poverty. His dad left his family when he was only eight. Due to that, his mother ended up taking the financial burden of the household. He despised his father for that. Reighley decided to take it upon himself to become the man of the house, eventually getting a job and enough wealth so that his mother and sister would never have to work again.

Reighley and his family lived in a small home with only two bedrooms and one bathroom. However, he wanted his sister to have her own room so Reighley lived in their garage. They had only been living in town for three months, but Reighley took up the challenge of making his room suitable to live in. He built himself a hammock and used some of the money he saved up during his summer job to buy a bunk bed. He took out the lower half of it and slotted in a couch he found from someone's curb. He considered the old proverb "one man's trash is another man's treasure" as a universal truth over time, as he had collected an abundance of things people would just throw away. TVs, sports gear, games, and even the bike he had. At this point, it became a hobby of his to ride his bike he found around looking for more treasures on the street.

"Reighley, come eat!" he heard a voice shout from outside the bathroom. It was his mom calling out for him.

"On my way," he answered, as he made his way to the dining room and arrived to see his mother Jericho, and his sister Isabelle, waiting for him to join them for breakfast. "Sorry to keep you waiting." Reighley apologized and sat down with his family and started eating.

"So, are you ready for today?" asked Jericho.

"Yep." both kids replied. Jericho was somewhere in her mid-thirties. She always made it a point to never tell anyone her age, trying the whole "forever thirty" thing. She had long brown hair, and green eyes, and looked no older than twenty-seven. Reighley thought of her as the hardest-working person he knew. She always pushed herself in order to provide for her family. She worked two jobs, with no days off just so she and her kids could get by. He felt bad about it all since she also did all the cleaning and cooking in the small amount of time she did have. She had a heart of gold according to him and her aura reflected it as it gave off a yellow hue. Yellow auras usually meant that the person in question was selfless, encouraging, and generous. Reighley feared she would work herself to death. That's why it was so important to him to graduate at the top of his class at Gilford High.

"I hear that Gilford Academy is pretty strict. You two do your best okay? Don't push yourself too hard for my sake." Jericho mentioned as she looked down at her watch. "We'll have to eat on the way, or I'll be late for work. Reighley, are you okay with walking to school?" His mom only had a two-seated vehicle, so he outed himself to start walking to school so his sister could have a ride. He made the excuse that it was a good exercise for him.

"Yeah, I'll be fine. You guys drive safely." Reighley replied with a smile. Both his sister and his mother said their goodbyes for the day and headed out to their car, leaving him all by himself. After some mental preparation and a good breakfast, he quickly made his way out toward school.

He had just moved to San Fran, Kyoto in the US. A city with a population of over 1,000,000. The city was made as a place of unison between cultures, as Japanese and Americans lived together. Although he would ride his bike around often he wasn't too familiar with the area just yet. Reighley walked for some time through the city, trying to remember the route he claimed he knew. He only told his mother that, so she wouldn't worry. Reighley didn't have a smartphone either, only an old flip phone to make calls, which meant there was no GPS for him to follow. He didn't worry too much though, as if things got dire he would simply ask for directions. He finally arrived at a crossroads and began to recognize his surroundings a bit. Since he rode his bike often he knew the area somewhat. He made sure not to overexert himself today as sweating a lot would make his curly hair look like an afro.

He would die from embarrassment on the first day of school if he showed up looking like that. Suddenly he noticed something on the road. Across from Reighley to his right, in the middle of the crosswalk was a cat. He quickly glanced up at the light and noticed that the oncoming traffic that way had a green light. The cat looked into his eyes, and he saw a light purple aura resonating from it. Light purple usually meant loyal, proud, and honorable. After a brief moment of hesitation, he panicked but then decided to save the cat. Reighley launched forward onto the road, with an explosive first step. With a high amount of adrenaline rushing through him, he rushed onto the crosswalk. When he reached the cat he bent down and scooped it up into his arms. At this point, oncoming traffic began to honk at him as they were several meters from him. On instinct alone, Reighley dove only to tumble and crash into the sidewalk on the other side. His head was spinning from the event, but he quickly gathered his senses as he heard the voice of someone shouting at him.

"Hey! Are you crazy? Get off the road maniac!" The noise came from an angry driver, presumably the one who almost hit him. Reighley got up and brushed himself off, and then proceeded to check if the cat was okay. To his relief, it didn't have a single scratch on it. He on the other hand was pretty bruised up. His glasses had cracks in them and his uniform got dirtied and had some tares in it. Seeing the man was waiting Reighley rushed over to him and began to apologize profusely.

"I'm so sorry sir! It's all completely my fault!" Reighley said with a bow. The driver had a partially bald head with a combover covering it and was stout looking. He seemed angry until he heard a meow coming from Reighleys hip. His demeanor changed as he saw the black cat with blue eyes Reighley had just rescued.

"Is the little guy all right?" The stranger asked.

"Yeah, it looks like it's fine, thankfully," Reighley answered.

"Don't be doing risky stuff like that. I don't want the thought of killing a boy and his cat in my conscience."

"Yes sir. Sorry sir!" Reighley apologized again.

"I'm holding up traffic so as long as you two are okay I'm going to head out."

"We are fine. Thank you, sir!" The driver took off soon after. When several vehicles passed, Reighley noticed a limousine passing by. It was white and had blue reflective windows. The limousine looked like it cost a small fortune as it didn't have any branding on it making him think it was a custom model. Reighley looked into the reflection of the glass making sure not to make direct eye contact with himself. He saw how dirty he had got his new uniform, and how he was riddled with bruises. He already knew his glasses were broken, but knowing that they cracked didn't help his mood either. His mood switched to relief of gratitude, as he was thankful that he was able to make it in time to save the poor helpless kitten. Reighley held up the cat in both arms and looked it in the eyes.

"You almost got me killed, you know?" He said and was given a meow in return. "You're just too cute to stay mad at."

A thought occurred in Reighley's head. His sister had been asking for a family pet for a while now. This was the perfect way to take care of the debt that he owed. Though, he wouldn't give her the cat as he was the one who risked his life for it. He would have to think of a name for it later. As for now, he needed to rush to school. He put the cat into his backpack, left the top unzipped for air, and made his way to Gilford High School. When he arrived he saw a large building that seemed a little exotic for his tastes. It looked as if someone dumped glitter into the paint mixture, as it almost had a blinding reflection to it. He walked towards the school gate and it looked like he had made it in time, as it was still open for him. When he passed his eyes met with a police officer that was on guard duty.

"Hey! Hold it right there mister." The officer held his arm in front of Reighley preventing him from going any further. "I recognize the face of trouble when I see it. If I hear that you cause any trouble to Ms. Young or her friends, you'll end up behind bars bucko."

"I don't even know who those people are sir." Great. He was being harassed only after taking his first step onto school grounds. The officer had a slightly dark green color to his aura. Green usually meant that the person was earnest, jolly, and easygoing. Since the officer's color was not completely dark, he assumed the man was missing the easygoing, and jolly part of him, and in its place was most likely some of the traits that came with a dark green. Those were envy, toxicity, and bitterness. He had no idea why a police officer would specify who he wasn't supposed to bother unless of course they were hired specifically for that individual's sake.

"Good. Now let's keep it that way. I don't want any assaults on the school grounds." The officer removed his hand out of the way letting Reighley pass, although being stopped by the cop grabbed the attention of several students nearby. Reighley wasn't too surprised that he knew about his record. To Gilford High, Reighley was a charity case. The only reason he had made it into the school was because of two things. His perfect grades since his incident, and the fact he knew the school nurse that worked there. She had recommended him to the principal, allowing Reighley to have just enough leverage to join the school.

When Reighley's eyes met the other students of the crowd ahead, he was astonished. The auras he saw were riddled with darkness. Not one aura he saw in the small crowd of students was brightly colored, though those colors varied.

Keeping his head down he decided to keep walking, making his way indoors. He was cursed. No matter where he looked, the eyes he met always gave off a dark aura behind them. This was the exact thing that happened to him in middle school. Everyone he knew except a few friends at Glasgow Middle School was riddled with dark auras. When he finally realized what the auras meant, it was too late and that's when the incident happened. His assault. Reighley knew it wasn't his fault, and that he did the right thing back then, but hoped there wouldn't be a repeat of what happened before.

While walking, an idea came to mind. What would he do with the cat in the backpack? He would just give it to Kaede, the school nurse until school was over. The plan was simple, but he didn't know where the Nurse's Office was. Desperate he looked around in the hope that perhaps someone would be kind here, and give him directions. In the end, all he got were weird looks and people whispering about his uniform. Finally, after searching in a sea of endless dark auras, a light shined through. It was a girl who was leaning up against her locker. She had blonde hair that was in a ponytail and green eyes. She had a pure light green aura to her. Seeing it was like feeling a cool breeze from outside after being in a sauna. She was chatting with another girl with brown eyes, freckles, and brown hair with a blue ribbon pinned to the side of it. This was his hope. A chance to find directions before class started and maybe a chance to make his first friend at school.

"Hello. Sorry to bother you… but do you know where the Nurse's Office is?" Reighley asked politely.

"Oh, I've never seen you before. Are you new here?" The blonde stranger replied.

"Yeah, I just transferred here so, I'm not actually sure where anything is."

"I thought so." The girl quickly explained to Reighley where the Nurse's Office was and then asked a question out of curiosity. "What happened to you? Your glasses are cracked and your uniform is a complete mess." While the stranger was talking he looked over at her friend to see her aura. To his surprise, it was a color he had never seen before. It was lighter turquoise. Occasionally, Reighley would see a blend of colors that would have some sort of combination of the traits that they were associated with, but it was rare to see. He wondered what traits she could have.

"Can you two keep a secret?" Reighley asked, looking at the two girls. They both nodded in response. "I saved a kitten from being run over while on my way to school." Both girls looked at him with disbelief. Reighley showed the two what was in his backpack, being careful not to draw too much attention their way.

"Aww! It's so cute." The brunette whispered.

"What's its name?" The blonde asked quietly.

"I haven't given it a name yet, but I should introduce myself. I'm Reighley Summers. Nice to meet the two of you." Reighley mentioned with a nod.

"Likewise. The name is Ash Fjord." The brunette said. "Don't let the teachers see you with that cutie or you might get suspended on the first day."

"My name is Samira Tempest. It's a pleasure to meet you." The blonde replied. Reighley chatted with the two and also asked for directions for class. He was quite relieved that he met some kind people on his first day. After saying his goodbyes, he couldn't help but think that others were staring at him the whole time secretly judging him. He had hoped that was not the case, as he had wished for a fresh start at Gilford Academy. With not much time to think about the matter, he made his way to the nurse's office.

Kaede was currently busy writing up an excuse note for a young boy who was a freshman with a sprained ankle before hearing a knock on her door. She helped the boy up after she treated his injury and gave him crutches as well as an extra wrap for his foot. When she held the door open to her surprise it was someone she hadn't seen since she went to nursing school. It was Reighley Summers. The last time she had seen him was at his family's Christmas party held four years ago. Of course, the two chatted every so often via text. She was the one who recommended him to the school. After waiting for the student she helped to leave, she hugged Reighley. She thought he looked adorable in his school uniform even though it was dirty. He was like family to her. They grew up in the same apartment complex and played a lot when they were younger.

"Reighley!" She said while latching on to him.

"Hey! What's wrong with you? Someone might have the wrong idea." He said while looking embarrassed. To Reighley, Kaede was family. Throughout his childhood the two's families were close. Always gathering and having parties. Those things happened less when Reighley's dad left but they still happened on occasion. However, Kaede always made sure to look out for him and check up on him. He appreciated her. So that's why he let her have this. He owed it to her at the very least. When he looked into her eyes he saw a pink aura telling him she hadn't changed in the slightest. Pink auras were inherently always light and usually meant that the person in question was loving, affectionate, and compassionate. He liked to think "overbearing" was included in some aspect of it all.

"Oh please. No one even comes in here." She said as she pulled him inside by the arm.

"You just had a patient!" Reighley yelped while being forcibly pulled in. Kaede looked at the young man standing in front of her and couldn't believe how tall he had become. She felt a bit somber realizing it had been so long since they last saw each other. He had completely outgrown her. He was roughly 183cm tall and his hair had grown out a noticeable amount, curling up at the tips. Gathering her thoughts she went into "nurse mode" to ask why he looked so battered and bruised.

"Just what on earth happened to you that you ended up looking like you got into a bar fight?" She immediately sat him down and began to check his face for any serious injuries.

"That's actually why I am here," Reighley said. He looked annoyed that Kaede started worrying about him. When he said this, Kaede paused what she was doing and waited for a response. "You see…" Reighley pulled the cat out of the bag, quite literally. "I rescued this little guy out on the road and I need you to watch after it for me until the end of class today." He held up the black feline and handed it out to Kaede.

"Wait just a second. You know I have allergies." Kaede said after an immediate sneeze.

"Yeah, but it's just a runny nose and besides, you're the only one I can turn to for this." Kaede stopped arguing and looked down at the cat now in her hand. She looked back up at Reighley who looked desperate for help. How could she turn him down in his time of need?

"Well fine, just this once." She couldn't say no. She found an old medical box, put the cat inside, and went back to make sure Reighley was okay. The kitten began to throw a fit in the box. It didn't like being cramped up after being in Reighley's bag all day.

"Thanks, Kaede. I owe you one." Reighley said with a grateful smile that melted her heart. After she finished checking his injuries. He got up and headed towards the door as it was almost time for his class to start.

"Take better care of yourself, okay?" she asked. Reighley paused while his hand was on the door handle and looked back and nodded, making his exit a quiet one.

Reighley made a quick haste since he wasn't concerned about being too rough with the cat out of his bag. He followed the directions that Ash and Samira gave him and headed upstairs to class 2-B. During the entire trip there he received weird looks from many of the students and several teachers as well. When he arrived the school bell rang signaling class was starting. Outside of the classroom door was a middle-aged man with glasses on. He looked like he was waiting for Reighley as once he saw him arrive, he perked up with a grimace. He had a brown aura to him. Brown auras usually meant that the person in question was conservative to a certain degree, and didn't like change much. It was one of those colors similar to pink as it wasn't light or dark, it was just brown.

"You were almost late." The man said.

"Sorry sir. I had to stop at the Nurse's Office because of an injury." Reighley obviously couldn't tell the teacher about the cat he brought into school, otherwise, he would be in for a lot of trouble.

"I see... Well don't let it happen again, and don't be causing any of the students here any problems, got it?" The teacher stated.

"Yes sir." He replied.

"Good, and that's Mr. Rugborn to you. Now wait out here until I call you inside. I'll have you introduce yourself to the whole class and then you'll sit by Ms. Young."

"Ms. Young?" Reighley questioned knowing that was the name the officer gave him a warning about.

"Yes. Her father is a large financial contributor to this establishment. I'm placing you near her so you'll behave." Reighley wasn't exactly sure what he meant by that but he nodded in agreement. Immediately Mr. Rugborn went into the class leaving Reighley alone in a now empty hall. A small amount of time went by before Reighley heard the signal for him to enter.

When Reighley entered the classroom, all eyes were on him.

"Come introduce yourself." Mr. Rugborn said. Reighley noticed his name was written in chalk on the whiteboard behind his teacher. He walked up to him and turned towards the class.

"Remember what I said. Don't cause any trouble for Ms. Young or her friends." Mr. Rugborn whispered into his ear. Reighley replied with a nod.

"Hello, I am Reighley Summers. Thanks for having me." Reighley said with a bow. He didn't like the attention too much but he used this moment as an opportunity to check the auras of the students in his class. The classroom setup was standard. The desks consisted of five rows. Each row has six students, with the exception of the last row. That row had an empty desk by the window. Reighley noticed that the people in the front row had dark auras. However, to his relief, every row after that had a couple or more people with lighter auras in each of them. He was starting to think that things might not be all that bad until his eyes met with a girl in the back row next to the empty desk. She had auburn red hair and shimmering blue eyes. On the surface, she was gorgeous. However, the girl's aura was quite shock-inducing to Reighley. It was a deep dark purple that almost appeared black. Unlike light purple auras that were affiliated with loyalty, pride, and honor, dark purple auras meant the person associated was greedy, arrogant, and pompous. The worst part of it was the aura had a shape. Occasionally auras attached to people with strong personalities would grow a form to them. Her aura was like an arrow pointing to what she wanted. It pointed directly at Reighley like a billboard sign to a restaurant or bar. He had never seen an aura quite like hers. He knew she was trouble so he decided he would attempt to ignore this crazed girl.

"Your desk is over there in the far back over by Ms. Young." Mr. Rugborn said as he pointed to the desk next to the empty desk by the girl whom he had just told himself not to acknowledge. Reighley finally understood the warnings he had been given. This was the girl that the police officer had mentioned, as well as his teacher. So after a brief pause, he walked over to his desk next to hers. On his way over he heard whispers from his new classmates. Some of them were glaring at him, while others mentioned his current appearance being dirty. When he had finally sat down he placed his bag on his desk and pulled out his history book that had plenty of cat hair on it. After cleaning it off, he paid close attention to the rest of the class. He noticed Ms, Young kept looking over at him whenever she had the chance. He made sure not to look back.

After an hour when class finally ended, Reighley began packing up his things when a crowd of people swarmed him. A few students immediately asked if he knew the crazy girl since she was staring at him the whole time. He told them that he didn't know anyone since he had just moved here recently.

"Say, it was Reighley, wasn't it? I am Freya Young. How about I give you a tour of the school grounds once our classes are over? It would be just the two of us." Reighley looked over and to his displeasure, it was Black Arrow Girl. She was looking at him like he was her next meal.

"Thanks, but no. I should be fine on my own," he replied. When he answered, the crowd around him and Freya appeared to be shocked by his response. Before he knew it, more people came in from outside of the class making the crowd larger. Freya however, looked like she completely ignored him.

"Well, aren't you shy? How about you come over to my private library and I help you get caught up with all the subjects you're behind on?" Reighley was severely annoyed with her persistence. To his surprise, her aura only became larger after his first answer.

"I'll have to pass. Sorry." Reighley turned her down politely. There was an awkward silence from the crowd. Freya's aura shrank a small bit as she looked at him with soulless eyes, then it grew to the point where the arrow wrapped around him entirely like a snake suffocating its prey. She would not back down even after he turned her down twice.

"I must need my ears checked because it sounded like you turned down my offer. I would like to make you my boyfriend. So, what do you say?" Freya got up from her desk, looking a little embarrassed, and placed her hand on his desk. Her aura was smothering him with pressure. This must have been how she got her way. A person's aura could affect other people if it was potent enough. However, Reighley's will was strong. He wouldn't be swayed into doing something he didn't choose for himself.

"I'm good, thanks. Besides, I don't even know you and something tells me that if I did say yes, you would just dump me the week after." Reighley replied. He didn't often take advantage of the knowledge he had of people's auras and use it against them, but he was left with no options. Immediately Freya's aura let go of him. The crowd around the two began to disperse as they seemingly were disappointed in his answer. Freya looked like she had been told a family member had recently passed, as she couldn't process what had just happened. Then her face turned a bright red. Angrily, she grabbed a girl from the desk in front of hers and pulled her out of it with the strength of a giant.

"This isn't over!" Freya exclaimed and then stormed out of the classroom dragging what he assumed was her friend behind her. What followed was a series of events that only reassured Reighley that he was cursed.

Chapter 3

The Sellout

Reighley closed his eyes for a moment and took a deep breath. He wasn't looking forward to spending the rest of the semester at school with Freya. He knew that their interaction would most likely bite him in the butt, but he needed to stand his ground. Reighley finished packing his things when he noticed a familiar person hovering over him.

"Looks like you're in for some trouble," Ash said sarcastically.

"Oh, hi," Reighley said, surprised to see her.

"I saw what happened, and you have quite the pair on you for telling that girl no," she said.

"She's pretty important around here I'm guessing?" He asked.

"You could say that." Ash crossed her arms.

"What do you mean?" Reighley questioned.

"Her dad helps pay for this place. He is some bigshot that gives his daughter everything that she wants. The principal kind of lets her get away with anything. Everyone in the school just does whatever she asks in fear that they might get expelled for defying her." Ash explained.

"You mean I might be expelled?" Reighley shuddered at the thought of getting expelled after all his hard work.

"Possibly. I doubt it though. I would be careful. Her fanboys are vicious dogs." Reighley was surprised to see Ash talk to him, but deep down inside it made him quite happy. He worried about his first impressions at school. He didn't need the entire school to like him, but having a few friends wouldn't hurt. Not to mention Ash's aura felt refreshing to be around. It was as if he had been at a coral reef in the ocean swimming on a perfect summer day.

"Fanboys?" Reighley asked.

"You live under a rock or something? Freya Young is extremely famous on a lot of social media. She has an army of trolls that she sends on anyone she doesn't like." Reighley laughed at the comment and then pulled out his flip phone showing it to Ash.

"I don't have any social media. My phone is too old." Ash looked shocked by what she had seen.

"Oh my! You found ancient technology under that rock you live at. Tell the dinosaurs I said hello." Ash joked. "But seriously, I wouldn't let anyone see you have that old brick or you would become the laughingstock of the school. Let's keep it between us." Reighley thanked her for the advice and the two went their separate ways.

While storming off in an embarrassed rage, Freya somehow ended up on the roof level of the school. Attached to her hand was a bruised and battered Destiny barely hanging on for dear life.

"I cannot believe the gall of that boy. He had the nerve to turn me down in front of our entire class." Freya complained while stomping back and forth.

"Freya... Let go please..." Destiny said with a whimper. When Freya stopped and looked at Destiny she instantly felt guilty and let go of her hand. She was the one who dragged her all the way up to the rooftop.

"Hang on Destiny. I'll have my private doctor come in and take a look at you later. For now, we have a real problem to deal with." Freya sent a text out to her maid Lily and had her make arrangements for her friend. Meanwhile, Destiny threw up a thumbs-up and a weak smile. "I need to get that boy to fall in love with me before rumors start to spread." Freya still couldn't believe what had just happened. Never in her life had anyone said no to her. She always got what she wanted. So, to better prepare herself for her next encounter with Reighley, she decided to do some light stalking on his social media account. She decided she wanted to learn more about him to gain the upper hand. While on her phone she went to her main social media application SocialLight. After it loaded she looked up Reighley Summers on the website. She was surprised to find nothing. She then looked at all the other applications she would use and still found nothing. Did she imagine it all? How could someone not exist on the internet?

"Is something the matter?" Destiny said after standing up and dusting herself off.

"I can't find him anywhere. It's like he doesn't exist."

"What? Are you talking about Summers? He's just downstairs."

"I mean on SocialLight or any website to be precise."

"Well, Maybe he's like a secret agent or something sent here to spy on the school. Maybe that's why he looked all beat up. He got into a gunfight before school." Destiny said, making her fingers look like pistols and accompanying them with sound effects.

"Don't be foolish. That happened because Reighley Summers is the boy who saved the cat." Freya explained. Destiny froze in disappointment and placed her finger guns back into her imaginary holsters. Freya was even more curious about him than before. He must have not known who she was when she asked him out. For now, she would see how things go, until she came up with a plan to get him to date her. After a discussion about what the plan could be between her and Destiny, the school bell rang signaling for them to return to class.

Reighley, while doing a bit of exploring, after tidying himself up, found a vending machine on a skywalk connecting two sections of the building. The school bell had just rang so he needed to hurry and buy something and then get back to class. He walked over to it and pulled out his wallet, only to see it empty. Although, it didn't surprise him. He spent all of his savings either on things for his room, or his younger sister's tuition. Though, it barely made a dent in her school debt. He told himself that he would help pay Isabelle's debt off first before his own. His mom was barely getting by with the rent and other house utilities, so it was the least he could do for his family. The drinks on the vending machine were ridiculously overpriced as well. Each beverage costs roughly 2800 yen. Which was about 21 US dollars. When Reighley turned back and walked towards his classroom he saw two people standing at the end of the hall. He was being spied on by Freya Young with a still arrow-like aura, and her friend she dragged along with her. Her friend had pink hair and was roughly the same height as his younger sister around 5'2. When he looked her in the eyes, he saw a pure white-as-snow aura coming from the girl. The aura had somewhat of a shape. It was as if a cloud had become a solid keeping its fluff and buoyancy. It shocked him that a girl like her would hang out with someone whose aura was almost the complete opposite. White auras usually meant that person was lighthearted, carefree, and honest.

Freya didn't expect to see Reighley again before class. The plan she had discussed beforehand was to send Destiny out to follow him after their next class. However, that was no longer needed as she found out something about him that she could use. He was broke.

"Short on cash?" Freya said followed by a chuckle. She figured he was poor, but didn't think he would be barely scraping by. An idea came into her head. A way to let her have her way.

"That's none of your business," Reighley said begrudgingly. He attempted to walk past the two girls only to be stopped by Freya standing in his way. She pulled out a stack of what looked like fifty bills each worth 10,000 yen out of the side of her bag. She held it right in front of him and Reighley was completely stunned. He had never seen that much money before. Each bill was roughly $74.00. It was more money than he had earned during his entire time working his summer job.

"Look Reighley, I think we got off on the wrong foot. I admit I was a little too aggressive. I mean you had no idea who I was right? So let's make a deal that would help both of us." Reighley felt a bit insulted by her statement, but it was true. He didn't know who she was nor did he care in all honesty. It was clear to Reighley that she wanted to control him and appeal to his greed.

"Are you trying to buy me?" Reighley asked. He was filled with a bit of disgust at the thought of being paid for. He was going to tell her no outright until the thought of his younger sister buried in a mountain of debt came to mind. He considered it. Swallowing his pride for his sister's best interest was something he was already quite good at.

"Don't make it sound weird. I am simply wanting to pay you to be my boyfriend." Freya said with a smirk. That was only half true. She also wanted to silence any of the rumors that she got rejected. "I'll give you a stack just like the one I'm holding for each week you spend with me."

"Sorry, but I am not for sale," Reighley said as he walked past Freya. He never would have thought those words would have come out of his mouth but he was glad they did. Reighley continued onward, not looking back at the two. He only thought about how awkward the rest of the day was since he had to sit next to her.

"Shouldn't you stop him?" Destiny mentioned seemingly confused.

"Just give him some time to think it over." Freya's face had turned red once again. She saw the look in his eye when she showed him the money. If he didn't accept her offer she would just increase the pay. Freya knew that everyone had a price, so it was just a matter of time before he would consider it.

"There is something odd about him," Destiny stated.

"How so?" Freya asked.

"He seemed pretty cold towards us both until he looked me in the eyes. Maybe he likes me?" When Freya heard this she became slightly jealous. Destiny was not one to lie. Her intuition was usually right. However, Freya knew she was the prettier one of the two so after some thought Freya decided to up the ante the next time she would see Reighley after class.

"We'll just have to wait and see. Everybody has a price." Freya said with a smirk. The two then hurried towards class.

Reighley sat down at his desk shortly after returning. Not even a minute later Freya and Destiny followed through the door and made their way to their seats. Reighley didn't bother looking at the two. He decided to focus his energy on school instead of being annoyed. After their English class had ended Reighley got up and attempted to walk out of the room.

"So have you considered-" Freya was caught off guard by an abrupt glare from Reighley when he had passed by. He completely ignored her and walked out the door. Every time Reighley would see Freya he would do the same thing. He refused to give her the time of day. Until finally school was over and it was time to go home. Reighley got up from his desk for the last time of the day when he heard the voice of Freya once again.

"Please! Would you just hear me out?" She asked. Reighley paused and looked back at her, not with a glare but with a sigh. The rest of the class, including the teacher, was watching with anticipation.

"Fine, what do you want?" Reighley asked. "I'm tired of this game of cat and mouse."

"Can we just talk in private?" She asked. The crowd looked confused and disappointed by her choice of words.

"Fine. Tomorrow after school. " Freya looked genuinely surprised that he said yes. She was feeling pretty defeated after being ignored so many times by him. It irritated her. So many people would do just about anything just to spend a single day with her but he wanted nothing to do with her. The crowd seemed completely engaged in their conversation.

"Okay." She replied. Afterward, Reighley stepped out of the class and headed towards the Nurse's Office. When he arrived he could hear a sneeze coming from the other side of the door. He opened the door only to see Kaede with a runny nose and his cat in her hands.

"It's finally growing on you huh?" Reighley said with a smile. Kaede was caught off guard. She was sitting at her desk. The trash next to it was filled to the brim with tissues. When she had seen who had entered her eyes lit up with excitement.

"Welcome back!" she said, immediately standing up and handing the black cat back to Reighley. "Do you have any idea how hard it is to breathe with that thing in here?"

"I didn't know I made you feel that way Kaede," Reighley said jokingly.

"That's- you know what I mean." Kaede turned red from embarrassment. Reighley knew Kaede couldn't handle the slightest comment about romance without turning red. So, he would tease her from time to time. Reighley was exhausted from his first day of school. So much had happened to him. He walked over to a bed in the center of the room and laid on his back letting out a deep breath.

"Today sucked buddy." He said while looking up at the cat he was holding. The cat meowed back at him. "You must be hungry."

"Have you thought of a name yet? If you need help, the cat is a boy." Kaede asked, still blowing her nose with tissues.

"Yes, yes I have. Right Morgana?" He decided to name the cat Morgana, based on one of his favorite game series. Morgana replied with a meow once more while Reighley petted its head.

"How was your first day of school?" Kaede asked.

"Well, I became the target of some crazy rich girl named Freya." When Reighley said this Kaede's jaw dropped from shock.

"Freya as in Freya Young?" Kaede couldn't believe her ears.

"Yep, that's the one." Reighley said while petting his new found friend.

"Well, what did she want?" Kaede questioned.

"She wanted to pay me to be her boyfriend." Reighley sighed.

"That's not that surprising. That girl is-" Kaede was cut off by Reighley.

"Yeah, Yeah, I know. I've heard it about ten times today. Look, as far as I am concerned, that girl is nothing special. She just has good looks and a lot of money." Reighley had heard enough about Freya for one day.

"Sounds pretty special to me. Well... what did you say?" Kaede asked.

"I told her no, obviously. Though honestly, she offered 500,000 yen a week so I can't say I wasn't tempted." Reighley said.

"500,000 yen!?" Kaede shouted. "That's more than what I make..." She whispered with a hint of jealousy.

"Yeah, I'm not completely sure why. It's not like I'm particularly special or anything."

"You are extraordinary to me. Well, whatever you decide to do make sure you're careful okay? I worry about you, you know?" Kaede said with concern.

"Stop being such a worry wart. I'll be fine. Besides, I already made a friend." Reighley grumbled.

"Well, if you say so. If you ever need anything just let me know. Now, can you help me clean all this cat hair up off the floor?" Kaede sneezed once again.

Reighley put Morgana back into his backpack after helping Kaede clean up as much cat hair as they could. The two caught up on how things were since they had last seen each other while they cleaned. Five minutes later they finished.

"Hey, how about you come to visit next weekend? I'm sure Isabelle and Mom would be happy to see you." Reighley asked.

"Sure, I can come over for dinner. It's not like I have anything better to do." She said with a sigh. Reighley knew that Kaede would usually indulge in wine on the weekends since she was a single woman who lived alone. He felt kind of bad for her, so he invited her so she wouldn't feel lonely.

"Well, I need to head home. Thanks again for helping me out."

"Anytime!" Kaede said with a wink. Soon after Reighley headed back out towards the school gates to make his commute home. It was already 5:30 PM. He had quite the walk before he would make it home.

Meanwhile, Destiny was panicking. She had lost something very important to her. It was a friendship bracelet Freya had made. The two girls made a matching pair of them. One for her and the other for Freya. She thought she must have lost it when she was being dragged about by Freya. She went to ask Freya for help, but it was too late. She had already left after Destiny realized she was missing the bracelet.

Destiny: Hey I lost my bracelet I need help finding it.

Freya: *Thumbs up Emoji*

Destiny was on her hands and knees in the second-floor hallway searching desperately when she noticed someone leave the Nurse's Office. It was the new guy Freya was currently obsessed with. Destiny looked up at him with tears in her eyes.

"Are you okay?" Reighley asked.

"I can't find it anywhere," Destiny replied.

"Find what?" Reighley questioned.

"My friendship bracelet. I've had it ever since I was seven."

"Well, do you know where you had it last?" Reighley felt bad for the girl. Destiny explained that she thought she may have lost it when she was dragged up to the rooftop by Freya. Reighley felt a bit guilty since he had some part to do with that, even though it was Freya's fault. "All right. I'll help you look for it."

"You will? You're so nice! No wonder Freya wants you to date her." Destiny said with a smile. Reighley looked a little confused by the girl's response but shrugged it off and started looking.

"So... I don't think the two of us have ever been properly introduced. I am Reighley."

"I'm Destiny! Nice to meet you." When Reighley heard what her name was he almost laughed, but made sure not to. He thought it sounded like the name of an exotic dancer, which was too ironic considering how pure of a soul she had. He had thought that her parents must have been the type to name their children something like that because they thought their child would be some special angel. They were half right but it was still a terrible name in his opinion.

After searching the first two floors of the building, the two had no luck finding her missing bracelet.

"So Destiny, why do you hang out with Freya anyway? Did she pay you to be her best friend or something?" He didn't understand why anyone would be friends with her without monetary compensation.

"No Freya and I grew up together. She's been a good friend of mine my whole life. Actually, the reason I'm looking for this bracelet is because she has the other half." Reighley was astonished by her answer. Never would he have imagined that Destiny would hang out with Freya on her own free will. Either Destiny was too nice or Freya wasn't as bad as he had made her out to be. After a while, the two found themselves outside of the hall of class 3-A. Through the window, Reighley could see someone very large standing by an open window. He saw a flicker of light come from the stranger. Destiny, however, couldn't see as she was too short.

"What is it?" Destiny asked.

"It's just some student." He explained.

"Let me see. Let me see!" Destiny started jumping in order to peek through the window but after no luck, she decided to open the door. When she did, the student looked like he was caught with his pants down as he attempted to cover up something in his hand.

"Hey! What's the deal?" The male stranger exclaimed.

"Sorry! We were just looking for something." Reighley answered immediately. Reighley looked into the young man's eyes and saw a blazing fiery red aura. He was surprised because on closer inspection it was a bright red aura. When he realized it, his worries quickly swept away. The stranger was incredibly well-built. He looked like he weighed well over 90kg. He had his blonde hair slicked back with a headband holding it down. Reighley guessed his stature was roughly 200cm tall.

"Oh… well do you need help?" The stranger asked politely. Reighley could tell he was an overall good guy. Red didn't just mean the person was passionate or had a desire of sorts, it also meant that the person was serious and straightforward.

"Yes! We lost something very important to me."

"Important? Very well... I will not rest until we find it. We will find it, for if my name isn't Ulysses Cinder. (You-Liss-Sees Sin-Dur)" He said with a nervous laugh.

"Right..." Destiny and Reighley said in unison. The three went on for the next ten minutes looking at each floor. Unable to find it, the three ended up on the rooftop.

"I don't think it's going to show up. We've checked everywhere." Reighley said with a sigh. "Maybe someone already found it and turned it in. You'll have to check tomorrow." Destiny looked truly disappointed almost to the point of tears, Until she got a notification from her phone.

Freya: Look up.

Destiny was confused by the text but after half a minute passed, off in the distance were three helicopters heading straight towards the school.

"What in the world?" Ulysses said with a dropped jaw. Soon after, the three choppers arrived. One of them went towards the entrance of the school, while the other two hovered over the school's rooftop. Freya was sticking her head out of the helicopter side looking down at the three. Immediately after, men began to pour out of the sides of each chopper. The men were in full swat suits. They looked like they were about to storm a hostage scenario. Freya grabbed the helicopter's intercom and spoke through it.

"They'll take it from here." Freya was attempting to save face. She wanted to impress Reighley and this was her best shot at turning the tables. However, she would have done it either way, since Destiny asked her for a favor for

56

once in her life. Freya knew it must have been that important because Destiny was usually pretty stubborn and tried to do everything by herself. For her to ask for help was very unlike her.

"She's an angel!" Ulysses said. His eyes were fixated on Freya. He looked at her like she descended heaven itself. Reighley thought to himself that he was the only sane person present at the moment. He wondered why Freya would go to such lengths for a bracelet. Finally, Freya's subordinates finished landing on the property using a rope connected to the chopper. Destiny was ecstatic, but Reighley wasn't fooled so easily. He figured this was all some ploy to show off to him. However, when he looked at Freya and saw her eyes he was shocked to see that her aura was not pointing at him, but at the building itself.

"She really did this for her friend..." Reighley whispered under the loud noises of the helicopter. Soon, Freya hooked onto the rope and descended to see the group face to face. Once she had landed, with the snap of her finger, all of her men stormed the building in search of the bracelet. Soon, after the helicopters flew south, just far enough so that they could hear themselves speak.

Reighley was impressed. He didn't think she had it in her to swoop down from the heavens, then all of that quickly faded away as he saw that she was recording the whole thing from an ActionPro hooked onto her shoulder. It was a video recorder that people who did extreme sports would use due to its durability. Destiny jumped into Freya's arms squeezing her tight.

"You really came through!" Destiny shouted with excitement.

"Of course. I wouldn't abandon a friend in need." Freya replied. When she said this Destiny burst into tears. Freya was quite embarrassed by the hug. She wasn't appreciated often and to this degree before and found it to be quite nice. It was different from her fans praising her or even her family. "Now, now, don't be crying on me Ms. Detective," Freya said jokingly.

"Okay," Destiny said sobbing. Reighley found it kind of sweet however he hid his face from the camera pointing at him from Freya. He didn't care for fame, nor did he want any part in helping Freya in her attempts to improve her status either.

"Can you turn that thing off?" Reighley said while looking the other way. Freya complied. She turned off the ActionPro after letting go of Destiny and then proceeded to walk to Reighley.

"One month." She said while looking at him intently.

"What?" Reighley asked.

"If you're not in love with me after one month, then I'll leave you alone. Regardless of the outcome, I'll pay you weekly as promised." Freya stated. Reighley was surprised that she was willing to compromise. He would have thought that she would have rather died than do that. She kept on surprising him. Whenever he would make an assumption about her, he ended up being wrong. So, Reighley decided he would give her a shot. Mainly for a paycheck since he needed the money. He thought that a month of his life surely would be worth that amount of money. All he needed to do was put up with someone.

"It's a deal". Reighley said. Freya was ecstatic. She finally had a shot to prove to him why she was amazing. She couldn't wait to restore balance to her universe. Now that she had him for a week, she could make him fall in love way easier.

Reighley didn't forget about the cat in his bag during the entire search. It had only been eighteen minutes of searching, but that was too long and Reighley began to worry. Freya was about to ask Reighley a question when he suddenly took off downstairs.

"I hope you find the bracelet!" He shouted on his way out the door. Even though she had gotten her way Freya couldn't help but feel annoyed that he didn't even say goodbye. It left her feeling like she didn't win. Regardless, the two would begin dating the next day so it was fine. It would all be the same in the end, according to her.

When Reighley finally reached the second floor, he went back towards the overpriced vending machine located on the skywalk. He looked over towards the spot and saw a purple bracelet on the floor near the wall. He had found it. He felt it quite ironic that the bracelet was purple but proceeded to pick it up and give it to a security team member that was nearby. The guard thanked him, and then Reighley quickly made his way home. Once he had left the school grounds he pulled Morgana out of his bag. It looked like it was going crazy because it was all cramped inside his backpack for so long.

"Sorry, Morgana. It won't happen again, buddy." Reighley said. When the cat heard him call it a name its wild nature calmed and turned into confusion, as it tilted its head 45 degrees. Reighley carried Morgana in his arms the rest of the way back home. Once they arrived, his sister Isabelle was pleasantly surprised by what he was holding. His mother, however, was very upset that he was late home.

"Hey, guys. I brought home a new member of the family." Reighley said. "His name is Morgana." The two girls became ecstatic as Reighley held up Morgana for the two to see.

"He's so cute!" the two girls said together. Morgana held his head up high almost like it was proud that the two ladies were all over him. After introductions were complete, Reighley let Morgana roam the floor for some time to help him get accommodated with the house while he had dinner with his family. When he had finished eating he then got ready and went to bed. He climbed up into his top bunk bed in his garage and brought Morgana along with him.

"This is your new home now," Reighley said. He ended up snuggling with the cat. He couldn't have been happier with what he had.

Chapter 4

Wanting More

Reighley had just left the school grounds while Freya, Destiny, and Ulysses were still on the rooftop. One of the private security team members rushed up the stairs holding the bracelet in his hand.

"We found it, Lady Freya!" The guard said with excitement. Destiny, filled with joy rushed over and snatched the bracelet from the guard.

"Thank you! Freya give this man a raise would you?" Destiny said with a golden smile.

"Actually, it was the boy who had just left the building. He found it and turned it in." The guard was honest. Freya knew that the guards were paid very well, and were extremely loyal to her and her family. They would have no reason to be dishonest.

"Very good. Tell those who remain downstairs that they are free to leave now." Freya replied.

"Freya, give Reighley a raise," Destiny said seriously.

"He doesn't work for me yet." Freya laughed. Deep down in her heart, she was thankful for him helping her best friend. He didn't have to go out of his way to do that for Destiny. Though she was confident that the task force would have found the bracelet eventually.

"I'll have to spoil him on our date tomorrow. It is the weekend of course."

"Date? I didn't know you and Reighley were dating." Ulysses said, slightly disappointed.

"It's complicated. Wait, who are you again?" Freya said with confusion.

"This is Ulysses, the guy who helped Reighley and me search the school. We found him in one of the rooms and he offered to help." Destiny retorted.

"Well, here." Freya handed Ulysses 10,000 yen, (75.00 USD). Ulysses was confused by the outcome but didn't refuse the payment. It would help with his cigarette addiction.

"Thanks. I really should get going." Ulysses awkwardly strutted towards the door and headed home. He wasn't sure how to talk to girls. He was quite shy when it came to simple interactions with them or anyone for that matter. Once he had left school grounds he wondered if he had made friends today. If not with the girls then at least with Reighley. Ulysses never had friends growing up. He only had his older brother and his father as role models for him. He was always alone. However, he knew the reason why. He was intimidating, his social skills were lacking, and he smelled like cigarettes. He tried to quit but just couldn't bring himself to do it. Not smoking for a day was like being in a desert without water for a week. He was nervous about what other people thought of him. He never wanted to make others feel uncomfortable. When Ulysses arrived home he played single-player video games to pass the time, as his father and his older brother both worked at their family's restaurant during the weekdays. They owned a small humble ramen shop called Back Alley Ramen. It was an underground walk-in wooden shack that had stools you could sit on once you walked over the sheet covering the entrance. Ulysses would help with the shop on the weekends. He was fairly proud of his ability to cook.

Their home was connected to the upstairs of the shack built into the structure. Ulysses shared a room with his older brother Sunny Cinder. Sunny had white hair and wasn't nearly as stout as his younger brother. He was already in college. He was two years older than Ulysses. Although the family lived in a restaurant, they were incredibly wealthy. Their family's wealth came from their mom's side of the family. She was born into it. She was often gone from home traveling the world and collecting art as a hobby. She had her two sons stay at home with their dad, so they could learn to live a normal honest life. After a long walk, Ulysses arrived home, and awaiting him in his room was his older brother.

"Hey bro, you think you can run the shop by yourself tomorrow?" Sunny asked.

"Yeah, I think I can manage," Ulysses replied.

"Good, because I'll be out of town. I am going to a group study thing for school." When Sunny said this Ulysses's eyes widened. Sunny was nothing like Ulysses. Though the two both got their education through Gilford High, Sunny was a popular student there at the time of his enrollment. He was everything Ulysses wanted to be, confident, with great social skills, and a perfect physique. Ulysses thought Sunny was the coolest big brother ever.

Ulysses was not jealous of his brother, instead, he was proud of him, as he was the top student in his class all while managing to work at the ramen shop. Ulysses knew he could never be as cool or awesome as his brother, but he still loved Sunny and supported him to the fullest.

Sunny was also a really good sword fighter. He practiced kendo daily throughout high school. However he didn't use a standard sword style, instead he applied Iaijutsu (居合術), a traditional quick-draw sword style. They called him the Yukime (ゆきめ) which in English meant Snow Blindness, because of his white hair and that he would swiftly strike his opponents with a blinding strike.

"Is it a date?" Ulysses probed.

"Yeah… kind of." Sunny got embarrassed. Being bad at talking to girls was something the two shared. It supposedly runs in the family, as their father Todoh (Toe-Doe) has trouble too, even while being married.

"You got this bro!" Ulysses gave Sunny a thumbs up.

"Thanks, buddy, let's hope for the best. I really like this girl."

The two brothers proceeded to talk about Sunny and his plan to ask this girl out on a real date with just the two of them. Ulysses, who thought himself unqualified to answer such important questions, suggested that he should just ask her outright, and be honest with himself. However, that was the harshest reality for Ulysses. He could say all these things and give great advice but he could never apply it in practice. When it came to taking that first step in making friends, he just couldn't do it. The only reason he decided to help look for the bracelet at school was to divert their attention from the fact that he was smoking on school grounds. Once the two finished talking, they went to bed. Ulysses and Sunny both were unable to sleep well due to their minds stressing about the future to come. When Ulysses reached into his pocket to grab a cigarette he realized that the pack was missing.

"Crap." He whispered.

Freya and Destiny chatted on the roof for quite some time after Ulysses had left. Freya's task force dispatched from the building before returning to their helicopters. Freya also had her private limousine waiting for her at the entrance. The two girls went inside the vehicle and Herald proceeded to drive the two home. Destiny was dropped off at her house which was about a ten-minute commute from school. The two said their goodbyes, and Freya was driven back home. When she arrived she was greeted by her personal handmaid Lily and the head maid Elise.

"Welcome back Lady Freya." The two maids said in unison, all while taking a bow. Freya waited for Herald to open the door for her, once he did she stepped out and made her way back to the front entrance of her family's estate. While on her way to the house elevator, Freya wondered if she looked cool in front of Reighley. A secret passion of hers was that she loved action movies and stunts, though she made sure not to tell a single soul. Not even Destiny. Her favorite actress was Chakie Jan, a Chinese movie star who would do her stunts in all of her movies. Freya made it a part of her live streams to do stunts of her own every so often, she would go rock climbing, hang gliding, skiing, ice climbing, and skydiving. On her outward appearance, she would remain calm, cool, and collected, but when she would do stunts like those it was one of the few moments in her life where Freya truly felt alive.

"Dinner will be ready shortly, Lady Freya," Lily informed.

"All right, I will come down after I finish getting ready. Don't bother me during that time." Freya replied.

"Very well," Lily answered. Freya made her way to her room alone. She had changed out of her current outfit she wore for the helicopter, into a set of comfortable clothes Lily had prepared for her beforehand. Freya wore a pink T-shirt with a star in the center and lime green shorts. She wanted to use this time alone to think of a plan for tomorrow. Freya decided that she was going to find out where Reighley lived and kidnap him for a date. During her commute home, she asked Herald to find out where the boy lived. She asked him to remain quiet about it to the other maids, as she didn't want it getting back to her father. Herald was the house worker that Freya trusted the most. He was often the one who went with her to all her extreme sports. He made sure not to snitch on her to her mother or father either, though they could find out through her livestreams on SocialLight. That was also part of the fun for Freya, as the risk of getting caught made her blood rush even more. In return, Freya would make sure Herald never worked any Holidays. She made the argument to her parents that there were no benefits to being the head butler, only more duties. It was their little secret that they shared. Freya assumed she had become this wild due to needing to act like a princess her whole life. The chains that were formalities, shackled her down.

Freya finished getting ready for dinner. Over her t-shirt and her shorts, she wore a navy blue dress shirt and a black skirt that went down past her knees. She usually wore something more modest for dinner for the off chance that her father would be joining. She knew that wasn't the case today since her dad left on a flight this morning but she did so anyway. She wore it because she had a small ounce of hope that he may have returned in time. Freya walked out of her room into the elongated hallway that was their second floor. Awaiting her was Lily, she was standing outside her door just off to the left.

"I left my clothes on the floor, take care of them would you?" Freya asked.

"As you wish, Lady Freya," Lily replied. Lily went inside Freya's room and cleaned up after her mess. She began rambling about how Freya couldn't make her life any easier.

"She could have at least put the clothes on her bed instead of being a complete slob," Lily whispered in frustration. This was Lily's general opinion of Freya. She thought of Freya to be a spoiled brat. Someone who would never change or fully mature, and most importantly, someone who would never be happy later in life. Lily was convinced that Freya would never find true love, for as long as she lived, because to her, Freya was the worst. Freya was the reason she was miserable. Lily was underpaid. This was because she made a mistake only a year into being Freya's maid. Lily had spilled coffee over Freya's clothes by accident. The outfit itself was a custom-made strapless white dress paired with a white hat with a flower pinned to it. It was worth 5,000,000 yen (37,500 USD).

It was Freya's birthday week. Freya pushed Lily very hard during that week, leaving plenty of messes to clean up and having Lily order things for her over the internet constantly. She also prepared all of Freya's outfits and helped her get ready for the day. At that time Lily was working sixteen-hour shifts daily. So, on the day of Freya's birthday, while holding Freya's coffee, she dozed off for a few seconds, spilling the drink on Freya and her extremely expensive dress. Now her paycheck has a deduction on it that is used to pay the dress off. In the end, what made Lily the most upset is that Freya never said thank you for all her hard work, or at least when she did, Lily was sure she didn't mean it.

Freya headed down the elevator and proceeded to the dining room. To her disappointment, her father had not returned.

"Welcome home darling!" Marine said while slightly tipping over, only to correct herself upright.

"Hello, Mother," Freya replied. Freya got a sense of Deja Vu, as her mother was still drinking wine. She worried about her mother, as normally she would stop drinking after she left for work. This time, however, Marine was outright drunk.

"Your Father hasn't returned home just yet. Don't worry he will be back eventually, just to leave again." Marine fumbled over her words. To Freya, this was hard to watch. Her mother drank because she was lonely. She was married to the richest and most successful man in the world, but rarely ever got to see him.

"Mother?" Freya asked.

"Yes, dearest darling?" Marine replied

"Let's watch a movie together," Freya said. Shortly after dinner, the two girls went into their private movie theater in their house on the second floor. The two then proceeded to watch "chick flicks" that Marine picked out, while Marine ate ice cream in her sorrows. The movie theater had a giant bean bag sac that the two sat in together. They watched movies until Marine sobered up.

"That was so good," Marine said while sobbing.

"I agree when the father said 'I love you, but I can't stay' it really had me tearing up," Freya said while tears were going down her face. The two realized that the movie correlated to their current situation. It was about a father who had a family and responsibilities. He was always busy to the point where his wife and his daughter became resentful of him for never being around. Their marriage began to crack, and the father ended up missing important moments in the daughter's life. It was all a little too "on the nose", for Freya. In the end, the dad realized his mistakes and ended up making time for the two and started being there for them. Freya, even though she got everything she wanted, wasn't sure if she would get the same ending.

"You know your Father loves you very much, Freya," Marine said.

"He loves you too," Freya replied. "Lily, bring me my milk."

"Of course, Lady Freya..." Lily reluctantly held a glass of warm milk on a heated disk under Freya's chin. Herald had prepared it, but somehow Lily ended up being the one holding the glass for Freya while she drank it from a straw.

"Hey Mother, I'm going on a date tomorrow."

"Is it with the criminal?" Marine asked.

"Well yeah, but he's a lot more kind than I expected," Freya said. "If you're going to spy on me, have Lily tail us, I don't want him uncomfortable on our date."

"Okay. Lily, you heard the girl. I'm entrusting my daughter's safety to you. If even the slightest thing goes wrong I want the proper authorities called." Marine said while looking towards the maid with a serious face.

"Excellent... As you wish, Lady Prismarine." Lily bowed, hiding a grimace on her face. Lily respected Mrs. Young. She was the one who gave her the job as a maid. Lily worked full time due to her parents both being hospitalized from a car accident as a child. When she was younger Lily met Elise by sheer luck. While Elise worked for Prismarine, she also volunteered as a registered nurse. She was assigned as Lily's parents' nurse at the hospital they stayed at. One day Prismarine was there speaking with Elise for reasons unknown to Lily and Lily recognized the woman from news articles and magazines. Elise had told Prismarine about Lily's situation, and Prismarine offered to hire Lily, and in return for her work her family's medical bills would be paid for. Lily was incredibly grateful to the Young family. The only reason she put up with Freya's antics was because she owed so much to her family.

Marine got up from the seat along with Freya. The two hugged each other goodnight and went their separate ways for the rest of the night. Freya made her way to her library to study. She figured out what her course of action was as well. Freya tapped into her knowledge of romance novels. She thought a good first date would be at an amusement park as there was a lot to do there. She needed to make Reighley fall in love with her. She was paying him, but she knew money alone wouldn't be enough. While studying for roughly an hour Freya heard a knock on the library's door.

"It's Herald, Miss Freya." The voice said.

"Come in," Freya replied. Herald entered and stood next to Freya. Lily was told to wait outside while Freya studied. "Did you find what I asked for?"

"Indeed," Herald answered. He proceeded to hand Freya a letter. Inside were pictures of Reighley entering and exiting his house letting out a cat. Next to the photos was a piece of paper with his address on it.

"So, he kept the cat?" Freya said curiously. "Herald, please have someone bring me cat litter, a litter box, and cat toys, as well as a bag of premium cat food. Nothing says generous more than a gift for the things he cares about."

"Very well, Lady Freya," Herald answered. Freya's plan to take Reighley to an amusement park changed slightly once she realized his living conditions. He lived in a tiny house, roughly 1200 square feet. It looked no bigger than her private bathroom. She was displeased by his social status, but wouldn't let this stop her. She asked Herald if he knew of any "poor people" restaurants that Reighley and her could go to that wouldn't be poison to her. He told her about an old friend that he trusted. He mentioned that he owned a ramen shop that served very delicious noodles for a commoner's price. However, Freya was skeptical due to the name of the shop. It was called Back Alley Ramen. Freya pictured what the place looked like in her mind. To her, she imagined a damp alleyway between buildings that had broken windows.

In the buildings were thugs flipping switch blades in unison. When she thought of what the shop looked like, she envisioned it being someplace that criminals and thugs would go to to talk about committing and planning crimes, all while eating food they could barely afford.

"You needn't worry Lady Freya. Todoh, the shop owner keeps the place very tidy and up to your standards. I eat there every so often." Herald reassured.

"Well, I trust your judgment, Herald, so very well, Reighley and I will stop there first for a meal," Freya replied. "Make all the preparations like I asked, we leave at 11:30 AM." Herald dispatched and began his duties assigned to him. Once he left, Freya spent the rest of her night studying and deciding what to wear for tomorrow before heading to bed.

The next day, Freya woke up at 7:00 AM with plenty of time to spare. It was a Saturday, so Freya had the day off. She conducted her morning routine and got ready for her date. Once Freya got ready she went around her entire house asking the maids what they thought of her outfit. They all agreed she looked wonderful, but Freya suspected they only said that due to her family being their means of income. Suddenly Freya took a step back. Why was she nervous about her appearance? She thought that he must think that she was beautiful. However, in the back of her mind, panic began to set in. What if he didn't think she was pretty? It was a possibility, as he was also the first person who turned her down. Reighley was a complete anomaly. The more Freya thought about it, the worst her nerves got.

Freya was wearing a red summer dress with white polka dots and green hooped earrings. On her feet, she wore red bare strap patterned sandals. Freya thought of red to be the color that demanded attention. Something that sticks out in the best way. She wanted Reighley to see her and be unable to take his eyes off her. Freya decided to ask Destiny about her conundrum via text.

Freya: Hey, how do I look? (Freya sent a picture of her attached to the message.)

Destiny: Like a Strawberry.

Freya: No seriously, how do I look? I need to know.

Destiny: Like a delicious Strawberry.

Freya soon realized that this was most likely the best she would get out of Destiny. Freya didn't want to tell her that she was worried that Reighley wouldn't like her appearance. So, completely out of options, she decided to do a quick live stream and ask her audience. Freya went live on the internet. Twelve thousand viewers joined in just under a few minutes. That was enough people to give her the confirmation bias she needed. After a short ten minutes of entertaining her viewers and answering their questions, she asked what they thought of her outfit and how she looked. Comments started flowing telling her she looked incredible.

FunnyUser232: You're gorgeous.

PrincessPlum7: I love your outfit!

Lucky_Luffy_x: Wish she was mine.

Moderator-DJ_Destiny has joined the chat.

Moderator-DJ_Destiny: STRAWBERRY!

Destiny started an unending virtual train of people spamming the word "STRAWBERRY" in her chat. This did not help Freya one bit as all of the confidence she had just gained flew out the window. Freya kept her poise and said goodbye as she ended the stream. Freya reassured herself that she looked good, and hoped for the best. When the time came for Freya to leave she met with Herald at the front entrance. At the door was Lily. She was wearing sunglasses, a scarf, and a cap. It was a fairly pitiful disguise, but Reighley wouldn't know of Lily anyway so it wouldn't be much of a problem. Freya didn't say a word to Lily, instead, she gave her a glare stating her intentions. It was the type of glare that stated "If you somehow ruin our date, I'll ruin you".

Lily only looked nervous underneath the getup she was wearing. Herald had pulled up the family limousine and opened the door for Freya letting her inside. Lily got inside and sat in the passenger seat. Freya planned to have Lily ride along with the two since you could not see through the reflective tinted windows. After picking up Reighley and dropping him and Freya off, Lily would get dropped off a short distance away to avoid suspicion. Freya pulled out a hand mirror to take one final look at herself. She looked wondrous but for some reason, she was not satisfied with the result. The only thing that would make her feel better is if Reighley told her she looked good. She would do everything in her power to know his opinion.

Isabelle always started her morning an hour and a half before Reighley. She did so, so she would have enough time to get ready for school. She always wanted her big brother to get enough sleep, so she became his alarm clock if he overslept. She knew about how hard Reighley worked himself and how much he'd sacrificed for her and their mother's sake. She was proud of him and considered herself lucky to have someone like him in her life. However, as of late, Isabelle began to worry. She worried that Reighley wasn't living out his life the way he wanted to, as he would forget to take care of himself from time to time and suffer from extreme burnout. She also feared that Reighley was giving up his youth for her sake. Reighley was fifteen years old but had never had a girlfriend or even shown interest in a girl. It's not that he was into guys as far as she knew, but that Reighley was too busy to have a social life.

It was 10:00 AM. Isabelle decided it was a good time to wake her brother up for brunch. She would let him sleep in on the weekends. Isabelle put her black curly hair up in twin ponytails and put on a black and white striped long-sleeved t-shirt that she tucked in. She then put on a brown skirt that went from her waist to her shins. She made a few friends on her first day of school. They invited her to go with them to the mall. She was scared that they would make fun of her since she couldn't afford to buy anything, so she lied to them saying that she had already used her family allowance for the month. She knew she couldn't keep up this charade forever, but she wouldn't make it seem like she was dirt poor either, even if that was the case. The outfit she was currently wearing was a birthday present from her brother. It was the nicest thing she had to wear. Isabelle asked Reighley how much it cost, but was only told "Don't worry about it", in response. She was sure it was expensive, and he must have used a good portion of his savings for such a nice outfit. That's why Isabelle was determined to become the financial provider of the family so Reighley could finally take a break and not work himself to death and maybe even start a family.

"Wake up sleepy head," Isabelle said as she opened the door from their kitchen to their garage. To her surprise, Morgana had already beaten her to wake up Reighley, as the kitten was standing on his chest as if demanding some sort of sacrifice. Reighley had fed Morgana some leftover chicken and rice that the family had the night prior, but they were all out and needed to get some actual cat food for Morgana.

"I'm already awake. Woke up with cat paws on my face." Reighley said with a yawn and a stretch.

"How do you plan on feeding him anyway? I know you're out of money." Isabelle asked sternly.

"Well, the original plan was to go on a bike ride and find some curb treasures, to pick up and sell, but things have been taken care of in the meantime," Reighley answered with a lax tone, lifting Morgana off his chest. "C'mon boy, let's see what we can scrounge up in the kitchen." Reighley climbed down his top bunk with Morgana in hand and made his way toward the kitchen door.

"You know, you could at least change out of your pajamas first."

"Yeah, you're right, hold this for me." Reighley handed Morgana to Isabelle and shooed her out the door.

Isabelle was standing by the kitchen door patiently waiting. She spent the time staring at Morgana in her arms and petting him. While waiting, Jericho returned through the front door. She had just returned from her first job and only had roughly thirty minutes of free time until she had to leave for her second job.

"Hey honey, I see you're ready for the mall. I can drop you off before I head to work. Make sure you bring the lunch I made you." Jericho mentioned while in a rush to get ready.

"Okay, I will." Isabelle went to the kitchen fridge and grabbed a premade lunch meat sandwich that was made for her and took it out. She unwrapped it and took the meat off it to feed it to Morgana. "Here you go kitty." Morgana meowed and ate the meat as if looking pleased with the offering. Reighley finished getting ready and opened the kitchen door and went through it. Reighley was wearing an all-gray outfit that looked loose and comfortable. When he saw Isabelle, he beckoned her to hand the cat over to him.

"C'mon hand him over. I have to feed him." Reighley asked.

"Fine..." Isabelle said with mild disappointment. Reighley took Morgana and walked over to the kitchen fridge, and noticed the premade lunch made for him.

"This will have to do for now." He said and proceeded to feed Morgana the meat from his sandwich as well. Morgana's eyes sparkled with awe, and after he ate the meat, he had an energy to him as if he was royalty. Immediately after, the doorbell rang. Isabelle turned towards the door and rushed over to it.

"I got it!" she exclaimed. When she arrived only a few meters away she opened it to see a sight that astonished her. It was a man that looked to be a butler in his late forties. He had a mustache and a monocle. Isabelle thought he looked straight out of a gentlemen's movie or something similar. In his arms was a container that looked like it was made from pure stainless steel. It had a cat paw emblem on the center of it and inside were two bags. One read Premium Cat Litter and the other Premium Cat Food. The two bags were surrounded by cat toys filling the inside area around them. What immediately grabbed Isabelle's attention was who was standing next to this stranger. It was the prettiest girl she had ever seen. She had long red auburn hair that looked silky to the touch. Her skin was fair and smooth, without a blemish and her eyes were like looking into an aquamarine gemstone. However, something was off about this mysterious beauty. She appeared nervous. It didn't make much sense to Isabelle. *"Why would a beauty like her be nervous?"* She thought.

"Good morning, Mr. Summers. I am Herald. Standing here beside me is Freya Young. We are here to acquire Reighley Summers."

"Acquire? I don't even know who you two are." Like a blow to the gut, Freya was shocked to the core. Not one, but two people didn't have a single clue who she was.

"Could you go and fetch Reighley for me? I need to speak with him." Freya asked.

"Yeah... Sure." Isabelle closed the door in the two's faces and went over to grab Reighley. Isabelle was suspicious. Not of the request, but because no girl that pretty would want anything to do with Reighley. It was out of nowhere. She wondered if this Freya girl was some secret girlfriend Reighley hid from the family. Then Isabelle thought she had figured it out. The cat food, litter box, and toys and the way Reighley said he had the money thing figured out, not to mention the way Freya said the words "Fetch". Isabelle guessed that he must have gotten another job working as a butler.

Still, something didn't add up to her. Freya was nervous. Isabelle knew that look on her face too. It was the look that she could best describe as hopeful anxiety. As if Freya was looking for approval. Isabelle snuck up behind Reighley who was bent over looking into the fridge for food and began to whisper.

"Hey. There is a pretty girl at the door waiting for you..." Isabelle stated.

"There is a what!?" Reighley exclaimed as he jerked his head banging against the freezer door. A nervous sweat started running down Reighley's brow as panic began to set in. Reighley stood up and rushed to the door in a hurry. It was as he feared. Somehow, Freya found out where he lived and now she showed up out of nowhere at his doorstep. The worst part of all was he wasn't sure how he was going to explain this all to his sister or his mom. It wasn't as if he could just tell them that he sold his pride as a man for some quick cash. When he made it to the door he closed it behind him, only to turn around to be a foot away from Freya. Meanwhile, Isabelle couldn't help but feel like something was wrong about the whole situation. Why was Reighley freaking out as well? She vowed to get to the bottom of it all, as she didn't want some random girl taking advantage of her brother. She would decide who would be a worthy partner for him.

Chapter 5

Many Firsts

Reighley was caught off guard. He was close to
Freya, too close. He paused for a moment, not sure where to
move. He didn't say a word. Freya was looking away from
him, and because of this Reighley couldn't tell what her aura
appeared like. However, Reighley thought he could make an
educated guess. Seeing what she was wearing, he bet she had
just come from a summer festival. Reighley then looked over
at the mysterious person standing next to Freya and could
only assume that he was her butler. When their eyes met, he
saw an ice-blue aura around the man. Reighley had shivers
sent down his spine, as ice-cold daggers for eyes were peering
into his soul, or at least that's what he thought. It was odd for
him to have such a bright aura just to have such a cold feeling
behind it. Reighley figured it was due to this butler not
approving of him, or not agreeing with Freya's choice of men.
It was unnerving, as most light blue auras meant kind, gentle,
or calm. This man, however, could only be described as calm.
Reighley took a step back nervously.

"What are you doing here exactly?" Reighley asked.

"What? Are you not happy to see me? You are my boyfriend starting today so I thought it best to have you join me for a date." Freya replied, finally looking into Reighley's eyes. Reighley noticed something unusual. The black billboard sign that was her aura wasn't snake-like, like the one that suffocated him before, instead, this one was more tame. However, It was still pointing at him.

"What? I thought that was starting next week."

"No. You said 'tomorrow after school. It's technically after school and tomorrow.'" Freya answered. Reighley fully admitted to saying that but didn't tell Freya that. He said after school tomorrow because it was a Friday and there was no school the next day, therefore he wouldn't have to talk with her. He thought it was a pretty clever way to make her leave him alone for the time being. He didn't think it would bite him in the butt.

"Okay, okay fine, but what's with all this cat stuff? I didn't order anything." Reighley asked. He was curious how Freya knew about Morgana, then it clicked in his head as he saw the limousine behind Freya and the butler. He remembered it being there during the whole predicament. However, that didn't explain to him how they found out where he lived.

"Consider it a 'boyfriend bonus.', and don't worry I plan on paying you a full week's worth of pay. " Freya stated. Reighley felt kind of dirty, in a gross way after hearing that. It was like he was property almost. However, Reighley couldn't afford to say no. He needed that money and the sooner he had it, the better.

"Well. How did you find out where I live?" Reighley asked.

"I had Herald here, find you. He's an expert at information gathering." Freya said proudly.

"Right..." Reighley replied with concern for his privacy. "Well anyway, thanks for the cat stuff. Could you give me a few minutes to get ready?" Reighley said while taking the stuff from Herald.

"Sure, but try not to keep me waiting too long," Freya answered. Reighley turned and opened the door behind him and brought all the gifts inside. While his back was turned Freya managed to peek through the door crack before it closed and saw a pair of suspicious eyes looking back at her. It was the girl who opened the door. Freya assumed it was Reighley's sister, so she hoped to make a good impression on the girl.

"Who is that?" Isabelle asked judgmentally while placing her hands on her hips.

"Just a friend," Reighley responded while avoiding eye contact.

"A friend hmm? Since when do friends bring a bundle of gifts, and show up looking like a pageant queen?" Isabelle probed.

"Okay, you got me. She's my employer." Reighley said with a sigh

"You got a job? Doing what?" Isabelle asked.

"Apparently as a part-time butler. Trust me, I know how it sounds, but she is offering to pay me good money. I'm doing this to better my future." For some reason, Isabelle didn't believe that Reighley was telling the truth or at least the whole truth.

"Are you sure this isn't your girlfriend?" Isabelle asked skeptically.

"I'm sure. I don't have any romantic feelings for this girl. I promise." Reighley replied. This time around Isabelle could tell he was telling the truth.

"Well okay. If you say so. Just don't work too hard, okay?" She shrugged her shoulders and walked back to her room. She would let it slide for now as she thought it was rude to keep people waiting at the door. However, she would do her own investigation of sorts at a later date.

Reighley left the hallway and went to his garage, closing the door behind him. He set the cat food and a litter box up in his garage. He placed Morgana in the litter box to get him familiar and then placed a bowl of cat food and water on the floor nearby. Reighley began to scratch his head about what he was going to wear.

"What should I do buddy?" Reighley asked the cat who was currently drinking out of his water bowl. "I can't turn her down. She just gave me all this free stuff. If I waste her time, she might not pay me either." Morgana twisted his head in confusion and looked at Reighley, who was pacing back and forth in his room, while also changing into the nicest outfit he had. "I suppose there is no other way around it is there? I guess I'll have to fake it till I make it. I mean she is paying me so, I might as well take it seriously. I'll just treat it like a real job." This plan all seemed well and good to Reighley until he realized he's never actually had a girlfriend before. Of course, he had liked people in the past, but he had never been in a serious relationship.

After taking a deep breath, and finishing getting dressed Reighley took a step towards the task at hand and headed to the door. When he arrived back outside, a slightly annoyed-looking Freya was waiting for him. Herald seemed to have already got into the limousine, as the engine was now running.

"Sorry to keep you waiting," Reighley said.

"It's fine," Freya said, trying to hide her impatience. Freya quickly scanned Reighley's outfit with her eyes and thought that he cleaned up nicely. He was wearing a green unbuttoned shirt over a white t-shirt and had black jeans on. She honestly expected him to wear mostly black but thought the colors looked nice, although cheap looking.

"Well let's be on our way. We don't have all day now." Freya stated.

"Right…" Reighley replied. Freya took two steps and then paused briefly. This was her first date. She knew it didn't mean anything, and that she wasn't going to marry Reighley let alone keep him for very long. Her goal in all this was to find out if Reighley thought she was pretty and to keep him for a long enough time that the rest of the school would think that the first encounter she had with him was merely a fluke. However, this was technically her first date, so it still made her somewhat nervous. All of her boyfriends she had in the past, she only spent time with them at school. She had never actually let any of them last longer than two weeks at most. She always kept them at an arm's length away as they would try to cling to her, both physically and emotionally. Reighley however was the opposite as far as she could tell. She would have to make moves toward him.

"Here," Reighley said. He held out his hand to grab a hold of hers and Freya was dumbfounded.

"Ah- yes," Freya said shocked. She slowly reached towards Reighley's hand but was unable to grab it. Suddenly Reighley took the initiative and grabbed her hand and held it tightly. Although Reighley was being confident he had no idea what he was doing. Normally he most likely wouldn't do this on a first date with a girl he liked. However, since it was Freya, it didn't bother him as much since he had no feelings for the girl. He thought he would just pretend to be brave and act like a confident boyfriend. Since Reighley was getting paid for it, he thought he might as well play the part.

Reighley went ahead and pulled Freya along to the limousine and opened the door for her. This put a light smile on Freya's face as this was the "bare minimum standard" told to her by Herald. Herald stated, "If a man cannot even hold the door for his maiden, then he is not worthy of her time." Freya sat down and Reighley made his way around to the other side of the vehicle and entered in from that door. While Reighley was doing this Freya looked at her hand, and could feel the heat leaving it. She clenched her fist and loosened it several times until Reighley opened the door, causing her to stop and act nonchalant about her actions. Her heart beat quickly. This was the first time a boy had ever held her hand.

"So, Where are we going?" Reighley asked while taking a seat.

"We are going out to eat. It's nothing too fancy. I have to ease you into this lifestyle. Anyone can be poor as you only need to worry about day-to-day things, but one must learn to be rich." Freya answered. Reighley took slight offense to the reply but shrugged it off as he wouldn't expect her to understand what it's like to be in his shoes, so he gave her the benefit of the doubt.

"Well, wherever we are going, I'm sure what they have is better than what I had for breakfast," Reighley said.

"What did you eat for breakfast?" Freya inquired.

"Nothing," Reighley said with a chuckle. Freya was baffled, but then let out a genuine giggle, only to catch herself mid-laugh. A few moments later Freya heard the sound of Reighley's stomach rumbling.

"Don't worry, you'll eat soon" Freya said to Reighley.

"Thank you for the reassurance." He replied.

The two sat in the back seat of the limousine in an awkward silence for the next few minutes. Desperate to break the silence, Freya thought she would ask Reighley about himself, as from her experience all guys liked to talk about themselves. Showing interest in them usually was the way she got guys to be wrapped around her finger.

"So, was that girl who answered the door your sister?"

"Yeah. Her name is Isabelle. Don't let her looks deceive you either, she can be a real villain sometimes." Reighley said sarcastically. "All jokes aside, she's actually pretty awesome. She's definitely smarter than I am, and works twice as hard."

"You must really care about her," Freya stated.

"Yeah. I do. Her future is paramount to me. The same applies to my Mom's retirement." Reighley mentioned.

"What about your father?" Freya asked.

"Well, I didn't think this would get so personal this quickly," answered Reighley.

"You don't have to answer if you don't want to," Freya replied.

"No, it's fine. He's not a part of my life anymore. He left the family when I was younger." Reighley said with distaste. Reighley lied about it being fine. He didn't like to talk about his father, but on the other hand, it was like therapy to him. He never wanted his family to carry the burden that was his emotional strife with his father so he kept it to himself.

"I see. I'm sorry to hear that." Freya said. She was surprised to see that Reighley had depth to him. That he was a real person. Most guys she talked to in the past would only talk about herself and would have borderline identity crises just to try to have similar interests with her, ending up making faux relationships.

"We have arrived." A voice over an intercom said. It was Herald as he proceeded to pull over to the side of the road to drop off the couple. Reighley stepped out of the limousine and opened the door for Freya, extending a hand for her to take. Freya allowed Reighley to help her up and then the two glanced at their surroundings.

It appeared that they had arrived in the Northern Higashisoma district. This place was fairly unique as it kept Japan's feudalism structure and design while implementing American techniques into the construction and overall appearance. This caused buildings to be far taller and built tightly together to make it appear more like a city. In front of the two appeared to be a small dimly lit alleyway in between two wooden buildings you could only describe as modern samurai temples. Each floor had an outer rooftop that had pointy corners that extended past the building. It was constructed almost as if someone built multiple buildings on top of each other, each one representing a level of the building. They were pagoda towers. Reighley guessed that the structures were business owned.

Meanwhile on the rooftop of the building across the street directly behind the arriving couple was Officer Templeton. He was posted up on the left-hand corner of the roof, dawning a pair of binoculars. The night before Officer Templeton had checked in after school ended with him speaking to Lady Prismarine. She told him that she would have assigned him to overwatch Freya on her date if it wasn't for her request to have Lily chaperone in his stead. Templeton was outraged with Reighley as the boy did not heed his warning. Frustrated that he wasn't selected for the job, Templeton decided to do his private surveillance of the boy.

"C'mon now, first you don't listen to my warning I went out of my way to give you, and then you had the nerve to date the one person I said to stay away from. I bet you're just taking advantage of the young family's kindness just to get an easy life. Just give me a reason to shoot you with this tranquilizer dart so I can drag your butt straight back into juvie." Templeton said while aiming a scoped dart rifle at the kid. "I can't wait to see the news articles that'll read 'Epic Police Officer Saves Billionaire's Daughter and Becomes Chief of Police'. Once I proved this kid is a criminal. I'll earn the respect of Jim Young, and potentially become his right-hand man on the security team!"

"It looks like our spot is down here," Freya said nervously.

"You are just asking to get mugged aren't you." Reighley criticized. Reighley was insulted again at the thought that Freya assumed this is what his life was like, but seeing how she appeared to be distraught he decided to let it slide once again. "Don't worry I'll keep you safe." Reighley took Freya's hand and the two proceeded down the alleyway.

Lily had stepped out of the limousine only a minute after the couple. She stealthily made her way to the designated meeting spot and waited for the two to go to the restaurant. Templeton noticed the two holding hands and was infuriated.

"How dare that street rat touch the Boss's daughter. Don't worry I'll keep that filth off of you." Templeton grimaced. He aimed his rifle at the boy ready to fire at any slight mishap Reighley would try, but then was suddenly blinded. It was a reflected light coming from a cell phone. Templeton lowered his rifle and pulled up his binoculars to see Lily looking him directly in the eyes. She gave him a death glare, it was as if she was saying that if he ruined this date she would ruin him. Lily shook her head 'no' several times and Templeton withdrew out of fear, putting his rifle away only to watch from a distance with binoculars.

"She's scary." Templeton quivered. He was terrified that she spotted him from that distance.

Reighley and Freya both walked for a bit down this elongated alleyway only to find that it was a strip mall, with many different walk-in shops built into the sides of the structures. Soon the two found their destination and stood before Back Alley Ramen. It was an underground restaurant. To enter, one would need to go down several stairs and turn left to reach the entrance.

"So this is it?" Reighley asked.

"It would appear so, yes," Freya answered.

"Shall we?" Reighley gestured towards the stairs which were dimly lit by lights from the ceiling. Freya nodded 'yes' and the two made their way down. Once the couple reached the bottom of the stairs, they saw that the entrance had a cloth that was parted through the middle. On it was a bowl of ramen with the characters (ラーメン) which Reighley could only assume meant ramen.

He was alone at work. Ulysses's father didn't work Saturdays. It was the only day he took off as he wished to leave it to his two sons so they could learn the restaurant business. However, Ulysses's brother was busy on his date today so the shop was left up to him. Though he feared failure, he was passionate about helping those he cared about, which in turn gave him strength. He wouldn't let his family down. It was not difficult for him either, as cooking was something he had been doing since he was three years old. He had no problem holding down the fort for his family so they could succeed in their own goals. Ulysses was preparing two signature ramen dishes for customers when he noticed Reighley and Freya walk in through the sheets at the entrance.

To the couple's surprise, the restaurant was the exact opposite of their expectations. Almost everything was made out of wood. It was tidy and the polished floor had a sparkle to it. The ceiling had lanterns with the same characters from the entrance on them. They set a beautiful atmosphere for the place. There were bamboo plants as well as a small fountain in one of the corners of the room. The restaurant was way larger than expected as it looked as if it could hold fifteen people at a time. In front of them was a table with stools you could sit on as you order your food and directly behind the table was a kitchen where said food would be prepared in front of you.

After the couple entered, their eyes immediately locked onto Ulysses. To their surprise, he was running the ramen shop.

"Wow. Small world." Reighley said.

"Oh! I didn't expect you two to come here." Ulysses was curious.

"Well, to be fair, neither did I," Reighley said. Ulysses gestured for Reighley and Freya to take a seat. When the two sat down Ulysses asked what the two would like to eat and pointed to a menu sign behind him. Reighley ordered the Spicy Shoyu Ramen, made with chicken broth and soy sauce as well as other vegetables, and Freya ordered the Miso Chashu Pork Ramen made with a soy-based broth with pork oil mixed into it. While preparing their orders, Ulysses made a promise to himself to make this meal perfect for the couple so he could be in good standing with Reighley. The two didn't talk much the first time they met, but he wanted that to change, as Reighley wasn't afraid of his outward appearance.

"You know I'm a little envious that you have such a pretty girlfriend Reighley. It being Freya Young no less." Ulysses said. After hearing this Freya looked at Reighley with anticipation. Ulysses gave Reighley a perfect opportunity to compliment Freya on her appearance.

"Yeah, she's pretty-" Freya's eyes widened in excitement until she heard the end of the sentence. "-great." Disappointed, Freya turned away to sulk for a brief moment.

When Ulysses heard the comment from Reighley it felt disingenuous. He thought that their relationship must have started recently. He knew that a good bowl of Miso soup to share between the two while they waited on their ramen would help them bond. While cooking Ulysses pulled out a large oval bowl and stuck a single soup spoon in front of the couple.

"On the house," Ulysses said. He looked directly at Reighley and gave him a sly wink and quick thumbs up. Ulysses thought that being a good wingman would help their bond as best friends begin to blossom. Reighley realized what the chef was attempting to do and decided to play along. He took the spoon and allowed some soup to fill it, and then proceeded to feed it to Freya.

"Here you go, darling. Say ah." Freya realized what was happening and immediately became flustered. Her face became as red as it did the first day the two met. Her head began to spin from embarrassment. She couldn't say no, as that would draw suspicion that the two weren't dating at all. Only their class and a few others knew that Reighley rejected her. Freya knew of Ulysses from school rumors and heard that no one would talk to him, so as far he was concerned the two could have been dating for several months. If that were the case, they wouldn't have any problem doing "lovey-dovey" stuff. The only problem was much like everything else in this "relationship" this was another first for her.

"Ahhh." Freya held her mouth open in an unflattering way, and Reighley proceeded to feed her the

Miso soup. Freya could have sworn that steam expelled out of her ears from how hot her face had become.

"Weird," Ulysses said under his breath. To him, it was almost like this was their first date. As they didn't appear to do this regularly. *"Is this their first date?"* He thought he might as well ask. "Hey not to question how long you two have been together or anything, but you two do not seem like you've been dating for very long," Ulysses stated. Reighley was about to answer when Freya chimed in, interrupting him.

"You're completely wrong. Reighley and I have been together for a month now!"

"Well, if you say so," Ulysses said. During this, he noticed a figure step through the sheets covering the entrance. It was a girl wearing sunglasses, a scarf, and a cap. The girl was fairly petite and had platinum blonde hair. It was Lily. After she entered she sat a few chairs away from Freya and Reighley.

Lily was irritated that she had to be here. She would much rather be at home sleeping than working on a weekend. However, if she had to be here, she might as well eat. Though she didn't think the place would amount to very much. Lily had a very picky palate when it came to food. There weren't too many things she liked. Although, she would still eat most things as it was necessary for survival. Regardless, most things tasted bland to her. Since she never had time to cook, she had no way to get tasty food except at events that Freya or her family were at.

"Welcome! What can I get for you today?" Ulysses asked.

"The daily bowl special is fine," Lily answered. Lily glanced over at Freya only to see Freya glaring at her. Ulysses began to fix her requested dish. He had just finished the couple's food but as he prepared to serve them, he looked at the couple only to see a nervous Reighley. He was holding the soup spoon a few inches from his mouth but was unable to drink the soup. Reighley realized that Freya put almost her entire mouth on the spoon he was about to drink from. If he took a sip it would be an "Indirect Kiss" from Freya. Remembering his job, Reighley mentally said goodbye to his first meal shared with a girl and drank the soup from the spoon.

Freya did not realize that Reighley indirectly kissed her. Her mind was still cooling down from being fed by Reighley. Ulysses served the couple their meals, disrupting them from their internal struggles. He couldn't help but not believe that the two were dating for a month now. Freya was too embarrassed to say a word. Reighley realized that he may have teased her a little too much and looked over at Freya.

"Hey, I'm sorry, was that too much?" He whispered.

"Yeah. I'm okay..." She answered. Hearing Reighley's concern for her made her heart skip a beat. All the previous things he did before now felt to Freya as if it was because he was obligated to do so, but he didn't have to ask her how she was. That made it mean more to her. When Ulysses saw this small interaction, his suspicions began to waver slightly. He knew what genuine concern looked like. To him, it wasn't something you could just fake.

The couple began to eat their food. When Reighley tried it, his facial expression was filled with joy.

"This is good! Like, really good! Is Gordan Romsly secretly hidden under all that muscle?" Reighley asked. Lily looked over at Freya and waited for her reaction. She figured Freya wouldn't like the food as much as her date. Freya had one of the best chefs in the world working for her family, so Lily compared eating here to going from a five-star restaurant to a fast food chain. Freya took a bite and she looked very surprised. Lily was shocked when she took a second bite, and then a third.

"Immaculate!" Freya exclaimed. Lily immediately became very eager to try this. She began to watch Ulysses cook. She realized that he was very detail oriented with his skills. He was massive in stature but was a gentle giant when it came to cooking food. When Lily's food was finally ready she stared at it intently. She eagerly grabbed her chopsticks and took a bite. Lily was shocked by the taste. It was the best ramen she had ever had. It truly was incredible. She looked up at the towering chef and viewed him as the god of ramen. He only looked back at her with confusion. Lily decided that she needed to marry this man. If he could create food that she could enjoy then she would gladly become his wife just to eat something this tasty daily.

Lily began eating in silence, this made Ulysses think that she did not like his food. He began to feel guilty about it.

He couldn't help but tremble in anticipation. Lily thought that at first glance Ulysses was just a punk in appearance. He was towering in the shop, almost cramped by the ceiling. His muscles looked like he trained them every day, and his dyed hair made her think he was your typical thug. She guessed that he was a troublemaker at school. At first glance that was what he appeared. However, someone who put that much care and consideration into something they did had to be a kind and gentle person on the inside. Meanwhile, Freya and Reighley got up and paid for their food. Freya left an extremely generous tip. The couple said their thanks and told Ulysses that they would return to eat there again. Ulysses stated that he would bring some for Reighley at school on Monday and Reighley took him up on that offer, though it left Freya uneasy as she wished to keep Reighley all to herself. After that, the couple left.

"Excuse me, sir, may I ask for your name?" Lily asked while batting her eyes, after removing her sunglasses.

"Ulysses." He introduced himself by saying only his name. It frustrated him, as his nerves made him unable to say the right words when it came to girls.

"Good," Ulysses said. He meant to ask her if she enjoyed the food. However, the words didn't come out as a question. It was phrased as an answer instead, making Ulysses feel more anxious. He began to freak out that the next thing he said would make him look idiotic.

"It was good!" Lily replied with a smile. It was a miracle. She understood him even when he messed up. Every girl he had trouble talking to usually walked away awkwardly as they didn't know how to talk to him.

"Back," Ulysses said. Again he couldn't speak well. He meant to say 'come back soon'. Ulysses worried that she might think he is some sort of muscle head, with no education.

"I have to go now, but I'll come back. I promise." Lily stated. The words promised echoed into Ulysses' head. She understood him. Even when he messed up she understood him and still wanted to return. Ulysses began to wonder if this was what it was like when his Dad met his Mom. Lily had to rush out. She needed to get into the limousine before the couple to not be seen and didn't want to keep Freya waiting.

Reighley saw the girl in the strange getup rush past him and Freya. She sprinted down the alley and out of sight. He thought it was weird but didn't question it. Freya couldn't help but feel frustrated. She put so much effort into making her maids do her makeup and prepare her clothes just so she would keep Reighley's gaze but to no avail. He was not infatuated with her, and nothing she did seemed to work. She would have to do things a little more apparent to make her stand out as the goddess she was.

The two made their way out of the alleyway and their ride arrived only seconds after. Reighley opened the door for Freya once again and the two got inside and began their route to the amusement park. Freya looked at Reighley, who was currently staring out the window watching the world through the glass. She thought he was cute. She liked his curly hair that coiled up from the humidity. Even though she had previously stared at him a multitude of times, this was the first time she realized that she was physically attracted to him.

Freya reached to grab Reighley's hand. When she touched it, his hand instinctively jerked away from her. Freya realized that the worst scenario had occurred. Reighley turned towards Freya awkwardly and tried to play it off. He then proceeded to hold her hand.

"You can stop," Freya said.

"Stop what?" Reighley asked.

"You can stop forcing yourself. If you hold my hand, do it because you want to, not because you have to." She answered and pulled her hand away. Reighley didn't know what to say. He was surprised that she considered his feelings. Even though he barely knew the girl, he thought it would be uncharacteristic of her to put him first. He wondered if her aura was wrong about her.

"I'll wait for you... until you're comfortable with me." Freya said.

"Right..." Something changed inside of Reighley. It was small and almost unnoticeable, but something began to stir.

Freya looked away from Reighley, hiding her face, and began to blush a tremendous amount from what she had just said.

"'I'll wait for you.' What am I thinking!? Why would I tell him that? It's not like I want him as my boyfriend forever. Just for a month..." She thought.

Reighley started to question if this was the right thing to do. Even if she was taking advantage of his poverty to buy his time just so she could appear perfect in the public eye. He wondered if it was okay to just be fake and not try to get to know her even though she was putting in all this effort for his sake. Reighley decided that once they arrived at their next location he would try to get to know Freya a little better. She was a complete stranger, and Reighley knew a good person, let alone a boyfriend, would try to get to know her regardless if he was getting paid or not.

"Here." Reighley handed Freya his flip phone. "So I can know in advance the next time you want to pick me up."

"I don't know how to use that." She replied. Reighley laughed as it didn't surprise him.

"Just tell me your number and I'll enter it in," Reighley said. Freya exchanged numbers with Reighley. She couldn't help but smile at the words "next time".

The limousine arrived at Distracto Land. Known for its crazy rollercoasters, its waterpark, and its characters. Distracto was a subsidiary owned by Freya's father. It was an entertainment industry that made movies, cartoons, and merchandise. When they exited the vehicle, the two were greeted by a security guard that escorted them inside the amusement park bypassing the line at the entrance.

Chapter 6

The Paid Date

The security guard guided the two toward the V.I.P. entrance, and a shiny golden lanyard was given to the two of them. This allowed them to skip to the front of the line on any ride. Freya pulled Reighley towards her and pulled out her phone readying to take a picture of the two.

"I have to post on SocialLight since I haven't today," Freya said.

"Hey, what if my family finds out!?" Reighley panicked.

"I've seen your phone. There is no way that 'that' ancient technology would be able to use SocialLight." Reighley reluctantly nodded in agreement. Freya took the photo of the two together. Freya was posing, holding her fingers up as a peace sign, while Reighley looked awkward and uncomfortable.

"Hey, let's retake it. Make sure to smile." The two attempted to take another ten photographs before Freya got a little upset from them all looking like she was holding Reighley hostage.

"Are you doing this on purpose?" Freya asked sternly.

"No! I just don't get my picture taken often. I hate photos of myself." Reighley said

"Why?" She asked.

"That's kind of hard to explain." Reighley couldn't tell her the reason why. Reighley had trouble looking at himself, whether that be in a photo or the mirror. He became incredibly talented at being able to avoid his own gaze in a reflection. The last time he had looked himself in the eye was after the incident in middle school. Freya decided not to press him further as she didn't want to push him away.

"Very well. You can tell me eventually."

Freya didn't delete the photos she took with Reighley, even if they looked questionable. She thought he looked cute in them. She sent a few of them to Destiny.

Freya: On a date with Reighley. (Photos Attached.)

Destiny: Geez, Freya! What on earth happened to him? He looks like he's being held there against his own will. Does he have shackles on his feet just underframe?

Freya: No! He just doesn't like his photo taken, but I plan on getting the perfect candid picture of him today. One I can keep as my wallpaper.

Destiny: I've never seen you do that before. You must really like this guy, huh?

Freya: Oh, whatever. I still plan on dumping him after a month. My parents would never allow me to marry someone of his social status.

Destiny: (Picture of someone's ankles with shackles on) "@Reighley"

Freya: LOL

Freya knew Destiny was technically right. She had never had one of her exes' photos as her wallpaper, even while dating. She wasn't sure about the other comment, however. Freya wondered if she did have feelings for him. She honestly didn't know. She had never been in love before and wasn't sure what that was like.

Reighley waited patiently for Freya to finish.

"So, what do you want to do first?" Reighley asked.

"Roller coaster. I want to ride all the roller coasters." Freya replied. Reighley looked at her aura which once was a giant billboard sign. It became multiple tiny black arrows pointing towards a multitude of directions that he only assumed were where roller coasters were located. Reighley thought to himself that his ability to see what she wanted would be pretty useful on their dates. He was sure many guys would be incredibly jealous to know exactly what their girlfriends wanted.

"All right. Lead the way." Reighley said. He thought he could probably find them all too using Freya's arrows, but he hadn't been here before so he didn't want to draw suspicion for himself. The two made their way to several roller coasters, some had loop-the-loops, others had you get inside while the coaster started upside down. Skipping the line had Reighley get deadly glares from some of the people waiting in line. Although, he could tell that some of them were because of who he was with. The security guard stayed nearby preventing anyone from going up to talk to Freya. During the rides, Reighley looked over at Freya and saw how excited she got from the coasters. It was like she was in an adrenaline rush. Afterward, she would regain her composure and act ladylike.

"You really like these rides, don't you?" Reighley said out of breath. He would get exhausted fairly quickly from the heights, and loops, as his heart could only take so much.

"Yes, they are quite grand. My father owns this entire park, so of course he would make the perfect coasters." Freya looked over at Reighley and saw him leaning over in exhaustion.

"Okay, you pick the next thing. I'll give you a short break for now." She said with a wink. Time and time again Reighley kept on getting surprised. She was quite considerate, even if it was only an obligation for dragging him along.

"You know, you're pretty sweet," Reighley said.

"Ah, thank you." Freya didn't know why, but even though she would receive thousands of compliments daily, through her maids and followers on SocialLight, this one meant more than all of those combined. Reighley smiled and stood up straight.

"All right. Mr. Security Guard, do you know of any horror attractions here?" Reighley asked. He loved horror. His favorite series of books growing up was a horror series called

Quiver. A collection of individual tales of obscure and odd things happening. Usually supernatural.

"Ah, yes. I would recommend the Hall of Shadows. Also, my name is Richard." The guard replied.

"Okay lead the way, Mr. Security Guard," Freya said. Richard wanted to correct her but feared losing his job. He knew exactly how scary Mr. Young was and didn't want to enrage his daughter, even by accident. Meanwhile, Lily was occupied keeping all those who wanted to interact with Freya at bay. She would swiftly interrupt any attempt of a fan to get close to Freya. She even asked Herald for help. The two secretly informed the severity of the situation to the security team, and how jobs were on the line if this date didn't go smoothly. The entire security team at the park then assembled and made an effort to keep all fans away from Freya and Reighley.

"I didn't realize being famous could be such a pain." Reighley said while watching a man holding a sign that said 'I Love You' on it be dragged away.

"It's not that bad. Being worshiped by people has its perks." Soon the two arrived at the Hall of Shadows. It was a black tent with a sheet thick enough to block out all sunlight covering the outside. The two entered the darkness only to be met by a strange figure surrounded by fake plastic candles standing behind a desk. Behind her were four doors that led into what can only be assumed as the hall of shadows.

"Welcome to my domain!" A woman in a vampire costume said. "To gain the treasure at the end one must put the blindfold of courage on and be placed in the center of the maze to start. Once you're inside you may remove the blindfold and attempt your escape."

"Sounds like fun," Reighley said while looking at Freya who seemed uneasy.

"Oh, but it is not! No mere mortal can escape the Hall of Shadows!" The vampire replied. Reighley could see an aura around the vampire girl. It appeared to be a red color indicating how serious this woman was taking her role.

"So what do you say, Freya?" Reighley asked.

"Let's do it," Freya replied. Deep down she was fairly scared. The reason this scared her, and extreme sports did not, was because with sports she had full control over most situations. Her own life was in her hands. However, with things like ghosts, she couldn't pepper spray a ghost or karate chop it. It wasn't like she carried a vacuum with her at all times either to suck the ghosts up, though in retrospect that didn't appear to be a bad idea to her. She could have sworn she had seen that in a game once.

The Vampire woman tied a piece of red cloth to Freya, and then to herself and then Reighley and Freya put on their blindfolds and held hands.

"I will guide you to the start. However, it is up to you to escape the maze!" The vampire said. "Once inside please locate your exit signs and enjoy!" After a short walk, the two were placed in the middle of a dark room. The vampire told them to wait to remove their blindfolds and to stay put. A few minutes later a voice was heard over an intercom.

"You may remove your blindfolds of courage!" The Vampire said. The two took off their blindfolds only to see a confusing scene. The floor was painted with glow-in-the-dark arrows pointing in many directions. The floor also had light paths dimly illuminating the area. Reighley tried to follow one only to bump into a wall.

"Ouch!" Reighley said after his face hit the wall. Reighley then began to panic as he had just realized what he got himself into. The hall of shadows was a hall of mirrors.

"Are you okay?" Freya asked. She was concerned.

"Yeah, I am..." Reighley answered anxiously.

"Are you sure? You don't sound like it." Freya replied. The hall of shadows wasn't nearly as bad as she expected, but she could tell that something was definitely wrong with Reighley. He fell apart, with his head looking towards the ground and knees bent. He couldn't bring himself to move. Eisoptrophobia. The fear of mirrors. More accurately in Reighley's case, it was the fear of his self-image. The mere thought that Reighley could see his own aura in a reflection, filled him with so much anxiety that it made him sick to his stomach. He could barely breathe.

"I can't... " Reighley said, gasping for air.

"Hey! What's wrong?" Freya said while bending down. She began to panic. To her, it looked like he was having a panic attack after he bumped into the mirror. It was dark but the lights on the floor allowed her to see Reighley. She noticed that Reighley had his eyes sealed shut. He needed help and she was the only one there.

"Just hang on. I'll get you out of here." Freya said.

"I can't open my eyes!" Reighley said.

"It's okay. You can keep them shut. I'll get you out of here." She replied. Freya took Reighley's hand and carefully helped him up. Reighley had no choice but to trust Freya. He held on tightly and didn't dare let go. After ten minutes went by of Freya leading Reighley, the two finally escaped the hall of mirrors through a door, only to enter into an elongated pitch-black hallway. From the other end of the hallway was a loud buzzing sound that pushed a breeze at the two.

"Hey, we're out now. You're safe." Freya said. Reighley paused nervously and slowly opened his eyes. Reighley looked behind him and saw a dimly lit glowing outlined door. In front of him was darkness. The door didn't illuminate anything past eight feet. Realizing it was safe Reighley collapsed against the door, with his back leaning on it. He slid down the wooden exterior and ended up on the floor. Freya looked at him with concern.

"Just let me catch my breath for a second," Reighley said.

"It's okay, take your time," Freya replied. Silence fell upon the two for a minute until Freya decided to ask about the hall of mirrors. "So what happened back there?"

"I... don't do mirrors," Reighley answered. "Well, to put it more accurately. I don't like looking at myself."

"Well, you were just fine when we took photos," Freya told

"That was different. I know I won't like what I see. I've gotten good at not looking directly at myself in the mirror." Reighley said. Freya bent down so she was face to face with Reighley. She used her hand to lift his head to the same level as her own.

"I don't know what you see in you, but you look great to me," Freya said with a smile. Reighley froze and the last of his anxiety dripped away. Her aura was small and pointed at his heart. Unsure what to say, he blushed from the comment and turned away from Freya.

"It's not the same," Reighley whispered, completely red. The two stood back up and Reighley took a deep breath. "Okay... I think I'm good now." Freya couldn't help but wonder how Reighley ended up afraid of his reflection but decided to leave it at that. "Thank you," Reighley said as he took Freya's hand. "Just so we don't get separated, all right?"

"Oh, all right..." Freya blushed. The two continued forward into the darkness.

"Ahhh!" Freya screamed. From the shadows were cloth streamers pitch black. They were completely hidden from the two. However, the strong breeze was blowing the cloth in their direction. It felt like the darkness was reaching out and enveloping the two. When this happened Freya let go of Reighley and jumped back. Reighley stopped and turned around looking toward Freya's silhouette.

"What's wrong?" Reighley asked.

"Something touched me. I don't like it!" Freya answered. Reighley realized that the tough cool exterior that Freya had fell apart.

"Are you scared of ghosts?" Reighley asked.

"Maybe..." She replied. Reighley thought it was cute, but decided not to give her any trouble for it since she had just saved him from his worst nightmare.

"Here, hold onto me," Reighley said

"Wait, what?" Freya answered. Reighley grabbed Freya's hands and placed them on his chest. He then wrapped his arms around her and pulled her close.

"Just ·hang on. I'll get you out of here." Reighley said.

"Copycat," Freya muttered, embarrassed. Reighley began to walk backward into the darkness while holding onto Freya. He acted like a shield from the cloth and the breeze. Freya's heart couldn't help but race. She was so close to him. Too close. She could smell his scent, and feel the warmth from his body. All her fears washed away. She felt truly safe in his arms. She hadn't felt something like this since she was a little girl. The two made their way through the darkness. To Reighley, it felt like the walls were closing in on him as the cloth got denser. However, this wasn't remotely close to as bad as the hall of mirrors made him feel. Soon the two arrived on the other side of the veil at the end of the hall. Freya looked up at Reighley who was looking back. He looked into her beautiful blue eyes and got lost in them for a moment. Freya's aura was surrounding him like before, but instead of entangling him, it embraced him gently. It was telling her that she felt comfortable like this.

It had finally dawned on Reighley, what he was doing. He was on a date with an incredibly beautiful girl that was clinging to him. He quickly let go, but Freya did not. He thought her eyes were dangerous. Looking at them was like looking at a beautiful blue gem found at the bottom of the ocean. They were a deep sunken treasure. He always thought she was pretty, but that didn't make him nervous until now.

"You can let go now..." Reighley asked politely. Freya let go and stepped back. The two finally realized that they were being watched by a couple of people. They made it to the end of the attraction and out of the other end of the tent. The two were completely embarrassed by the display they put on for everyone else, and awkwardly left the area.

"Sorry, you had to see me like that back there." Reighley apologized.

"It's okay. Thanks for keeping me safe." Freya said.

"You're welcome," Reighley replied.

Meanwhile, while the two were in the hall of shadows, the security guard team at Distracto Land switched into outfits to blend in as civilians. Officer Templeton was standing at the top of the skyscraper that was the Moon Launcher ride. A towering machine that launched groups of people strapped in, several hundred feet in the air, and then back down to give them the sense of falling. Templeton had a camera in hand, taking photos of the date to bring back to his boss Mr. Young. Templeton was determined to expose Reighley for who he "really" was.

The couple were walking towards the Ferris Wheel to relax a bit after the intense attractions they experienced. While they made their way there, the two stopped for ice cream. During this time, a man attempted a stealthy leap toward Freya.

"Freya, Marr-" The man was abruptly snatched mid-jump by Lily and the security team and taken behind an alley. It was almost as if the man disappeared out of thin air.

"Did you hear that?" Reighley asked

"Whatever are you talking about?" Freya answered. She knew the situation was most likely a crazed fan. However, this happened often and she didn't want Reighley's guard to raise, both emotionally and physically. The two arrived at the Ferris Wheel and once again skipped the line thanks to their pass. Reighley looked at those waiting in envy and couldn't help but feel guilty. He knew what it was like in their shoes as he too should be waiting in line like the rest. It made him wonder why Freya even chose him in the first place. He was grateful for it since it was a relatively easy income, but he wondered if it was just pure luck or if there was another motivation behind it.

The two entered the Ferris Wheels pod and sat down across from each other. Freya thought that overall today went fairly well. She would have to thank Lily for making the date go smoothly. It was 4:00 p.m. and she planned on returning Reighley home on time for dinner so she would be in the good graces of his sister. Then it occurred to her. Why did she care what his sister thought about her? If she planned on leaving him after a month, then she should have no reason to get invested. She pondered this thought but couldn't find an answer.

"Well, how did I do?" Reighley asked. "I mean as your boyfriend. I'm sure you've had plenty in the past."

"Well that is true but, this is my first official date," Freya answered as the wheel began to turn, lifting the two enough for the next group of people to switch out in the pod just under them.

"Really? I would have thought a pretty girl like you, who could have anything she ever wanted, would have wanted to go on a date." Reighley said, confused. Freya was overjoyed to hear the word "pretty" come from Reighley's mouth. It truly was a mission success. She finally got her answer. Beauty was half the battle, however, it still didn't sit right with her. Out of all the adjectives he could have used to describe her, she felt "pretty" was somewhat of an insult. He could have said beautiful, gorgeous, or "the prettiest girl in the world". "Pretty" alone just wasn't enough to satisfy her, but it would have to suffice for the time being.

"There aren't many guys out there worth dating, in all honesty," Freya replied.

"So then why me? I'm not special, and I definitely don't have money, so why?" Reighley asked.

"Because I couldn't have you and I always get what I want. Desperate times, call for desperate measures." Freya said honestly. Reighley felt slightly sickened by the answer, but it made sense and he was glad she was at least honest about it. However, it stung a bit, knowing he was disposable to her.

"I see..." Reighley answered. At this point, the two were halfway to the top of the wheel and Reighley looked out towards the crowd below and then surveyed the landscape. Freya got nervous from the silence.

"*Did I say the wrong thing?*" She thought. She was the one who told him she would make him fall in love with her in only a single month. She thought being truthful was the correct course of action. Freya looked at Reighley and thought this was the perfect time to get herself a candid picture of him, so she took out her phone and took a picture stealthily. The photo was surreal. It had a melancholy feeling to it, like a memory captured in time. While looking at the photo she couldn't help but think back to the Hall of Shadows, and how Reighley panicked at the mere thought of seeing his reflection. "*Was he the real vampire here? What kind of life does someone have to live to be that insecure with themselves?*" She wondered. Freya felt like he had too many emotions that had been bottled up and needed to be let out.

The silence lingered until the two reached the apex of the Ferris Wheel, only to abruptly stop once again. Reighley looked back over at Freya, the wind blowing in her hair. Reighley thought it was something out of a movie. He thought it was too bad she wasn't as nice as she looked or he might actively try to pursue her. He noticed her aura was almost riveting. It was as if she had nine elusive and aloft tails with the shape of an arrowhead coming behind her. All of which were pointing toward him. It was a captivating sight to behold. To him she looked like a mythical creature heard in fairytales, but real and only a few feet away. She was a complete mystery to him. It was like he was stranded out at sea, only to discover that there was a deep bottomless ocean below. He was a mere step from drowning.

"Just who is Freya Young?" Reighley asked.

"What do you mean?" Freya questioned.

"I know nothing about you. We are complete strangers, and yet here I am on a date with a girl I don't know. If you really plan on making me fall for you, I think getting to know you better would be a good start." Freya didn't know why, but to her, it felt like Reighley was giving her a hint to gain access to his heart. Meanwhile, the Ferris Wheel began to spin in full motion as there were no more passengers to load or unload.

"Well, I am a famous, beautiful, talented, rich, multi-billion dollar girl," Freya said with a smug expression.

"I already knew that," Reighley replied. He couldn't help but scoff at how conceded she sounded with that comment regardless if it was true or not.

"Well, my father owns Slowsoft and I am the eventual heir to the company," Freya said proudly.

"Okay, but I kind of figured that one out on my own," Reighley replied.

"Fine, ask me a question, since you know everything apparently," Freya said, annoyed.

"Back on the roller coasters, you were like a completely different person. Your face looked like someone who truly was living life to the fullest. What was up with that?" He asked.

"Extreme sports…" Freya muttered.

"What?" Reighley asked.

"I do extreme sports, okay? I do it because it makes me feel alive, but you absolutely cannot tell my family."

"Wait seriously?" Reighley asked, confused.

"I keep it a secret from them, even though I occasionally live stream myself sometimes doing it. There is something about the risk involved that gets my blood running." Freya answered. Reighley was blown away completely. When he asked to know more about her he didn't expect to learn that she was an adrenaline junky of sorts. He figured she would have said she was into modeling or something similar. He thought she would tell him that roller coasters made her feel like she wasn't some peppy princess and could let loose and not worry about things just for a little bit.

"Well, I didn't know that," Reighley said sarcastically. "You just keep on surprising me."

"Well, is that a good thing or a bad thing?" Freya asked.

"It keeps things interesting, at the very least," Reighley answered. The two began to talk about Freya's hobby until the end of the ride. Reighley discovered her passion for doing dangerous things and couldn't exactly wrap his head around it. Roller coasters alone were enough to make him fatigued. He couldn't even begin to imagine himself skydiving, ice climbing, or even hang gliding.

Finally, the Ferris Wheel came to a halt, and it was time to exit the ride. Freya could have easily just asked her father to let her have the park all to herself allowing her and Reighley to spend the entire day alone together with the exception of the security, but feared that would make the date even more artificial than it already was. The two stepped out of the pod and Freya informed Reighley that it was time to head home.

The two walked back towards the entrance and on their way a group of three female students from Gilford High School spotted the couple. One of the students took a photo of the two from a distance and began to gossip about Freya and her love life to the other two. One of the girls in the group was Samira Tempest.

"We should totally post this on SocialLight. I'm sure the school would go crazy knowing Freya Young had an official boyfriend." The girl who took the photo said with an almost greed-filled grin. This girl's name was Yula Figthorn. She had green highlights in her hair, was a second-year student, and was a member of class 2-D.

"Yeah, and that boy she's with must be a real catch if he got with her. Maybe we could try and steal him away." The other girl said. This student's name was Matilda Key. She had half black and white hair split right down the middle of her scalp, was also a second-year student, and was a member of class 2-D.

"We should give them their privacy!" Samira said sternly. She was surprised to see who Freya was with. From what she could tell, Reighley had no idea Freya even existed on his first day of school. So she wasn't sure why he would be on a date with Freya. Even though their meeting was brief, Samira couldn't forget the first impression he left on her. Soon after Reighley showed Samira the cat he rescued she couldn't believe the rumors that were being spread around school about him. His eyes were too kind to be some criminal. He already had it rough enough from what she could tell. "Look, I dislike Freya just as much as the two of you, but we should at least respect Reighley's privacy."

"Why? Who cares? He is a lost cause all things considered, especially if he ended up with that wench." Yula said with a shrug.

"I'm not so sure. The whole 'bad boy' thing is pretty hot." Matilda said.

"I won't allow it!" Samira exclaimed, stepping towards Yula. "We 'ALL' know very well the full extent of being harassed by Gilford Academy. That boy had nothing to do with that, so we should just leave him out of it." Samira's sense of justice was compelling to the two girls. Samira had a heart of gold, and her friends knew that. She prided herself on doing what was right even in trifling times. It was that exact reason Yula and Matilda became friends with her.

Yula saw the fire in her eyes. She was serious. It was the same as when she first met Samira. How she could keep herself like that was a mystery to her, but she couldn't help but give in to her demands.

"Geez! I get it. You don't have to yell okay? I won't post the photo."

When Samira shouted, Reighley caught wind of it. He looked over and recognized one of the three girls. Samira looked back at him and their eyes interlocked. Reighley could see that her aura was different from the day prior. The once light green, soft, and gentle breeze was now an intense pressure on his shoulders. It was like her conviction had weight to it. When she realized he spotted her the aura's pressure let up. Reighley was about to raise his hand and say hi to Samira when Freya stepped in front of him.

"Don't bother giving that trailer trash attention," Freya said, filled with jealousy. For the first time, Reighley didn't recognize Freya. She looked almost sinister with her intent being abundantly clear. Her aura blocked out the world around the two. It encompassed them, filling the space with pitch-black darkness. Reighley knew what this meant. Freya wanted complete control over who he was allowed to see.

"What?" Reighley asked.

"I said don't bother with that trailer trash. Only focus on me." Freya said.

"No…" Reighley's heart was filled with anger, and his eyes with pity. "Today's date is over, right? I'm going home." Reighley turned and left Freya out in the open. He put up with a lot of her comments, but this was a potential deal breaker for him. Samira was one of the first people to treat him with kindness at school. Almost everyone else there was against him, but she was kind. He felt as though he would lose all respect for himself if he stayed near her for even a second longer, so he left.

"Wait. Come back! You can't just leave me here! You're mine! How do you plan to get home anyway?"

"I'll walk," Reighley replied while looking over his shoulder with cold eyes. He then proceeded through the exit and made his way toward home.

Chapter 7

I'm Sorry

Freya did not understand what went wrong. The date was going perfectly until now. Just what happened? What would make Reighley want to leave her side? The look Reighley gave her kept replaying in her head. She had a roller coaster of emotions going all at once. She felt as though their date ending had to do with some external factor. She looked over at the group of girls whom Reighley was going to greet. It appeared that they were watching the whole time.

"It must be because of them," Freya said angrily. "This is all Lily's fault. She should have kept that stupid group of girls from being near Reighley. Worst of all it was Samira and company. They just had to interfere again." Even so, she didn't understand why Reighley would have just left. She guessed they must have told him something about her at school. Freya approached the group of girls. When Samira, Yula, and Matilda saw Freya head their way they all prepared themselves for the worse.

"Look, here comes the red devil," Yula said. Soon, Freya was right in front of the group and looked as upset as ever.

"What did you tell him?" Freya questioned Samira with crossed arms.

"Tell who?" Matilda said, stepping in front of Samira.

"Don't play dumb with me. Reighley recognized you three." Freya accused.

"Why don't you just leave us alone?" Yula asked, joining Matilda.

"Girls, it's all right," Samira said while having Matilda and Yula step out of the way. "I met Reighley on his first day of school, but the only thing I told him was where the Nurse's Office was that day. Nothing else. Besides, if I did mention bad things about you, then why would he have agreed to spend time with you?"

"Yeah, instead of accusing us, why don't you just ask him yourself why he's mad?" Matilda asked. As upset as Freya was, she thought they did have a point. However, Freya would not show any weakness.

"Stay away from him. All three of you, unless you want a repeat of what happened at last year's school festival." Freya threatened and then turned away. The trio heeded Freya's warning and then went deeper into Distraco Land to get as far away from Freya as possible.

Soon Freya met up with Lily and Herald. Freya explained that Reighley left on his own accord.

"Herald. I would like you to make sure Reighley arrives home safely. I will call Elise and have her pick Lily and me up."

"As you wish, Lady Freya. The boy will return home without a scratch." Herald replied and swiftly took off towards the limousine. Once he was out of earshot, Freya turned towards Lily.

"Lily, what happened?" Freya asked.

"I am unsure what you are referring to as Lady Freya," Lily replied.

"You were supposed to make sure the date went smoothly, yet somehow Reighley ended up leaving. You should have done a better job clearing the area of unwanted people."

"I am sorry Lady Freya, please forgive me. It appears my best was not enough." Lily said with a bow. This struck a nerve in Lily. She had spent the entire day working hard to prevent the failure of the date, but in the end, she still got blamed for Freya's failures. Lily assumed Reighley just left because Freya was too self-centered.

After hearing Lily's response Freya felt bad about her comment. Freya knew Lily was giving it her all for her sake, and until the point of Reighley's departure, things were going perfectly. Deep down she knew that Lily had nothing to do with Reighley's departure. Even so, she couldn't figure out what went wrong.

"No, forget what I said. You did a great job today." Freya said. Lily noticed how Freya looked and could see she was visibly upset about the thing she said. This response was enough to soothe Lily's anger. She didn't expect Freya to second guess herself, let alone praise her afterward. She wondered if Reighley had some sort of positive influence on her.

Freya took out her phone and made a call to Elise, asking her to pick them up, and the two waited around for the next 15 minutes for their ride to arrive.

Reighley was walking on the sidewalk in a random direction. He didn't want to admit it but he wasn't sure how to get home from here. However, he didn't regret his decision either. He knew that he would like himself even less if he stayed around Freya after what she said. He decided he wasn't going to end things with her either. In the end, for the most part, he thought Freya was kind and compassionate, be it, in her selfish way. He even enjoyed the date, despite a few scares along the way. So, he figured he would ask Samira and her friends about Freya to learn more about their situation the next time he saw them at school.

While walking aimlessly, Reighley noticed a familiar white limousine pull up next to him. The window rolled down revealing Herald holding a bag in hand.

"Care for a lift Master Summers?" Herald asked. Reighley was about to interject, but Herald knew what he was going to say. "Do not fret. Lady Freya is not here. She asked me to make sure you get home safely, and to respect your privacy."

Reighley looked into Herald's eyes and no longer saw the cold-as-ice aura emanating from him. It was now a simple light blue aura.

"What's in the bag?" Reighley asked.

"Your money," Herald said. "I was given the responsibility of paying you your weekly checks." Reighley thought it over for a second, and after thinking about it decided to get inside the vehicle. Herald rolled down the window separating him and Reighley and he handed him the bag of money. Reighley could not believe his eyes. He was given 500,000 yen, (3,517 USD). He made more money in this one weekend than he did his entire summer job the year prior. He thought it was crazy that Freya could just throw money around like this as if it was no big deal.

"I'm guessing I don't have to tell you my address," Reighley said.

"You are correct. I am well aware of where you and your family live." Herald replied. Reighley wasn't sure how to take that comment. He didn't know if it was a threat or something harmless.

"Right..." Reighley replied with a false smile. As it turned out Reighley wasn't too far from home as it only took fifteen minutes to get there. When they arrived Reighley stepped out of the vehicle with his bag of money in hand. Before he had the chance to walk away, Herald rolled down the window once again.

"Master Summers," Herald said

"Uhh... Yes?" Reighley replied.

"I have watched over Freya since she was a newborn. Never have I once seen her truly chase after or show interest in someone or something to the degree she does with you. Do not play with her heart." Herald said. Reighley looked at Herald for a brief moment. Was it advice or a warning? He couldn't know for sure. Without a word spoken to each other, Herald rolled up his window and took off speeding away.

Finally, Reighley was home, but his work was not over just yet. He went inside and awaiting him with a stubborn glare was Isabelle.

"So how was this Job?" She questioned, with hands on her hips.

"It was a rough first day, but it was bearable." He replied. Isabelle noticed the bag of money in Reighley's hand and became incredibly confused.

"Did you guys rob a bank or something!?" Isabelle asked.

"No, no, I am not doing criminal activity. I am an upstanding citizen."

"Yeah, sure. Whatever you say Mr. Bank Robber." Isabelle said with rolled eyes.

"Well, what about you? How did the trip to the mall go?" Reighley asked.

"It went okay. My new friends bought a lot of stuff while we were there." Isabelle said. Feeling bad for his younger sister, Reighley pulled out 14,200 yen (100 USD) and gave it to Isabelle. Her eyes widened from the amount handed to her. It truly made her question the validity of her older brother's work.

"Here. You can have this, the rest is going towards our school debt and mom's bills."

"I don't want your blood money." Isabelle jested. "Besides, it's your money."

"It's not blood money, but I may need to pay you to keep your mouth shut. I'll need you to keep this a secret from Mom." Reighley replied.

"Okay partner, you have yourself a deal," Isabelle said, shaking his hand. Isabelle pocketed the cash and headed towards the kitchen to cook dinner for the family. Reighley lied to his sister. He didn't plan on taking a cut from that money he had just earned. He just made an excuse so she would take the money from him. With that out of the way, Reighley made his way to his room. Once inside, his leg was pounced upon by Morgana. Reighley picked up the small kitten and played with him.

"Hey, buddy. Sorry, I was gone on your first day here." Reighley said while petting Morgana behind the ear. He looked over at all the expensive cat essentials Freya and Herald gave him before abruptly stealing him for the day. He felt it was a bit much, but he did appreciate it, as it was more money he saved in the end. "Here. Let's get you some food." Reighley spent the next half hour taking care of Morgana until dinner was ready. He ate with Isabelle, and couldn't help but look at the two empty chairs in the dining room. Afterward, he spent the rest of his night studying.

Elise picked up Freya and Lily and returned the two to the Young family estate. The three went inside and Freya had Elise prepare a change of clothes for her to wear for dinner. Once ready, Freya went into the dining room to eat with her mother, with her father still absent.

"So, how was the date? What I wouldn't give to experience being young and in love again." Marine asked. She put both hands on her cheeks and sighed longing for the past.

"Mother, I am not in love, but it was nice, up until the end..." Freya said with rosy cheeks.

"Oh, What happened dear? Did you break his heart?" Marine leaned forward attentively.

"No. He was kind and I felt like we grew a lot closer from such a small amount of time spent together." Freya answered.

"Then I don't see the problem," Marine said, confused.

"Well, something happened right before we were about to leave and then he ended up walking away," Freya explained.

"Care to elaborate?" Marine questioned.

"Well, the thing is, I don't know why he walked away, but he had a look in his eyes. It was like all that enjoyment he had on the date was suddenly gone in a single moment." Freya told.

"I see... Well, why don't you ask him? If there was one thing I wish was better with my relationship with your father, it would be communication. That man is so busy that he barely has time for a phone call. If you're considering this boy to be a real boyfriend, you should think about these things. On the other hand, if you plan on treating him like the flavor of the week, then it may not be worth the time."

Freya pondered the thought. She remembered she had Reighley's phone number, so she could ask him via text. However, Freya had several problems at hand. What was the appropriate amount of time to wait before texting someone you just went on a date with? If she texted him too soon, would she seem needy? It wasn't as if he could just text her. He didn't have her number on his phone, and even if she did text him, what would she say? All these thoughts stormed Freya's mind at once until Marine interrupted her train of thought eager to know more.

"Anyway, what else happened?" Marine asked.

Freya then told Marine all that happened during the date, and Marine felt a thirst for more romantic tales. She was giddy with each bit told. Freya left out the part with Reighley having a mental breakdown in the Hall of Shadows. She didn't wish her mother to think less of him and felt as though it was a secret that she and Reighley shared.

Finally, once dinner was finished the two made their separate ways. Freya needed to study, so she proceeded to her personal library. Sometime during dinner, Herald also returned to the manor. While studying, Freya couldn't help but stare at her cell phone on her nightstand. She would glance over at it briefly and consider texting Reighley, only to perish the thought. This reoccurred a multitude of times, distracting her from getting any work done. This continued even while Freya was in bed. She couldn't sleep with the thought of disdain in Reighley's eyes; she couldn't bear him ignoring her the next day or any day after. Finally, after a short burst of vigorously spazzing in frustration, she decided to text him.

Freya: Hey it's Freya.

"Hey? Is that the best that I could come up with?" Freya said and then screamed into her pillow in embarrassment, kicking her feet. Reighley was still studying on his desk. Morgana was sleeping curled up in a ball next to his textbooks, when Reighley's phone made a notification sound, waking the kitten up. Surprised he got a message at all, he wondered who would be texting him at 11:32 P.M. He wondered if it was Kaede, as she would sometimes send him drunk texts telling him she missed him. Reighley looked at his phone and to his surprise it was Freya.

"Hey?" Reighley said aloud while petting Morgana. "Why on earth is she texting me at this hour?" He wasn't sure what to do, but decided things would be worse if he didn't reply, he answered. Freya stared at her phone, waiting for a response. She wondered if he may be asleep, or even worse, he saw it and didn't reply. It was driving her crazy, but then suddenly her phone received a text back.

Reighley: Shouldn't you be asleep?

Freya: I couldn't sleep. Not without knowing how things stand between us.

Reighley: Us? I'll still work for you if that's what you're asking. I'll be your pretend boyfriend on Monday.

Freya couldn't help but be frustrated with his response. It was what she wanted to hear, but it wasn't what she needed. She needed to know why he left her out in the open at the amusement park. It boggled her mind. It made less sense the more she thought about it.

Freya: I'm glad to hear that but that isn't it. I need to know what made you leave.

Reighley: I'll tell you, but I need to figure some things out first. Anyway, I just finished studying so I'm going to bed. I'll talk to you later.

Freya: Okay. Goodnight.

Reighley: Night.

Freya held her phone up while lying on her back. She stood still, staring at the messages. Their short conversation left her with more questions than answers. Freya was surprised Reighley was studying this late at night. She bet it was that exact work ethic that got him accepted into Gilford High. Still, she felt completely unsatisfied with the result of her conversation. This feeling made it difficult to sleep. She went to her photo gallery on her phone and looked at all the pictures she had taken from their date, stopping at the one she took of Reighley on the Ferris Wheel. She then proceeded to set it as her wallpaper. She stared at the photo on her phone screen. Her heart began to beat out of her chest. She could not stop thinking about him.

Sunday came, and Freya spent most of her day live-streaming to distract herself and even tried several extreme sports to get her mind off of things, but no matter what she did, she kept thinking about Reighley. She would constantly check her phone for messages just on the off chance that she missed a text from him. Reighley on the other hand spent his time storing the money he had earned in his bank account, then he went on a treasure hunt for curbside throwaway items. He ended up finding an old VHS TV set with a bunch of old movies. This was a great find. He couldn't wait to set it up in his bedroom and have vintage movies playing while he studied. Soon Monday arrived and it was time for school. Freya was driven to school by Herald, and Reighley walked to school. When he was just down the block from Gilford High, he saw Ulysses just a few houses down. Reighley quickly caught up to Ulysses. When he arrived he realized just how big he was in comparison to his height.

"Ulysses! Hey big man, what's up?" Reighley said, patting Ulysses on the shoulder.

"Hi, Reighley. Uhh… Not a whole lot." Ulysses said. He was pleasantly surprised that Reighley came up to greet him. "Here, I made this for you, like I said I would." Ulysses pulled off his large backpack and handed Reighley a metal-insulated food container from inside it. "It's your ramen. You can return the container when the day is over."

"Thanks. You didn't have to do this for me. Do you want me to pay for this?" Reighley asked.

"No. I said I would, so I did. It's that simple." Ulysses answered. Reighley was genuinely happy he was about to get free amazing-tasting ramen. He thought he may have gotten a read on Ulysses at this point. His aura was misleading. At first on the outward appearance Ulysses seemed intimidating to Reighley, but after he saw him in action, he was just an earnest young man doing his best. He was like a big teddy bear but with all the might of a real bear.

"Well, thanks. I appreciate it. I owe you one." Reighley humbly accepted the gift and the two continued.

Ulysses looked over at Reighley and had a moment of reflection. Although he knew he would never be as good a cook as his other family members, all the hardships he faced while learning to cook truly paid off and this made him proud of himself. His skill helped earn him a friend.

The two walked the rest of their way to school together and chatted about the video games they both played. Reighley took notice of Ulysses' choice of games. The majority of the ones he recognized were new single-player games, it made him wonder if he just liked being alone or didn't have many friends to play with. Ulysses was shocked to hear that Reighley didn't have many games. The games he would mention were quite dated as well. He wondered what his financial situation was at home since it sounded like Reighley wanted to play those games but just didn't have them for some reason or another.

Finally, the two were at the school gates. Reighley thought it strange that the school guard from the week prior wasn't on duty, instead it was the history teacher Mr. Rugborn.

"Hold it right there." Mr. Rugborn held his arm, preventing the two from passing.

"You didn't hear my warning, did you? I told you to not be a burden on Ms. Freya and yet you started trouble in my class. Do you have any idea-"

"Any idea of what Mr Rugborn?" Freya answered from behind the two boys. She glared at the teacher and then proceeded to walk up next to Reighley and grab his hand. The students who were filing into the front entrance all froze in astonishment.

"Do you have any idea how well you did on your entrance exams boy? I checked your results and you aced the test, with a 100% score. Congratulations." The teacher said with a nervous sweat, even though he truly believed Reighley cheated and didn't deserve to be here.

"Well, thank you," Reighley replied, and then three made their way into school.

Although Reighley wasn't too fond of Freya coming to his rescue for the second time, he did appreciate that she ended the harassment towards him even if it was only temporary.

Freya was terrified of what she just did, not because of the repercussions at school as that wouldn't happen to her, but because she was placed in a position where she had no idea what she should do next. She tried to play it off all cool, but she didn't know what to say to Reighley since their date.

While walking, Freya didn't say anything at all. The three stopped in front of the school lockers. These were small boxed lockers you could use so you could switch your shoes, as one of the customs was to have a pair of shoes for both outdoors and indoors.

"You can let go now," Reighley said to Freya, who was still gripping his hand.

"Yeah, right..." Freya said. She released Reighley's hand and made her way to her locker, which was head-level. She opened it and hid her face behind the door and then immediately blushed from her actions. "Why can't I talk to him?" she whispered. "It shouldn't be this difficult." Freya was paralyzed, unsure where to go, when she felt a poke on her lower back, causing her to jump with a yelp.

"Hello, goddess of love!" Destiny said with a giggle.

"Destiny! Thank goodness you're here." Freya said. She decided to disregard Destiny's comment since she was going to become Freya's means of escape. Freya grabbed Destiny by the arm and took off deeper into the school. "Come, let's not be late for class now!"

Ulysses noticed the two scurry off and wondered what their deal was. He turned towards Reighley who was nearby and gave him a thumbs up.

"See you later bestie," Ulysses said, with a goofy smile.

"Later," Reighley said, throwing up a peace sign with his fingers. He was a little confused by Ulysses calling him bestie, but he couldn't bring himself to crush the guy's spirit. It wasn't as if he didn't think of him as a friend. Reighley was more than happy to have someone he could approach, and potentially hang out with. He figured they would become good friends eventually.

Now that Reighley was finally alone he planned on finding Samira at her locker before class. He still remembered where her locker was from when they first met, so he retraced his steps until he arrived. Lo and behold, she was there again with Ash Fjord. This time however the two other girls Reighley had seen at the amusement park were with her as well. Reighley was a little nervous. The previous time they talked it was because Reighley was in a desperate situation to find Kaede. However, this time Reighley was about to approach a group of very attractive girls. Going up to pretty girls wasn't something he thought any guy could get used to. If it was one, like Freya, then it wouldn't be as difficult. Deciding not to think about it anymore he made his way to Samira and her friends.

"Hey guys, could I talk with you?" Reighley asked with a nervous smile.

"You sure can, handsome," Matilda said, stepping towards Reighley. When Reighley looked into her eyes, he saw a gray aura. Gray auras usually meant the person was mischievous, cunning, or aloof. Reighley internally warned himself to watch out for this girl as she could cause trouble for him in the future.

"Leave him alone Matilda. He doesn't need another Freya in his life." Yula said. Reighley looked at Yula's eyes and saw a brown aura, just like Mr. Rugborn. Although brown auras meant that the person usually was conservative and didn't like change, it also could mean that the person in question had a hard exterior that was hard to break. This meant it was tough to get close to these people as they let very few in.

"Hey, I take offense to that!" Matilda replied. The group of girls laughed, and Reighley couldn't help but agree with Yula's comment. One Freya was more than enough for him.

"So what's up? I see you fixed your glasses. Did you ever name your little friend?" Ash asked.

"Yeah, I ended up naming him Morgana. I decided to keep him. Also, I know it's none of my business but, do you guys and Freya have a history?" Reighley answered and asked.

"It's good to see you again, Reighley, and yes, You could say that." Samira joined.

"That's a bit of an understatement if you ask me." Matilda chimed in.

"The girl's basically our Arch Nemesis," Yula answered. Reighley thought it weird by their choice of wording. He expected them to say Archenemy, not nemesis. Arch Nemesis implied that Freya did something she thought was justified retribution.

"So. What happened then?" Reighley asked.

"Well, Freya told us not to talk with you, but I don't mind. It all happened during last year's school festival in November." Samira explained.

"Festival?" Reighley asked.

"Our culture festival. It only lasts a total of two days, and during it, all classes participate in a group project, one for each class. The four of us girls were all in class 1-D at the time and the class came up with the idea to hold a dance in our school's gym."

"Okay, so where was Freya during all of this?" Reighley asked

"Her class was performing some sort of play in a theater room and from what I understand, she couldn't stand the fact that our dance was more popular than her play," Yula added. "So, when the second day of the school festival arrived everyone was looking forward to the dance. That's when Freya decided to take things into her own hands."

"I see." Reighley acknowledged.

"Believe it or not, Freya used to hang out with us. Even though she was in a separate class, we used to consider her a friend." Samira answered. "The problem happened when our class dance became the most popular school attraction. Freya didn't like that."

"Being the witch that she is, Freya targeted the students in charge of the dance to get it canceled. Which were Samira and the rest of us." Matilda said. "Samira was in charge of organizing the dance and the class couldn't do it without her. Knowing this, Freya mentioned this issue to her father who then hired security to keep us out of the school for the remainder of the festival. We weren't even allowed on the school grounds."

"In the end, we got blamed by the entire school for being unable to show up and host the dance for everyone and the school harassed us for it. We brought it up to the teachers, but they completely overlooked it because of the power Freya and her family held over the school. Even worse is that Samira lost all of her privileges to host things in the future. The only reason we could even have a dance was because Samira was highly regarded as the most responsible student by all the teachers." Ash said.

"So, now you know," Samira said.

Reighley stood there, taking it all in. It was fairly surprising to him to know how far out of her way Freya would go, to be number one. He didn't take her as such a petty person. However, he felt as though she got her punishment, because besides Destiny, Freya was alone, and that must have been the result of her actions.

"Well, are you going to break up with her?" Matilda asked.

"You would like that wouldn't you?" Yula said. Matilda was flustered, but didn't let it show, and instead rolled her eyes.

"No. I won't and she isn't a witch. I appreciate you guys being honest with me, but I have my reasons for being with her." Reighley answered. He couldn't tell them that he was getting paid to be with her, but he also felt as though abandoning her wasn't the right answer either. "I'm going to have a talk with her."

Reighley thanked the girls once again and headed to class. He felt as though he could fix this. Freya, despite her shortcomings, wasn't all that bad in his eyes. Granted she did some things that are unacceptable, but not unforgivable. He decided he would ask her to talk to him on the rooftop after school and settle things.

Meanwhile, Freya was running out of options. The way things stood, she would lose any chance of Reighley sticking around. She arrived in class with Destiny and Freya sat at her desk without a word.

"Hey, are you okay?" Destiny asked. "You just don't seem like yourself." Freya looked towards Destiny. Freya had a concerned look on her face which was unusual for her. It was so unusual that it was drawing unwanted attention from the class. Some students were wondering why she looked like that and began chatting with other class members whispering rumors, while others were filled with righteous anger as they thought Freya should never look upset. For once, Freya wasn't craving to be the center of attention. She looked back at the class and silenced them with a glare. Afterward, the rest of the class returned to their normal routine.

"Well, I think I did something wrong to someone, but I'm not sure what to do," Freya mentioned

"Then apologize," Destiny said with an immediate answer. "Even if you don't know what you did for sure, it's better to apologize and make up right? That's what you do with the people you care about." This answer surprised Freya as usually, Destiny was the last person she would ask for advice, as Destiny hardly took anything seriously.

Freya thought it through and concluded that Destiny was right, whatever she did, it made Reighley upset enough to walk away. She didn't know if it was romantic feelings or not, but she did care about Reighley. He was different from the other guys she dated, she wasn't sure how, but he was, and she wanted to get to know him better.

Reighley arrived in class 2-B. When he entered he saw Freya. She looked directly at him when he walked through the door. When the two's eyes met, Reighley saw Freya's aura. It was dark purple. The hue changed from being borderline black. The typical arrows that angulated around her were now uniform. They pointed towards Reighley but instead of being jagged and direct, they kept venturing off of him as if nervous. Reighley walked over to his desk and sat down. He heard Freya begin to speak to the right of him.

"Here." She whispered and handed Reighley a note. It read

(Meet me on the roof after class. There is something I would like to talk with you about.)

After Reighley read the note he nodded at Freya, signaling he would agree to meet with her. Soon, class started and the two kept their focus on their studies. When the bell rang and class finally ended Reighley and Freya both awkwardly got up and walked to the roof of the school. They didn't have much time before their next class but Freya needed to say what she wanted. Reighley watched as she walked out to the center of the rooftop. The wind bellowed her red hair. She turned around and began to speak.

"I'm sorry," Freya said.

"For?" Reighley asked. Reighley saw her aura. It was a single, lone arrow, pointing at him yet again. He could tell just how serious she was just from looking at it. Reighley didn't expect her to apologize. He was actually coming up here to tell her that things don't need to be awkward between the two and to ask her about what happened the other day.

"Whatever I did that made you walk away," Freya replied. It was as he suspected. He figured she didn't know what she did wrong, but the fact she apologized was a step in the right direction.

"Look Freya, I'm not upset with you. At least not anymore."

"Then tell me why you walked away! I need to know." Freya asked. She raised her voice so it wouldn't be drowned out by the wind. Reighley walked up to her to answer. The two were now five feet apart.

"There were two reasons I was upset. The first was because you tried to control what I do and who I can be friends with. That's not okay. The second is because you spoke poorly about genuinely nice people. They don't deserve that. I appreciate the apology, but I don't think I should be the one you should be saying sorry to." Reighley answered.

"They didn't even hear me say those things," Freya interjected.

"That's not the point. I know what happened between you and those girls and no they didn't tell me." Reighley said. He didn't want more drama to start because Freya knew he found out from them. Freya's face was riddled with guilt.

"What was I supposed to do? They never treated me right. All they did was want things from me." Freya yelled. Reighley felt as though he pushed too hard. He could tell she was bitter as well, so he decided to dial it back.

"Look, if you're serious about having me fall in love with you. Here's some advice. I love girls who do the right thing."

Silence fell between the two, and Reighley turned blushed with embarrassment.

Chapter 8

Better Between Us

The two were at a loss for words. They both attempted to say something when the school bell rang signaling for them to return to class.

"We should probably get back to class," Reighley said.

"Okay," Freya replied. The two made their way back to class 2-B. On their way back Freya stopped Reighley before the two entered the classroom.

"So are things okay?" Freya asked.

"For now," Reighley answered. Finally, the two entered the classroom and took a seat at their desks. When the two walked by Destiny, they both noticed a smug look on her face. They thought she looked as if she knew something they didn't. Destiny looked over at the two and leaned in to whisper.

"How was the smooching?" Destiny said. Reighley and Freya both choked on the air itself in response to her comment.

"That didn't happen," Freya whispered. She looked over towards Reighley who couldn't bear to look her way after that comment and blushed.

"Yeah, whatever you say love birds," Destiny said. Afterward, the class's next teacher entered the room and proceeded to teach math to the students.

During class, Reighley couldn't help but cloud his mind with thoughts of what he told Freya on the rooftop.

"Why did I say that? That's so lame!" Reighley internally screamed. "I can't believe I said love. What did I even mean by that?" While the teacher was in the middle of a lesson, a loud slam noise could be heard in the back corner of the classroom. It was Reighley. He slammed his forehead on his desk loud enough to disrupt the entire class.

"Mr. Summers, do we have a problem?" The math teacher asked. Her name was Cynthia Clevens. She always wore white business attire and had black hair and green eyes. She was twenty-one years old, single, and unmarried.

"No ma'am," Reighley answered. Afterward, he sank into his desk chair and almost couldn't contain his embarrassment. This answer infuriated Ms. Clevens.

"*I am not a ma'am.*" She thought. "*I am an attractive young woman.*" At this point, the entire class was looking toward Reighley. Freya looked over at him with concern as she had no clue why he would do that to himself.

"Are you okay?" She whispered. "I could get my best doctors in, to check on you, if you're not feeling alright."

"No. I'm okay." Reighley replied and shook his head no. Reighley looked back toward his teacher Ms. Clevens and noticed she was looking directly at him. He didn't need to see her aura to recognize that hostile expression she was giving him. Her aura, however, once looking at it, appeared in both red and black colors. The colors were separate but also melded in and out of each other. Reighley thought it reminded him of magma. He wondered how much anger was built up in his teacher. It was as if she was a volcano. He could only pray he wasn't on the receiving end of the irruption.

Freya found it hard to focus. Unlike the embarrassed Reighley, Freya found conviction in the words she was told. *"What does it mean to be a good person?"* she thought. *"Does he think I'm not one? I'm super nice."* Freya began to doubt herself but then convinced herself that she could figure it out. *"I want him to know me better. I want him to think I'm a good person."* Freya looked over at Reighley during class and came up with an idea. She was going to learn more about Reighley through his younger sister. *"I'll just take her out on a shopping trip and spoil her, and maybe exploit her for information on her brother."* She felt as though she couldn't just pry into his personal life through him just yet. Freya knew Reighley didn't have a father in his life, and assumed that might be part of why he is the way that he is, but couldn't be certain. She figured this would be the best way to learn more about Reighley without bugging him.

Reighley felt as though something was off with Freya. When he looked at her, he saw a flash of gray around her aura, and he could only prepare for the worst as it meant she was planning something. Soon the class was over and it was time for their homeroom period. This was a short break to eat or do other things. This break usually only lasted between five to ten minutes before their next class started. A couple of female students went up to Freya and Reighley and stood in front of their two desks.

"So we heard the rumors. You held Reighley's hand when you entered the school, right?" The female student asked.

"Yeah, are you two dating?" The second female student questioned.

Reighley glanced at Freya waiting for her to brag about how the two went on a date but noticed something was off. She looked back at him, anticipating an answer. Realizing that the ball was in his court he decided to reply.

"Yeah, Freya is my girlfriend now. We went on a date this weekend." Reighley answered.

"Wow! No way, she really did tame the beast like the rumors said." One student said to the other. Reighley took offense to the comment, but at this point, sly comments toward him began to affect him less and less.

"Don't call my boyfriend a beast," Freya said with an angry expression. The two girls looked at each other and then bowed to Freya in fear.

"We're sorry!" The two girls said in unison and then scurried out of class. Freya made a mental note to trash the two girls on social media for having the audacity to disrespect Reighley after knowing they were dating.

Freya began to realize that people tended to see Reighley poorly due to his past, but she knew that he was a nice guy. She decided to post one of the photos of them at the amusement park together on SocialLight. She thought if people knew Reighley was her boyfriend. They would stop harassing him. Freya was scrolling through her photos, attempting to find the perfect one to post. She thought about posting the one she saved as her phone wallpaper but after considering it, decided that it was for her eyes only. In the end, she couldn't decide.

Suddenly Ms. Clevens, who was currently gone, reentered the classroom and approached Reighley.

"Mr. Summers. Since you interrupted class earlier, I decided to assign you on clean-up duty after school." Ms. Clevens said. After School Clean Up Duty was assigned to students to do after school. It was mandatory because it taught students to clean up after themselves and be responsible. However, in some rare cases, teachers would assign it to students who weren't on duty for that day as a way to reprimand students who misbehaved.

"Okay, sure." Reighley didn't mind. He didn't think of it as unfair treatment as he did slam his head into his desk disrupting the class. Ms. Clevens was unhappy with this response.

"What do you mean, 'okay sure?' You're not supposed to be okay with it." Ms. Clevens thought. "Alright well, at least you understand your mistake and are willing to own up to it." Ms. Clevens said.

Freya was watching this all unfold when Reighley's words echoed into her mind. This was her chance to be a good person.

"I'll help too!" Freya interjected. When she said this the whole classroom uproared. Freya was the only student who didn't have to participate in after-school clean-up duty. Due to her father owning eighty percent of the school as an investor, the Gilford High School Teachers Union decided it would be unsightly for Freya to work.

"That isn't necessary Ms. Young." Ms. Clevens said. "I am sure you are aware, you are not required to participate in clean-up duty."

"I know, but even still, I want to do it." Freya thought this would be a good way to nonchalantly ask Reighley if she could come over so she could take his younger sister out for some shopping.

Reighley was shocked to hear this. "Does she even know how to clean?" He thought. He bet that Freya had never done physical manual labor a day in her life. "Was this because of what I said? He wondered if something began to stir up inside her heart."

"Well, if it is what you want, I cannot say no." Ms. Clevens answered. It wasn't as if she could deny her wishes. She hoped that it wouldn't come and bite her later on. Ms.

Clevens walked away from the two and felt dissatisfied with her results from the intervention. She felt it best that since Freya Young was involved she wouldn't press it any further, so she made her way to the nurse's office. She often spent most of her time during her breaks there speaking with her good friend Kaede. The two would chat about things that happened in and out of school to help Cynthia get her mind off stressful things and relax.

After Ms. Clevens left, Reighley noticed Freya looking toward him. She had a look in her eyes, and he was sure he knew exactly what was going on inside her head. It was like her face had, "See look, I can be a good person." written all over it. Although Reighley appreciated the help, he needed a break from Freya and other people. He was an introvert at heart and was reaching his limit on how much social interaction he could handle before he needed to be alone.

"Looks like it will be just the three of us!" Destiny chimed in. Freya and Reighley leaned over and looked at Destiny who was smiling at the two.

"What?" The two said together.

"I'm on clean-up duty too! Oh boy, was I surprised you volunteered to help Freya. Even when we were kids you always made me clean up the toys we played with together."

"Well, that's very true," Freya said. When she was younger she liked bossing Destiny around. There wasn't any need for Destiny to pick up all their toys as children since that was what the maids were for. She did it because, near the start of their friendship, she found Destiny annoying.

Reighley, glancing at Freya began to question the type of "friendship" Destiny and Freya had when they were younger, he guessed if it was more of a servant and master type of relationship than a friendship, but decided not to think about it.

The school bell rang yet again and class started shortly after. During the remainder of their breaks, Destiny spent time informing both Reighley and Freya of the duties they would help with after school was over. During lunchtime, Reighley ate the ramen that Ulysses made for him and couldn't have been more satisfied. He was given cold soba noodles soaked in a dripping sauce. It was even tastier since it was free. When classes finally ended for the day, the three stayed behind to work together. After school, clean-up duty only took a maximum of fifteen minutes and normally it was done with two students. They would use brooms, vacuums, and mops, to clean the floor, and then take the trash out as well as clean the chalkboards.

Reighley began to sweep the floors, and Freya was given a vacuum. Freya began to move the vacuum without it being on. She ended up getting instantly frustrated as she wasn't sure how to operate it. Reighley noticed her struggling and decided to help.

"Here, you need to turn it on, after it's plugged in," Reighley said, afterwards he plugged the vacuum in and showed Freya how to use it. Freya was embarrassed by her incompetence, but Reighley didn't blame her for it. He figured by the way people treated her, that she had everything done for her in her life. He thought this was a good opportunity to learn what it was like to be a normal everyday person. Destiny was on the mop and trash duty. After a spot was swept and vacuumed she would mop the area that was just cleaned. After twelve minutes passed the three were done cleaning, and all that remained was taking the trash bags out of the room. Destiny lifted two filled trash bags but couldn't swing them over her shoulders. Reighley didn't know if she was being dramatic or not but it looked like she was struggling from it.

"Here, I'll take one," Reighley said. Destiny looked at Reighley in awe, as if he was an angel sent down from heaven above. Reighley was handed a bag and was impressed Destiny was able to lift two of them at once, as they were not light in the slightest. Reighley being kind made Freya irritated. She wanted Destiny to take the trash out alone so she could be alone with Reighley, but she couldn't fault him for ruining her plans and being a nice person. Suddenly the classroom door opened up behind the two.

"Hello, bestie," Ulysses said, acting coy.

"Hey dude! What's up, what are you doing here?" Reighley asked.

"Well, I was waiting at the school entrance so I could get that ramen container back," Ulysses said. Although that was true, he also wanted to hang out with his new friend for a little bit before they had to go home. Ulysses noticed Reighley and Destiny looked like they were struggling with what they were holding. He looked over and saw Freya who seemed impatient with the situation. He wondered if he and Destiny were interrupting Freya and Reighley from having a moment. Ulysses saw this as a moment to prove himself once again. Deciding to be a true friend, Ulysses went into wingman mode.

"Hey, would you two like some help with those?" Ulysses asked.

"Sure that would be great" Reighley replied before immediately getting interrupted. Ulysses hoisted both bags out of Reighley and Destiny's hands and single-handedly swung them over his shoulder. Reighley was flabbergasted, as those bags combined weighed well over 60kg. He thought Ulysses truly was a powerhouse and wondered if he was involved with any sports.

"Hey Destiny, can you show me where to take this stuff?" Ulysses asked.

"Oh don't be shy now Uly. You can call me D. We're friends, right? We have been since you helped me the other day." Destiny replied.

"Umm... Okay, D, can you show me where this goes?" Ulysses said.

"Sure Uly," Destiny replied while going out the classroom door. Ulysses looked at Reighley and Freya and gave his signature thumbs-up before following Destiny. Freya's opinion of Ulysses improved once again. "It *looks like I owe him one, yet again.*" She thought.

Reighley was putting away the cleaning equipment back into the cleaning closet that was in the corner of the room. When he was done he turned around to see Freya too close to him. He looked into her eyes and could see her aura. Her dark purple aura arrow was pointed in a random direction which made him confused. He expected her to have the arrow pointed at him since he was alone with her. Nevertheless, he still wasn't comfortable being ambushed by her.

"Hey Reighley, could I come over?" Freya asked.

"What, why!?" Reighley asked. Reighley had many questions. Why would she ask to come over, and wasn't it improper for her to be at his house? "Just what are you planning?" He thought.

"I want to see your house." She claimed. Freya got closer to Reighley. He was almost pinned against the wall.

"Freya please, you already tried this tactic once, it doesn't work on me. I don't break that easily." Reighley said.

"Tch, fine." Freya scowled. "What do you want then, more money? I can pay you."

"Are you trying to bribe me, again?" Reighley asked.

"It worked last time." She jested.

"Just tell me what you're planning. I just want you to be honest. You can't solve everything with money, Freya." Reighley told. Reighley knew she wasn't wrong. The only reason he dated her is because she was his ticket to get his family out of crippling debt. It was to pay off the house they lived in, and their tuition. Even so, it wasn't going to help her in this case. Reighley strengthened his resolve and decided that no amount of money she offered him would tilt his favor towards her, as that wasn't good for her in the long run.

"How about 1,000,000 yen? (6,875 USD)" Freya asked.

"1,000,000 yen!" Reighley thought. "That would cover a quarter of a semester here at Gilford High. I could really use- ``No!" Reighley stopped his train of thought. "I can't. I told myself I wouldn't be bribed by her." Reighley gulped and then stood tall. "No." He said.

"It really won't work huh?" She asked. "Fine, I want to meet your sister." It finally clicked with Reighley. That dangerous arrow was pointing toward his house. The fact that she knew the exact direction of his home was astounding to him. He stood there and thought it through. It wouldn't hurt if she met Isabelle. He thought it may even lower Isabelle's suspicions of him. She was already thinking Reighley was robbing places, even if it was a joke. Reighley thought this could be a good step forward for Freya and he knew he couldn't lie to his sister forever.

"Okay fine, you can come over this weekend, but only because you were honest. Just so you know, you're not coming inside! I'll introduce you at the door and you can meet her there." Reighley answered

"Yay!" Freya hugged Reighley. Reighley froze in astonishment, he wasn't sure how to react. Freya looked at Reighley and saw he appeared aloof from the physical touch, but she could see through his guise. He was blushing, though she could barely see it. Freya guessed he had never received a hug from a girl that wasn't family. She thought it was cute. She made a mental note to ask his sister if he had ever had a girlfriend before her.

"Oo, spicy." Destiny said as her head peaked through the door.

"This isn't what you think!" Reighley tried to explain and Freya didn't say a word, but instead only blushed.

"Yeah, yeah, get a room," Destiny said with a familiar smug look on her face. Ulysses walked in behind Destiny and saw Reighley backed into a corner by Freya. He wondered what all happened in the few minutes he and Destiny were gone.

"I'm like the greatest wingman ever." Ulysses thought.

While Freya was distracted by Destiny's comment, Reighley took this opportunity to escape by sneaking past her. Once he escaped he scurried towards Ulysses.

"Here, bro." Reighley handed Ulysses his container back. "Thanks again.

"No problem," Ulysses answered.

"Hey, I was wondering for a while now, but do you play any sports?"

"Uh, no." He replied.

"What, how come!? You're an absolute unit! You would dominate in any physical sport." Reighley questioned.

"I'd rather cook." He replied. Ulysses was constantly asked to join sports clubs, but he didn't like sports. Seeing people's reactions to eating the food he made was far more rewarding.

"Wow, I didn't expect that out of you. Although it makes sense, your cooking is incredible. Would you like to work for my family when you're older?" Freya asked.

"I don't know if my parents would be too happy if I abandoned the family shop," Ulysses replied. This was true, but the future scared him. He wasn't sure if he was good enough to become the head chef of his family's restaurant. He always pictured his older brother Sunny who ended up being the one who ran things.

"Freya, you really should get to know Ulysses better. He's kind and like a big brother!" Destiny replied.

"I've never had a brother before. Well, I wouldn't be opposed to inviting him to future gatherings." Freya said. She didn't mind having him around, as he has time and time again, proved himself to be on her side when it came to Reighley and her being together. "I'll throw some event together that the four of us can go to."

Freya's words unnerved Reighley from the thought of what plan she may come up with. He figured it would be something as crazy and extravagant as when the group met together on the school rooftop for the first time. He knew it was out of his hands now as Freya was like a force of nature.

The four soon finished chatting in the classroom and made their way to the entrance of the school. Waiting there for Freya was Herald. He was standing outside of the Young family's limousine. Herald looked towards Freya and noticed something he hadn't seen in quite some time. Freya was smiling with friends other than Destiny.

"Lady Freya, I'm glad to see you are doing well," Herald stated.

"Hello, Herald. Thank you for waiting." Freya replied. She turned towards Destiny, Reighley, and Ulysses and spoke. "I'll be seeing you all soon."

"Later," Reighley replied.

"Bye-bye!" Destiny said.

"See ya," Ulysses said while raising his hand briefly to wave.

Herald assisted Freya with her stuff and opened the door for her to enter then the two left the school. Reighley Destiny and Ulysses were standing at the entrance and Destiny was picked up by who the two could only guess was her father. Once it was just Ulysses and Reighley, the two began to walk from school together back to their houses. Reighley talked with Ulysses about how they were some of the only students who walked to school. The other students of Gilford High usually had a ride. He asked Ulysses why he didn't ride to school like other students and he was told that his parents wanted him to grow up like a normal student. Ulysses told Reighley about his family being born into wealth from his mother's side of the family and how he hardly got to see her. Reighley felt as though the two had something in common, as neither of them was able to see their mother often. Reighley thought it best to exchange phone numbers with Ulysses so the two could chat more. Soon the two made it to a point where they could no longer walk together and needed to go their separate ways to return home. So, the two said their goodbyes and left.

While walking home alone, Reighley reflected on the day. He thought back to the events that happened. However, whenever he tried to think of anything, he pictured Freya, either when she cornered him, or on the rooftop. The more he spoke with her, the more he thought she was growing on him. Though he may be getting special treatment because Freya wanted his attention, he knew she was compassionate. With the addition of Ulysses and potentially Destiny as a friend as well, he thought things were getting better at school.

Reighley was interrupted from his thoughts by the sound of his phone in his pocket. He received a text from Kaede.

Kaede: Hey Reighley! Miss you. You haven't stopped by the nurse's office to see me recently. I spoke with Ms. Clevens and she told me you got in trouble in class today.

Reighley: Yeah, sorry. I've been busy. I'll stop by soon.

Kaede: Well, I still plan on coming over for dinner this weekend. You invited me over last week, remember?

Reighley: I remember. I'll see you then.

Kaede: It's not good to keep a lady waiting, you know. I'll be there Saturday at 6:00 p.m.

He lied. Reighley had completely forgotten he invited her over. He placed his hands on his head and began to panic a little.

"Oh, shoot," Reighley said aloud. He realized that Freya was also coming over that day. Reighley worried that if Freya saw how overbearing Kaede was, things could get ugly. Thinking quickly he pulled his phone out to send a text message to Freya, but heard another beeping sound from his phone. His fears came true. He checked his phone and saw he received a text from Freya.

Freya: Hey. You never told me what was a good time to come over. How does 6:00 p.m. sound?

Reighley: You could come over a little earlier. Around 5:00 p.m.

Freya: I can't come over any earlier. I have a movie shoot I need to go to. I won't be done until 5:30 p.m. It would probably take 20-30 minutes to get to your house.

Reighley: Okay, sounds like a plan.

Reighley's heart was filled with anxiety. Things were set in stone. He worried that if Freya didn't like Kaede, then Freya could cause Kaede to lose her job as the school's nurse. He hoped that Freya would arrive at 5:50 p.m. so he could introduce her to Isabelle and then kick her out. He felt bad about having to do something like that to Freya since she was looking forward to coming over, but he thought it would be for the best. When Reighley arrived home he was greeted by his younger sister Isabelle.

"You're later than usual again," Isabelle stated.

"Had after-school cleaning duty," Reighley replied. "Is Mom home?"

"No. She's working overtime again. She picked me up from school on her break. She won't be back until tonight." She answered.

"Okay. Well, Kaede is coming over for dinner this weekend." He explained.

"Really! I haven't seen her in so long! I'll be sure to whip up her favorite food for dinner."

"Also, you know my boss is coming over for a few minutes as well." He didn't want to tell her they were technically dating just yet. "She said she wanted to meet you since you were my sister and all."

"Okay. Well, I'll make some extra food for her as well." Isabelle said.

"Oh, no need. She is only stopping by for a few minutes." Reighley told.

"Well, I'll have some just in case," Isabelle said. Reighley knew there was no winning with her so he let it slide. Reighley went to his bedroom and somehow ended up with a cat in his curly hair. Morgana leaped from the top of Reighley's bunk bed and attached his claws to his scalp. After a brief yelp, Reighley unhooked Morgana from his head and held him in his arms. He played with the cat for a while before studying.

"Hey, buddy. What do you think, should I just cancel the dinner date?" Reighley asked the cat.

"Mow." The cat replied.

"Yeah. I thought so too." Reighley replied. "Looks like I'm screwed." Reighley spent the rest of his night studying after dinner. When Jericho finally arrived home from work it was almost time for bed. She approached the garage door and gave it several knocks.

"Hey. How's my boy doing." Jericho asked.

"Mom!" Reighley replied with excitement. He opened the door and hugged his mother. When he saw her, he could see how worn out and exhausted she was. She was only 38 but was starting to get gray hairs from all the stress due to working so much. "How was your day?" He asked. Jericho told Reighley about her work as a Certified Nursing Assistant. She loved sharing stories about her kids with the elderly she worked with. She informed Reighley that he had in essence, a bunch of grandparents he hadn't met yet.

Reighley couldn't help but feel guilty. His mother was working herself to death for his future. He reminded himself that he was running out of time. He needed to work harder before her condition got worse. Even if that meant graduating a year early. The sooner he got into a university the more time his mom could take it easy and finally relax.

"I'm sorry Mom. You're working so hard for our sake. I wish we weren't such a burden on you." He said.

"You watch your mouth, young man. You two kids are my pride and joy. You are not a burden." Jericho said sternly.

"Sorry," Reighley replied. "Hey, by the way, Kaede is coming over this weekend for dinner. Also, there is something I need to talk with you about."

"Oh, I hope I will be home by then. That girl absolutely adores you, you know?" Jericho said.

"More like she absolutely smothers me," Reighley muttered, with rolled eyes.

"You used to say you wanted to marry her when you two were younger." Jericho teased.

"Mom, Stop!" Reighley coiled up from embarrassment. "Please don't bring that up during dinner."

"No promises," Jericho said. "So, what is it that you would like to tell me?"

"Well, a friend of mine may be coming over around that time for a little bit as well."

"Oh, I'll ask Isabelle to cook some extra food!" Jericho insisted.

"No, no, she will only be around for a few minutes. There is no need for that." Reighley interjected.

''She?'" Jericho said with a grin.

"Oh, crap," Reighley said, facepalming his forehead. "Mom, it's not what you think. She is just a friend."

"Hmm, whatever you say. Isabelle!" Jericho shouted.

"Yes, Mom?" Isabelle yelled from her room.

"Make sure you make extra food on Saturday for our guests." She told

"I already planned on it!" Isabelle replied.

"*Please somebody kill me.*" Reighley thought. He grunted in frustration and embarrassment and proceeded to kick his mom out of his room. "I'm going to bed. Night Mom, love you." Reighley said while slamming his door shut.

"Night dear, love you too," Jericho called with a mischievous tone and went off to her room.

Reighley climbed into bed with Mornaga and began to dread the upcoming weekend.

"What is wrong with the women in my life?" Reighley thought. *"Can't a guy catch a break?"*

Morgana began to claim a section in the center of his bed forcing Reighley to be uncomfortable. His mind wandered back to when he first saw how his mother appeared at the door. His mood was soured by the thought of his absent father. Every time he saw his mother exhausted, he became more and more jaded and resentful towards him. He blamed his dad for being the sole reason his mother was working so hard. When Reighley was five, his mother was assaulted by his drunken father. It was the first time and last time something like that had ever happened in his life. During the attack, Reighley attempted to hold his father back but was thrown aside. His mom was forced to tell Isabelle to call 911. Later that night, his father was arrested. Soon after he lost his job and he refused to look for work, blaming his wife for all of his problems. Without his job, he fell into a depressive state. From this, he continued to spiral out of control with his abuse of alcohol. Jericho, running out of options, had enough. She left him, taking the kids with her. Reighley hated the similarities he and his father shared. The fact that they both had the same blood and had criminal records infuriated him. He refused to continue to follow down his father's path. Reighley promised himself long ago that he would become the true man of the household and take care of his family. This was his duty. He had to put them first no matter the cost.

Lost in thought, Reighley dozed off and fell asleep cuddling Morgana. For the rest of the work week, Reighley spent most of his free time studying, only socializing during school hours. He made an effort to text Freya, as he was afraid he would lose his job if he completely ignored her outside of school.

Chapter 9

Dinner Date

Jim Young had just returned home after a couple of long work weeks traveling the world. It was Friday night and he was exhausted. He wished to see his family. However, it was 9:00 p.m. and he had to get up early in the morning after filling out some documents in his office upstairs. So, he made his way up the elevator and got to work. While working he heard a knock on his door. He knew it must have been semi-important, as he told his workers not to bother him unless necessary.

"Good evening Master Young. I am glad to see you have returned safely. " Herald greeted with a bow.

"Thank you, Herald. Now what is it, can't you see I am busy?" Jim replied, slightly annoyed at the fact he was interrupted.

"Forgive me, sir. It seems that Officer Templeton is here and wishes to speak with you about important business." Herald replied. Jim scoffed at the thought. He guessed that Templeton had anything but something important to say, as he was a major suck-up in the worst way. The reason he was kept around was that he was paid cheaply and did what he was told. It had been a long week, so he looked forward to hearing updates about what had happened since he left on his two-week-long endeavor.

"Very well. Send him up. Make sure he is aware he has but five minutes of my time." Jim asked.

"As you wish Master Young," Herald said and quickly exited the room and descended the staircase to the lower levels.

After arriving at the entrance, Herald opened the door and welcomed Mr. Templeton into their home. He informed him that he only had five minutes to speak with Jim. Herald noticed the officer had what he thought was a photography bag in hand as well as a smirk that stretched on his smarmy face from one cheek to the other. Soon the two were back upstairs and Herald and Templeton were standing at the door frame of Jim's Office.

"Herald, leave us," Jim commanded.

"Very well," Herald said, leaving Templeton and Jim alone to their own devices.

"Well now, don't waste my time Templeton. What is it that brings you here at this hour?" Jim asked.

"Yes sir. Thank you, sir." Templeton said while nervously walking in. Although Officer Templeton wished nothing more than to serve as Jim's right-hand man, he couldn't have been more terrified and intimidated by him. "You see, some concerning things have come to my attention. It has to do with Ms. Freya, your daughter sir."

"Oh? What are these concerns of yours." Jim asked curiously.

"You see, she is in a relationship with a boy," Templeton said with a gulp.

"I see. This is nothing new Mr. Templeton. Freya has been in plenty of relationships since she started high school. Did you really come up here to tell me that? I told you not to waste my time." Jim said, slightly irritated.

"Well sir, take a look at these and decide for yourself," Templeton said while taking out a few printed photographs and placing them on Jim's desk. Jim looked at the pictures and jumped out of his seat in surprise. It was a photo of his daughter and some boy he did not recognize, embracing each other outside of a tent house. He recognized the location as well. It was at DistracoLand, the very amusement park he built for his precious little girl.

"The nerve of this kid," Jim said aloud, breaking his elegant posture. "Who is he?" Jim asked.

"His name is Reighley, and here is everything we know about him," Templeton said while handing Jim a file he pulled out of his bag.

It was a new day. Saturday had quickly snuck up on Isabelle, but she knew that today was the day she would find the truth. Isabelle was looking in her full body mirror in her room and pictured a detective outfit on herself, but in reality, she was in her pajamas.

"Today's the big day!" She told herself. Isabelle was waiting all week for tonight's dinner as she had a plan to weed out any troublemakers trying to impede her brother from living a normal life. Isabelle had the entire day planned out from start to finish. This was a skill she prided herself in. The ability to plan extremely far ahead and organize. As much as she hated to admit it, she wasn't as smart as her older brother, so she had to come up with a diligent student study guide to complete. The regiment she assigned for herself involved brutal amounts of studying, both in and out of school. Because of this, she was ranked top ten out of all the students in her middle school.

Isabelle woke Reighley up as part of her daily routine at 10:00 a.m. so the two of them would eat breakfast together. She then fixed Reighley's favorite meal to butter him up to make him more prone to answering her questions. She fixed him chicken and waffles, smothered in syrup, which was usually something she saved for special occasions as it was unhealthy. Reighley came out of his room ready for the rest of the day. He had a long-sleeved red hoodie on and was wearing black jeans. He sat down in his seat at the table and started salivating from the food.

"Wow, you went all out today!" Reighley said with excitement.

"Oh, you know, I just wanted to pay you back for the money you gave me earlier this week," Isabelle replied.

"I appreciate it. Thank you." Reighley said while scarfing down his breakfast. After letting Reighley enjoy a couple of bites of his breakfast, Isabelle decided to pop the question.

"So, your boss, is she single?" Isabelle asked. Astonished, Reighley choked on his food and began coughing harshly.

"What makes you ask that?" Reighley asked.

"Just answer," Isabelle told.

"No, she's not," Reighley replied. He technically wasn't lying to her since he was her boyfriend but felt bad nonetheless.

"I see. That's all I needed to know." Isabelle said and stood up from her chair. Before Reighley knew it, her food was already gone and she entered her room. He had a sneaking suspicion that his sister was up to something. He had a premonition that something bad was going to occur in the foreseeable future and his stomach began to sink from the nerves, ruining his appetite.

Isabelle concluded that Reighley's boss was trying to play him. She remembered the way she looked at Reighley and how nervous she was back when she picked him up the weekend prior.

"She is trying to swoon Reighley like a side chick," Isabelle said while pacing back and forth in her room. "Sure my brother is cheap, but still that's unacceptable! There is no way that she would look at him like that if she didn't plan on making moves on him." Isabelle slapped her cheeks with her hands and hyped herself up. "It's up to me to stop this love tyrant and save my brother's dignity and I have just the plan." She thought aloud.

Freya was nervous. She had been acting at her movie shoot since 10:00 a.m. but couldn't think of anything other than meeting Reighley's sister tonight. She even dragged Destiny over to her place every day after school to help her pick an outfit for the visit. Freya was currently playing the role in a movie called Princess Charming, Sleeping Handsome. It was a twist on the old tale, where the princess would be locked away in an old castle trapped in a perpetual sleep and the charming prince would come in and rescue her while slaying a dragon. However, the movie roles were gender swapped and she was the princess on a quest to save the sleeping prince.

"Cut!" The director said. "Good work everyone. Freya, you were amazing. An absolutely stunning performance."

"Did you expect anything less?" Freya asked.

"Of course not! Okay, now it's time for the kissing scene."

"The what!?" Freya said completely stumped.

"You know, the part where a kiss from someone who truly loves you will wake you up?" The director answered. "Here's the scenario. You have just beaten the evil warlock, Mallace the dragon and you have found the prince sleeping in the castle. No matter what you try, he won't wake up. So remembering what you were told about the magic of love, you bend down and give him a smooch."

"A smooch…" Freya looked over at the other actor, his name was Deven Stallik and was also someone Freya despised. Although, she kept it professional during filming as it was all just show business in the end. Deven was laying on a bed of Delphiniums, a blue flower that was known for being a protective plant, and looked over towards Freya and gave her a wink. Freya's face grimaced. It wasn't as though she found Deven unattractive, but that he was one of her ex's she dumped the year prior. She considered him creepy and a sleazebag. The reason she dumped him was because he cheated on her only a week into their dating. He ended up using their relationship to gain a cult following of girls on SocialLight, but this was WollyHood, the movie business, and things like this happen all the time.

"Have my stunt double do the kiss," Freya asked.

"Yes, finally!" Freya's stunt double screamed from backstage. Freya did all of her own movie stunts, like her favorite actress, so her stunt double was there for the show. Her father assigned her one to make sure she was safe, but he didn't know about the extreme side of Freya's life and how she had different plans. Freya would make it clear to those around her not to tell these things to her parents, with passive-aggressive warnings, saying things like her father would believe her over anyone else.

"What? Are you crazy!? This is the climax of the film. All hope is lost. You need to be the one who does it." The director complained.

"Let me remind you who is in charge here. My father paid for this movie's entire budget. He can take those funds away at any time." Freya threatened. It wasn't simply the fact that she had to kiss Deven, that alone made her want to vomit, but also that it was her first kiss and she felt as though it was too important to just throw away at a movie she barely cared for.

"Yes of course. You are the star of the show. We will do things your way." The director said in frustration while beckoning to the nearby stunt double to fill in the scene.

Freya pictured herself standing over the bed of flowers with Reighley laying on top of it, sleeping peacefully. She imagined leaning in to kiss him and immediately woke up from that daydream due to it being too embarrassing to think about.

The rest of the filming went by fairly quickly to Freya. Deven attempted to chat with her several times but Freya completely ignored him. Soon it was time to leave and Freya had all her things packed and ready to go. She changed into a separate outfit, one that was presentable enough to be seen by her standards. Freya was wearing a large salmon-colored cardigan, over a white and pink zig-zagged t-shirt, with blue skinny jeans and a pair of brown boots. She thought she looked as amazing as she could while keeping it casual.

Herald picked Freya up at the entrance and the two began their route to Reighley's house. Herald looked in his rearview mirror and could see a nervous yet smiling girl in his back seat. Freya could not contain her excitement, nor control her nerves. She was antsy in her seat, twiddling her thumbs. To her, this was new and exciting, yet mildly terrifying. If she messed up with her first initial impressions with Reighley's family, then she might be rejected as his girlfriend.

"Just how am I supposed to face his family? What if they don't like me?" She thought to herself. "If Reighley doesn't see me as a good person, would they?" Up until recently, Freya had unshakable confidence in herself. She could always find her answers through a guide or some advice online, but there wasn't an answer for the unprecedented. This was a brave new world for her. She tried dating advice from social media in past relationships but those all failed, partially due to her methods and lack of trying. Results were everything to her when it came to advice.

"Herald... May I ask you something?" Freya said while looking at the man through the rearview mirror.

"Of course," Herald replied gently.

"How did you and Molly meet again?" Freya asked. Molly was Herald's late wife. Freya was far too young to remember her, but she was all he talked about when Herald and Freya were out together. He would tell her stories about their life from before Molly passed.

"We met thanks to your father," Herald replied as he began to reminisce about the past. "It was when I first started working for him. Molly was a waitress at a high-end restaurant your father was attending and I just so happened to be the only butler available at the time. She was beautiful. I glanced into her eyes and the way she looked at me said everything. She didn't want anything to do with me at all. The rest of the night was uneventful and we never even spoke a word."

"What? You're saying Molly wasn't interested in you? Then how did you get together?" Freya asked.

"On my one day off I went back to the restaurant. Right when I walked in our eyes met yet again, and she continued to completely ignore me. As luck would have it, they were short staffed and she was assigned to my table. When she finally approached I told her something that got her attention. I said 'It would be an honor if I could serve you for the rest of my life.' Of course, Molly thought that was corny and all. If she were around today she would still be teasing me about such a quip. Nonetheless, it worked in the end. From then onward, I would use every day I had off to visit her until I finally mustered up the courage to ask her to dinner."

"That's sweet," Freya replied.

"Don't get confused Lady Freya. She said no to dinner as well." Herald interjected.

"I don't understand. If it was going well, then why say no?" Freya said.

"It was because she was unsure of herself. Uncertainty prevented her life from moving forward." Herald answered.

"But, you didn't give up did you?" Freya questioned.

"The ones that are hard to get are usually worth the effort," Herald claimed.

Several words Herald said stuck out to Freya. She knew she was unsure of herself, but Herald's words sharpened her resolve. She needed to take that next step or nothing would change.

Meanwhile, while Freya was heading over to Reighley's house, Reighley was sweating profusely. He prayed that Freya would show up before Kaede. Suddenly, he heard a sound from his phone, he checked and saw that Freya had sent him a text.

Freya: On my way. I'll be there soon.

Reighley: Cool. I'll let Isabelle know.

He quickly went from panicking to relief as his eyes glanced at the time in the corner of his phone screen.

"*It's 5:35 p.m, hopefully, Freya will arrive around 5:50-5:55 p.m.*" Reighley thought. He knew the sooner she arrived, the sooner he could get her out of his hair. The real test was to make sure Isabelle didn't invite her inside. Reighley informed Isabelle that Freya was on her way when he noticed a feast that Isabelle was preparing.

"Woah now, isn't this a bit much for just the four of us?" Reighley asked.

"Nope," Isabelle said.

"Where did you even get the money to buy all this- wait, you didn't use the money I gave you did you?" Reighley asked.

"Nope," Isabelle said. "Mom paid for it. You didn't want Mom to find out you've been making side cash. It would make it pretty obvious if money appeared out of thin air."

"That is true. Also, you're not planning on inviting my boss into our house right?" Reighley asked.

"No promises," Isabelle said. Reighley realized it was a lost cause to attempt to persuade his younger sister. The only option he had left was to wait until Freya arrived and block the entrance if he had to. Reighley left the kitchen and went back into his room. He stared at his phone and the current time, waiting for a message from Freya. He hoped she didn't show up unannounced. Soon it was 5:55 p.m. and Reighley received the long-awaited text.

Freya: I'm here.

"Crap," Reighley said aloud. Swiftly Reighley rushed to his front door, but before he got there the doorbell rang. Isabelle was about to finish fixing dinner and was working on preparing the table when she heard the bell. With almost inhuman-like speed and skill, she finished setting the plates and then ran to the front entrance, not wasting a single second. When Reighley opened the door he was greeted by

Freya, who was waving at him. To Reighley, Freya looked flawless. It made him second-guess how a girl of her stature would end up at his doorstep.

"Hi! I'm Isabelle. Nice to meet you." Isabelle said, squeezing right past Reighley through the door frame. Freya took a few steps back and made room for a hasty Isabelle. She could smell the food from inside and the aroma was delightful.

"Hello. I'm Freya Young. Nice to meet you as well." Freya replied.

"Won't you come in for a bit?" Isabelle asked.

"Isabelle!" Reighley immediately interjected. He looked over at Freya, glancing into her eyes. Her aura was pointing past both him and his sister. She wanted to go inside their home. He could only hope Freya remembered what she agreed on when she asked to come over. Freya knew what she had to do. If she ended up lying to Reighley after saying she agreed, she guessed he wouldn't trust her in the future. Deciding to make the tough decision, Freya answered Isabelle.

"Oh, that shouldn't be necessary-" Freya objected before she was abruptly interrupted. Her arm was grabbed by Isabelle and she was pulled through the front door. This action forced Reighley to step out of the way of his guest as Freya let out a shriek, narrowly avoiding him. Reighley groaned, and could only watch the horrors that were about to unfold.

"We'll be in my room for a bit. Don't bother us. Oh, and make sure that the food doesn't burn" Isabelle called back towards him as she continued to drag Freya through the hallway, past the kitchen, into her room.

Freya was in a panic. This was all happening so quickly that she couldn't get a chance to react or decline the offer. While passing through the kitchen Freya glanced at the dining room table and saw how much food was prepared. She was curious if there was a special occasion tonight. Once they entered the room the door was slammed shut behind her and she could see nothing. There was an audible click as the lock was set in place. It was completely dark and somehow Freya ended up seated on a cold metal chair. Alarmed, she decided to speak up.

"What's going on here? Why did you put me in this closet?"

"It's my room..." Isabelle muttered. Suddenly a single light illuminated the room slightly blinding Freya. In front of her was a silhouette of a figure in what appeared to be a heavy trench coat, wearing a duckbill cap, leaning back in a chair. However, Freya couldn't know for sure. Freya realized that the source of light came from a small lamp placed on the corner of a cold steel table. It was like something out of a noir detective film. Before Freya could completely get her bearing, Isabelle's voice emanated from the dark figure.

"So, tell me, chump, what are your intentions with my brother?" the mysterious female voice with a Brooklyn accent said.

"What?" Freya squealed.

"You're his boss, right? I've seen the way you've been looking at Reighley. Don't play dumb with me." She replied.

"What!?" Freya said, completely confused. She lost her composer and began to freak out. "Just what on earth is going on?" This was the last thing Freya expected to happen this evening. She thought that the two girls were going to have a nice quick chat about getting together so they could go shopping. Instead, she was being interrogated by Reighley's younger sister.

"C'mon now. Spill the beans. You have a boyfriend, right?" she said

"Uh, Yes..." Freya replied. Isabelle finally revealed herself from the shadows, as if it was a plot twist in a movie. Freya looked at the girl and saw that she didn't have a trench coat, but an oversize winter coat that looked like it could fit her brother. The hat the girl was wearing was a scarf folded over on top of her head.

"Aha! I caught you red-handed. You are trying to play my brother, keeping him in your back pocket. While you have a boyfriend no less!" Isabelle shouted, pointing her finger toward Freya. Freya realized the situation and immediately decided to clear things up. She took a deep breath and spoke, while Isabelle stood there proud of herself.

"Isabelle. Reighley is my boyfriend." Freya answered.

"What?" Isabelle said, taking several steps back, completely stumped.

"This is all some big misunderstanding," Freya replied. "Yes, technically I am Reighley's boss, but also he and I are dating." Isabelle was standing there unable to speak. She had put so much effort into this interrogation and none of it mattered.

"That can't be right. You must be lying! Reighley is way too mediocre to be your first pick!" Isabelle couldn't accept the facts. She insisted it wasn't the truth.

"It is the truth. Ask him yourself." Freya replied.

Soon Isabelle turned the lights on and rushed out the door to see a very irritated Reighley standing with arms crossed in the hallway.

"Reighley is it true, is she your girlfriend!?" Isabelle asked.

"Ah, yeah..." Reighley answered sheepishly, rubbing the back of his head. He couldn't hide it from his perceptive sister any longer. A minute passed and Freya left Isabelle's room, exiting back into the hallway. She was confused by the sound of a loud banging noise. Isabelle was slamming her head into the drywall from embarrassment. Her face was completely red. Freya giggled and thought back to when Reighley slammed his head into his desk at school. She could tell that the two were siblings. Soon Isabelle regained her composure and walked over to Freya.

"I'm sorry! Why don't you stay for dinner to make up for my mistake." Isabelle said to Freya.

"I'd love to!" Freya answered. She sent a text to Herald letting him know to return in an hour or so. After speaking the three heard the doorbell ring. Isabelle looked towards Reighley and smiled manically. Her plan was complete. She knew that the two were most likely dating in secret. It was obvious from the start, but she wanted to make sure. However, she stalled long enough for Kaede to arrive, and this was where her true test for Freya began.

"I'll get it." Reighley had daggers for eyes pointing at Isabelle. He realized that this was likely something his sister planned out. Isabelle felt shivers down her spine from her brother's leering eyes and immediately hid behind Freya only to stick her tongue out, making a crude face at Reighley as he walked away.

"Mission accomplished," Isabelle muttered.

"What?" Freya said, confused by her comment.

"Nothing…" Isabelle smirked.

"My not-so-sweet sister is trying to ruin my life." Reighley thought to himself. He walked towards the front door yet again and opened it, only to immediately be pounced on by Kaede who was wearing a business casual dress.

"Reighley, I missed you!" Kaede said with a gleeful tone. She wrapped her arms around Reighley and squeezed the life out of him. Standing behind her at the entrance of the house was Jericho. She had returned home just in time for dinner.

"Yep, definitely cursed." Reighley thought. Suddenly, he felt a malicious chill down his spine. For the first time in his life, he could feel an aura emanating from behind him. He turned his head around to see a pair of deep blue leering eyes shrouded in a darkness that filled the entire hallway. It made his glare from earlier seem harmless. Reighley began to question whether or not he would survive the evening and regretted not having written a will.

"Dinner time!" Isabelle shouted from the kitchen.

"Great! I'm starving." Jericho said, sliding past Reighley who was being smothered by Kaede. "You must be Reighley's friend who happens to be a girl," Jericho said to Freya with a mischievous tone.

"Hello. I am Freya Young. Nice to meet you-" Freya's voice was drowned out by an overly obnoxious loud voice. Jericho told Freya that the two would talk more later, moving on toward the kitchen.

"You haven't visited me in a while. Jerk." Kaede teased, pulling Reighley's cheeks.

"Yeah sorry, you can let go of me now." He shrugged.

"No! Not until you promise to visit- Achoo!" Kaede said before immediately sneezing, letting go of Reighley. "Is that cat here?"

"Yeah, but he's in my room. We tried to clean up as much as we could." He replied. Reighley used this chance to escape her grasp only to turn around and run headlong toward a fuming Freya.

Kaede was shocked to see that Freya Young was there. Her dad was her boss's boss. She had heard the rumors at school from the teachers. Many of the rumors ended up being true. Freya was the queen of Gilford High School. She made some teachers' lives miserable in the past. She was the sole reason they lost their jobs. However, it was unlike Kaede to treat someone poorly just from rumors regardless if they were accurate or not. She thought it was best to treat everyone kindly, no matter their past. The last thing she heard was that Reighley was offered money to date her. She guessed Reighley had accepted that offer for one reason or another and wondered how serious he was about her. No matter what, she would support him in his endeavors like she always had. He was becoming a fine young man in her eyes.

Chapter 10

Sweet Dessert

Freya was filled with a multitude of emotions. She had thought that up until this point, coming over to Reighley's place turned out better than expected, only until *"she"* showed up. For the first time, Freya felt inferior to another woman, and the epicenter of that inferiority stemmed from hugging her boyfriend.

"Is this the type of woman Reighley likes?" Freya thought, *"What does she have that I don't?"*. Freya wondered, but her thoughts were interrupted by Reighley who was now standing in front of her.

"Hey, it's not what you think, I swear!" Reighley explained. Kaede walked up next to Reighley and began to introduce herself.

"Hello, Ms. Young. You may recognize me from Gilford High School. I am the school's nurse. My name is Kaede." Kaede said while bowing. Freya did recognize Kaede after she got close. She was the woman who did her school physical the year prior. "I wasn't expecting you to be here, but the more the merrier!"

"Reighley, how do you know her?" Freya asked. At this point, Freya was visibly upset with her arms completely crossed.

"I've known her the majority of my life. We grew up in the same neighborhood." He answered. Reighley began to worry that Freya may have gotten the wrong impression.

"*So this is the legendary childhood friend I've read about in so many books.*" Freya thought. If Reighley had someone like her around him growing up, it made sense to her why he was so distant when girls were all over him. He gave the same expression when she hugged him as well. Freya glanced up and down at Kaede. Estimating her beauty on a scale. "*Yep. She's a mature adult, and beautiful. I can't believe he never told me he had a girl on the side.*" Freya pretended to be unimpressed and replied to Kaede, "Well I think I remember you, it's hard to tell." She acted standoffish toward the two standing in front of her.

"Well, let's not keep Isabelle waiting..." Reighley said awkwardly.

"Okay!" Kaede said. She linked arms with Reighley and dragged him towards the kitchen.

Freya was infuriated, "*The gall of that woman!*" she thought. She considered leaving the house but quickly squashed those thoughts as that would mean she conceded to Kaede. Before Reighley and Kaede made it to the kitchen, Reighley extracted himself from Kaede and went back for Freya.

"This entire time, I've been letting these girls walk all over me. Didn't I say I was going to be the man of the house?" Reighley questioned himself and walked over to Freya. "Why do I even care what she thinks anyway? It's not like she's my actual girlfriend." Reighley grabbed Freya by the hand and led her to the kitchen. "Come on, let's go eat," he said. Freya was overjoyed that he came back for her, but wouldn't let him know it. She was still upset that he let Kaede smother him in affection.

Jericho had just finished helping her daughter place the food on the table when she noticed her son and two beautiful young ladies walk into the kitchen dining room. She looked over at her son who was holding the hand of his friend who just so happened to be a girl and thought, "I am so proud of my baby boy," he was growing up and this was a big moment in his life. He was entering a popular phase, and could potentially have a genuine girlfriend. Jericho's eyes turned towards the food and her mouth began to water from how delectable it looked. There were an assortment of different things to eat. The table had a pot roast filled with carrots, potatoes, and broccoli. Around it were two casseroles, one was beef, and the other chicken. There was bread and butter on several plates and there were even two pies on the table for dessert. They looked to be cherry and blueberry. Jericho patted Isabelle on the shoulder and began to praise her.

"Isabelle, You really outdid yourself," Jericho said.

"Thanks, Mom!" She replied.

Jericho looked back over at her son and mouthed the words *pull out the chairs for our guests*, as that was not only polite but gentlemen-like. Reighley noticed the gesture and did as told, pulling out the chairs for the two.

"Oh my, what a gentleman. Thank you very much." Kaede thanked gleefully.

"Hmph…" Freya hummed.

"*What did I do?*" Reighley thought. After Reighley let go of Freya's hand and sat down, the five began to eat dinner. He was seated between Freya and Kaede and across the table were his mother and sister. He couldn't help but feel like he was trapped between a rock and a hard place. Reighley looked at everyone around the table while using his abilities to prepare himself for what was to come. He started with Kaede. Her aura was as prominent as ever, still pink and fluffy almost like cotton candy. Knowing sugar was bad for him, he reminded himself to keep some physical distance from her. Freya's aura was an anomaly. Her arrows which normally pointed themselves toward her desires were on fire and embedded in the ground. He could only guess that meant she wanted to stay here at all costs. When he glanced over toward his sister and his mother, his alarms were set off. Isabelle and Jericho both had hues of Gray around their standard blue and gold aurae respectively. He knew they were up to something and he needed to find out what that was before it was too late.

Freya had a spoonful of the casserole only inches from her mouth. She was hesitant to eat it, as her palate for food was set at a high standard. She was afraid that she might spit the food out instinctively and didn't want to be offensive to Reighley's family. She put on a brave face and gave it a shot, taking a bite. To her surprise, it tasted as good as it smelled, but not good enough to fix her mood. As she was eating she was glaring towards Kaede who was off in her world, enjoying her meal. Jericho noticed Freya was not amused by the competition and decided to probe her.

"So Freya, how did you meet my son?" Jericho asked.

"Umm... Well, we go to school together and we sit next to each other in class." Freya didn't want to admit it but she was intimidated. The three girls across from her were like the final boss in a game or show. Combined, it was like they were an amalgamation of pressure, looming over her.

"Didn't you ask Reighley out on the first day of school? He told me he turned you down." Kaede asked. "You even offered to pay him to date you." The entire time she was speaking Reighley was dragging his finger across his neck while looking towards Kaede, hoping to signal to her to not bring that up in front of his mom. Freya was startled by the question, but she couldn't back down. It was her time to fight back.

"Those are fighting words," Reighley thought. He looked over at Freya to see her reaction and was surprised to see her flames engulf her. He could tell she wasn't going to back down.

"Yes, I did offer to pay him. It was the only way I could get his attention after he completely turned me down three times in a row, but he and I are dating now." Freya said, almost proud-like.

"Oh really!? Reighley I thought you said she was a friend that just happened to be a girl." Jericho said with excitement. She raised a brow toward her son. Reighley let out a sigh. He knew the gig was up. He wondered if Freya had mentioned the two were dating to have one up on Kaede for whatever reason.

"I turned her down because she came on too strong. It was like she decided I belonged to her from the moment I walked into the classroom," Reighley said, "It wasn't until I heard her out that I decided to give her a chance."

"Yes! My son has a girlfriend!" Jericho internally shouted for joy and then began speaking, "So, do you belong to her? I thought you said you were going to marry Kaede back when you were younger?" she asked mischievously. Reighley looked completely flustered by the comment. *"He's so adorable when he's embarrassed,"* She thought.

"I remember that! It was so cute. Try asking me again in a few years, Reighley." Kaede teased with a wink. Freya's jealousy shot through the roof. The fact Kaede said that after Freya announced she was his girlfriend made it worse. Her mood soured. She wanted to get Kaede fired. Even though the two weren't truly dating as of yet, she felt as though she was being cheated on by him right in front of her. She imagined Kaede and Reighley at a spectacular wedding getting married, and that ignited a fiery rage in her soul. Reighley looked over in Freya's eyes and saw that her aura was a dark purple flame that, if were real, would burn the entire house down.

"I don't belong to anyone." Reighley said defensively, "It's just that her reputation depended on me saying yes... That's all." Soon the five were done eating and the group sat around the table.

"*Is that your true feelings?*" Jericho wondered, "*The boy I know wouldn't commit to something that serious with a reason as trivial as that. You've grown up too fast. You're always serious about your future and taking care of the family. You have never done something without a good reason and you rarely do anything for yourself.*" Jericho looked at her son and then glanced over at the quiet Isabelle and couldn't help but smile. She couldn't have asked for better children.

Freya was disappointed in his answer but knew deep down she didn't have his heart. She knew that wasn't the real reason they were together. He was only dating her to support his family. "*He was being selfless, while I was being selfish,*" She thought. While eating, she looked at Reighley and then glanced around the kitchen and couldn't help but think his ambitions were admirable. She started to wonder if she had things too good back at home. For starters, her kitchen and her dining room were separate, and she called Isabelle's room a closet. The Summers family's household was the size of her walk-in closet, yet they didn't feel cramped. She felt as if she should be upset with Reighley, but felt like he had suffered enough. "*I should spoil him more.*" She thought. "*He is the type of guy that would give up everything for those he cares about, but what do I even do for him besides pay him?*" Freya thought about that question while eating a piece of roast beef. "*I should support him.*"

Freya's deep thoughts were disrupted by Isabelle and Jericho who caught her eye. The two would glance at her and then at each other, repeating those motions several times.

"So who wants to see Reighley's baby photos?" The two said in unison.

"N-no, no!" Reighley choked on his word. He panicked and got up from the table, he knew the location of the photo book and immediately ran in its direction, hoping to seal it away in his room for the night.

"I want to!" Kaede said.

"Me too," Freya said. Her spirits were lifted by the thought of seeing Reighley as a cute baby.

"All right, here we go." Isabelle pulled a photobook from underneath the table as if prepared for this moment and it was too late for Reighley. He was pure red from embarrassment. He wanted to hide in his room and wait until the suffering ended, but he said he was going to be the man of the house so he decided to take it like a man. He wouldn't be able to unlive this in his mind if he ran away. Soon Isabelle cleared the table to make enough room for the photobook and Jericho began to flip it open.

Reighley sat back down in his chair and began to preemptively cringe internally. However, he thought that some good would come of this. He looked at Freya and saw that her fiery aura was doused. Now in its place was a heart-shaped cupid's arrow pointed toward the album. Her face was amused as well. Freya wanted to see him as a toddler. She had a smile on her face that was hard to hide.

"She must want to see it. If it will make her happy then I guess it's not all that bad," Reighley thought, *"Wait... why do I want to make her happy?"* He couldn't answer that question and shrugged it off, but there was something about her smile that made Reighley fulfilled. Soon the five gathered closely together and started looking at the book.

"He's so cute!" Kaede said. The girls were looking at a Polaroid photograph of Reighley in front of a TV. The photo had a written note next to it that said (Saturday Morning Cartoons!).

"Groverman, Right?" Jericho asked Reighley. In the photo, Reighley was pumping his fist to the television. There was almost a sparkle in his eyes. "You used to tell me you were going to grow up and be like Groverman when you grew up."

"Hey, he was pretty cool when I was a kid."

"What's Groverman?" Freya asked.

"He was this forest ranger that was chosen by the trees. He could control nature around him because of it." He replied. Freya giggled as she thought it was adorable. Reighley realized how embarrassing this all was but was attempting to hold onto any dignity he had left; he felt like he was managing somehow. Freya pointed out a costume

195

Reighley was wearing in the next photo, it was titled (Groverman saves Halloween!) The picture showed Reighley on top of a pumpkin. In one hand was a wooden sword pointed towards the sky, the other had a bag full of candy.

"These are too cute." Freya chuckled.

"This one is Reighley and me eating ice cream," Isabelle said. There was a huge contrast between the two children. Isabelle was tidy, licking the ice cream cone in her hand, while Reighley had ice cream all over his shirt and the floor. "He's still this messy," Isabelle jested. The group laughed and then turned the page. The room went a little quiet as the next photo was a picture of Reighley sitting on his dad's lap. It was titled (Reighley found out Santa wasn't real.) It was a photo of Reighley crying while his father was wearing a Santa outfit.

"Who's that?" Freya asked. She knew it was his father but wanted confirmation. Reighley and Isabelle took after their dad in a lot of ways. They both inherited his curly black hair, and they had similar facial structures.

"That's my dad," Reighley said. His tone was bittersweet. He longed for the simpler days when his family was together. When he would look at himself in pictures, he could only see his father. It was a reminder of who Reighley was in the past. "He isn't a part of our life anymore." Freya felt bad for the Summers family and decided not to press further. The photo afterward was a picture of Kaede kissing Reighley on the cheek. Freya was jealous that Kaede got to spend so much time with Reighley throughout his life. She was marginally older than him, Freya estimated 5 years. Freya swore to herself that she wouldn't lose. She felt as though to win, she needed Reighley's first kiss.

Soon the group was halfway through the book and Freya noticed that they were out of photos. It stopped right when he was in middle school.

"What happened? Is this everything?" She asked.

"Yep. Reighley stopped letting me take pictures of him after middle school." Jericho answered. "It's a shame too. My little boy has become so handsome."

"I have some photos of Reighley on my phone..." Freya said.

"What!?" The three girls said as they all began crowding Freya.

"He let you take pictures of him!? Let me see!" Kaede asked.

"Yeah, is that a big deal or something?" Freya asked while showing the photos from the amusement park. Reighley was quiet ever since they passed the photo with his father. Freya looked over at him for answers but he avoided her gaze being completely silent. Reighley didn't let other people take photos of him after middle school. If he looked in a photo he wouldn't see his aura, unlike with mirrors, but it would remind him of the last time he saw his aura.

"Yeah. I don't even have any photos with him." Kaede stated.

"He must really like you in order to do that," Isabelle said, looking to get a reaction out of Reighley, however, when she saw the look on his face, he appeared distant. As if he didn't even hear her words, completely lost in thought. Everyone paused and looked over towards Reighley, anticipating a response from him. The silence lasted over five seconds. The group collectively thought that he was spacing off in his own world thinking about things, but yet something was off about him.

"Hello, earth to Reighley," Kaede said while pinching his cheek.

"Ouch!" He yelped, snapping out of his clouded mind. "Sorry... what?".

"You were zoning out," Isabelle said.

"My, bad..." Reighley laughed awkwardly. Freya couldn't help but wonder what was going on inside his head. She was about to ask him a question before she heard a ringing noise coming from her phone. She was receiving a call from a number she did not recognize.

"Who is it?" Jericho asked.

"I'm not sure," She replied. She stared directly at the screen for a brief moment and then decided to answer it. "Hello?"

("Hello, is this Freya?") The voice asked.

"Who's asking?" She snarled.

("It's your Father.") Jim said. Freya's expression turned somber. ("Where are you? You weren't at home all day today.")

"I'm at a friend's house." She explained.

("Well you need to come home, now.") Jim commanded.

"What, Why?" She replied puzzled.

("Just do as I say.") Jim said.

"Yes Father... I'll be home as soon as I can," Freya replied and then hung up the phone. *"Normally I would be happy to see Father since it has been weeks since I had seen him last or even spoken to him, but this, this is different. If I was home right now, I would be laying in bed bored senseless, or doing homework. The only company I would have is the people I would live stream for on SocialLight,"* Freya thought as she scanned around the table seeing the smiling faces looking back at her. *"but this is so much fun! I don't want it to end."*

"That was your dad? Why didn't you recognize his number?" Reighley questioned. He noticed her aura's arrows were pointing at everyone in the room, he wasn't sure what that meant.

"It must have been a new phone. He gets the newest models from his cell phone company and tries them out himself." She replied and began standing from her seat. "Anyway, I have to get going."

"Aww... do you have to? Things were just getting fun." Isabelle said heartbroken.

"Yes. I'm sorry. I'll take you out shopping next time."

"Really!?" She jumped out of her chair in excitement.

"Yes. I promise," Freya reassured.

"That's such a shame..." Jericho replied. "Know you are welcome to stop by at any time. I'm sure my kids would love the company." Freya turned towards Kaede and whispered in her ear.

"I'm not going to lose to you." She muttered, however, Kaede only gave a confused look back as she was unsure what she meant by that, but decided to be supportive.

"Do your best!" Kaede said with a smile.

"Reighley why don't you walk her home?" Jericho asked.

"Yeah, sure- wait, what!? She lives super far away." He mentioned.

"Yes, but it's the gentlemanly thing to do. I raised a gentleman, didn't I?" Jericho questioned.

"Yes Mom," he replied. Looking over at Freya, Reighley noticed a glimmer in her eyes. Her aura said it all. She wanted to hold his hand. "Hold on, let me grab my shoes from my room." Reighley swiftly rushed towards his door, entering it and making sure Morgana wasn't let loose. When he opened the door Freya saw the inside of his room.

"His room is a garage?" She asked.

"That's right. This small house only has two rooms, so Reighley opted himself out so Isabelle here could have her room," Jericho said.

"He's such a good brother," Kaede mentioned.

"Yeah, he's okay," Isabelle said jokingly. She didn't mean it as she thought the world of her brother.

"Just how much does he give up for his family?" Freya thought. Soon Reighley exited his room and met Freya at the

front door, and the two said their goodbyes and left the house.

The two started walking towards the sidewalk and Freya fell behind sending a text to Herald letting him know that Reighley was taking her home. Reighley looked back at her and waited for her to finish, and extended his hand for her to take it. Freya smiled and grabbed it and the two began walking.

It was a cool night outside, just warm enough to not need a coat. It was 7:15 p.m. The sun had just set and the horizon was orange and pink. A purple hue stretched across the night sky. There wasn't a cloud in sight. The stars were visible and the moon was crescent in shape, hovering in the direction that they faced. It loomed over them. The two walked the sidewalk's path as Freya led the way, passing under street lights, one after the other. Birds could be heard chirping in the distance, and vehicles would pass the two every few minutes.

"You wanted to stay didn't you?" Reighley asked.

"Yes, but I need to listen to my parents," She answered.

"It sounds like they're pretty strict," he stated.

"Yes. They run businesses and do fashion shoots. Meeting with people all around the world. They don't have time for fun and games like your family does. Still... It was nice." Freya said with a small smile. This warmed Reighley's heart. He figured he could get used to seeing her smile.

"Feel free to come back. That's what you're paying me for, right? Besides, you left a good impression on my family, so I'm sure they wouldn't mind." Reighley extended an offer towards her in the hopes to make her feel better.

"You think so?" She asked.

"Definitely," he reassured. Freya was carrying a purse on her person. She pulled out a large stack of money and handed it to Reighley.

"Here. This week's pay. You've been doing a good job."

"Thanks. You really shouldn't carry all that cash with you, unless you're looking to get mugged." Reighley took the money and pocketed it in the red hoodie he was wearing.

"I can take care of myself just fine, thank you," Freya said, slightly irritated.

"Okay fine. Whatever you say." Reighley replied.

"Don't patronize me," Freya said, upset.

"There is no winning with you, is there? Look, I was just trying to watch out for you. It's dangerous at night," Reighley said sternly.

Freya stopped walking, jaunting Reighley backward a bit. She realized she was being self-centered once again. *"This was his way of showing he cared and I completely shut it down,"* she thought. Freya took a deep breath and apologized. "No, you're right. I'm sorry. I'll be more careful."

"You're getting better at that," he said.

"At what?" She asked.

"Apologizing," he joked.

"Tch, jerk," she scoffed, and then the two laughed out their grievances and continued onward. Soon they were passing by an ice cream shop.

"You never got to try my sister's pie did you?" Reighley asked.

"Sadly no, but I'm sure it was good," Freya answered.

Reighley pointed to the ice cream shop and asked, "How about we stop there for dessert?"

"I would love to. It's not like my father is tracking me or something crazy like that," she said as the two made their way to stop for ice cream.

Meanwhile at the Young Manor, Jim Young was currently tracking Freya through G.P.S. (Global Person Searcher) on his laptop in his bedroom. It tracked Freya's location via cell phone. He was already suspicious of her travel speed, as they were moving at a very slow pace and wouldn't arrive for another hour or so, but his suspicions peaked when the two stopped entirely on the side of the road.

"*She sure is taking her sweet time. What happened to my little girl who used to run to her father's side, right when he arrived home? I bet she is with that criminal! That Reighley kid is a bad influence on her. I will never accept him, especially after knowing his status. He is not fit for my daughter.*" Prismarine was standing next to the bed and noticed Jim constantly staring at his laptop. She checked it and saw that he was tracking Freya.

"Would you leave the girl alone, Jim?" Prismarine commanded. "She is enjoying her youth, and I have heard great things about this Reighley character. There's a real chance our daughter could find true love and your prying eyes won't help anyone but yourself." Prismarine closed Jim's laptop and crossed her arms in disappointment.

"Yeah, well, love is blind and it doesn't pay the bills. The boy has a criminal record Prismarine! A criminal record for goodness sake!" Jim shouted.

"'For goodness sake' is right. You have your lovely wife with you, whom you haven't seen in weeks and you're busy worrying about our daughter's playdate. Besides, I am positive they are doing just fine. I made sure Herald was tailing them just in case," Prismarine complained.

"How do you know for sure?" Jim interrogated.

"He gives me updates," Prismarine's phone began buzzing and she pulled it out of her bag to check her texts, "Look, that's him now. The two are at an Ice Cream shop. Isn't that just adorable? Now let's go watch a chick flick in the movie theater, and no laptops!" she admonished.

"Yes, Ma'am..." Jim groaned. The two went on to watch the movie The Joke Book, to distract him for the time being.

Back at the Ice Cream shop, Freya and Reighley had just entered inside. The interior was designed to be themed like a 60's diner. The decor was covered in racing stripes and the stools with red leather tops. The two walked to the register and noticed a familiar face.

"Hi, welcome to Freeze Frames! How may I help you?" Ash Fjord asked. She was taken aback by the fact Freya Young had just entered her store with Reighley by her side. She put on a fake smile and began to serve.

"Great, just great. Freya is going to take a picture of me and post it all over SocialLight. I'm going to be the laughingstock of Gilford High," Ash thought. *"Not to mention I could get in a lot of trouble for working since Gilford High prevents students from working while attending."*

"Hey, Ash! I didn't know you worked here," Reighley greeted. "Could I get a banana split?"

"I better not get too friendly with Reighley while she's around," Ash thought. "Of course, and for the lady?" Reighley immediately recognized that fake smile she put on. Her turquoise aura was translucent. It was like it was telling him she wanted to disappear. Reighley knew that feeling all too well.

"I would like a Berry Parfait Romanoff with a strawberry dipped in chocolate on top and the cream boiled for an extra thirty seconds," Freya asked.

"Uh, Freya, I think they sell like normal ice cream here," Reighley interjected. Freya stopped and checked the menu and picked something she thought she would like.

"Oh… Then a single scoop of strawberry on a cone please." Freya asked.

"Woah, she said please!? Reighley must have taught her a thing or two. Well done," Ash thought. "Very well. I'll get that to you right away. Please take your seats and we will bring

205

your stuff to you," she recommended. The two began to sit at a table in the corner of the shop waiting for their food, when suddenly Freya had an epiphany. Her birthday party was coming up. It was around the deadline when she and Reighley's deal to be a "couple" would come to an end. She realized she hadn't even invited Reighley to it either.

"Hey, Reighley..." Freya suddenly became embarrassed.

"What's up?" He asked.

"So, my birthday party is coming up here in a few weeks and you are my boyfriend, so I thought I would ask if you would come to it," she asked while twiddling her fingers. Reighley felt as though this was a good opportunity to help rekindle an old friendship, while also helping Freya think for herself.

"I'll go, but only if you invite Ash," He said.

"What? Why on earth would I invite her?" Freya was outraged.

"Why do you think so?" Reighley interrogated. Freya stopped, calmed her emotions, and gave it some thought.

"Is it because he thinks it would be a good starting point to make things better between us?" Freya reminisces. She had known Ash since middle school. She remembered a simpler time when Ash and her would spend time together talking about books the two would read simultaneously. Freya would invite her and the rest of the girls to a movie night in her at-home theater and then the group would spend the night

having sleepovers. However, Freya had a deeper respect for Ash when they were friends. Ash was a tomboy and wasn't afraid of getting her hands dirty. She was a 1st Kyu, also known as a brown belt in Jiu-Jitsu, which was a form of lethal martial arts that combined throws and practical techniques one could apply in a street fight. Freya picked up Karate in middle school simply because she didn't want to lose to Ash. Once she was confident in her ability to defend herself if it came down to it, she quit, causing some distance between the two.

"I'm still not quite sure if it's a good idea," Freya worried.

"Just think about it. If you ask her, the worst she can say is 'no'," Reighley explained, "but if she says yes then that means that she wants to make things work too." Freya thought about it some more, and realized that making up with Ash was a start if anything, and if she said *"no"* at least she tried to do the right thing.

"Well… do you have your answer?" Reighley questioned.

"Is it because it's the right thing to do?" Freya asked.

"Bingo," Reighley said. "I don't know Ash that well, but I can tell she is not a bad person. However, she definitely didn't want to be seen by you tonight."

"Fine, I'll give her a chance," Freya said, "but you're coming to my party."

"Did I have a choice in the first place?" Reighley asked.

"I won't force you if you don't want to," Freya chuckled, "but I want you there." Reighley blushed, looking into her eyes. He wasn't used to being told he was wanted. He noticed her aura was calm and comforting. It was the brightest he had seen it be. It was still a dark purple, but it was almost a normal color and it was pointing towards him but giving him space. He realized he started getting used to her laugh. Her smile was infectious. For a moment he forgot that their relationship was a farce.

"Was she always this happy? It's weird seeing her like this. It's like she is my girlfriend or something... Is she really the same girl I met two weeks ago; Can a person change this fast or is her aura lying to me?" Reighley doubted and then replied, "You got yourself a deal." Soon after, Ash arrived at their table with their desserts in hand and handed them to the couple.

"Here you go! One banana split and a strawberry scoop," Ash stated. She attempted to get in and out as fast as possible, turning away after Reighley and Freya thanked her. However, she heard the voice of Freya reach out to her.

"Hey Ash, I don't hate you and I won't tell anyone you work here so you don't have to worry about that, but in return... would you come to my birthday party in a few weeks?" Freya asked. Ash was shocked. Never in a million years did she think Freya would invite her to her party after how things went the year prior. She wondered if it was a setup as Freya was known to do that every so often.

"Is it a trap? Is she just saying this to get me comfortable so she can embarrass me later? No, I don't think Reighley would let her... He must have been influencing her, or perhaps she is just inviting me to appeal to him."

Chapter 11

Changes From Within

Ash was torn. She couldn't decide whether or not she should say yes and if Freya was being honest about what she was saying. She turned and faced Freya and Reighley sitting at the table.

"*What do I do?*" She thought. "*Is it really worth giving her another shot?*" Ash looked over towards Reighley, and he gave her a nod indicating it was right to say yes. "*Can he read my mind or something? It's like he could tell exactly what I was thinking.*" Ash took a deep breath and let out a long sigh. "All right, what time is this party?" She asked. Freya's eyes lit up from her answer. She went into it expecting Ash to say no to her.

"Really!? You'll come?" She asked.

"Yep. Don't make me regret it, okay?" Ash pestered. Freya agreed and explained the details of the party to her and then Ash went back to work. Soon the couple finished their desserts and waved goodbye to Ash, exiting the building. Once Reighley and Freya left Ash sent text messages to her friend group letting them know what happened. When Herald saw the two leave he began tailing them yet again, headlights off, displaying tactful yet prudent espionage. It wasn't much longer until Reighley noticed Herald. The white limousine he drove could only stay hidden for so long.

"Looks like we're being followed," Reighley mentioned. Freya looked back at the vehicle following the two and then took hold of Reighley's hand. She had the same feeling from before back at Reighley's house. She didn't want the night to end, for things to slip away from her, and for some reason, the thought of going home without spending some alone time with Reighley made her sad, until she remembered the words Herald told her.

"Uncertainty prevented Molly's life from moving forward," she thought. *"I'm sorry Herald, but I'm not going to just wait around for something to change!"*

"Come on, let's make a run for it!" Freya said with a courageous smile, taking off in a sprint.

"What!?" Reighley exclaimed, being pulled along by Freya's antics. Herald was astonished by Freya's actions. Giving them an encouraging smile, he immediately gave chase.

"My goodness Lady Freya, just look how much you've grown," Herald thought. He decided he would play the part of the hunter to make things more memorable for the two.

"Where are we going!?" Reighley yelled, attempting to maintain the same pace as Freya.

"Just as far away as possible!" She answered. The two ran for a while until their next available turn in the city. Once they found one they quickly took a sharp turn left down an alleyway too small for vehicles. "This way." They made their way through and arrived on the other side and continued to run for a while. Through every twist and turn somehow Herald and his limousine would appear, almost like out of thin air.

"What has gotten into her?" Reighley thought, *"I want to stop... but how can I when she looks like that?"* He looked at the girl who was pulling him along and saw an excited smile on her face as if she was having the time of her life. Her aura's arrow was brimming with life as it pointed toward a random direction. *"I forgot. Freya loves the thrill of things."* While the two were escaping their hunter, Reighley realized that Freya was going in what would be considered a large circle. He knew the city fairly well after his last treasure hunt downtown. Exhausted, he conjured strength from within and sprinted in front of Freya, deciding to lead the way.

"Come on. Follow me!" He shouted. "I know my way around these parts."

"Okay!" She replied. Freya let Reighley lead her, placing her full trust in him. The two started making some progress making distance between them and Herald. They would stop every so often taking quick rests, only for Herald to catch up, like a game of hide and seek on a massive scale. Then while running away, heart racing, Reighley realized something as he began to smile.

"Actually... This is pretty fun! I think I get why Freya enjoys the rush!" He thought.

When they thought they had finally lost Herald, the two arrived at the edge of the city limits. What awaited them was a steep hill that led down to a coastline. In front of them off to their right was the famous Crimson Gate Bridge. An infamous San Fran, Kyoto piece of history. The bridge was a bright yellow, which made many people confused about why it was called the Crimson Gate Bridge. It's 1.7 miles long and stretches across the sea connecting to a nearby city for vehicles to cross. On the sides of the bridge were Japanese lanterns that were lined up on the sides of the bridge. They would light up during the night causing the water below to illuminate.

Freya pointed out a staircase to their left and gestured the two should go down to the shore. Completely out of breath exhausted by the running, they leaned on each other for support as the two slowly descended the stairs to the shores below. Once they arrived Reighley collapsed on the floor on his back on the soft sand. The tide was low, and seagulls could be heard off in the distance. A cool breeze swept through their hair as the moon reflected off of the sea.

"I think we lost him," She said. This entire time she had been running she hadn't realized how sweaty she had gotten.

"I don't... get paid... enough for this..." He said out of breath. Freya was leaning forward, hands on her knees attempting to catch her breath when the two stopped and looked at each other and started bursting out laughing making it more difficult to breathe.

"Oh no… I got carried away. I don't want Reighley to see how gross I am," she thought. She turned away from Reighley and pulled out a handkerchief from her bag. She wiped her face and arms off with it. When she was done Reighley got up from the ground and checked his hoodie's pocket and to his relief, the money he had earned was still bundled up inside. Sand stuck to the back of his hair due to the moisture. He brushed himself off and attempted to clean the sand off him, during this, Freya walked up to Reighley and when he finally got his bearings she grabbed a hold of his shirt with both hands. She pulled herself close and put her forehead on his chest.

"Hey, I'm kind of gross right now, and aren't your parents going to be upset with you?" he said flustered.

"I don't care… I just wanted to be alone with you," she said, with her voice muffled by his clothes. Reighley wasn't sure what to do. He couldn't see her aura while her head was down. How could he tell if she was telling the truth? He always had her aura to confirm his suspicions about how she felt. Unsure how to respond he lifted Freya's head upward by her chin to see her eyes. When he looked into them, a familiar occurrence happened. He was embraced once again by Freya's aura. It circled the two and coiled up. It was like she had captured him. He was losing all sense of reason staring into her eyes. The light from the bridge behind them made her aquamarine blue eyes emanate through the darkness of her aura. He was captivated. With eyes locked the two lips were only inches away from each other. Freya began closing her eyes in anticipation, unsure what would happen next.

"*What am I doing?*" Reighley thought, "*How did things end up like this? If I were someone else, would she act differently?*" The warning Herald gave him echoed in his mind. "*Don't play with her heart,*" he recalled. Abruptly, Reighley put his pointer and middle finger on Freya's lips and pushed himself back gently.

"What's wrong?" She asked. Freya was confused, the setting was beautiful. To her, Reighley's silhouette was something out of a movie. The Crimson Gate Bridge behind him was brighter than the rest of the city off to the right of them. "*It was perfect... so, why, why did he stop?*"

"This isn't right. You should save things like that for someone special," he said. Freya's aura unraveled and then dispersed and the smile that Reighley was growing comfortable with was now absent.

"You *are* special to me," Freya said.

"You hardly know me, and plus, I don't think something like this should happen because of a transaction," Reighley replied. "I mean, besides, how well do you even know me?" This hurt Freya, several tears began to swell up in her eyes.

"Did I do something wrong?" she sniffled.

"No, no, I just don't want to be the thirtieth guy you've done stuff with if I'm not actually your boyfriend," he answered.

"Well, you wouldn't be. You would be the first," she retorted, "and I do know you! You're a kind-hearted, selfless, and considerate person, who always puts others first. I bet the only reason you pushed me away is because you think it would be best for me, but you're wrong. I'm taking this seriously!" This response made Reighley's heart skip a beat.

"Why would she go to such lengths just for me? The last I knew, she most likely had a crush on me at the bare minimum," he thought. *"There is no reason for her to say these things if she's just planning on getting rid of me in a few weeks."* Reighley, unsure what to do with the now emotional Freya, placed a hand on the back of his head, scratched his hair, and apologized. "Look, I'm sorry. That was a pretty uncool thing for a fake boyfriend to say," he said. Freya took a deep breath, regaining her composure before tears began to stream down her face, and replied.

"Dummy," she said, wiping her eyes with a few chuckles.

"Ahmm," a voice scoffed from the hill beside them. The two looked over and saw Herald waiting at the bottom of the steps. "I do not wish to interrupt Lady Freya, but your father requested you return. He is quite unhappy with tonight's outcome. I ordered Elise to take you home, she is waiting up above. I will give Master Summers a ride home as well."

"Very well," she sighed. The two made their way to the top of the hill and Freya hugged Reighley before they got inside separate vehicles, "Thanks for today. Sorry for making you run so much," she said while squeezing him tightly.

"Yeah, no problem. Next time you come over you can meet Morgana," he said, flustered.

"Who's that?" She asked.

"My cat," he said. Soon both got inside the separate vehicles and made their separate ways home.

It had been a while since Reighley had last ridden in a vehicle. He was staring out the window, his eyes jumping from building to building.

"So how much did you see, Herald?" Reighley asked.

"I saw the entire thing," Herald replied.

"Well that's both mortifying and *embarrassing...*" Reighley thought.

"Master Summers?" Herald said.

"Uh, yeah?" Reighley replied.

"You have done well to listen to my advice."

"*So it was advice!*" He internally sighed in relief. "*You know what? Herald is all right.*"

"However, let me give you a warning. If you happen to make that girl cry again without a good reason, you will disappear," Herald threatened.

"Yes sir," Reighley replied with trepidation. "*Wait, wait, wait, what!? Did he just threaten to kill me if I made Freya cry?*" He thought.

"Very well, that is all I have to say," Herald replied. The rest of the ride home was spent in an awkward silence.

When Freya arrived home she was met by her mother outside at the entrance of their manor.

"Hello dear. How was your time with Reighley?" Prismarine asked. From just behind the doors was a muffled angry-sounding Jim Young. Freya could hear him ranting on and on but couldn't quite understand what he was shouting about. She could only pity the person who was taking the heat from him on the other side.

"It was wonderful Mother. I see Father is upset," Freya pointed out.

"Yes, he is very upset with your actions. Don't worry though dear. I'm on your side in this," Prismarine encouraged. Freya took a deep breath to prepare herself for the wrath to come and walked inside her home. When she entered she saw Lily almost in tears, being yelled at by her father. Freya knew it wasn't right for him to take his anger out on her and stepped in.

"Leave her alone!" Freya yelled. Jim stopped what he was doing and turned to his daughter who was only a few feet away. The last thing Lily expected was for Freya to defend her. She was so surprised that she dropped the broom and dustpan she was carrying.

"You're in big trouble missy! He yelled.

"What, Why!?" Freya asked.

"I work my tail off every day, weeks at a time, all for you, and this is how you repay me? You go running around downtown with some boy!? I don't think so. Throughout your entire life I've always given everything you've asked for, but this time I will put my foot down. He is banned from this household. If he takes one step inside of here I'll have Officer Templeton arrest him for trespassing," Jim yelled. Freya was incredibly frustrated. She had always wanted her father to be there, but he was too busy for her, and for the first time in a while she finally found someone to fill that void in her life. She had given up on him coming home one too many times. All her bottled-up emotions needed to be released.

"Well, it's not like you would be around to know if he was here or not," she sassed.

"You watch your mouth young lady," Jim scolded in a blind rage. " You ungrateful child. Do you have even the slightest idea of what I do on a daily basis? You will not speak to me in such a manner. Now, go to your room!"

"Jim! That's enough! Prismarine shouted, snapping Jim back into reality. When he came to, his heart broke. He saw his daughter in front of him with tears flowing down her face like a waterfall.

Freya let out a scream in frustration and then shouted, "Just go back to work already, I don't want you here!" She then proceeded to sprint past Jim towards the spiral staircase, making her way upward to her room, stomping the entire time to prove her point.

"Lily, make sure she's all right and pick that stuff off the floor!" Jim commanded. Lily was astonished but didn't show it.

"*Shouldn't you be doing that!?*" Lily thought but was too afraid to voice her opinion. "Yes sir," she answered, picking up the cleaning equipment she dropped, and then immediately followed suit.

Jim was silent. So many thoughts came to mind. *"Did I go overboard? She's never spoken to me like that. Either way, she'll appreciate it when she's older."* His train of thought was interrupted by Prismarine tapping his shoulder.

"Jim?" she said.

"Yes Marine," he answered.

"Tell me, have you ever seen our daughter take the stairs before?" She asked. Jim pondered for a moment, but he couldn't recall a single time Freya had done that in the past. Even when she was younger she would use the elevator.

"No, I haven't," he muttered.

"Our daughter is changing Jim. You need to accept her for who she is. She is not your little girl anymore. She's growing up now." Prismarine explained.

He couldn't accept it. *"She must be wrong. This is all because of that Reighley kid. It's his fault, not mine,"* he thought. His facial expression became bitter.

"Would you stop being so stubborn!" Prismarine scolded. "I know exactly what you're thinking. You think it's the boy's fault that things turned up like this. Look in the mirror, Jim. If you do anything to that boy-"

"Freya will get over it," Jim interjected.

"Jim!" Prismarine shouted.

"Watch it, Marine, and quit reading my mind!" Jim said while storming off to his office.

"What a happy family we have here..." Prismarine muttered.

When Lily arrived upstairs in Freya's room, she saw that Freya was sitting on her bed face down with her face smushed into her pillow sobbing.

"Are you alright Lady Freya?" Lily asked with concern. Normally she wouldn't care one way or another how Freya felt even after being ordered to check on her, but seeing how she was defended by her she felt as though she owed her one, "If you would like someone to talk to, I would be more than happy to oblige."

Freya popped her head out from her pillow and looked back at Lily "Really, you mean it?" she sniffled.

"Yes. It is the least I can do to repay you for earlier." Lily answered. Freya sat upward and patted a spot on her large bed for Lily to sit. Lily sat on the edge of Freya's bed and turned towards her, ready to listen.

"He's never around..." Freya said, wiping her eyes. "I get that he's busy running everything, but I can't even remember the last time I spent an entire day with him."

"*I don't recall him doing that either,*" Lily thought. "I see...," she replied.

"I finally have someone willing to spend time with me. Yes, I have to pay him, but he does care about me, and Father just wants to take that away from me. It's like Father just wants to make me miserable," Freya said.

"*So that Reighley boy is being paid? Interesting...,*" Lily pondered. This was the first time Lily had seen Freya open up. Lily decided to sit back and listen, she knew better than most that just having someone to listen to your problems was the best treatment for frustration. She had Elise as her confidant to complain to whenever Freya would do things that irritated her.

Freya got up from her bedside and began pacing back and forth in silence. She raised both of her arms upward and then swung them down to her sides with a loud grunt. Afterward, she began ranting to Lily. All the built-up emotions she had never once spoken out loud about her father all came out at once. "Stupid Father, getting in the way of things! Why is it now of all times that he finally takes an interest in my life? I've worked so hard just for him to spend a little bit of time with me. I've been the perfect daughter up until now." Freya stopped speaking abruptly. She had a realization. *"I'm doing the exact thing my father just did to Lily... She doesn't deserve this,"* Freya stopped moving, and took a deep breath, exhaling loudly. "I'm sorry Lily. I'm sorry about my Father. He shouldn't have treated you like that downstairs, and I'm sorry for shouting at you. You don't deserve that..." Freya was scouring her mind for anything else to apologize about. For a minute Lily didn't recognize Freya. It was like a completely different person was standing in front of her. A thought occurred in her head but she ended up unintentionally saying what she was thinking.

"Just what happened to you in the last two weeks?" Lily asked. She almost couldn't bring herself to hate Freya anymore. She still wished she wasn't in debt, and she blamed

Freya for that partially. However, she couldn't possibly stay mad at someone who defended her and then apologized to her for her parent's actions. It was so unlike Freya that it scared Lily a bit.

"What...? What do you mean?" Freya asked. She was shocked by Lily's lack of composure. She was always calm and collected, and never once broke her maid etiquette in front of Freya. Although, it wasn't as if she was prohibited from doing so. Freya had told Lily countless times in the past to speak with her normally from time to time, but Lily refused.

"You're different now. I don't know what it is, but something about you has changed," she said.

"Is that a good thing or a bad thing," Freya asked with concern.

"It's a good thing. Now if you'll excuse me I need to prepare your bath and clothes for you to sleep in," she stated. Lily got up from the bed and walked towards the door when she heard Freya speak once again.

"Hey, Lily?" She asked.

"Yes, Lady Freya?" Lily stopped and answered.

"Thanks again, for letting me rant. I feel a bit better now," Freya said. Lily looked back over her shoulder and saw Freya with a smile on her face that Lily hadn't seen throughout all the days she worked for her. It was genuine gratitude. Something Freya had never given Lily since she started as a maid. She wasn't sure how to respond so she gave a nod and walked out of the room towards the bathhouse.

"Just who does she think she is?" Lily fumed, *"She has no right to become a better person, not after all the horrible things she's done... Don't think this means I forgive you, Freya. Actions speak louder than words and I'm sure you'll go back to your former self sooner or later."*

When Reighley finally arrived back home, he said, "Goodbye Sir," as he waved Herald off and headed back inside. He checked his phone to see the time and it was 10:00 p.m. *"Shoot... it's pretty late. I still need to get some homework done before bed. Looks like it's going to be another late night,"* he thought. When he arrived at the front door, it opened preemptively.

"Welcome home," Jericho said.

"You were waiting for me?" Reighley asked.

"Of course. I couldn't sleep knowing that my son was out roaming the city in the middle of the night," she replied.

"So, am I in trouble?" Reighley asked, worried.

"Nope," Jericho answered.

"-and you're not going to ask what happened or why I came home so late all sweaty?" He questioned.

"Nope, I trust you. I'm sure you had your reasons. As for that girl, there was no need for me to interrogate her or anything like that. Your Mama didn't raise a fool for a son. Besides, I'm sure Isabelle had that part covered and then some," she said, with a laugh.

"Huh..." Reighley said with relief. He couldn't understate how much he appreciated that his mom wasn't overbearing and not breathing down his neck, unlike a certain someone he knew. It made him happy to know he had her trust to do the right thing and make good choices.

"Thanks, Mom," he said with a smile.

"*Although I may be a little young to be a grandmother.*" Jericho thought. "Now, go take a bath, you smell awful," she ordered.

"Yes Ma'am," he replied. Reighley walked inside past his mother and went to his room to grab clothes and a towel to change into. When he entered, he was ready for the daily pounce that he would receive from Morgana. He looked around the room waiting for the attack and then saw his cat on his desk ready to jump. However, something was off. Morgana looked like he had frozen in place. When Reighley got close to him Morgana scurried away in a panic.

"That bad, huh?" He said. This interaction hurt Reighley a bit, but he thought it was a fair response. He looked Morgana in the eyes and saw its aura. Its normal purple was flowing away from Reighley like a smoke in the wind indicating the cat wanted to be left alone. "All right, hold on Morgana, I'll be right back," he explained. Soon Reighley had gathered everything he needed, while storing the money he earned away, and then made his way to the bathroom. Afterward, he conducted his nightly routines of taking a bath, brushing his teeth, and changing into his nightwear. He didn't wear normal pajamas to bed, instead, he would wear casual comfortable clothing. He would put on a white T-shirt and black joggers then he was ready for bed.

Reighley then returned to his room to begin his homework. After a couple of wary sniffs from Morgana, it finally deemed Reighley worthy of its affection, now that he smelled better.

Reighley couldn't help but think about the threat from Herald, as well as the silent ride home. *"I'm definitely cursed. I really should consider writing a will,"* he thought. Soon Reighley had finished all of his school work. He looked at Morgana who was curled up sleeping on a few of his papers on his desk and picked him up.

"Alright Morgana, it's bedtime," he said. Reighley walked over to his bunk bed and climbed up it with his cat in hand and once the two made their way up top, they laid down getting comfortable, but not until Morgana made it clear that it had first say on where it lay.

"What a crazy weekend, right buddy?" Reighley asked while looking at Morgana's eyes to see his aura. It was back to its normal purple form. He didn't need to check it often as animals' aura's very rarely changed. They were constant and consistent in how they lived their lives, unlike people. Sometimes he wished he could pick and choose when to use his ability, but it wasn't as if he could turn it off.

"Meow..." The cat said and then stretched its paws.

"Yeah, I'm tired too," Reighley said and paused. He recollected the events of the day. They stormed his mind, one by one. When it finally came to mind, he kept reliving the moment he spent with Freya at the beach. "I can't believe I almost-" he turned red with embarrassment from the thought of almost kissing Freya. He took a second to gather his composure and then while laying on his back he raised his hand towards the ceiling. He stared at the back of his hand and muttered, "What am I doing?" He sighed and began thinking about him taking the lead in the escape from Herald, *"I acted selfish again, but it was a lot of fun. My life used to be so simple and straightforward before I met Freya, but now that I have her in it, things have changed so much."* With his hand still upward, his vision shifted as it refocused on the ceiling. He remembered that all of this would come to an end in just two weeks. *"That's right… Everything will go back to the way it was before soon. Freya and I will have our fake breakup and we won't see each other anymore outside of school. It was a short-lived spring romance,"* his thoughts were melancholic. He let his arm rest as he let out a yawn, conjuring a final thought before falling asleep. *"But I guess it was fun while it lasted."*

Throughout the evening Freya was waiting for a text from Reighley. She felt as though she always initiated their conversations and hoped that after tonight Reighley would be thinking about her enough to send her a message when she heard a knock on her door.

"Honey, it's me." Freya recognized the voice as her mother Prismarine.

"Yes Mother, what is it?" Freya answered.

Prismarine peered her head through the door and asked, "Are you doing okay, Freya dear?"

Freya nodded yes, in response, "Lily was able to help me feel a bit better,

"Well, that's good. I'm glad you are all right…" She replied. There was a moment of silence between the two until Prismarine felt like speaking up, "Look, Freya, I'm sorry about your father. I wish I could have done more to help you out."

"It's okay Mother. It's enough to just have you on my side," Freya said, "Besides, Father hasn't even met Reighley. I won't let his opinion change what I see in Reighley. I really like him, you know?" Prismarine halted completely and looked at her daughter, as tears began to start streaming down her face ruining her mascara. "Mother!? What's wrong?" Freya asked.

Prismarine began wiping her face, "It's just my little girl is growing up so fast," she sniffled. "Okay, okay," she said, gathering herself. "I will continue to be on your side dear. If this is what you truly want then I'll do what mothers do best and support you all the way through. Well, I'll leave you be for now. Have a good night Freya, dear," she said. She slid her head back through the door. Only a small crevice was left open when Prismarine heard her daughter speak.

"Hey, Mom? Thanks." Freya said with a smile.

With her back facing the door Prismarine looked over her shoulder and spoke through the crevice of the door before closing it. "You're welcome, dear."

Moments after walking away from the door, far out of earshot, Prismarine was incredibly giddy. *"OH, MY, GOSH. She called me Mom!"* she thought, while jumping up and down in excitement and letting out a tiny squeal, *"She hadn't called me that since she was a little girl."* Prismarine gathered herself once again, pumped her fist and encouraged herself, *"All right, Prismarine, just keep being a 'rockin' mom. You've got this!"* Afterward, she made her way toward Jim's office to scold him.

Reighley opened his eyes and somehow found himself inside a dark office, in front of him was a desk with a silhouette of a man sitting in a chair facing backward towards a window. The moonlight gleamed through it shining on Reighley, making it hard for his eyes to adjust to the brightness. He looked down and saw that he was tied up by a rope to a chair. His arms were completely restrained with his arms tied down.

"What!? Just what is going on!" Reighley shouted. His voice echoed into the darkness. The chair slowly yet menacingly began to rotate towards facing Reighley, and a voice came from the silhouetted man.

"I'd stop squirming if I were you. Unless of course, you would like to be stopped by force." The silhouetted man said. From the right corner of the office room, footsteps were heard walking towards Reighley from the darkness. Out from the corner, was Herald, shrouded in darkness. He was holding a butter knife in one hand and a handkerchief in the other.

"I warned you, Master Summers," Herald said. Reighley saw a cold icy unforgiving aura emanating from him. When the silhouetted man finally turned around to face Reighley, Reighley looked into his eyes and saw a pure black aura that blocked out the light of the moon from the window. All he could see was the man's devilish red eyes and to his horror, he was holding a photo of Freya in tears. Reighley didn't recognize the photo or the location in it and defended himself.

"It wasn't me! I swear!" He shouted.

"There's no point in denying it," said a feminine voice from the shadows. Reighley was confused by this as the voice he heard came from the left corner of the room. Out from the shadows was Isabelle who dramatically revealed herself with maniacal evil laughter. In her hand was a frying pan and she would knock on it with her knuckles making a menacingly clanging metal sound.

"Isabelle? Is that you!? How could you!?" Reighley shouted.

"Mwahahaha! Quiet Brother... This is all because you failed to get a satisfying present for Freya," she blamed.

"No, I swear! She told me she loved it-" Reighley tried to justify himself when the voice from the silhouetted man was heard.

"Silence! Don't think your "*Insight*" on others will save you this time. You've failed my daughter for the last time boy! Herald, Isabelle, get rid of him." Reighley began to panic as the two were walking towards him brandishing their weapons. Reighley could only let out a helpless scream before waking up.

Chapter 12

The Perfect Gift

Reighley woke up in a panic, the look of fear enveloped his face. He let in a sharp and heavy gasp for air, the shock of fear shunting him upright. The noise woke up Morgana, which made the cat yowl and jump a meter into the air causing it to ricochet off the ceiling. Reighley took a moment to gather himself. Glancing towards the cat he noticed a look of astonishment and betrayal. It glared and hissed at him while its fur was bristling.

"I'm sorry Morgana!" Reighley said. He attempted to ease its distress by petting him, but he dodged Reighley's hand and scurried off towards the end of the bed. Reighley let out a sigh from the response. He began thinking about his dream and how in retrospect it was fairly comical and far too absurd to be real. "'*Insight*'... *huh?*" Reighley remembered the last thing the man in the center of the room in his dream told him before he woke up, "*that's a pretty cool name for my ability to see auras.*" Then he remembered why he got shanked by a butter knife and whacked by a frying pan. "Crap," he muttered. It occurred to him that he would have to get something for Freya's birthday since he agreed to go. "I have to get her something," he said. Reighley placed his hand on the corner of his bed's guardrail and hoisted himself over, landing two feet on the concrete floor. Once down he grabbed Morgana from off the top bunk and used Insight on it. He noticed its aura was going wild like a bird slamming into a cage it was locked in indicating it needed freedom, so he let the kitten loose into the house. Afterward, he went over to his desk.

"Let's see, let's see," he said to himself while digging through several garbage bags full of gadgets and trinkets on the floor by his desk. The bags held a portion of his collection of treasures he found throughout his various expeditions through the city. He kept them all by his work desk as he would use some of them for spare parts to fix other treasures he found. The rest of his room was tidy, but his desk was an organized mess. Reighley searched through several bags attempting to find things he thought Freya would like. He pulled out an old silver stopwatch he fixed several years ago. The glass on the inside was cracked and the battery was dead, but it had a beautiful lavender flower engraved on it. It was only then that he realized that she probably had or could get a better version of anything he could pull out. Discouraged, Reighley put the stopwatch on his desk.

"What on earth do you give a girl who has everything?" He said after a grunt. Completely stumped on what to do next he decided to give Ulysses a call. He figured two heads were better than one, and it was a Sunday, so he had time to go shopping at the mall for a present. Reighley pulled his phone off his desk and unlocked it. To his surprise, Freya hadn't messaged him yet. "That's weird..." he muttered. "She normally texts me by now." He took a moment to think it through and wondered if she had been upset with him from the night before. Deciding to check in on her, he sent her a text.

Reighley: Hey Freya, are you doing alright?

Freya was in the middle of streaming on SocialLight on an expensive computer she owned placed in the corner of her library. She was chatting with her followers. They would watch her do her online shopping for clothing and other miscellaneous things. She made sure to spend no less than 300,000 yen (2,138 USD) with each purchase as she knew her followers wanted to know what it was like to be rich. This was no problem for Freya as her wallet was bottomless. Most of her fans were around the age range of twelve to thirty, with the fanbase split roughly fifty-fifty with both males and females alike. She scrolled through various websites buying dresses from designer clothes companies as well as things she felt were good for entertainment.

Her most recent purchase was a mechanical bull she ordered. She planned on placing the bull in her enormous backyard. Her family's estate is 1800 acres in size, so it was large enough to hold just about anything she put there within "reason". Freya enjoyed including her best friend in the things she did live on stream. However, Destiny was the only guest that was allowed as Freya made it a point to never

233

collaborate with any other famous people or streamers for fear that they would outshine her and steal the spotlight from her. To her that was unacceptable. Once the things she bought lost entertainment value, she would give them away to her fans through a random raffle for those who paid a subscription to her.

"Alright! Mechanical Bull purchased. What's next?" Freya said. From the chat in her stream, she saw Destiny reply.

Moderator-DJ_Destiny: Yee-Haw! Ride-em Cowgirl!

Doctor_Respectful_007: Moo!

Social_Lightus204: You would look great in overalls.

"Destiny you're coming over and riding it first when this thing arrives," Freya said as she heard a noise come from her phone. She received the text from Reighley. She knew it was him since she set a specific notification sound for when he contacted her. When she heard the tune, she stopped everything she was doing and looked over at her phone which was on the desk. Displayed on the center of its screen was a message from Reighley.

"Hey Freya, are you alright?" She read to herself. Her immediate reaction was filled with excitement. This was the first time she had ever received a message from Reighley, and it was even better that he was concerned about her. To her that could only mean one thing. *"He's thinking about me,"* she thought while blushing with a smile on her face. She forgot that she was live streaming in front of over 80,000 people on the internet.

Gullible_Guillotine_X: Who's got you smiling like that?

Moderator-DJ_Destiny: It's Loverboy!

QueenyFishy12: She's so cute when she's embarrassed.

"'Loverboy!?' Destiny just what on earth are you saying?" She panicked in her head. Soon the entire chat was saying things like *"Loverboy!"* and *"I wonder who Freya's new boyfriend is,"* which was all too much for Freya to handle. Fans began to argue in her chat, debating whether or not she had a boyfriend and if she did, they wondered if he was good enough to match her likeness and beauty. Freya could only sit there in a quiet panic as she didn't know how to proceed. The view count began to rise from 80,000 to 85,000 and then 120,000 all within the span of a few minutes. The chat was a mob that could not be silenced.

Young_Fan_Boy_Jin: There is no way Freya has an actual boyfriend. There is no one in this world worthy of her. #DestroyLoverBoy

Taco_Panda: Guys he's the real deal. All her exes never made her smile like that. #FindLoverboy

"There is no 'Loverboy', now stop talking-" Freya was interrupted by reading a comment sent by her best friend.

Moderator-DJ_Destiny: Loverboy is real.

This was all that was needed for the rest of the internet to run wild with theories. Freya's fans knew Destiny was a reliable source of information and Freya could only watch as the world found out that she was in a serious relationship regardless if it was fake or not.

Completely out of options, knowing that if she denied it things would get much worse, Freya scoffed, stuck up her nose, and decided she wasn't going down without a fight. "That's right! This mysterious '*Loverboy*' is real and I'll let you know he is the best boyfriend ever! All will be revealed to the public at my birthday party on May 6th, and the entire party will be streamed!" she said. "*Oh, no... Why did I say that? Reighley hates the idea of being famous. I should have kept my mouth shut,*" she mentally scolded herself. "*I guess there is no way out of this now.*"

She let the chat talk about it as trends like "*#Loverboyisreal*" began trending throughout social media. Her viewer count went up to 180,000. It was out of her hands now all she could do was wait for a moment to change topics. When that moment arrived she quickly switched the topic to be about things that were going to happen at her party. She had many things planned, like the arrival of famous chef Gordan Romsly; a world renowned chef who would be making the food for her guests, an ice sculpture modeled after herself, and a highly advanced laser tag system that her father had recently manufactured. It would use a laser that discerned its targets based on core body temperature, and she even hired over one hundred actors to play as undead zombies, all while wearing professional makeup. She did it for Reighley because she thought he would love it since she remembered he liked things in the horror genre, but she didn't dare tell anyone that.

Freya kept looking at her phone and knew that situation would get worse if she replied to him as every so often people in chat would mention things about this mysterious "Loverboy".

"Destiny why do you do this to me!? Sorry, Reighley... Looks like I can't reply just yet," she complained to herself in her head. She made a mental note to herself to crank the mechanical bull she purchased up to eleven when Destiny would ride it as a sort of payback.

Reighley sat down at his desk after sending his text to Freya. With each passing minute with no response, anxiety began to set in, and then sweat started to run down his brow. *"Somethings wrong. Why isn't she replying!? Is she mad?"* He thought. Reighley knew this was very much unlike Freya as whenever the two would text each other, it was always him who would reply after periods passed. Freya on the other hand, always had her phone on her and always replied instantaneously. *"Did I mess up? Did I say something wrong? What should I do?"* Reighley tried to reason with himself, *"Okay, okay, hold on Reighley. There has to be a reasonable explanation for this. Maybe she's busy. Just because you're used to being messaged first thing in the morning doesn't mean she's upset just because she didn't text you back instantly. Wait, what am I thinking? Why does that matter?"* He asked himself mentally. *"If only she was here, then I could use Insight on her to find out."* Reighley groaned and then snapped himself out of the panic remembering the task at hand. He needed to call Ulysses, so with his cell phone still in hand, he dialed Ulysses's number and waited for him to answer. After a few rings a click noise was heard indicating the phone was answered.

("Hey Bestie!") Ulysses was overjoyed with the fact Reighley, his best friend, called him out of nowhere.

("Hey dude. How's it going?") Reighley was still unsure where Ulysses got the term *"Bestie"* but at this point, he didn't mind.

("Things are going well. What about you?") He replied.

("Well I got myself a bit of a problem. You see, I was wondering if you could help me out today. I need to go shopping for a birthday present for Freya,") Reighley explained.

Ulysses let out a signature prideful laugh. ("Aha! What a good boyfriend. I expect nothing less from my Bestie.")

("Uh… Are you okay dude?") Reighley remembered the first time he met Ulysses he acted the same way but changed shortly afterward.

("Umm yeah… Sorry, I don't know how to talk over the phone. I'm trying to get better at talking to people,") Ulysses awkwardly replied. There was a silence that stretched into the ether. Reighley understood him now. He knew Ulysses had trouble talking to people. He was socially awkward, but self-aware that he was socially awkward. It was something he was trying to improve on.

("Don't worry about it, man. No judgment here. We all have things we need to improve on.") Reighley encouraged. In reality, Reighley meant that about himself. He hadn't even begun to improve on the things he needed to work on, ("Anyway, can you make it?")

("Thanks, man. However, I don't know if I can help you out. I'm working at the shop today. I'm sorry.") Ulysses apologized.

("Well... That sucks. You're like my only friend, that's a guy. I could use the help.") Reighley explained. The words *"Friend"* reverberated in Ulysses's head like an echo in a hallowed chamber. How could he let his best friend down in his time of need? Not to mention he was Ulysses only male friend.

"He's relying on me." Ulysses thought. He was currently busy cooking with his brother Sunny at the Back Alley Ramen shop. The restaurant had its fair share of regular customers, but today was a particularly slow day. Not enough to say that the shop was *"dead,"* but enough that they would only have a customer every so often. Sunny took notice of his younger brother's expression. He appeared torn. Like someone who was stuck between choices, placed in a moral dilemma of sorts.

"Hey Ulysses, what's wrong?" Sunny asked. Ulysses was startled by his brother's question. The surprise caused his cell phone to slip out from his hand from underneath his neck, and almost fall into a bowl of Ramen Ulysses was preparing if not for Sunny's lightning-fast reflexes. Sunny quickly stretched out with a pair of chopsticks and snatched the phone out of the air. Once caught Sunny returned the phone to his brother.

"That was a close call... Thanks, bro, and it's nothing, a friend just asked if I wanted to hang out today. That's all." Ulysses explained.

"Dude. Why don't you just go?" Sunny asked. From what he understood, this was the first time Ulysses had mentioned having any sort of friend since he entered high school.

"You know... We have the shop to take care of while Dad is out." He explained.

"It's fine big man, go. I can take care of it. Think of it as a way for me to pay you back for helping me the other week. That date was a success because of you, so if you want to go and hang out with a friend, do it," Sunny encouraged, "and besides, I get a feeling we are going to be slow here for the time being, it's a job for one man, not two."

Ulysses looked towards his brother and hugged him. "Thanks, Sunny! You're the best," he praised. The size comparison between the two was night and day. Ulysses squeezed Sunny, almost to the point of suffocation. He didn't know his own strength but knew not to squeeze for very long as in the past he knocked his brother unconscious when the two were younger.

"Yeah, yeah. Now, go and get out of here and have some fun." Sunny said with an embarrassed expression. He was a sucker for praise, especially from those he cared about. This made him a bit of a pushover.

After, Ulysses let his brother go and placed his phone back up to his ear. "(Bestie, it looks like I can go after all.)"

("Really!? That's great. How about you meet me at the Midori Mall in an hour,") Reighley suggested. *"Well... That was wholesome,"* he thought. He had heard the entire conversation over the phone, it made him wish he had an older brother who looked out for him.

("Alright.") Ulysses replied.

("Cool! See you soon.") Reighley said. The two ended their phone call with each other.

Reighley began getting ready for his trip to the mall when he heard a knock on his door.

"Hey, are you awake? What was all that noise earlier?" Isabelle asked.

"That was like ten minutes ago. I could have fallen off my bed and you're just now checking on me?" Reighley shouted.

"Eh, you're fine. Now come eat breakfast," Isabelle claimed.

"Fine..." Reighley groaned. Once presentable, he stepped out into the dining room and began to quickly scarf down the breakfast that was prepared for him. Isabelle fixed him eggs, sausage, and buttered toast, with a side of orange juice to wash it down.

"So what are you in a hurry for?" Isabelle interrogated. Reighley took a second to swallow his food and then replied.

"I'm going out to the mall with a friend to try and find a birthday present for Freya.

"What!? You have a different friend besides Freya?" Isabelle asked, completely surprised.

"Yeah. His name is Ulysses and he is over 200cm tall and super strong, but he's basically like a big teddy bear," he explained. Isabelle could only picture Ulysses as a Viking who had just come off the coast. Ready to storm a nearby village and pillage it for supplies. She then glanced at Reighley who one could argue was average in build and athleticism, and couldn't help but idolize whoever this Ulysses was, at least in her head compared to her brother.

"I want to see how tall he is! Warriors are super cool!"

"He's not a warrior, silly. He's a goofball if anything, but he's a really nice guy." Reighley said.

"Don't ruin it for me. I watched one of those movies on your desk on your old VHS TV in your room last night," she explained. Her eyes were sparkling as if she was fantasizing about something. Reighley used his Insight on her to see if he could figure out what was going on inside her head. To his surprise, her light blue aura was blown up out of proportion. It was twice her size. It was shaped like a Viking with heavy snow raining down on it. It had a long braided neckbeard that dropped past its gut, a horned helmet that had a face guard covering the eyes, and it was holding a great axe. It appeared to have a bear pelt mantle over its shoulder as well. He guessed that was because of the teddy bear comment from before. Reighley knew she must have watched one of the old Viking movies he found. He didn't even want to question whether or not the film was appropriate for a fourteen-year-old girl to watch. Disregarding it for now, without hesitation Reighley squashed her active imagination.

"Don't use my stuff without asking," Reighley said while flicking Isabelle in the forehead.

"Ouch!" Isabelle complained, "Fine... Sorry, I'll ask next time."

"It's fine. You can repay me by taking care of Morgana while I'm gone." Reighley gestured towards the cat who was currently on the kitchen countertop cleaning its fur.

"I do that anyway," she said.

"I'd hope so. Anyway, I have to go now."

At last, Reighley finished eating. He quickly cleaned off his plate and made his way back into his room. He pulled out some spare cash from his refurbished dresser, which he salvaged shortly after moving into town and then he double-checked Morgana's bowls for food and water before leaving his room. Afterward, he dashed out towards the city after shouting goodbye on his way out the door to make it to Midori Mall on time.

Ulysses was halfway towards the subway system when he reached into his left pocket. This was where he usually kept his pack of cigarettes. When he realized they were not in that pocket he stopped moving. He started to scramble around frantically looking through the rest of his pockets on his person in the hope of finding it. To his horror, every pocket was empty. He realized he had forgotten his pack of cigarettes he would keep on him and began to shutter in a cold sweat. He had a tough decision to make. Either go to Midori Mall and risk Reighley finding out about his smoking habits, or turn back and be late, letting his friend down.

"He's counting on me this time. How could I let him down?" He asked himself. *"Alright! I'll press onward and endure for my bestie's sake."*

San Fran Kyoto is a peninsula divided into five major districts. Each district has its major drop-off and pick-up points and all are connected to the central district transportation hub. These interconnecting bullet trains allow for an easy commute to any district. In the northeast section of the city was Higashi Pier 78. The Young Family owns the majority of the properties that reside within the area which includes several supermarkets, malls, and the amusement park; Distracto Land, turning the port into a tourist trap. San Fran Kyoto Peak is a district located in the center of the city acting as the central hub point between the other four. It was here where businesses came to flourish. The competition in the area was cut-throat and many companies aspired to rise to the top of their echelons, but those who failed were soon forgotten as they were bought out or had to file for bankruptcy.

The other remaining districts are Clothstone Town, Koko Rich Coast, and Wazuka Bayview. Clothstone Town is located in the southwest part of the city and is primarily a rural, countryside town. Koko Rich Coast is the northwest district that is known for the ever-present fog that layered itself above the city, and the fact that it was connected to Kanpan Beach located just west of the Crimson Gate Bridge. Wazuka Bayview is a historical district that is known for the quaint use of traditional architecture for its residential houses.

Ulysses's family shop was located in San Fran Kyoto Peak. His family was wealthy and had several properties around the city. He lived there because it was a direct request from his mother Kokeisha (Co-Key-Shah), and it was a close walk to Gilford High.

Kokeisha was the one who indirectly supplied Ulysses with cigarettes. She stored an abundance of them in an antique cabinet in her room and would always restock them at the end of the month. Both of Ulysses's parents smoked, so he was sure his mother was unaware of his addiction because she most likely assumed it was his father Todoh who was using her supply.

When Ulysses arrived at the station, he scanned his subway pass at the entrance to receive a ticket. He then proceeded towards the gate that led to Higashi Pier 78's train. The gate was a turnstile that blocked the path. Which had a one-way revolving wheel that would spin forward if someone scanned their ticket and passed through it. Ulysses was almost too big to fit so he had to turn his body sideways to squeeze through.

"*Skinny thoughts. Skinny thoughts,*" he mentally encouraged himself.

When he finally arrived at the Higashi Pier 78's platform, many of the people hurried out of his way, in fear of being trampled on. To board the train, he needed to slouch downward and squeeze his arms to his chest to make it inside. When he stepped in, the crowd around him parted, making room between them and himself.

"*Great. Everyone is scared of me again... This is why I hate trains,*" he thought. It wasn't until then that he noticed a single girl who stood her ground. "*It's her! The girl who came to the shop a while ago.*"

Standing in front of him, only a few feet away, was the girl who came into the shop during Reighley and Freya's date. He couldn't forget her that easily, in fact, he often thought about her as she was the only one who understood him when he could barely speak.

Lily was on her way to visit Ulysses at his ramen shop since it was one of her rare days off. She even picked one of her cutest casual outfits. A simple zebra striped short-sleeved shirt, and jeans as well as sneakers. She was excited to see her future husband and try more of his delicious food. When she saw a large teenager squeeze through the train door beyond the crowd, her eyes lit up.

"*It's Ulysses! I can't believe it. What are the odds I would run into him halfway there?*" She thought. "*I must speak with him. That's why I came all this way here in the first place."* Her heart wasn't fully prepared for this encounter.

Ulysses was staring at her in a way that one could only describe as ominous. However, this was the stare he would give anyone when he was frozen in fear unable to decide on what to do next. *"What should I do? She's right in front of me and I can't move a muscle."* Completely lost in thought, he felt a tug on the end of his sleeve.

"Excuse me, sir? You do remember me, right?" Lily asked.

It was another miracle. As if the weight of the world had lifted off his shoulders. His heart fluttered with anticipation as she spoke, and when she stopped, words finally came out of his mouth.

"Yes, I do," he answered. Internally, Ulysses shouted to the heavens with joy as this was the first time he could say more than a single word to the girl. When Lily heard that he remembered who she was, she was elated. She let out a big smile in response.

"I'm glad," she said. "I never introduced myself last time. My name is Lily."

"L-Lily," Ulysses stuttered. "Nice…"

"That's right," she replied. "So, where are you headed to?" Lily asked. She thought it was cute seeing him struggling to talk. She found it easy to understand him due to her time spent with her grandmother, who also spoke similarly due to her old age.

"Present. Mall. Friend," he said with a deep cough afterward. *"Holy crap! I'm doing it! I'm talking to a girl,"* he reflected. Meanwhile, the train doors closed behind Ulysses and the crowd around them looked at the two with utter confusion. The crowd looked at Lily in awe and considered her a heroine for standing up to the large ogre of a man.

"Oh, you're going shopping with a friend at the mall to buy a present?" She asked him. Ulysses nodded in complete astonishment, as even he would have interpreted it as him going to the mall to buy a friend a gift. "That's great! Would you like some company!?" She enthusiastically asked. Ulysses nodded again, without giving it a second thought.

Soon the train began moving and Lily was shunted forward by the sudden momentum. Lily lost her balance and fell over, only to be caught by Ulysses. Lily, who was always good at hiding her emotions, couldn't help but turn red from looking at Ulysses. She regained her footing and stood up straight. "I'm sorry! Thank you," she said with gratitude.

"Yeah, be careful," he commanded. Ulysses took Lily by the hand and placed it on a support handle that was hanging from the ceiling. After, he immediately realized he touched her hand and freaked out inside his head. *"Ah! I did something stupid. She is going to think I'm creepy now,"* he thought.

When he did this Lily's heart skipped a beat. At first, she was going to marry Ulysses since he could cook, but he was also a gentleman who prevented her from falling in front of a crowd. This combination swept her off her feet in one fell swoop. She didn't expect him to be so considerate. Lily held onto the support handle on the train and couldn't help but stare at the hand he had just touched. Her heart was beating rapidly, and she didn't know what else to say.

Finally, the train arrived at Higashi Pier 78. The crowd, who were still wary of Ulysses, decided to wait for him to leave before they carried on with their business. Once off the train, the passengers nodded to Lily in deference as they walked by, giving her their thanks. Lily was slightly confused by the passengers' peculiar behavior but ultimately decided to ignore it.

"Let's go," Ulysses commanded. Lily gave a nod and the two made their way outside of the station entrance. From there Ulysses looked around and saw Reighley who was standing by a clock, posted into the ground. The two made their way towards him and Lily had a sudden realization.

"Wait. Isn't that-?" Lily immediately recognized Reighley from her Back Alley Ramen escapade.

"Hey man! Glad to see you made it here okay," Reighley called and then stopped and looked at the young lady next to him. "You never told me you had a girlfriend!" He shouted.

The two stopped in their tracks almost crashing from the statement. "No, no, you got it all wrong! I've only just met her recently," Ulysses said. Lily was surprised he was able to speak so clearly to Reighley. She figured it just meant he was comfortable with him. She was slightly envious because of this.

"Ah, I see," Reighley said, discreetly giving the exact thumbs up that Ulysses had given him in the past. He immediately used his Insight on Lily to try and see what she was like. To his surprise, it was a new color that he hadn't seen before on a person. It was beige and he had no idea what it meant. While the two were approaching him something strange happened to Reighley, he went into an almost trance-like state of mind, and the color he was looking at began to bisect until it was a tripartite of its three original colors.

"*What the-,*" he thought, as the colors split off into three, being gray, bright yellow, and brown. "*This has never happened before. Is this her aura? I've never met someone with such complex traits like this before. It must mean she has something from all three colors, but I can't tell which specifics she has.*" When the two arrived at the clock post Reighley snapped out of his trance.

"Hello. My name is Lily. It's a pleasure to officially meet you," she said with a bow.

"Officially?" Reighley asked.

"Oh, ah, I mean yes! Ulysses told me he was going shopping with a friend." Lily said sporadically. "*Oops, that was close. I almost let it slip that I knew who he was already,*" she thought.

"Right... Well, I'm Reighley. Nice to meet you as well. Did Ulysses tell you what we are doing?" He introduced himself with a quaint wave.

"Umm… sort of. He said he was going to the mall with a friend to get a present. Midori Mall I presume?" Lily answered.

"Wow, she's amazing," Ulysses thought while looking back and forth, switching whenever the other talked. He was completely infatuated at this point, but yet at the same time terrified. *"Thank goodness Reighley is here or I wouldn't know what to do with myself."*

"Yeah. That's the plan. However, I am the one in need of some assistance. You see, I am getting a present for Frey- I mean, my girlfriend and I needed help on what to pick for her," Reighley said. *"I probably shouldn't tell a random stranger that the girl I'm dating is Freya Young. I don't think that would end up going very well if they knew who she was,"* he considered.

"Just my luck," Lily said out loud.

"What?" the two replied.

"Uh… I mean, I am a girl, so I should be able to help you get the right gift for her," she answered. *"Great. I have to go shopping with my future husband and my boss's boyfriend for the person I dislike the most,"* suddenly Lily had a thought. *"Wait… I could try and make them get her a lame gift that she won't like."*

"Really! Thanks a bunch! With your help, I'm sure that we can get a gift that she will like. I really want her to like it." Reighley said with joy and slight relief as he relived the nightmare in his head from the night before.

"Dang it. He's so sincere," she thought.

"Lily, I'm counting on you," Ulysses said. Like an arrow straight through the heart, Lily's feelings changed.

"*Fine. I suppose if it's for Ulysses's sake, I'll take it seriously,*" she reconsidered. "Right," she nodded.

"Alright. Let's head out," Reighley said. The three left the station entrance and made their way to Midori Mall which was several blocks away. The group passed through what seemed to be a strip mall with an assortment of different shops and Ulysses pointed out a restaurant that was popular in the area. Reighley took note of the expensive restaurant and the fact that Ulysses praised it, meant it must be a good place to eat. He knew he couldn't afford it, but thought it would be a nice place to go on a date. The restaurant was named the Garden Shores and the majority of its seating was outside. Above the tables were white interwoven pieces of wood that blocked the majority of the sun from the customers.

While on their way the three crossed over a brick bridge that was near the sea. Seagulls could be heard off into the distance. The sound of the birds caused Reighley to glance over towards the beach to his right. It was hard to see at first due to how bright the sun was. It took a second for his eyes to adjust from the light, but Reighley blocked it out with his hand and what lay past was a beautiful beach. The heat from the sun's rays gently graced their skin. Reighley looked out towards the ocean as they walked. The beach was as clean as could be. He hadn't swam in the ocean before, but not from lack of trying. He never had an opportunity as the previous home he lived in was landlocked. Reighley couldn't help but think how great it would be to cool off in the bay. He wanted to try it during this summer break.

The trio arrived at Midori Mall. It was a massive structure that was four stories tall. It had a multitude of fake vines all around its exterior. The face of the building had a sign on it stating "(WEST ENTRANCE)". Wasting no time, they headed through the revolving doors at the entrance. Once in, the three approached the large map that was made available to all patrons of the mall. The map showed a multitude of shops and stores that were listed and displayed in bright colors. Once in front of the display they began reading some of the store names aloud that sounded promising.

Reighley turned to Ulysses and asked. "So, what do you think she would like?

"I don't think I am qualified to answer that," Ulysses replied. The three laughed at his quip.

After a brief moment of trepidation, Lily replied."Well, I am single so I wouldn't know for sure, but if I was in a relationship, I wouldn't mind some jewelry." With concern, she thought, "*I know Freya very well, but the problem is that I don't recall her valuing anything that she has been given in the past.*"

"Well. That's the thing. Since she is pretty wealthy, I'm not sure if the thing I buy won't be just another shiny thing that she could have bought herself…" Reighley replied.

"I'm sure she will love whatever you get her," Ulysses encouraged.

"Yes, but this is the first one, so it has to be special," Reighley replied while thinking, *"Especially since it's also the last."* Unable to decide, the three looked at the map and pondered on where to go first. Taking a shot in the dark, the group decided on a store called Goalds. Lily recognized it as a place Freya frequented before. She mentioned to the group that it had golden trinkets you could purchase for your significant other.

The three arrived at the shop and were greeted at the entrance. The trio began browsing through the items when Ulysses spotted something.

"Hey, what about this?" He asked.

"Let me see," Reighley peaked over and noticed a giant gold chain necklace with a large dollar sign pendant on it. "Uh, I know she likes money, but I don't see her wearing this," Reighley explained, thinking *"It's not like she's a rapper."*

"How about this?" Lily asked. It was a golden necklace with a brown recluse spider on it.

"Um... I think that's a bit offensive," Reighley said nicely. *"What is up with this place? Don't they have anything romantic?"* He thought. The three spent a few more minutes browsing the items on display before deciding that there was nothing there worth buying. They left and continued to explore the mall in search of the perfect gift. They tried many different stores. They started with a clothing place but most of the clothes were probably too cheap for Freya's tastes. Next, they went to a store that sold stuffed pillows and cushions. The only issue was they only sold plain fruits without any characteristics that could be deemed as cute.

Reighley thought to himself *"Who would buy these? They don't even have cute little faces on them. They're just plain fruit."* Immediately after the thought a group of couples entered the store.

"Look, it's so adorable! You have to buy me one." a female customer said. Her boyfriend had a look of bewilderment on his face but soon acquiesced to her request. Soon there was a long line at the cash register as more couples flooded in buying fruits. All the while the men of the groups looked at their significant others with doubt and confusion on their faces. Reighley didn't understand what was so great either and decided to move on. They then visited Richards Sporting Goods, an extreme sports store, in search of adventure gear for her. Even this didn't feel quite right because he figured she most likely had everything in the entire mall let alone the store itself.

After their search, the three stopped at the cafeteria for a break and got some food.

"Man, this is tough!" Reighley sighed while seating himself at a table with the other two. *"It makes me wonder if I even know her at this point,"* he thought glumly. Once seated he heard hysterical laughter coming from a few tables away to his left. Reighley looked over to see the commotion and realized it was just the person he needed. It was Destiny, and she was one person who most likely knew what Freya liked most.

"Hold on a second guys, I see someone I know," he said and immediately got up from his chair and made his way toward the laughing girl. Lily looked over at who he was talking about and began to panic as she knew Destiny would tell just about everyone in the mall that she was Freya's maid. She turned her head to the right, shielding her face with her hair, in hopes she wouldn't be found out. She felt sick to her stomach from the thought of being discovered in her daily life.

"You okay?" Ulysses asked.

"Yep, just some neck pain that's all," Lily said nonchalantly.

Reighley made his way to her table when she noticed him.

"Oh, hey look, it's Loverboy!" Destiny said with a laugh.

"Loverboy? What are you talking about?" He asked. He could hear Freya talk through her phone's speaker. *"Phew... Looks like I was right and she was just busy,"* he thought.

Meanwhile, back at Freya's place, she was reading the messages when Destiny sent another in her chat.

Moderator-DJ_Destiny: Attention All, Attention All. I am with Loverboy as we speak!

It was one message but it made Freya explode with emotions. "What!?" she said. "Destiny, You're with Re-" she quickly covered her mouth in fear of exposing him, but it was too late.

Gullible_Guillotine_X: Loverboy 'R'

Lucky_Luffy_x: Ladies and Gentlemen, we got 'em.

Marine_Fan: R, R, R, R, R, R!

Freya instinctively froze on the spot. *"That girl. Ugh! What am I going to do with you, Destiny?"* Freya thought in frustration.

Reighley looked at Destiny with extreme confusion and asked, "What just happened?"

"Oh I've been teasing Freya since this morning," she answered. Reighley used Insight on her and saw the same aura as before. A pure white aura without waver. He knew she was the honest type with no reason to lie, but he could have sworn there was gray in there.

"That's great and all but why was she about to say my name?" He asked.

"Oh, because I told the internet that Freya had a boyfriend with a special codename, Loverboy!" She said with a laugh.

"I'm sorry, you what?" Reighley angrily said. When Destiny saw his expression she felt a bit of fear, as shivers went down her spine.

"Was I not supposed to?" She asked.

"No," he said, irritated. "You're her best friend, right? Then you are supposed to know these things. I don't want the world to find out we're dating." He said.

"I'm sorry... I didn't know, I swear," she apologized. Reighley looked at her and she was about to cry. He thought it through and felt as though it was an honest mistake taken too far. He took a deep breath and let out a long sigh with eyes closed and comforted her.

"It's fine, it's not like it was going to stay hidden forever," he said. "Destiny, why don't you join Ulysses, Lily, and I for lunch?"

"Lily and Uly are here!?" She said excitedly.

"You know Lily?" He asked.

"Yep! She's-" Destiny suddenly received a call from Freya and ignored it. *"I better let it sink in a bit before talking back with her."* The two returned to the table with Lily and Ulysses and both were feeling sick to their stomach. Ulysses was ill from withdrawals, having not smoked this entire time. He had a cold sweat running down his brow and looked irate, while Lily on the other hand was still hiding her appearance.

"Are you two alright? You don't look well." Reighley asked. When he arrived back at the table, both Ulysses and Lily quickly scurried toward the female and male restrooms respectively. "Must have been bad food..." Reighley muttered as he turned towards Destiny.

"Anyway, I am trying to buy Freya a present for her birthday but I haven't had much luck," Reighley explained the events of what had happened thus far to Destiny and she could only cross her arms with disappointment.

"You were the chosen one, Reighley," She said with disappointment. "How can you guys suck so bad at getting her a gift?"

"Look. It's not like it's that easy to buy a girl who has everything, anything," he explained.

"Heh. I've done just fine each year and I don't even need to buy her anything," she boasted.

"What? You know a good gift I could give her?" Reighley asked with desperation. Destiny nodded in silence and slowly lifted her wrist. "The friendship bracelet?" He asked.

"Yep. She never takes it off. Not even when she does fashion shoots or movie scenes. She's all like, 'I pay you enough money, just edit it out in post,' or something like that," she explained. "That is just one of the many things I've made for her over the years."

"I see..." he said and began to ponder, "*So if I make her something unique, then maybe she would value it more than some store-bought item.*"

Destiny was looking critically at Reighley when she saw his face subtly relaxed and a smile spread across his face. "Think of something, young padawan?" She asked. Reighley let out a laugh and answered confidently.

"Yeah, I got this," he said.

Inside the single-stall men's restroom, Ulysses was gagging. "*This is bad... I didn't think it would become this awful so fast. This is the longest that I have held off smoking before, but I can't let them find out. I don't want to risk losing them as*" *friends…"* He thought desperately. While completely blue in the face from his exertion, he attempted to rouse himself by saying "Especially Lily, I'm sure she would skip town if she saw me like this. C'mon Ulysses, toughen up!" He slapped himself in the face with both hands in an attempt to stem the next wave of nausea using sheer willpower, but it made little difference.

Meanwhile in the single-stall women's restroom, Lily was busy preparing herself. She figured something like this would happen, so she brought her disguise kit that she used during her ramen escapade, just in case. She pulled her disguise out of her bag and stopped to look at herself in the mirror. Sighing dejectedly, she wondered what her life would have been like if she wasn't a maid. If she was in the same world as Freya, would they have been friends? She envisioned having friends around her in the mirror, picturing Freya, Ulysses, Destiny, and Reighley standing beside her smiling. For a moment she thought that this was a future she could have seen herself in if things were different. Her heart aching, she quickly squashed the idea, as she was simply a maid, first and above all else.

"I'm sorry Ulysses, but I have to go…" she whispered as she put on the disguise. She peaked out of the restroom to see if anyone was watching, and once she was sure the coast was clear she snuck away.

Chapter 13

New Blossom

Reighley was chatting with Destiny while glancing over at the restrooms every so often awaiting the return of both Ulysses and Lily. He noticed a woman leave the restroom that Lily was in. She looked vaguely familiar to him. *"That's odd… Did I miss Lily leaving the restroom?"* He thought, *"And that woman, I feel like I have seen her somewhere before."* Reighley tried to use *Insight* on the woman but it was no use. She was wearing a pair of black sunglasses that stopped him from using it. Suddenly a loud sound was heard from the men's restroom behind the lady, she looked backward at it in concern.

"Ulysses! What's wrong?" Lily thought, *"I have to help him, but I need to leave. I can't compromise my identity."* Her caretaker instincts that were ingrained into her very soul caused her to halt in hesitation, this caused Lily to recall a time when Elise had just dropped her off at home after work…

Before Lily was Freya's handmaiden, she lived with her Grandmother in Clothstone Town in a small little cottage out in the countryside. She moved in with her Grandmother after her parents were caught up in an accident. It wasn't soon after that before she was taken in by the Young family to work as a maid. Even though she was young in age, she still worked full-time for the Young family. They would pick her up every morning and she would spend her days learning all the mannerisms and duties that being a handmaiden entailed, to the point of exhaustion. Only after a long day's work would she return home to spend time with her grandmother.

Lily had just been dropped off home by Elise who waved her off and took off shortly after. Lily made it to the front door and opened it to see her grandmother using a duster on the cracks and corners of the front room.

"Welcome home, Lily. How was your day at work dear?" Her grandmother Daffodil said.

"It was hard, Grandma. My legs and arms hurt, and I can't even have fun there," Lily replied.

"I know dear. It must be very very hard on you. It was never supposed to be this way, but I want you to know that I'm proud of how committed you are to this. It's not an easy task for an adult let alone a seven year old my dear," Daffodil praised her while patting Lily on the head. "I am very, very, proud of you."

"But Grandma, I am eight years old now! We just had my birthday party last week, remember?" Lily corrected.

"Oh, yes, silly me, how could I forget?" She stated. "How about you go and change out of your uniform and go play for a bit while the sun is still out? Go and have that fun you've been missing out on. How does that sound?" Daffodil asked.

"Okay! I'm going to go see if Miko (Me-Co) wants to play." Lily replied and quickly got her into clothes she could wear outside.

"Very well. Be careful." Daffodil replied.

When Lily rushed past her to go outside. She ran over towards her neighbor who was a young girl named Miko. Miko was slightly older than Lily, being the age of twelve. She lived with her mother whose home was built next to a nearby shrine house.

Miko's mother, who was utterly devoted to the shrine, gave her daughter a name that literally meant Shrine Maiden. Miko had her profession chosen for her at birth by her mother. Shrine Maiden's started their intense training from the early years of adolescence and it would persist anywhere between three to seven years. Concluding only when one became qualified to become a shaman priestess. Their attire would consist of bright red long divided pleated trousers, a white fold-over dress with long droopy sleeves that was tucked into the pants called a Kosode, which was the predecessor to the Kimono, and a red or white ribbon. They would be trained to maintain immense concentration entering a trance-like state to communicate with kami (gods) or spirits of the deceased, as well as practicing fortune telling.

To get to Miko's house Lily had to travel a dirt path and then climb several hundred stone steps with bamboo stalks on both sides. Out of breath, Lily was about to knock on the wooden door to their house when she heard a scream come from inside. She recognized the screamer as Miko. Lily was fairly familiar with her voice due to Miko often screaming from being afraid of many critters like bugs. Instinctively Lily opened the door and rushed inside. She rushed into the hall to see Miko standing on top of a small table in the room beyond having a meltdown.

"Miko, what's wrong!?" Lily asked.

"There… there… there's a snake!" Miko replied, "It's over there!" She pointed towards the corner of the room. Lily rushed inside and looked at the corner of the room. She recognized the snake as a Yamakagashi (Rhabdophis Tigrinus/Japanese Garter Snake), which, unlike common American garter snakes, was venomous. She learned this because part of her training as a maid consisted of gardening. She was required to know of potentially dangerous animals that she might come across while she was at work. She always felt as though the information was useless, until now.

"Get rid of it!" Miko begged.

"Hold on, Miko. It's venomous, so I need to be careful." Lily stretched her arm out and the snake hissed at her, and in a single motion, she swiftly picked the small snake up behind its head by wrapping her fingers around the nape of its neck. Lily let out a shuddering breath. Things like these bothered her. Lily was terrified of snakes to the point that it would have paralyzed her in fear, but since it was for someone else's well-being, she felt as if she could do anything.

"Get it out of here, and please don't let my mom find out it's poisonous!" Miko yelled.

"It's venomous, not poisonous, which means as long as it doesn't bite you, you'll be okay."

"As long as what doesn't bite you? What's all this commotion!" A voice behind Lily came from the door.

"I'm sorry Mother, there was a snake inside the house!" Miko explained. The woman looked to see that Lily was holding the snake, then at the disarrayed room. After seeing how messy the area had become, a look of distaste was evident on her face. She was disgusted by the behavior that she had seen.

"Remove that thing from this house if you'd please," she told Lily, "and Miko, calm yourself, girl, there is no reason for you to lose your composer over a simple creature. It appears you have not learned well enough to keep yourself stable from our training. It looks like you'll require more supplementary lessons, starting tomorrow."

Lily went outside and placed the snake on some leaves a little ways from the house, hearing a subdued "Yes Mother," reply from inside the building. Lily patiently waited and watched the snake until it slithered away.

"Psst! Is it gone?" Lily, looking up from the snake, saw Miko peeking her head out the front door.

"Yeah... It is." Lily said. Suddenly, Lily began quietly sobbing, trying hard not to attract attention from Miko's mother.

"Lily?" Miko asked.

"It was so scary!" She cried. "I thought it was going to bite me!" Seeing that she needed comforting she went over to Lily and patted her head.

"Thank you, Lily. You really saved me back there!" Miko praised. After a couple of minutes, Lily wiped the tears from her eyes and sniffled. Soon the two made their way back down the stone staircase toward Lily's house.

"So how did you know about the snake and stuff?" Miko questioned.

"It's part of my maid training. I have to do garden work so they taught me about all sorts of creatures to watch out for." Lily answered.

"Wow... Being a maid must be hard." Miko stated.

"Yeah. It's a lot of boring stuff too though, but it's nice to be needed," Lily said. "I bet being a shrine maiden isn't fun either. Your mom is strict."

"She can be, but it's not like I have any choice in the matter. She named me Miko, because she decided for me that I was going to be a shrine maiden before I was even born," she explained. Miko stopped on the staircase and fell behind a few steps causing Lily to pause and turn back towards her. "Hey, Lily?"

"Yes, Miko?" She replied.

"Promise me that once your parents are out of the hospital, you'll do what you want to do," Miko said.

"What do you mean?" Lily asked, confused.

"Well... I'm going to be stuck here like this, on the path *'she'* chose for me. I mean, you have the chance to do anything you want, to go and live a normal life."

"You can live a normal life too," Lily said.

"It's not that simple... I'll lose everything if I do that. That's why it has to be you." Miko sorrowfully explained.

"I'm not sure I understand, but if you say so." she conceded.

Soon the two girls descended the moss-covered stone staircase making their way through the bamboo stalks on their way towards a dirt trail that led to Lily's house. Once at the bottom of the stairs, through the cover of the bamboo, the girls could feel the shedding warmth of the evening sun. The girls looked out over the expanse of the countryside seeing little to no clouds overhead. All the while, feeling the light cool breeze sweeping through their hair as they hurried toward the house. When the girls arrived Grandma Daffodil was in a chair out on the front porch of the home in the shade.

"Hi Grandma, we're home!" Lily said with excitement.

"Oh! Hello sweetie. Welcome back," she said towards Lily and then looked over towards Miko. "Ah, Miko, look how grown up you've become."

"Hello Mrs. Monet (Moe-Nay)," Miko said with a bow.

"No need to be so polite dear. You come here all the time, so just have fun while you're here," she said. Immediately, Miko's posture relaxed as she slouched a bit.

"Okay! Mrs. Monet," Miko perked up with excitement and explained what happened at her house. "Oh, Yeah! You should have seen Lily back at my house. She was so cool. She came to my rescue and saved me from a snake." She left out the part about the snake being venomous as she didn't want Lily to get in trouble.

"Is that so? Lily, come here." She waved towards her, signaling her to come stand by her side and Lily walked over to Daffodil, as she was told. Lily was unsure of what her grandmother's response was going to be like but didn't worry about it too much. "It's not too surprising. Lily here has always had a servant's heart, putting others before herself and doing things without ever being asked or told," she said fondly while looking back toward her granddaughter. "I'm sure she will grow up to become a fine young lady."

In a single moment in time, memories flooded into Lily's head as a wave of nostalgia swept over her. She paused as she heard the groans and coughing coming from Ulysses in the men's restroom. *"How could I have forgotten this feeling? The urge to help someone."* She thought. *"I had been locked away, slaving away for Freya for so long I forgot what it felt like. That calling... The call to help someone in need."* She had a tough choice to make. She couldn't just abandon Ulysses. It wasn't because he was her future husband, but because he sounded like he needed help.

For a brief moment, for just a second, Reighley got a glimpse of Lily's eyes from the side of her face. Even though she was wearing sunglasses, a hat, and a scarf, this was all he needed to understand whom he was looking at. He saw the beige aura from before. However, it looked like it was ripping itself in two. There were two different versions of Lily projected above her and both were fighting for control. One was tugging the other away from the back of its shirt, attempting to leave, while the other tried to charge towards the men's restroom in the opposite direction.

"I'm not sure what her deal is, or why she is wearing a disguise but..." He thought, as he stood up from his chair and walked towards Lily. *"Ulysses would be devastated if she left and I don't need a full picture to understand what's going on."* During this, Destiny looked at him with confusion but idly sat back deciding that it might be more fun to just watch as the scene unfolds.

Lily noticed Reighley approaching. She let her urges to help die inside her as she turned away ready to leave it all behind. *"I suppose it's better off this way,"* she frowned.

"You want to stay right!? Then stay!" Reighley shouted. Those are the words he wished he had told Freya when she had come over. He was growing tired of watching people shy away from their true feelings.

Lily froze in her tracks with her back still turned, "How did you know it was me?" She asked while removing her disguise.

"I knew because you seemed concerned for Ulysses." He answered. Over by the table Destiny reacted to this revelation as if she had her mind blown. She couldn't believe it was Lily in disguise.

"I can't stay. In fact, I shouldn't even be here." Lily explained before turning to face Reighley.

"Why not?" Reighley asked.

"We live in separate worlds. Mine is different from the normal one you all live in," she said. Reighley was confused by her statement but wondered if it had to do with the two different versions of herself that he saw within her aura.

"It doesn't matter what world you live in if you live in it with regret." Reighley paused briefly and thought of Freya, "You see... I have this friend of mine. A friend that you kind of remind me of... She was put in a similar position as you. My friend had to leave, but she wanted to stay. I wish I had told her to, but I didn't. I knew exactly what she wanted, and I didn't stop her from leaving. I regret that, and I don't want to make the same mistake twice, so if you want to stay, then stay." Reighley pleaded.

His words struck a chord in Lily's heart. She could only think of the sad eyes she had seen on Miko's face seven years ago. When Lily said to her, *"You can live a normal life too,"* remembering this caused Lily to stop and think about it. *"I wondered if those words ever reached her. To this day Miko still lives as a shrine maiden, unable to do what she wants to do. I wonder if she is full of regret?"*

Suddenly a loud painful sound of someone throwing up in the restroom was heard, and Reighley watched Lily as the aura above her that was holding her back, finally let go. Lily rushed past Reighley towards the restroom and thought to herself, *"Freya, I think I get it now. I get how you could have fallen for such a guy. How he could make even someone like you change."* When Lily arrived at the door with Reighley following behind her only seconds later, the two knocked on it.

"Ulysses!? Are you okay?" Lily asked with concern. Belching noises could be heard from the other side.

"Uh, just constipated," he fibbed trying to hide the fact he was nauseous.

"You okay in there, man? You don't sound very good." Reighley asked.

"I heard the sound of you throwing up. Look, I know you don't know me very well, but I can help you. You don't have to worry about scaring me away!" She said to reassure him.

"You guys can just go on without me, I'll catch back up with you later!" He couldn't let them see him like this.

"We aren't leaving without you," Reighley stated.

"You just don't get it," Ulysses said.

"Get what?" Lily asked.

"I can't leave," Ulysses answered.

"Why not?" The two said in unison.

"I don't want to ruin everything for everyone." Ulysses explained.

"Dude, what are you talking about? There aren't even any issues between us." Reighley consoled.

"This is the first time things have been this good. I'm tired of being the reason that everything falls apart." Ulysses was sitting in front of the door, with his back towards it, blocking all entry. He had just thrown up from the nausea. He felt terrible. He felt like a fool for coming all this way without his cigarettes. He was so busy working at his shop that he forgot to smoke after work the day before. He assumed that was why his body was acting this way and why he was having withdrawals. His mood was beginning to shift and he couldn't help but be irritable.

"You won't do that man. You are such a reliable guy-," Reighley tried to say before suddenly interrupted.

"I'm not! I'm a coward. I am afraid of heights, and the dark, and I can't even talk to girls, but you know what terrifies me the most? That I'm going to mess it up. That's what I've always done. These stupid hands of mine destroy everything I touch! People avoid me because they are scared of me, but in reality, I'm the one who's terrified." He explained. Lily lowered herself a bit hoping her voice would reach Ulysses on the other side of the door.

"That's not true. Back on the train, when I was falling, you caught me and I didn't break. You kept me safe. The way you cook your food is so careful and soft. Those hands you speak of are the most gentle and kind hands I've ever seen. So please, Ulysses. Come out." Lily begged.

"Uly? Are you okay buddy?" Destiny asked. She had seen the commotion and couldn't stay on the sidelines any longer. She wondered how deep the wounds from which those feelings stemmed. A long silence occurred. The three waited in anticipation for what Ulysses's decision would be until finally, the door opened with his head facing the ground.

"I smoke. It's why I'm feeling ill," he said disappointed in himself. Ulysses braced himself for looks of disgust. He couldn't bear to look at his friends and see their reaction. The group looked at each other and then faced Ulysses again. Reighley reached up and placed his hand on Ulysses's shoulder, patting him a few times.

"I already knew that dude," He said comfortingly. Ulysses looked at his friend with astonishment.

"When did you find out?" He asked.

"When we first met. I saw you sneaking a cigarette in the classroom," Reighley explained.

"You knew since then? Why didn't you say anything?" Ulysses asked.

"Because it didn't matter." He answered. Ulysses looked at his friend with surprise and then gratefulness. "Besides, it's not like you were good at hiding it either," Reighley said with a chuckle.

"I always assumed it was your parents that smoked and it happened to stick on you," Destiny said.

"It doesn't bother me," Lily answered. *Something so trivial as that wouldn't cause my feelings to waiver.*" Lily thought.

"But... I could get you guys in serious trouble. It's not legal." Ulysses said with a worried appearance.

"Do you want to quit?" Reighley asked.

"I'm not sure if I can," The more he thought about it, the more he realized he most likely began smoking because of anxiety, and the fact he was lonely. He remembered his mother Kokeisha telling him when he was younger that it took the edge off of her.

"That's not what I asked," Reighley said.

"Yeah. I think I don't need it anymore." Ulysses answered.

"That's all I needed to hear. I'll help you out. That's what best friends do right?" Reighley said. Ulysses's eyes began to water and he hugged Reighley, smothering him in his arms while sobbing.

"Thanks, Bestie!" He said.

"Hey, you should probably stop calling me 'Bestie,' that's what girls do. Call me bro." Reighley explained.

"Aniki! (兄 あに 貴 き • slang for a big brother or gang leader.)"

"Well, I guess that's better than Bestie," Reighley said jokingly.

Suddenly a ringtone could be heard coming from Destiny's pocket. She pulled out her phone and stared at it. It was Freya calling once again.

"Who keeps calling you?" Reighley asked.

"Oh look, it's Freya." Destiny said and then immediately proceeded to end the call with a single swipe of her finger. The rest of the group looked at Destiny with a terrified look. They began to wonder if she had some sort of dirt on Freya that allowed her to treat her friend like that.

"Hey don't let her find out we are getting her presents for her birthday, okay?" Reighley asked.

"Roger that Loverboy!" A few seconds later Destiny received a text from Freya. She read it out loud to the group. "'Stop ignoring my calls, and pick up the phone. Why are you with my boyfriend anyway?' Yikes, someone isn't a happy camper. By the way, Lily, aren't you supposed to be with Freya today, don't you have maid stuff to do?"

Lily's worst fears came to fruition as her identity was revealed. It happened the exact way she thought it would too, but somehow, things were different. She wasn't scared like before, so she decided to own up to it.

"Today is one of my rare days off." Lily replied. The two guys paused for a second until what she said registered in their heads.

"You work for Freya!?" the two asked in conjunction.

"That's correct. I act as her handmaiden." Lily replied. She spent the next minute explaining her situation to the group. She told them about how long she had been working for Freya, and how she owes a great debt to the Young family, both metaphorically and monetarily. She didn't, however, go into too much detail about it. Once she had explained everything she let the two boys take it all in and waited for a response.

"So… does this mean I won't get to see you for a while?" Ulysses asked.

"I'm afraid so. I only get two days off a month as a maid for the Young family household. So it will be some time before I can visit you again."

"I can wait," Ulysses said. It was three simple words but Lily didn't expect them to mean so much to her. She assumed that because her life would be so busy people who got to know her would simply forget about her, or either fail or be unable to make time for her.

"I'll hang out with you at Freya's house! I can never have too many friends." Destiny said.

"Yeah, whenever you have some time, you are more than welcome to hang out with us. I'll talk to Freya about it, and make sure she's fine with it."

"Th-Thank you." Lily couldn't help but let out a grateful smile. The thought she had previously in the restroom, being surrounded by friends of her own was potentially becoming a reality. She was usually pessimistic these days because of her heavy workload, but her future was looking brighter for once.

"Hey! Just what is going on here!?" An angry voice yelled from a distance. The group glanced over towards the loud familiar female voice. The people in the food court began to look towards the group from the yelling.

"Freya!? What are you doing here?" Reighley asked. Almost instinctively the group stood in front of Lily in fear that Freya would potentially lash out or blame her.

"Hello." Ulysses said.

"Freya. Hey girlfriend." Destiny said nervously.

"Guys, it's alright. You've done enough." Lily said, stepping between the three.

"I see you've made some friends Lily," Freya said. Lily looked down in shame, as she failed her job as a maid. She wasn't supposed to let anyone know she worked for Freya.

"I-I..." Lily couldn't get a word out before Freya interrupted her.

"Good for you," Freya said with a pure-hearted smile. "I'm glad to see you have a life outside of work."

"So you're not mad?" Lily asked. It was surprising to her. If she had been asked a month ago whether or not Freya would have freaked out on her, the answer would have been a definitive *yes*. However, Lily knew that something had changed inside Freya's heart for the better and she figured out where the source of that goodness came from.

"Of course not. That would be entirely uncool." Freya looked towards Reighley and winked. Reighley could only imagine what was going on inside of Freya, as he looked at her aura arrows and they all pointed towards herself. He put two and two together and bet she was trying to be a good person, but he was surprised they weren't pointed at him. He would have thought Freya would try to impress him by doing the right thing, but her aura said otherwise. He guessed she wanted to work on herself more than anything.

"You know you really shouldn't be here. We are all birthday present shopping for you. You would ruin the surprise," Reighley explained, "and how did you even get here so fast?"

"Helicopter. I have my own landing pad. " Freya explained.

"Why am I not surprised?" Reighley sighed but then thought it was exactly something she would do. "Look, we already got our gifts for your party. If you see them I'll be upset. How about you join us for food and we all disperse for the day."

"Are you sure?" Freya asked. She felt bad about intruding after they went out of their way to get her something.

"Yeah. It's fine. I have to do something when I get home as well, so I can't stay for much longer." Reighley explained. During this time many people around the food court began to recognize Freya and began whispering about her off in the distance, some even taking photos of her.

"Which one is 'R'?" Someone whispered.

Soon the group sat back down and ate their now lukewarm food. Freya scolded Destiny for ignoring her calls and trolling, and then the group ended up making their way to the exit. After eating and enjoying time together, Freya invited Ulysses to her party as well after a reminder from Destiny.

When it was finally time to say their goodbyes Lily's expression was bittersweet. She couldn't help but worry that her first friend group would be too busy for her on her days off. She didn't have school like the rest of them, nor did she have homework on the weekends. Only time could answer her questions so she decided to be patient. Freya offered her a ride and Lily accepted it, and Destiny decided to tag along too. Herald was already warned about their departure during their meal, so he was ready to pick the girls up. Once the girls said their goodbyes, Lily hugged Ulysses.

"Fix some ramen for me next time, won't you?" Lily looked up towards Ulysses with gentle eyes.

"Yes." Ulysses reverted to speaking poorly as the hug from a girl sapped all of his bravado away. Soon the three girls took off as Herald chauffeured them home and Ulysses and Reighley were left to their own devices. As the two headed towards the station Reighley came up with a plan to help Ulysses quit smoking. Ulysses agreed to the plan and told his friend he would give it his best shot. Finally the two parted ways at the station and went home.

During the girl's car ride home Lily sat in the back of the limousine for the first time in her career as a maid.

"You know... I approve." Lily said.

"Approve of what?" Freya asked.

"Of your relationship. I think he is good for you." Lily said. Freya wasn't sure how to take the answer and unexpectedly was embarrassed. Up front, driving was Herald who nodded in accordance with Lily.

"Would both of you stop teasing me? And Destiny, don't say another word!" It was as if Freya could see the future as she preemptively silenced Destiny before she could get a word out.

"But I didn't say anything!" Destiny complained.

"I have had enough trolling from you today," Freya explained. Destiny decided to pick a new target to tease.

"Well, what about you Lily? That was quite the hug you gave Ulysses back there." Destiny interrogated.

"Hey, I-I, that has nothing to do with anything." Lily couldn't think of a response and could only blush in embarrassment. Herald recognized the name of the boy and gave Lily the nod of approval.

"I've become quite the matchmaker in your absence, my dearest." Herald thought.

The group let out a chuckle in unison and continued their way home.

Reighley and Ulysses had to part ways, so the two said their goodbyes, and Reighley left towards the station that boarded those wishing to go to Koko Rich Coast. Reighley's family lived on the cusp of the district on the southeastern side of town towards San Fran Kyoto Peak. When he boarded the train he comfortably sat on a chair and waited for the train to take off. Once it did, Reighley looked out of the window at the city passing him by once again taking care to not look himself in the eyes.

"I'm pretty lame, huh." He thought to himself. *"I talk a big game, trying to get people to express their true feelings, but I can't even look at my reflection in the mirror without having a potential mental breakdown. In the end, I'm just a hypocrite."*

When Reighley arrived at the station after a relatively short trip he quickly left. On his way home he found himself at a crossroad in a street he didn't recognize.

Wanting to familiarize himself with the city he took a small detour down the block to check out the area. The street was filled with a multitude of strip malls. Most were privately owned restaurants while others were clothing outlets. A particular building caught Reighley's eye. It demanded the attention of all who passed by it. It had a neon sign of a computer motherboard chip with pink and blue alternating lights. The store's name was Motherboards. It appeared to be quite popular as there was nowhere left to park. Reighley approached the building to see what the commotion was about. He read a sign that said (Gamers and Mothers are Welcome. Preferable if you're both. Daycare Available!) Reighley ended up getting a peek inside through the window until he realized the implications of spying on moms playing video games. From what he saw, it was an internet café that mothers could bring their children to so they could play video games.

"What an incredibly niche idea," Reighley thought. *"Well, I better get going before I get spotted and called a creep for the rest of my life. Wait, is that-?"* Reighley recognized a game he used to play in his old hometown. *"Fusion Fighter X!? I haven't played that in forever."* He thought. It was a fighting game that let the player pick any two characters and combine the moves and abilities that the two had into a single character. Reighley then took notice of the familiar face playing the game. *"It's her! I'm sure it's the lady who gave Freya a ride home when she and I ran away from Herald downtown."*

Later that evening when the girls returned to the Young family estate, Lily was summoned to Jim Young's office. She had many concerns as she was never summoned for anything. Every problem Jim had, fell upon Elise to take care of in the manor. Jim had just returned home from a strenuous day of work, so Lily assumed it must be fairly important. Nervous, she hesitantly knocked on the office door.

"Come in," Jim said. Lily opened the door and entered inside.

"You summoned me, Master Young?" Lily asked with a bow. Jim was sitting in his chair eating a bowl of Ramen that looked and smelled like it came directly from the Back Alley Ramen shop. Lily recognized the scent and could only assume he must have had someone get him something from there. She thought it was odd that Jim had gotten food from there of all places, but she wasn't paid to ask questions.

"Yes. You see, I have an important task that only you can accomplish that involves my daughter." Jim explained.

"Only me, Sir?" Lily asked in confusion.

Chapter 14

Away From Those We Share

Elise Chamberlain is the Young family's Head Maid and the personal handmaiden of Prismarine. Like most of the servants of the household, she too lived in the manor. She was one of the first maids to be hired on by the Young family. She started when she was 18 years old. At the beginning of her career, her duties laid an incredibly heavy burden on her as she was only one of a few servants of the house. As the Young Family became a more prominent figure within society, their staffing increased and by the time Elise turned 27, she became the head maid of the house. Her duties included organization, training, and scheduling of the other maids. Lily was her favorite staff member. She showed the most promise, which was why Elise hand-picked her to attend Freya. Elise also attended Prismarine, who was a fairly independent employer. She would chafe at constantly being waited on. This gave Elise far more free time than she anticipated, allowing her to pursue her hobbies. Her role as the head maid came with many benefits, which included free lodging, meals, education, and transportation. These benefits came at the price of always being on call, without a day off. This didn't bother Elise as the exorbitant amount of free time she had could be considered days off.

Elise has been living with the young family for the last 18 years, making her 36 years old. She may not consider her life outside of work to be productive, but "Ch@mberM@de" her handle and alter ego flourished. While she was not at the manor she would spend her time exercising. People considered her a pillar of health, but she used working out as an excuse to spend the rest of her time at an internet café called Motherboard. The Café was packed with everything from high-spec computer games to tabletop classics, from role-playing to shooters, and every genre in between. Customers could also spend their time there watching Japanese animations. The building was unique because it targeted mothers in the area as its general customers. It had a daycare that parents could bring their children to while they indulged in gaming. Mothers could only have their kids stay for a max of three hours a day as the Café had a policy stating they did not condone negligence. Elise was addicted to spending time here. She spent every possible second of her free time gaming. Motherboard was owned by Slowsoft and she would use the fact that she worked for the Young family as an excuse to get free access whenever she pleased. To Elise, Motherboard was the perfect place. It is predominantly run by women in their thirties who love video games. She made plenty of friends and rivals in the community. Within the last month, Elise went back to playing a fairly old game called Fusion Fighter X. The game had a resurgence in popularity, due to the developers adding additional content.

"G. G," Elise said while delivering the final blow to her enemy. She was facing a new challenger who was trash-talking her. Nothing was more satisfying to Elise than shutting down someone's ego with her skills. When she crushed her opponents, the look of rage and frustration on their faces was more fulfilling than a hearty meal. To her, results were everything. Words mean nothing if you cannot back it up with actions. This was Elise's life philosophy.

"That's not fair! You cheated!" The challenger accused.

"You thought you were good because you spammed the same overpowered attack. Here's some advice. Go back in time and don't challenge me. You'll save yourself the embarrassment." Elise advised. She wasn't often mean to new challengers as she enjoyed a good rivalry, but she despised those who trash talk without the skills to back them up. Elise was a registered nurse and she thought the best remedy for pride was a humble pie. Elise's passions weren't only for destroying egos, but for sharing things loved with the people who expressed genuine interest in the things she cared about. She couldn't count the number of times she helped a newcomer join the community by showing them the ropes in whatever game she was playing.

Elise had an uncanny ability to tell if someone was looking at her. Especially if it was a new pair of eyes. She called it her "Gamer Sense".

"Wow, she's actually really good. I'm not sure if I could beat her." Reighley thought while peeking through the Café window.

Instinctively, Elise looked at the person in the window with prying eyes and recognized who it was. *"It's Reighley. The young lady's paramour,"* She thought. Although she heard from Jim that he did not approve of the boy, Herald informed Elise that he had had a positive influence on Freya. Immediately she became embarrassed that she was seen in such a state. She couldn't bear the thought of people seeing her this way. She needed him to keep his mouth shut. Out of options, she beckoned Reighley to come inside for a chat.

Reighley used his Insight on Elise and saw a magenta aura that was given shape in the form of a crown. It hovered like a halo atop her head. It was as if she was the Queen of Motherboards. He could tell it wasn't a self-proclaimed title either as her aura was regal and bright.

"Looks like I've been spotted…" Reighley reluctantly hunkered over towards the entrance and entered inside. When he entered, he casually took a good look around. The café had a retro gaming decor. Neon light displays of video game characters, and arcade machines were remodeled into table booths. There were many love sacks and couches designed to look like cute game creatures. It was a café so it had a barista. The countertop you would order from contained real computer motherboards sealed underneath a glass panel. They were rigged with RGB (Red Green and Blue) LEDs that illuminated the tabletop. In the far back was a large room that Reighley could only assume was the daycare as he could hear and see children playing inside. The daycare room had a glowing neon baby rattle sign above it signaling its importance. It had a glass panel of reinforced glass around it so all the mothers could see their kids inside. *"I can see the appeal to this place,"* he thought. He noticed a large stop sign at the entrance as well. It stated:

(NO HITTING ON THE WOMEN! ALL ATTEMPTS WILL BE CONSIDERED HARASSMENT AND YOU WILL BE ASKED TO LEAVE.)

Reighley thought this policy made sense. He guessed most women came here to play video games, relax, and drink coffee while someone watched their kids, not to be hit on by guys. That's what bars were for in his opinion.

Reighley walked over to the woman who was still staring at him and greeted her with a wave. She appeared to be a brunette in her thirties. She had her hair pulled back into a tight ponytail and she seemed to perpetually have a serious expression on her face. The cool calm and collected type. The glasses she wore helped pull off the persona nicely.

"How can I help you?" Reighley asked nervously. He felt as though he was in trouble.

"Mr. Summers. I didn't take you for a fool. We both know why I brought you in here." Elise gave a disappointed stare.

"Oh no. She is totally going to misunderstand that I was just passing by." He thought.

"Come. Have a seat. Let's play a few rounds." Elise asked, gesturing to sit next to her.

"What?" Reighley questioned.

"Are you familiar with Fusion Fighter X?" Elise asked.

"Uh, yeah. I played it a lot. I heard there was new content."

"I see. Well, what's taking you so long? Are you not up for the challenge?" Elise asked.

"Uh… Okay…" Reighley hesitantly took a seat and picked up a controller.

As the two were selecting characters and picking a stage to battle on, Elise paused before starting the game.

"My name is Elise. I know you recognized me. I need you to keep *this* a secret between us. It is of utmost importance that no one finds out I spend my free time here." Elise explained while starting the game. She gave an impromptu fist bump and wished Reighley good luck. Before he could notice it, a small crowd of women idly sat back and watched their match.

"I don't understand," Reighley said as the game started.

"(Round 1. Fight!)"

"Let me ask you this. Do you know how to dance?" Elise asked.

"No, what does that have to do with anything?" Reighley questioned.

"If you keep this a secret, I will teach you how to slow dance for the young lady's party." Elise explained.

"Wait, there's going to be a dance!?" Reighley said, panicking.

"I see. So you weren't aware." Elise said. The first round was going in Elise's favor, but Reighley didn't intend to go down without a fight. Fighting games were something he got obsessed with for a while. He played in the competitive scene a year ago. Their fight was a constant struggle. Reighley realized just how rusty he had become.

"It's over," Elise said while briefly pushing up her glasses and then she proceeded to finish Reighley off with a twenty-two-hit combo, causing him to lose the first round. The crowd behind the two nodded in agreement as they expected nothing less from their best player.

"You know, you don't have to bribe me to keep it a secret. All you have to do is ask." Reighley explained.

"(Round 2. Fight!)"

"Oh. I was under the impression that you were dating Freya for the money." Elise said while starting aggressively in the game, giving her a lead in health.

"Haha... I wonder what gave you that idea." Reighley laughed awkwardly.

"Well, she *is* a modern-day princess. Most people would desire her for status and power." Elise said.

"I don't desire her!" This comment caused Reighley to lose focus and inadvertently falter on the battlefield.

"(K.O.)"

"G.G." Elise said. The crowd behind her clapped subtly. They were surprised by the amount of trouble Reighley caused Elise. After a few moments, the group of women went back to their normal routines.

"Dang, well played." Reighley said.

"So, have you considered my offer?" Elise asked.

He paused and gave it some thought. *"Would it be worth learning how to dance for someone I'm not going to end up with? Things are going well now, but for how long? She'll just get bored of me, right? Girls like her only like something for so long until they move on to the next thing, so what's keeping her here? I'm nothing special compared to her exes. She's famous, so I'm definitely not the most attractive guy she's ever dated and I don't have money either."* Reighley took a deep breath and slowly exhaled. *"But for some reason, even if at her party, our dance was both our first and last, I still feel like I owe it to her not to end things on bad terms."*

Elise extended a hand for Reighley to shake. "Deal?" Elise asked.

"So can you teach me how to dance?" Reighley questioned.

"Yes." Elise replied. Reighley extended his hand out towards Elise and shook her hand in agreement.

"You have yourself a deal." He complied.

Reighley looked over at the clock and realized the time. He needed to go home as he had things to do. He exchanged numbers with Elise, and she informed him that whenever he needed a challenge he was more than welcome to play video games with her as she considered him a worthy adversary.

Soon Reighley left after a quick goodbye and made his way back home. When he arrived, he rushed into his room without wasting a single second. He poured some cat food and water for Morgana and immediately began digging through his treasure collection.

"I found you!" He said as his creativity began to flood throughout his mind.

The weekend was almost over and Reighley had just barely finished his present for Freya before it was time for bed. He had put it in a box and wrapped it up in red wrapping paper with a knotted bow on top. This was how he envisioned what rich gifts looked like, although he wasn't sure. He didn't want to embarrass himself or Freya at her party by giving her something unpresentable. He looked at the gift resting on his desk, and couldn't help but be proud of what he created for her. Morgana batted at his hand impatiently waiting for him to finish. Reighley picked up the cat and the two made their way to bed. After getting into bed Morgana promptly laid on Reighley's chest and began incessantly bathing himself. While scratching Morgana's ear, Reighley asked,

"You haven't met Freya yet have you?"

"Meeeow." said Morgana.

"I hope she likes cats. If she doesn't, that will be the dealbreaker." Reighley said with a laugh. Soon the two fell asleep

The following morning Reighley woke up to the aroma of bacon. When he came to his senses he could hear the sizzling of eggs being cooked on the stove. Curious about what was being made, he stretched his arms, got out of bed, and headed towards the smell. He walked into the kitchen after placing Morgana on the floor and as per usual noticed Isabelle was fixing breakfast.

Isabelle turned her head at the sound of Reighley walking in. She noticed he was headed towards a piece of toast with a similar form to a zombie. She opted to wake him up with a shot to the head with her TERF blaster.

"Ow! What was that for?" Reighley growled.

"Good morning. Are you ready for midterms?" Isabelle asked. Choking on the bread that was now in his mouth, it was like reality slapped Reighley in the face. He had been keeping up with his studies, but he had forgotten that this week was midterms and he was caught completely unaware.

"You're joking, right? Is that this week?" A wave of anxiety swept over Reighley.

"It's not like you to forget these things." Isabelle stated. "Are you sure you didn't get your brain eaten by an undead?" Opting to shoot him again with the blaster.

"Okay... I have to make sure I'm ready. Also, stop watching zombie films! I could do without the headshots."

"It's the only way to kill them." Isabelle said while blowing on the tip of her TERF gun. Reighley mournfully decided to skip the well-cooked breakfast, and with a piece of toast in his mouth, he rushed back into his room to get ready. He was multitasking as he went out the door with a textbook in hand and toast in his mouth. He was speed reading through the subjects of the day, studying on his way to school. When he arrived he was confronted by his Math teacher, Ms. Cynthia Clevens, who was at the entrance.

"Mr. Summers! Just what do you think you're doing?" She asked.

"Good Morning, Ms. Clevens. What seems to be the problem?" Reighley questioned.

"This is an elite school young man. You cannot just waltz right in with crumbs on your face, messy hair, and a backpack wide open." She answered. "That is improper school etiquette."

"I'm sorry Ma'am. I am just trying to keep up my good grades. I'll go take care of it once I'm inside." Reighley explained. *"Why does every teacher here have it out for me? I'm just trying to do my best here."* He thought. He felt like there was no light at the end of the tunnel. Reighley was getting annoyed that every adult except for Kaede seemed to have some sort of negative feeling toward him. He also knew he needed to stand up for himself as the previous harassment attempts had been foiled by Freya before.

"You need to do better, young man." she said. "*It's people who have a bad attitude like him that are the problem with most men today. He doesn't show a great woman like me an ounce of respect, calling me Ma'am again. As if I am some old hag.*" she thought.

"I'm sorry. I'll do better." Reighley said. He just couldn't risk insubordination at this type of school. His future was far too important to risk it all on being sassy with a teacher.

Cynthia noticed the fire in his eyes extinguished. It looked like he had just accepted that this was the way things were in his school life.

"Good," she said. "Now, carry on..." Reighley gave a nod to her in response and proceeded inside, sulking away. While Cynthia was watching the boy walk away, a feeling crept up on her. "*Gosh... Why do I feel like I am the bad guy here? He didn't even fight it or explain his situation.*" Cynthia felt guilty. This feeling persisted even after she entered the school, so she made the decision to do what she normally would when she had a lot on her mind. Speak with Kaede. Cynthia proceeded down the hall to the nurse's office and knocked a specific way. She would knock twice, pause, and then knock three more times. This was how she let Kaede know it was her.

"Come in! Therapy time?" Kaede asked. The door opened up and Cynthia walked inside greeting her friend. "What's on your mind this time? Let me guess, boy troubles?"

"It has to do with that new troublemaker student. There is something up with him." Cynthia claimed.

"What! Are you talking about Reighley? What's wrong with him? Is he okay?" Kaede said, sounding concerned.

"I ran into him this morning. The kid was a complete mess. His backpack was left wide open, his hair was completely unkempt, and he had bread crumbs all over his face. When we are in class, he rudely disrespects me as a woman. He even called me "Ma'am," even though I am young and beautiful. Yet when I confronted him about it, I felt like he had just accepted the fact I was against him. It made me feel sort of guilty. Why are you so worried about him anyway?" Cynthia asked.

"Because that boy has the whole world stacked against him. I worry about him sometimes, like the weight may be too much for him to bear."

"Weight? What on earth are you talking about?" Cynthia inquired.

"Reighley Summers. He has so much on his plate and he never tells anyone about his problems. He's always been like that. He is one of the most hard-working people I know," Kaede explained.

"How do you even know so much about him?" Cynthia asked.

"We grew up together." Kaede explained. She went on to tell Cynthia about Reighley's life. She told her how his father left at a young age, and what drives him to work so hard. She explained what he was like outside of school. However, before Kaede could finish telling everything, she was interrupted by a voice over the intercom.

("Attention all members of the Teachers Union. Please meet me at the office for an important meeting. All classes will be delayed until then. Thank you.")

"That's odd. We never have these." Cynthia said, looking up towards the intercom speaker.

"We'll talk later, but stop being so harsh on Reighley. He's a fine young man and from what I know about him, he'll grow up into the type of man you would wish to marry." Kaede explained.

"What!? That's-" Cynthia was embarrassed to contemplate it, but Kaede was right. After hearing about his character, he would be the type of man she would be interested in. However, she could never see him in that type of way as he was a student. After waving goodbye to Kaede, she got up and proceeded to her teachers' meeting. *"I don't want him to become bitter towards me..."* She thought. *"I'll try and be a little easier on him."*

Reighley arrived at his classroom after tidying himself up in the nearby restroom. When he entered he saw Freya impatiently waiting for him. She was standing beside his desk with her arms crossed while tapping her foot in annoyance. Reighley felt like he was in trouble for some reason. He noticed that her school uniform wasn't fully up to its usual standards. He used Insight on her and saw nothing unusual with her purple arrow auras. They all seemed tamed in his opinion. Destiny who was sitting closer to the door waved at him nonchalantly.

"Hey. Is something the matter with Freya?" Reighley whispered.

"Yeah. It's her time of the," With blinding speed, Freya covered the mouth of Destiny before she could say another word.

"Mmm!" Destiny said with a muffled mouth.

"Year to appreciate best friends who keep their mouths shut in front of their friends' boyfriends," Freya said, still covering Destiny's mouth.

"Mmm, mhm! (Translation: You traitor!")

"I had a different maid prepare my stuff today. Lily was nowhere to be found. I haven't seen her since we were at the mall." Freya explained.

"What? You think she's missing?" Reighley questioned.

"No. I asked Elise about it and she said that my father had some sort of special task for her. That's why my uniform isn't perfect the way it normally is. It makes me sort of appreciate having her around." Freya answered.

Suddenly Mr. Rugborn entered the classroom and the students returned to their seats.

"I hope you're all ready, midterm week starts today," he said. The class around him began to sigh in unison. "But before that starts I have an important announcement to make."

"What do you think it is?" Destiny whispered to Freya and Reighley.

"Maybe a new student?" Reighley questioned.

"No. I would have known about it already." Freya said.

"You may come in now." Mr. Rugborn said, looking towards the door. "Class I would like to introduce you all to one of our newest students to join Gilford High.

"Yes sir." A voice from behind the door spoke.

Freya stiffened at the voice. *"I know that voice. Don't tell me..."* Freya instantly recognized the person who entered the classroom. It was Lily and she was in a Gilford High School uniform.

"What is she doing here!?" Freya thought. Lily walked toward the center of the classroom and was handed a piece of chalk. She then wrote her name on the blackboard.

(Lily Monet.)

"Greetings... I'm Lily. It's a pleasure to meet you." Lily said with a bow. The entire class went into an uproar.

"She's so pretty!" A girl upfront said.

"Finally a girl!" A boy whispered.

"Is she half Japanese?" a voice whispered loud enough to be heard over the crowd.

"Settle down class!" Mr. Rugborn said, attempting to reestablish order. Once the class quieted down he began to explain her situation. "Lily here had been given special permission by the founder Jim Young to transfer into this school." The students all gazed at her wondering how she knew Jim Young. They were curious if she was a model or someone of extreme importance like a princess from a foreign country. However, Reighley felt as though something was wrong. He looked around the classroom and noticed that there were no empty seats. He raised his hand and was called upon by Mr. Rugborn.

"Yes, Mr. Summers?" Mr. Rugborn asked. *"Glad to see he's learned some manners at least. Good for nothing commoner. Soon, you'll be out of here. The student council only agreed upon this with Mr. Young so we could prove you are a cheater."* He reflected. Although this was true for Mr. Rugborn, the true proposal that caused everyone to agree came from Cynthia Cleven. Mr. Rugborn thought back to the Teachers Union meeting…

(A few minutes prior, during the teachers' meeting.)

"I know you all have your qualms with Reighley Summers. I think this is a perfect opportunity to set the record straight. Mr. Young, can the girl be trusted?" She said to a live video of Jim.

"Yes." He answered.

"Then have her not only keep an eye on him but have her closely watch to see if he is cheating during the exams." Cynthia pleaded.

"Interesting proposal. Very well. The girl will observe the boy to see if he is a fraud." Jim agreed.

"Uh.. Mr. Young, when will she be joining?" Mr. Rugborn asked.

"Today. In class 2-B. However, she will not be participating in the curriculum until after the exams." Jim explained.

"But sir, that class has no extra seats as of yet…" Mr. Rugborn said.

"I'm well aware," Jim reassured.

(Back in the present.)

"I noticed that there is nowhere for her to sit." Reighley pointed out.

"That isn't true Mr. Summers. Her seat is to the right of yours."

"…" Reighley along with the rest of the class fell silent. All heads turned over to the desk just right of Reighley. Their attention was drawn towards Freya. The class had a realization of the implications of what Lily joining class 2-B meant. The expression on Freya's face could only be described as astonished then furious. It took Freya a moment to process what had just been said.

"That's correct. As of today, Freya will be transferring classes." Mr. Rugborn said.

"Our goddess!" A few boys wailed in despair.

"No, why is she leaving!?" student A cried.

"I don't understand." student B said.

Freya looked over towards her best friend Destiny. Freya saw a look of horror on Destiny's face.

"*Wait… No, no, no, no, no. That's not fair. Freya's leaving? We've always been together.*" Destiny's anxiety began to swell up inside her. She was always by her best friend's side.

The mere thought of spending the rest of the school year without Freya by her side sent shivers down her spine. Goosebumps began stockpiling on her body. Her temperature fell far below normal. She looked like she had just seen a ghost.

"Surely I misheard you Mr. Rugborn," Freya answered with a threatening tone. She was the only one in class who knew that Destiny had a sort of separation anxiety when the two were apart for too long.

"I'm afraid not, Ms. Young. It was a request by your father." Mr. Rugborn replied. Freya looked Lily in the eyes, hoping and praying that this was all some sort of misunderstanding, but Lily only shook her head confirming Freya's fears. "Come now, it's time for you to leave. Your new classroom is in 2-D."

"Mr. Rugborn, can I take her place?" Reighley pleaded. He saw the teary-eyed Destiny and couldn't help but feel guilty. He used his *Insight* on the teacher and saw a malevolent dark green tint to his familiar brown aura.

"I'm afraid not Mr. Summers." He answered. *"Besides, Lily here will be keeping a close eye on you from now on, you dirty cheater."* The teacher thought. His aura turned into a subtle yet maniacal grin.

"Freya-" Reighley looked at her in the hope of seeing her aura, but she wouldn't look him in the eyes. He didn't know what to say to her. *"This is all because of me."* He thought. Feeling responsible, Reighley knew he had to make things right. *"Don't worry Freya, I'll fix this."* This event only reinforced the thought in his mind that things should end between the two of them after the party. He felt like he was only causing trouble for her. He wanted Freya to be with her best friend. What was his relationship with her in comparison with that of Destiny? Freya and him hadn't even known each other for a month. Regardless, to Reighley that didn't seem like the right answer either. Freya gathered her things and walked towards the door while the classroom stayed silent. When she passed Lily, Freya interrupted any chance Lily had to speak.

"It's not your fault," After saying her piece Freya arrived at the door and Reighley couldn't help but feel bitter and frustrated.

"I won't let it end this way!" Freya shouted to the heavens looking towards the ceiling, hoping that somehow her father was listening in to this interaction. "Do you hear me, Jim!? This isn't over!" With one final rebellious roar, Freya stormed out of the classroom. The entire class was awkwardly quiet for a brief moment before the teacher spoke up to break the silence.

"All right, Ms. Monet, go take *your* seat." Mr. Rugborn commanded while glaring at Reighley. Lily sat down at Freya's now vacant desk. She felt ashamed. To her, things were finally starting to get brighter, even between her and Freya. She was sure Freya must have been resentful towards her even if she didn't show it.

"*Freya... I'm so sorry,*" Lily thought. Soon the rest of the class went on but the atmosphere was gloomy at best.

Freya was struggling with a multitude of emotions while she headed toward class 2-D. Her world had just been flipped upside down on her as if she had the rug pulled out from under her feet. She felt powerless. This was a new feeling for her. She hadn't faced off against her father before, but she felt as if the two were enemies. He was butting into things that were in her opinion, none of his business.

"I cannot believe him! He separated Destiny and me without even considering what that would do to my life and my friends. I bet he didn't even consider Destiny a part of the equation. That jerk! I'm telling Mom. She will have my back on this, but until things are fixed I'm not saying a word to him." Freya was livid. She walked with purpose until she arrived at the classroom door. Waiting for her there was a teacher Freya didn't know very well.

"Ms. Young. Welcome to your new class-" The teacher fell silent as Freya completely ignored him and walked inside the classroom. When she entered she scanned the room, being fairly sure she wouldn't care about anyone in there. She hoped that would be the case as it would reinforce her motivation to return to class 2-B.

"Ulysses?" Freya muttered. To her surprise, out of sheer coincidence, a friend was here. Seeing a familiar face helped calm the storm that raged inside of her. She could have sworn that he was a third year, which made her all the more confused to see him here. The rest of the class began to praise the gods that Freya was transferred into their class except for Ulysses who looked incredibly dumbfounded.

They treated this as a miracle. Cheers could be heard echoing around the room as the class rejoiced. To Freya, what was strange wasn't the cheers the class made but the composition of the room. It appeared that the room was filled with almost every misfit and commoner that the grade had. Only a few students were in their actual uniform, Ulysses being one of them. Most of the class wore biker jackets with hoodies on them each with ripped sleeves. They also wore blue jeans, with a white tank top. It was a classroom of punks. Freya put both pointer fingers on her temples and let out an audible sigh that was drowned out by the crowd.

"Class, settle down." The teacher said without a care in his tone. The group all nodded in agreement and they all fell silent. At a second glance, Freya looked at the school equipment that the students were using and saw that it all had her face on it. On the wall were posters of Freya doing various movie scenes.

"This isn't a classroom, it's a fan club!" She thought. *"Normally this would take obsession to a whole new level, but I've seen worse…"*

"Freya, please sit wherever you'd like, I'm sure the class will adjust accordingly." The teacher said as he sat in the corner of the room and pulled out his cellphone. Freya was in awe of the whole situation. Mainly she was shocked that the school allowed this behavior in Gilford High. She wondered if it was because of the social status of the classroom, that the school just didn't care about what went on in there.

"Oh... Well then, I'll sit next to my friend and bodyguard Ulysses." She said while pointing out a seat next to him. She obviously lied about the bodyguard part but feared if she told them he was just a friend the class would soon shift their anger towards Ulysses. She didn't wish to bring him any trouble, especially since she planned to leave this classroom as soon as possible. The student in the chair Freya pointed towards, packed up all their things and moved to the empty seat that was in the front row. While the rest of the class had their eyes on Ulysses while Freya sat down in her new warm chair.

"Haha... Hi Freya." Ulysses laughed and then whispered to Freya frantically. "What are you doing here!?"

"Good to see you too, Ulysses, and I'll explain in more detail later. More importantly, why is there no actual school going on in here!?"

"You didn't know? Everyone in class 2-D is a member of the Freya Fanclub. Well, everyone except me who is just stuck here." Ulysses explained.

"I'm slightly offended you didn't join." Freya jested.

"Nothing against you, but if I did, I think these guys would make me their leader or something... I'm just not cut out for that type of stuff." Ulysses informed.

"Ahem!" A student with a red headband scoffed and Ulysses and Freya quieted down for him. He stood in front of the teacher's desk and began to speak. "Now that Ulysses has been appointed by Freya as the Bodyguard, we shall refer to him as Boss, or Sir Odysseus from this point forward." He commanded.

"Yes sir!" The rest of the class agreed.

"Geez, the teacher does not care in the slightest," Freya thought.

"Now if you would all pay close attention, today we are going to watch the movie *Landmind.*" The student turned on a projector in the room and on the screen was Freya.

"What the!? That's one of the films I starred in," Freya was incredibly weirded out. It made her a bit uncomfortable knowing that all these students were watching movies about her instead of doing actual school stuff. It felt wrong. "If they had asked me a month ago, I think I definitely would have used this class and most likely taken advantage of everyone in here. These guys treat me like the most important thing in their life, but I've never even met any of them. They need to try and learn while they are in school instead of wasting their time on me. "She pictured Reighley in her mind and then the rest of her new friends, "Besides, I think there are things more important than me. I guess it wouldn't hurt to be their guide out of this mess."

Soon the movie was over and Ulysses was quivering from the anxiety of being in the spotlight. He wasn't a leader. He couldn't even hold a conversation with people other than his Aniki, Reighley.

"Boss? Sir? I can't handle that level of responsibility!" Ulysses thought. *"Why is the spotlight on me now?"* Before each

student left on their short break between classes, they would stop by Ulysses's desk to say something to him.

"Good work today Boss!" Girl Punk A said with a thumbs up.

"Yeah keep it up, Sir Odysseus." Girl Punk B said.

"Odysseus!? That isn't even my name and why are they thanking me? I didn't even do anything!" Ulysses began to panic. Girls were talking to him all of a sudden. He needed his heart to stay loyal to Lily. He looked over at Freya, who was strangely calm. The students around her left her gifts in the form of snacks and drinks at her desk as they passed by. They wouldn't say a word as if they felt unworthy to speak and simply bowed towards her with each gift. Once every student left the class, the two remaining were Freya and Ulysses.

"Freya... I... Need... Help..." Ulysses said. The words barely were able to escape from under his breath. Freya looked over at Ulysses and saw he looked worse than someone with motion sickness out in a stormy sea. He looked blue in the face.

"What's wrong Ulysses?" Freya asked with concern.

"Everyone is talking to me and thanks to my genetic 'Y' chromosome, I am inherently awkward... I can't even speak, I get so nervous," Ulysses said. Freya felt empathetic for Ulysses. She couldn't help but feel bad for him.

"Well. You seem to be talking to me just fine, and I'm not only a girl but a woman of high value." Freya reassured him. Ulysses stopped shaking when he heard this and paused gathering it all in.

"Oh no. You're right. You're a girl too!" Ulysses immediately got up and ran to the nearby trash can and gagged over it.

"Ouch…" Freya whispered, very offended. However, putting her feelings aside she went over to him and patted his back. She felt like helping him was the right thing to do. "There, there. Looks like we have a lot of work to do, but don't worry, I'll help you, young one."

"We're the same age, and help me with what?" Ulysses laughed.

"I'm going to be your wingwoman for Lily, just like you were my wingman to help Reighley and I be together," Freya explained.

"What…" Ulysses said, very confused. He began to blush immediately afterward.

"I know you have the hots for my maid and you have a shot with her too." Freya said with a smug look, bumping her elbow towards Ulysses's side.

"What? Really? You think I have a chance with her?" Ulysses's eyes were filled with a glimmer of hope.

"Of course you do," Freya said.

"Well… how do I win her over?" Ulysses asked.

"For starters, why don't you ask her to slow dance at my party? That will steal her heart away." Freya suggested.

"Dance?" Ulysses gulped.

"Yes, there is going to be a dance at my birthday party." Freya explained.

"Oh… Well can you teach me how to dance, and when is it again?" Ulysses asked nervously.

"It's on May 6th. Less than a week from now." Freya explained. Ulysses pulled out his phone and looked at the date. It was May 1st. He swiftly placed his head back over the trash can and gagged from the stress.

"Hire… a stunt double… for me…" Ulysses said. Freya thought it over for a minute.

"Hmm… that could work. Wait no! He needs to be able to do this on his own." she contemplated and then replied. "No. You can do this." Freya encouraged him.

After a few minutes passed Ulysses gathered his composure and began to ask why Freya was even here in the first place. Freya explained that her father did this in an attempt to separate her and Reighley.

"Your dad sounds as scary as my dad…" Ulysses explained. Freya could only imagine Ulysses' father as some sort of biomechanically engineered superhuman. That was the only explanation Ulysses gained in his physique.

"Well, regardless, we will start your training after school. Consider it a thanks for being a friend I could talk to to cool my temper. I'm not sure what I would have done if there was no one I knew in this class. I probably would have gone insane. Besides, that's what friends are for right?" Freya said with a friendly smile.

"Thanks…" Ulysses said with gratitude. For the first time, he felt as though he could consider Freya a friend. He didn't think it was possible in his opinion. Not that he was unwilling, but from what he knew of her, she just was too focused on other things and didn't have time for a big oaf like himself.

The bell rang signaling the next class to start and all the students reentered into the classroom. The same teacher entered in as well.

"Alright class, it's time for film number two!" The student with the Red headband instructed.

"Yes sir!" The class roared.

While the class was starting, Freya came up with a way to get back at her father.

"You wanted me to be in the misfit class right? Fine. I'll be a misfit." Freya thought. *"The sooner I handle this, the quicker I can get back to Destiny."*

Chapter 15

Homogeneous Ones

Reighley was astonished by Freya's sudden outburst. He didn't expect her to do something to that degree. *"She called him 'Jim"*, he thought. *"That's the first time I've seen her genuinely angry... oh, gosh, when we break up, is she going to be as upset as that? Would she get mad at me? Our agreement ends in less than a week. C'mon, Reighley! That doesn't matter right now. I need to come up with a plan to fix this."* Reighley looked over towards Lily who seemed like she was in a depressive state. When she glanced back at him, Reighley saw her aura using Insight. It was beige as usual but with a layer of deep dark blue surrounding it. Looking at the desk in front of Lily he noticed Destiny who was looking towards him with teary eyes. The typical white fluffy cloud that was her aura looked now like a rainstorm pouring down solely on her. Like a personal cloud of sadness in cartoons he had seen as a child. His Insight was interrupted by the whispers of Lily.

Long time no see…" Lily said.

"What are you doing here?" Reighley questioned.

"Freya's father sent me here to keep an eye on you and to separate you from her," Lily explained.

"Well... I see where Freya gets her abrasive side from." Reighley said. Class began and Reighley turned his head to pay attention. While looking away he whispered. "We'll talk more later." Reighley couldn't help but be worried about Destiny's mental state. He always remembered seeing her with a pure white, happy-go-lucky aura. It was troubling that it looked the way it did. For now, he had to put those thoughts aside and focus on up-and-coming tests. For the rest of the class period, Reighley was somewhat pressured by Lily.

"Is she watching me? It's subtle, but I swear she is glancing at me while I take my notes." Reighley thought.

Soon class was over and it was time for Reighley to figure out why Lily was keeping an eye on him. She never let him out of her peripheral vision. The moment Mr. Rugborn stepped out of the classroom, Reighley turned towards Lily.

"Care to explain the whole 'observing' thing you've been doing?" Reighley asked.

"I'm surprised you noticed. It was the secondary task assigned to me." Lily said.

"What? They asked you to watch me?" Reighley asked, very confused.

"Yes." Lily wasn't told she couldn't tell Reighley what she was up to. Even if she was, she would tell him anyway. She felt like she owed him for his previous intervention at the mall. "Many teachers are under the assumption that you are cheating to be the number one student here at Gilford High. They asked me to watch you closely this week and to report any suspicious behavior. Personally, I don't believe it's necessary."

"Well thank you for having some faith in me," Reighley said with a chuckle. "But still, I guess that explains the poor treatment, even after becoming Freya's boyfriend." Reighley then looked over at Destiny who was hunkered over on her chair at her desk.

"Are you doing all right Destiny?" Reighley asked. With no verbal response, Destiny shook her head no, while it was tucked into her arms. Reighley knew he needed to try and make her feel better since Freya wasn't around. In reality, Destiny always felt like more of a third wheel than a friend to him. It wasn't as though he disliked her or anything of the sort. He found her normal demeanor quite enduring. It was more or less that he wouldn't have gone out of his way to make plans or hang out with her, outside of her being around when he was with Freya. The more he thought about it, the more he realized he barely knew Destiny. He wasn't sure if she was one-dimensional or if there was depth to her. Either was fine. Sometimes Reighley wished he had things as simple in life as Destiny made her life appear. Although clearly, everything wasn't perfect. The moment Freya was removed, Destiny began having a mental breakdown of sorts.

"I'm worried about her." Destiny sniffled.

"About Freya?" Reighley replied.

"Yeah… You may not know this but Freya is kind of an idiot." Destiny explained. "She gets herself into trouble all the time if I'm not constantly watching out for her. It's why I moderate her streams. She is the type of person to click on links that her viewers post in chat during her streams. I was the one who had to point out that, that's virus bait 101."

"Really? I didn't expect that." Reighley assumed Destiny was always watching from the sidelines. Always ready to troll at any moment. Learning that she was acting more as a guardian of sorts was sweet in his opinion. Even Lily, who was sitting near Reighley and Destiny, was surprised to hear this revelation.

"It's true… One time, when we were younger, Freya went to a tropical private island for vacation without me. She ended up doing one of her dangerous stunts and climbing the side of a mountain without any gear. She ended up falling and breaking her arm. It was the one time I decided I didn't want to go. If I was there, I could have prevented that from happening." Destiny shared.

"So, despite appearances, you are Freya's voice of reason," Lily said.

"I guess you could say that," Destiny replied. "I'm afraid she is going to do something stupid like paraglide off the school's rooftop. She tried that once. I had to stop her. I need to get back to her before she gets herself hurt." Reighley got up from his seat and approached Destiny.

"Hey, don't worry! We'll see her at lunchtime. I'm sure nothing bad could happen in the few hours that you've been apart." Reighley said, comforting her with a pat on the back.

Meanwhile, back in class 2-D Freya was chatting with Ulysses after the second class of the day finished.

"Alright Ulysses. Listen closely. You and I are going to run this classroom." Freya suggested.

"What! Why would we do that?" Ulysses asked.

"Well for starters. This behavior is unacceptable. These students are learning nothing watching movies of mine, regardless of how flattering that may be. Second off, if you become the quote-on-quote 'Boss' that would boost your social skills tenfold, which in turn will help you better talk to Lily. This will make you more manly, I swear." Freya explained.

"More manly?" Ulysses questioned.

"That's right. A real man has underlings serving him. Lily will be all over you. You need to help me run this place."

Ulysses thought it over. *"Lily needs a real man in her life? What even is a real man? The only real man I know is my dad. I guess that makes Sunny and me his underlings…"* Ulysses, realizing that he didn't count as a man according to Freya's description, decided it was best to try and listen to the only girl he could ask for help. "If it's to win her heart, okay… but what do you have to gain from it?" Ulysses asked.

"I need to get back at my dad for putting me in here," Freya said. "Here, watch this…" Freya got up from her chair and walked over to a random female student. "Here, I need your jacket." Freya pulled out a wad of cash. It was stacked with five, 10,000 yen bills.

"No, no, I don't need your money, please take it and this too!" The girl said, immediately taking her jacket off and a choker, handing it to Freya.

"Thanks..." Freya said while taking the jacket. She felt as if that was too easy. She looked back toward Ulysses and saw that his jaw had dropped. Deciding to take her fate into her own hands she put on the black spiked jacket and choker walked towards the teacher's desk and sat on it with her legs crossed.

"Umm... Freya, what are you doing?" The teacher looked very confused. Freya took a moment and quietly asked the teacher a question and shortly after he shrugged and gave her a nod of approval.

"Listen up! As of today, all of you are now under my guidance! Do you have any idea how much potential you all are missing out on? It's midterms and you are watching movies! Movies for goodness sake!" Freya shouted. "If you have a problem with it, you can take it up with Odysseus. As for now, for now, I'm going to teach this class!" The entire class was shocked by this. It was as if they were experiencing a truly life-changing event. Freya pulled out some black eyeliner, mascara, and eyeshadow she had in her purse and applied a heavy amount to her face using a tiny mirror. She then put on some reading glasses, pulled up the dusty textbook that was on the teacher's desk, and wiped it down with a tissue from a box nearby. "I'm going to save all of you from expulsion, is that clear?"

"Yes, Ma'am...?" The class shouted.

"You didn't put your heart into it!" Freya claimed. "I said, is that CLEAR!?"

"YES MA'AM!" The class shouted.

"She can't save them. They're beyond help. Freya this, Freya that. It's all they talk about these days. Why did I have to get assigned to this classroom?" Dante thought. He had tried for the entire semester to get the students to listen but to no avail. He figured if they were projecting their energy towards something that was at least not negative, then maybe there was a chance that he could get moved to a new classroom to keep the students well-behaved. At this point, he just didn't care.

"She's... She's... Awesome!" Ulysses thought. It was pandemonium and Ulysses couldn't believe what had just unfolded. In an instant, Freya showed a charisma he could only dream of having. It almost gave him the courage to make some sort of order. Almost. *"If I become more like her, then I won't have any trouble talking to Lily."* Suddenly two of the girls from the class approached Ulysses.

"Umm... Odysseus sir?" Punk girl A said.

"Hmm!?" Ulysses couldn't get any words out so the only sound that came out was an irritated grunt of annoyance. Because of this, he turned red from embarrassment. The two girls saw this and worried they angered him.

"We're so sorry to bother you, Boss! Please forgive us. Joy and I are a part of the cosplay club and we were wondering if you wanted a cool black leather jacket made in your size!" Punk girl B said, bowing to Ulysses. She also took the head of the girl named Joy and forced her to bow as well.

"Your name," Ulysses answered.

"Uh! My name is Lillie." The girl answered. Ulysses's head began to spin. He was talking to a girl, with the same name as the one he liked. He looked at her and her face began to warp to look like Lily's.

"*Uh-oh...*" Freya, upon hearing this, hopped off the desk and rushed to his aid. When she arrived she stepped in between the two girls and intervened. "Yes, he would very much need a jacket custom-made in his size. Here is some money for the materials." Freya said handing the previous wad of cash she had to the two girls.

"Thank you so much! We'll work on it right away!" Joy exclaimed. After the two girls walked away, Freya turned towards Ulysses and whispered.

"Get a hold of yourself, Ulysses! How are you ever supposed to slow dance with Lily, let alone date her, when you can't even speak properly to a girl with the same name as her." Freya said. She was right. Ulysses couldn't help but agree with her. He was pathetic in that aspect. Something in him needed to change in order for things to progress. Otherwise, he might be better off bringing a mop with sunglasses and a scarf to slow dance with instead. To him that would be less embarrassing than messing up in front of Lily.

"You're right... I need to be brave," Ulysses said with a sigh.

"Of course I am. Besides, I know of that girl, and her name isn't even spelled the same." Freya said. "Her name is spelled with an 'L, I, E,' instead of a 'Y'."

"Freya, how do you act so bravely in front of others?" Ulysses asked.

"It's simple actually. When I feel stressed out, or anxious about what comes next. I tell myself to 'remember to breathe.'"

"That's it?" Ulysses asked skeptically.

"Yep. That's it. You would be surprised how often we forget to do just that when things get stressful." Freya explained.

"Okay... I'll give that a try next time. By the way, how do you plan on teaching all of these students? Unlike them, I just study in my own time..." Ulysses said, worried.

"It will be fine. Besides, these people are nicer than I expected. I think it's about time people started caring about class 2-D," Freya reassured.

The clock struck noon, and the school bell rang, signifying it was time for lunch. Reighley asked Lily and Destiny if the two would like to join him. He planned on meeting up with Freya with the hope that he could figure out what his next course of action would be. The group arrived in the cafeteria. It was overly crowded near the center, as a bunch of students gathered around a sectioned-off area where students were sitting. There was a large commotion in the outer crowd and many students looked as if the thing in the center was awe-inspiring.

"What's happening?" Destiny asked, intrigued. "You're tall, right? You should be able to tell." She looked at Reighley who was just as confused as she was. Curious, she pulled out her cell phone and checked SocialLight for anything trending at her school. *"What!?"* Destiny was completely shocked. The front page on SocialLight was one of Freya in a punk getup. She took a selfie, of her sitting on the teacher's desk, and behind her was the entire class of 2-D. *"I leave her alone for only a day and she starts a gang!?"* Destiny immediately recognized some students in the crowd as those in Freya's picture. Distraught, she rushed towards the crowd and pushed through it in the hope of finding her best friend on the other side. She forced her way in, completely smothered by other people. When she peered at the crowd of students she saw Freya through the gap. Freya was surrounded by students from class 2-D. They formed an almost human barrier around her like they were protecting a mafia boss or president. *"This... is too much. I can't reach her. She's slipping out of reach again."* Destiny thought while struggling to push through.

Destiny couldn't help but feel like this moment reminded her of back then. Back when the two were younger. *"I know I lied to Reighley earlier. The truth is, I was invited to that vacation. The trip to Solstis Island. Where you fell. You kept it a secret. All this time. That's how I knew you were a true friend."*

"I got you!" A voice said. With her train of thought interrupted, a large hand grabbed a hold of Destiny from the gap. Ulysses pulled her through to the other side.

"Uly!" Destiny.

"Hey D," Ulysses said. "All right Ulysses, time to be brave. Remember what Freya taught you."

(*"When you feel stressed out, or anxious about what comes next. Remember to breathe."*)

Ulysses took a deep breath, and let out a loud shout towards a few of the fan club members.

"Guys, make some room!" Ulysses ordered.

"Yes, boss!" The students replied and started to clear some space and break up the crowd. Soon there was more than enough space for three and a half people. When Ulysses stepped aside, behind him was Freya, who was sitting on a table eating an apple with one hand and texting on her phone with the other.

"Destiny!" She said with a smile. "I was just about to text you."

"Freya, are you crazy? Starting a gang?" Destiny said.

"They're not a gang. It's my fan club." Freya explained.

"Okay. I know you were just explaining it, but I don't think you realize how much you sound like Guinevere. " Destiny said.

"Good to see you too," Freya said sarcastically.

"Freya, you look like the sun just burnt out," Destiny said looking at the all-black goth girl get-up Freya was wearing."You're right... I need to go all out. I need to show Jim that he can't control me anymore." Freya steeled her resolve, reaching in her handbag for more black makeup to apply.

"That's not what I was getting at! Look, Freya, I'm worried about you. I'm worried you are going to do something stupid and get yourself into something you can't get out of. Are you sure this isn't dangerous? What if the other school gangs heard of this startup? You could incite a gang war between our high schools, or even worse, what if your dad withdraws you from Gilford High?" Destiny asked.

"No. This isn't dangerous at all. Most of these students are struggling here with school. I want to help them. I planned on asking the number one student for some study tips as well." Freya elaborated.

"You just want to talk with your Loverboy," Destiny teased.

"No! Well, yes, but that's beside the point. Destiny I need you to trust me this time. Please. I know I get myself into a lot of trouble and you're always the one bailing me out, but this is different. It's about making a point by not judging a book by its cover. Something I learned very recently. So please have my back on this." Freya said. After a brief pause, Destiny stopped Freya's tangent and held out her hand towards her. "What are you-?"

"Get me a jacket!" Destiny exclaimed. "You are going to need a VP. I can see that you already have your Sergeant of Arms. Destiny said as she glanced over at Ulysses." Freya's eyes began to water up a tiny bit, and then she immediately hugged Destiny.

"I won't even ask how you know about all of that, but thank you, Destiny." Freya said with gratitude.

"Yeah, yeah, I know. I rock." Destiny said with a smug look." After the embrace, Freya looked towards Joy who was standing at the edge of the inner circle.

"Joy, Lillie Two, I need a jacket for Destiny, pronto!" She commanded.

"All right! Lillie Two, You heard the lady. Let's go fetch the girl a jacket." Joy said.

"Lillie Two!? Oh, all right…" Lillie Two said.

"Blue if possible," Freya added.

"You know me so well," Destiny added dramatically. The two girls went out of the crowd towards the cosplay club room but before leaving, Freya quickly glanced around attempting to find Reighley in the cafeteria. With no luck due to the crowd around her, she left.

On the other side of the crowd, Reighley stood there with Lily.

"There's no getting through that crowd," Reighley said. He guessed there were at least one hundred students surrounding them.

"I hope Destiny is all right," Lily mentioned.

"Me too. Well. I'm going to eat lunch on the roof. Want to tag along?" Reighley asked.

"I don't think it's proper for a boy and a girl to be alone together," Lily said.

"Fair point. Ulysses might get the wrong idea. How about out by the garden? There will be others around." Reighley said.

"Sure." Lily agreed. "I have to keep an eye on you anyway." The two made their way towards the center of the school, which was outdoors. It had a fountain in the center of it with a statue of Gilford Manning. It depicted him as an elderly man with sunglasses. He helped create the prestigious education system Gilford High was renowned for. Reighley and Lily sat on a bench near the fountain and pulled out their lunches. The two began to eat and chat with one another.

"I was meaning to ask, but how long have you been working for Freya's family?" Reighley questioned.

"Since I was eight," Lily said. "I would have returned to a normal life by now if I wasn't indebted to the Young family."

"You don't like the life you're living?" Reighley asked.

"Before I would have said yes, but now, I'm not sure. So much has changed in this past month." Lily replied.

"How so?" Reighley questioned.

"My life was pretty miserable working for Freya all these years. I was constantly cleaning up the messes she would deliberately leave me. I take care of pretty much everything for her. However, things are different now. Now I'm in a sort of gray area. She's changed because of you."

"You have my sympathy," Reighley said, jokingly. Lily paused after swallowing her food and looked at Reighley.

To her, he looked serious, but looking into his eyes she could tell something was off about him.

"Why do your eyes look so sad?" Lily thought while looking at Reighley. *"Is it because Freya left the class? No... It's deeper than that."* Lily put her food aside and thought it was time for some answers. "Reighley, how do you feel about Freya?" She asked.

"What!? What brings this up?" Reighley said with a slight blush.

"Well. I know she pays you each week." Lily teased.

"How does everybody know that?" Reighley wasn't surprised at this point.

"Never underestimate the Young staff's observation skills," Lily said proudly.

"Now that she mentions it, Elise has uncanny perception too," Reighley thought. "Look, I don't know to be honest. If we are going by the rules of the deal the two of us made, we'll break up after her party."

"What? Why?" Lily asked.

"It was a part of our agreement. This was never about dating. It was about Freya saving face amongst her peers. If I didn't fall in love with her after a month of being together, then we would 'break up' and she would leave me alone. She just wanted me because she couldn't have me. At least at first." Reighley explained.

"Do you want her to leave you alone?" Lily probed. She wanted to know the truth.

"No... but, this is bigger than what I want. There is something deeper going on in Freya's life. "

"What do you plan on doing?" Lily asked.

"I don't know yet. I'll figure it out after I meet with *him*." Reighley answered.

Soon lunch was over and the two went back to class.

The rest of the school day went by and Reighley left early without seeing Freya once. On his way out he sent a text message to her.

(Sorry. I have plans. I can't see you after school. I'll text you later tonight.)

A few moments later she replied.

(I miss you.)

It was three simple words but they were as bitter-sweet as could be. He didn't know how to respond to something like this. It hurt his heart slightly. It was the first text she had sent him that made him feel like she was his real girlfriend.

"She's getting attached to me... I'd be lying if I told myself I didn't miss her too, but I can't tell her that. If I did, It would only make my decision more painful. I don't want her to get hurt because of me."

Deciding not to reply, Reighley left the school grounds towards his meeting place with Elise. The two planned for Reighley to be picked up at Motherboards. He also thought it was best no one he knew saw him and Elise together. On his walk there he noticed a strange mansion during his commute. It was atop a green hill. The driveway was well over one thousand feet. He had never been down this particular path before. He guessed this area was where the upper class resided. He wondered if Freya's home was nearby as well. Before passing the mansion entirely, he noticed something by the curbside.

Guinevere was blessed and highly favored. The extremity of her elegance remained unmatched. She is as beautiful as the sky itself. Models have wept with envy knowing they could not compare to her majesty. The life she lived thus far was absolutely perfect. This is reflected in her surroundings to a literal degree. Everything from her household to her person was symmetrical in design. She would have her hairstylist cut her cyan blue dyed hair in a perfectly even bob cut. Each of her outfits was custom-made. She couldn't bear to wear the same clothes as those who dared to breathe the same air as her. They were filth in comparison. Guinevere had just finished her daily education. She spent a large quantity of her life at home as she had private tutors who would come to her mansion. Her parents insisted they bring the school to her, to protect her. The lessons were a breeze for her. Since she could simply cheat. At birth, Guinevere was gifted with the telepathic ability she called *Reverie*. It was the ability to read the minds of those around her. Their thoughts would appear like subtitles. This was how she knew other people were scum. Their opinions, intentions, and feelings were all written in plain view above their heads. This caused many of her servants to get fired. If they thought even the slightest negative thought about her in any way then they were instantly removed from the job.

Guinevere was sitting in the center of a three-seater leather couch in her family lounge and snapped her fingers at her butler signaling for a refill. She drank tea as it was her preferred source of caffeine even though the beverage was barely acceptable to a person of her station. After the butler approached to fill her porcelain teacup, she took a sip. To her disgust, it was lukewarm. Guinevere displayed a grimace on her face and tossed the expensive porcelain set shattering it on the floor.

"This tastes like mud! You might as well poison me while you're at it. What do I even pay you for!?" Guinevere said while looking at her butler.

"I'm sorry madam. I'll clean this up and get you a new fresh glass of tea." The butler said. *"How could I be so stupid? I upset Madam Guinevere. I must fix this immediately!"*

"Hmph!" Guinevere scoffed. Using her ability *Reverie*, she was pleased by his response. Occasionally she would test her servants' loyalty towards her. She'd intentionally overreact to see if their opinions of her had changed. *"As expected. It seems he has taken full responsibility. I suppose he can keep his job despite his mistake."* Guinevere thought. Suddenly on the small tables on both sides of her, phones began to vibrate and buzz. She glanced over at each of the phone screens and noticed an alarm was going off.

"I suppose it's that time already, isn't it? Forget the tea." She said while silencing the alarms. She stood up from the couch she was lounging on and pocketed both of her phones into separate handbags. Guinevere carried two purses on her to counteract the asymmetry. She had two of everything. She could not feel at peace unless she knew everything was placed exactly where it should be.

"Madam?" The butler asked, confused.

"Donald, get the vehicle ready. I have an appointment." She asked.

"Yes Madam Guinevere. What is the appointment for?" Donald asked. *"I don't recall her having me schedule any appointments."* He thought. Again, Guinevere read these thoughts like an open book above Donald's head. No thought could hide from her *Reverie.*

"Your job isn't to ask questions but to do what I ask Donald. Now leave me." Guinevere reprimanded.

"Yes Madam Guinevere." Donald replied. *"She's completely right. I must do what she asks of me with no questions asked."*

"Good." She said, reading his thoughts. Once Donald left the room, Guinevere headed up a center staircase in the entrance hall. Her room was in the core center of the house. She had full control of the structure of the home. Her parents spent a fortune simply remodeling the mansion to her liking. She had the place all to herself. She felt it unbalanced having her parents' room be a part of her home. There wasn't any place she felt she could place them without things becoming uneven, so she kicked them out. They always listened to her, as she knew the secrets each of them held close to their hearts. All the skeletons they kept in their closets made for perfect blackmail to use if they ever told her no. They too were imperfect. The only good things she could think of that her parents did for her were bringing her into this world and buying her things.

While in her room, Guinevere readied herself for the day. Her room was spotless. Her bed hadn't a single wrinkle on it. Yet she was nervous for what was to come. There was only one person who frightened her. Freya Young, and making matters worse she had just been invited to her party a few days ago. She held feelings of contempt towards Freya as she was the only person in this world that she even remotely considered perfect. The two girls had traded barbs in the past. Guinevere was the one who always started the conversations. Most of their talks however never went farther than a terse sentence or two. This didn't bode well with Guinevere, but this party was her chance to finally outdo Freya.

"This time… you won't be better than me." She said with anger.

Guinevere headed out of her room making her way towards the front of her home where Donald was waiting for her in their blue limousine. Once she entered the back, the vehicle headed down the elongated driveway. When the vehicle was about halfway down Donald warned Guinevere.

"Madam. It seems someone is rummaging through the trash you had thrown to the curb," he said with disdain. Guinevere looked out the window of the vehicle and in the distance, she saw someone hunkered over near a trash pile. Although *Reverie* was perfect in appearance it did have three flaws that Guinevere was well aware of. The first was that it could only see subtitles of thoughts, not images conjured up in people's minds. The second was that it had a range that was limited to Guinevere's ability to read from a distance. The third and final flaw was that she couldn't tell what people were feeling. She could only make inferences with what words she was given. From the distance she was at, she was unable to depict what was above the stranger's head. Usually, she would use binoculars to spy on others but felt it was a wasted effort as the vehicle was approaching anyway. When the vehicle pulled up next to the stranger Guinevere rolled down her window and spoke to the boy.

"I'd appreciate it if filthy rats didn't rubbage through my garbage, thank you," she said. Of course, Reighley saw the vehicle coming towards him, but nothing prepared him for the rudeness that followed.

"Um... excuse me? I'm sorry I assumed this stuff was all being thrown away." Reighley said mildly annoyed. *"I guess I'll play nice since I am technically on their property."*

"This is private property and a monkey like you should leave-" Guinevere stopped for a moment as she read Reighley's thoughts above his head. She was incredibly efficient at reading and speaking simultaneously.

"Monkey? Tch... I can't get a read on this girl with Insight. It's like her eyes won't stay still. No, they aren't even looking at me, but above me?" Guinevere read Reighley's thoughts.

"Insight? What's Insight?" She thought. "What are you doing here?"

"I was just passing by when I saw this new game station that was sitting here on the curve. I was hoping to ask if I could have it since it was tossed out." Reighley explained with a fake smile. *"With this, I could play the games Ulysses recommended to me."* Finally, Guinevere looked into Reighley's eyes, and *Insight* activated on her. A chill went down his spine as he stared into her eyes causing her aura to appear. The area around him morphed into what he could only explain as black ice. He had only seen one aura that was ever this dark before. He wasn't aware ice-cool auras could even become like this. It was almost as if he took one wrong step he would slip and fall into a void beneath and that would be the end. *"This girl is bad news. This whole situation reminds me of Freya, but only worse."* Reighley thought.

"Freya!? What do you mean Freya? How do you know my intentions?" Guinevere thought after using *Reverie.* Suddenly she recognized the uniform Reighley was wearing. *"That's a Gilford High uniform! This boy must know Freya Young."* Guinevere, quick with her wit, decided to fib about his connection with Freya. "Oh my, if only I noticed sooner that you were a member of Gilford High School. I take back what I said before. They wouldn't let Monkeys into that place. Say, you wouldn't happen to know of a Freya Young would you?" Guinevere asked.

"No, I'm sorry." He answered. *"There is no way this girl and Freya are 'buddy buddy'."* He thought.

"Now, now, you must have heard of her. She is the grossest- I mean goddess of Gilford High. You know, Extraordinary movie star, internet celebrity?" Guinevere felt as though she and this stranger were in the same boat. It was the first time she felt like she had found someone like her. Someone gifted with some sort of ability. *"This Insight he thought of, must be how he could get a feel for who I am. His face completely changed after he looked me in the eyes. Not to mention he said he couldn't get a read on me because of the lack of eye contact. That must be it."*

Reighley paused for a second feeling like the ice beneath him was cracking. He took notice of the Freudian slip that escaped her thoughts. "Oh, you mean *that* Freya Young," Reighley replied. "Yeah, I think I've seen her a few times." In every fiber of his being this stranger was giving off a bad feel. He could tell her intentions were as pure as tar. *"I need to get out of here. I just get this feeling I shouldn't let her find out Freya and I are dating."*

"Bingo," Guinevere said out loud.

"What?" Reighley answered.

"Oh, nothing. Feel free to keep the Gamestation 5. I really must be going before I'm late. May I ask for your name?" Guinevere asked with a smug look.

"It's Ray." Reighley lied.

"Is that short for something?" She questioned.

"This girl just won't let up, will she?" Reighley thought. "Nope. Thanks for the console," he said while picking up the Gamestation 5 as fast as possible. As much as

he despised people like this, there was no way he was passing up a free Gamestation 5. His treasure-hunting self wouldn't forgive him if he passed up this opportunity despite how annoying it would be to carry the thing across town.

"Not so fast," Guinevere said.

"Yes?" Reighley said with his back turned. *"Ugh! What now, Karen?"*

"My name is Guinevere and the next time you see Freya, tell her that I'll be taking what's hers!" She said irritated with his thoughts. "Now Donald, drive." She commanded.

"Yes, Madam." He replied immediately, taking off.

After the vehicle left earshot, Reighley let off a sigh of relief. *"Well, that was just awful. What is wrong with that girl? That was by far the worst encounter I've had with a person since I've lived here. Not to mention her aura. Freya's an angel compared to that snob and it's not because she pays me. I think I've had more than a lifetime's worth of rich people messing with my life."* He thought. Reighley looked down at his phone and realized the time. *"Shoot! I'm going to be late."*

Meanwhile, back in the limousine, Guinevere was fuming. While the vehicle was driving away she turned behind in the back seat and used the pair of opera binoculars she kept in her bags. Allowing her to use *Reverie* on him for his final thoughts.

"THE NERVE OF HIM!" She shouted as she dropped her binoculars to her waist.

"I felt he was quite pleasant for a hobo," Donald replied.

"Shut it, Donald! I didn't ask for your opinion."

"Yes, Madam. Sorry, Madam."

"Whatever. That doesn't matter now, because I've hit double bingo!" Guinevere said with a maniacal grin. *"Freya Young has to pay her boyfriend to stay around. I finally have some dirt on you, Little Miss Perfect! Did you want to dance Freya? Fine, let's dance. If your boyfriend can be bought, I'll buy him. That'll teach you not to threaten exposing my family secrets, you witch. I'm the only one who is allowed to blackmail my family. The world only has room for one perfect girl and that's me!"* Guinevere thought. She couldn't help but get excited about what was to come. *"Now to more important matters. Why did Ray call me Karen?"* Confused, she looked up what it meant on the internet.

"THAT INSOLENT LITTLE-" Guinevere roared.

Chapter 16

The Calm

He was watching from the shadows, despite not receiving any orders to. Officer Templeton needed to know what had happened that day. What had become of the delinquent and his boss's daughter? This was something he couldn't just sit and wait around for. He decided to stake out the school to follow Reighley afterward. To his surprise, he noticed Reighley walk out of the school building immediately after the bell rang. He decided to discreetly follow the boy. While vowing to keep a close eye on him. He assumed that Reighley would look defeated, and he was right. The young boy had his head down when he exited. Templeton was slightly worried that the boy would turn to violence to get his way like he did in middle school. However, he was fully prepared for such an outcome and even somewhat expected it. Throughout his years of experience serving on the police force, he learned several things about criminals. They showed their true nature when backed into a corner.

"Now where are you running off to?" He whispered to himself. Officer Templeton was in his civilian vehicle following at a discreet distance. He brought along his binoculars so he could continue to spy on Reighley. He figured a patrol vehicle would stick out far too much. Reighley pulled his cell phone out. It appeared he had gotten a notification of sorts. He looked at his phone and immediately stopped in his tracks. After a long pause, Reighley remained frozen from what he had seen. Templeton could see slight anguish in his eyes.

"Why the long face, kid?" Templeton asked himself. He knew exactly why the boy would be in low spirits. Jim made his move to separate the two. This was it. The moment Templeton had been waiting for since Reighley had taken his first steps on the school grounds. *"You should have listened to me when I warned you back then. This is what happens when you play games with the best on the force."*

Eventually, Reighley ended up on Yufuku (裕福 - Wealthy) Street. Known to house the top one percent of earners in San Fran Kyoto. He began to wonder if the boy was here to burglarize the homes of the rich. However, he soon watched as Reighley began to walk up to a trash pile on the curb. Templeton began to wonder if things were so bad at home that he needed to dig through trash. Then Reighley pulled out a Gamestation 5 from the rubble. Seeing this caused Templeton's jaw to drop. He had been trying to obtain one for the past year but had no luck due to scalpers on the internet, and yet somehow Reighley was lucky enough to stumble upon one on the side of the road. Templeton seethed in jealousy over the luck of this brat. He decided he would just have to confiscate it from the kid since it didn't belong to him. He obviously didn't have permission to just take it. Templeton began to pull forward a bit before he saw a vehicle leave the property Reighley was at. When the vehicle pulled up to Reighley, Templeton rolled down his passenger window in order to overhear the conversation going on. He couldn't catch much but did hear the words, "You can keep the Gamestation," come from the vehicle.

"You're kidding, just how lucky is this kid?" Templeton questioned. "First he got the attention of one of the richest girls in the world, but then just happened to find a Gamestation 5 for free? Lucky rat. Karma is coming for you kid. Karma is coming..." Once the vehicle drove away, Templeton recognized the household. It was one of the Pendragon's family homes. Specifically, one that was used to house Guinevere Pendragon. He knew of this place as he was assigned several times in the past to escort Prismarine and Freya here. However, the building looked different since then. It was like everything had been redesigned to be in perfect shape in every way.

After a while, the boy proceeded on to his next destination. Templeton followed Reighley to Motherboards, the gaming café. A place he knew fairly well as he had been a part of a few calls that involved disreputable men who hit on women there. He was a white knight in their community, and his popularity with the ladies there was fairly well-received. During one of those escorts, however, there was only one woman he had set his eyes on who truly captivated him. It was none other than the queen of the café. He didn't know her name, instead only the name the girls called her. Ch@mberM@de. Queen of Motherboards. There was something about her that Templeton couldn't help but be drawn to. It was as if she emitted a radiance that enlightened everyone and everything around her. He couldn't help but want that in his own life. It was like she offered peace to his aching soul. Regardless, he hadn't built up the courage to speak with her, and with the inclusion of the rule that men cannot hit on women inside, he felt that he would be the one who would be escorted out.

Templeton parked his vehicle shortly after Reighley arrived and watched the young boy enter into the establishment. He watched the boy be greeted by several mothers inside.

"Tch… you lose Freya and immediately hit on some moms huh? Disgusting." Templeton grunted. His eyes widened as he watched Reighley head straight for Ch@mberM@de. "Hah! He thinks he has a chance with the queen of the castle! What a joke-" Templeton ate his own words as the woman greeted him with a bow and the two proceeded towards the exit. "What… is happening?" He said while he watched Reighley enter a vehicle with Ch@mberM@ade. He was at a loss for words. "This kid is blessed by the gods!" He shouted. He watched in both jealousy and awe as the two left the establishment leaving the parking lot.

Templeton followed the two in his vehicle and began rambling to himself about the absurdity of it all.

"There's no way the kid has that much game. All he did was walk in, and walk out with a bride! Are you telling me if I would have waltzed right in, I could have had a wife by now!?" He said with jealousy.

Meanwhile, inside Elise's vehicle, Reighley was sitting in the passenger seat with a lot on his mind. He couldn't help but think back on how Freya acted in class. He knew she had been pushed to a breaking point. He figured now was the perfect time for answers.

"So how long have you been working for the Young family?" Reighley asked.

"For the past eighteen years," she replied.

"So you've been there in the house since Freya was a child, right?" Reighley questioned.

"Yes. Why the sudden questions?" Elise asked intrigued.

"Well... I wanted to ask about Freya's relationship with her father," he explained.

"I see. Well, to put it bluntly, there is no relationship as of right now. Master Jim hasn't spent time with Freya since she was a little girl. They two would have a meal together now and then but that is as far as it goes."

"I see, so that explains it. So what about her birthday party? Will he spend the day with her during that?" Reighley asked.

"I'm afraid not. If I remember correctly he only planned to stop by for an hour or two. The master is an incredibly busy man. He works fourteen to sixteen hours a day with no breaks, or time off." Elise answered.

"Sounds like a pretty miserable way to live," Reighley said with contempt. "You would think, with how much money he is making he could just hire people to reduce his workload so he could at least spend a day with his family."

"Being a businessman is not that simple. There is a lot of time, resources, dedication, and energy spent in doing that sort of job." Elise explained.

"Sure, but what is the point of having all that money, success, and power, if you can't even spend time with your family?" Reighley asked. Elise didn't have an answer. She felt like she didn't have the right to say whether or not Reighley was right since she never pursued a family life. She knew she threw her best years away as a potential wife. She felt that she was still fairly attractive for her age, but she knew she had nothing on the younger more fertile woman around her. Deep down, part of her knew that it was too late for her to start a family with her current lifestyle. She had focused so much on her career and the wealth that came along with it that by the time she realized what she had done, it was too late. She put her financial future in front of a future with a family. This was the reason she went to Motherboards. It was an escapist fantasy for her. Seeing the mothers come in and out of the place with their children allowed her to imagine a life where she too could be in their shoes.

"Reighley. Success is not fulfillment." Elise said, looking over at him. Reighley looked at the woman driving him and immediately felt a sort of sadness cast over him. For a brief moment, he could see her aura and with it, Elise disappeared. It was no longer the bright magenta crown he had seen prior, instead, it was a dimly lit, isolated wedding band, completely in solitude. He could feel a fear emanating from it. It was the fear of ending up alone.

"I agree. That's why I need your help. I want to speak with Freya's father before her birthday party. I need to let him know to be there for her." Reighley answered.

"I see." Elise smiled. She was unsure of Reighley up until now, but she is sure Freya is in good hands. "Very well. I will help you. However, we will need some help. I suggest we inform Herald as well. He thinks highly of you. You'll have to convince him for this to work."

"All right, I'll do it! Thank you, Elise." He replied. Elise paused and looked at the grateful young man's smile and couldn't help but be slightly envious of Freya.

"Lady Freya is a lucky girl," Elise claimed.

"What do you mean?" Reighley asked.

"Not all of us are lucky enough to have someone care as deeply as you do for her," Elise responded. Reighley didn't know what to say, instead, he awkwardly blushed in embarrassment as the two drove in a somber silence.

Regret began to settle in Elise's heart. She had to accept the consequences of her life choices.

"Just what life did I give up to become who I am?" Elise thought to herself. Results were important to her and yet she couldn't get the results she wanted. *"There were plenty of men who were suitable husbands that I completely ignored. Was it because of my income? Did I become so independent that I refused to rely on a man, or were my standards just too high? Whatever the reason, it's far too late now. I cannot have children of my own now. There is no changing the past…"* While thinking, she looked in her rearview mirror and noticed a vehicle. She realized it had been following them for some time now.

"It seems we are being followed," Elise said.

"What? By who?" Reighley asked, fighting his impulse to turn around and look.

"I'm not sure. I can't tell who it is because of the tinted windows." Elise said. "Well, I wouldn't worry too much about it. Besides, we're here." The two pulled into a large parking lot full of minivans and other suburban vehicles. They arrived at a dance studio named Yoshi's Studios. From the entrance, plenty of dance moms could be seen entering and exiting with their children. The place was entirely festered with people of all sorts. Some in suits and dresses, others in costumes and tutus. Although in different clothing Reighley could tell by the demeanor of these people that they were in the upper class. He had been around enough rich people to spot one. It was like an aroma of importance aired off of them, or at least that was the impression he got.

"Let me guess. Freya's family owns this place as well?"

"That is correct. The Young family owns a sort of monopoly. However, most of these companies were bought simply because of Freya. Whenever she showed interest in something, her father would buy a business that could help her to the fullest. Even if Freya's interest died in a week or two." Elise explained.

"Not surprising," Reighley said. *"Hmm... So Jim spoils her to make up for not being around. Money is nice and all, but nothing can replace a father being there for their kid,"* He thought. He knew that all too well. It broke his heart as he watched Isabelle grow up without a dad in her life. He knew that every birthday his dad was absent from would chip away at her soul. He didn't want Freya to keep hurting like that. These thoughts only strengthened his conviction. *"A father that's there but isn't around is still a deadbeat dad."*

Once they parked their vehicle, Elise pointed out which vehicle was tailing them. Given their options, they decided to enter the studio. Once inside Elise spoke with the receptionist about rental clothing Reighley could wear. When the woman asked for payment she showed an emblem and instantaneously the mannerism of the woman at the desk changed completely. She treated Elise as if she ran the place and began bossing other employees around to fulfill Elise's request. After a short wait, Reighley was handed a suit to change into. He went into the men's changing room to get dressed. He had never worn a suit before and was struggling to look presentable.

"How do I even get this thing on?" Reighley said, struggling to tie a tie around his neck. He was embarrassed to admit it but, this was the nicest thing he had ever worn besides his school uniform, and it didn't even belong to him. *"Come on Reighley, remember why you are here. You have to learn how to dance for Freya."* He convinced himself. Eventually, he gave up on the tie. *"I don't have the time or the luxury to learn how to put this thing on... I'll have to ask Elise for help."* Suddenly, before he could exit, a man who was exiting a changing room noticed Reighley struggling and got his attention.

"Excuse me, would you like some help?" The stranger asked.

"Uh, yes that would be very helpful," Reighley replied. He looked at the man and his aura was a normal yellow color, just like his mother's. *"I guess not everyone here is that bad."* He thought. The man helped Reighley tie his red necktie around his collar and straightened everything out for him.

"Nice! You look sharp, kid." The stranger said.

"Thank you," Reighley said with a bow. He looked at his outfit in the mirror while avoiding eye contact with himself and attempted to bolster his confidence. He looked like he belonged at Gilford High or to some prestigious elite family.

"No problem kid. Take care!" The stranger said waving goodbye. Reighley couldn't help but feel like he recognized the face of this man, but couldn't pinpoint it.

Reighley then began to wonder to himself. *"Does money really make a person more standoffish? I'm starting to think that isn't the case. It's like money only reveals someone's character. If they were bad from the start then getting rich wouldn't have changed anything. Then again, it's not like rich people can't change even if they are unbearable to be around. Freya is the perfect example of that. I mean, I like her enough to learn how to dance."*

Afterward, Reighley stepped out of the changing room and Elise was there waiting for him. "You clean up nicely young man. Come now, we mustn't waste time." Elise said.

"Right!" He replied. The two entered the studio and Reighley looked at his surroundings. The studio was packed. The walls were covered with mirrors so one could see oneself dancing. The studio also had a balcony up a staircase. It led to a V.I.P. studio for those better off financially. When he entered many people stopped what they were doing and looked directly at him. He was overdressed.

"What's everyone's deal?" He whispered to Elise.

"They are just admiring the fact you were able to rent a suit like the one you're in," Elise answered.

"Huh, why?" Reighley questioned. Elise leaned over and whispered into Reighley's ear. "WHAT! 2,000,000 yen!? (USD 15,096.)" He frantically whispered.

"What's the big idea? This outfit is worth more than all of the money Freya has given me."

"The boyfriend of Freya Young must appear to have status, otherwise you'll bring shame to the Young Family," Elise explained.

"I'm not her actual boyfriend you know?" Reighley explained.

"Hmm, is that so? Then why are you learning to dance? You wouldn't do something like that for someone who meant nothing to you." Elise interrogated. Reighley had no answer. She was right. The last thing he wanted was to embarrass Freya. He just wanted to make her happy. He wouldn't do that for just anyone.

"Stop teasing me and just teach me how to dance okay?" Reighley replied embarrassed. Elise couldn't help but smile. She found his devotion to be somewhat adorable. The two made their way toward the center of the floor, and with all eyes on them, the two began practicing.

"There he is… I almost didn't recognize him in that outfit. Not to mention he has his grubby hands all over my queen. That boy is pure evil! Swooning such a pure and innocent heart such as hers! Is Freya not enough to satisfy his carnal desires." Templeton thought to himself while spinning next to a mirror. He had entered the studio and asked if he could rent a costume. He was wearing a masquerade mask. He thought it was perfect. "How did he afford that outfit anyway!? That is a Featherwork original suit. There is no way he could afford something like that."

Suddenly two girls dressed up in similar outfits as Templeton appeared in front of him.

"Um, excuse me, sir! Your pirouette is flawless. Could you show us how you're spinning like that?" One of the girls asked.

"Oh, haha. Of course!" He replied. *"Dang it all! I'm too good at this."* He thought. He began teaching the two girls how to pirouette. This made him unable to see everything going on between Reighley and Ch@mberM@de.

Standing over in the corner of the studio, completely lost in thought was Matilda Key. She had her half-black and half-white hair put up in a ponytail. She was a dancer at heart. She had only recently been coming to Yoshi's Studios to practice after school. It had been over a year since she came here regularly.

"I don't get it…" She said, dismayed. In her hand was an infinite pass to freely practice at the studio. It showed up in her shoe locker a week prior. With it was an apology note.

(I'm sorry. Freya.)

"Why would she give me this? Is she trying to trick me? I wouldn't put it past her." She said to herself. She thought back to a recent conversation she had with Ash Fjord.

("What!? You were invited to her party?" Matilda asked.)

("Yeah. She invited me the other day. Reighley was with her. She seemed different." Ash said.)

("She is going to pull something." Matilda claimed. "I wouldn't go if I were you.")

("I'm not so sure... It felt like she was trying to make amends with me," Ash replied.)

("Don't say I didn't warn you. Feel free to call me after you get publicly embarrassed at the party. Matilda said.")

("Oh gee, thanks for the kindness." Ash replied sarcastically.")

Her train of thought was interrupted by the sound of someone tripping and falling near the entrance of the studio. When she looked over at who had fallen, she was surprised to see it was Reighley Summers. He looked like he was freaking out over getting his suit dirty. When she recognized the brand her eyes widened as it wasn't cheap. She found him very attractive and became somewhat envious that Freya managed to find someone like him.

"Just looking at him gets my blood boiling... That's probably why he sticks around her all the time. Look at all the benefits he gets from just being her boyfriend." Matilda thought. *"But... I'm no better am I? I did the same thing over a year ago. I was using her to get in for free. Even now, I showed up here without even accepting her apology."* Deciding she had enough, Matilda decided she would head out for the day. When she walked past Reighley, she watched as he tripped and fell over his own two feet.

"He's really bad. In a cute and enduring way." She thought, letting out a slight giggle. Matilda recognized the

woman Reighley was dancing with as Elise. Although it had been a while since she had seen her, she couldn't forget the face of the Young family's headmaid. *"He must be getting dancing lessons for the party."*

"Matilda?" Reighley questioned, spotting her while on the ground.

"Ah! Oh, hi Reighley. I didn't see you there... Haha." She laughed awkwardly. Reighley stood up and walked over to her.

"I didn't know you danced." He said.

"I didn't know you couldn't dance." She said, with a laugh.

"Ouch. Yeah, who knew using your feet could be so difficult." He replied. He looked at her familiar gray aura. It appeared like a cloak around her. She was shrouded in mystery. It was like she didn't want to be noticed.

"Say. Are you sure you don't want to date me instead of Freya?" Matilda asked. Reighley was caught off guard by this sudden question but attempted to play it off.

"I'm flattered but, I'll have to pass," Reighley answered. Something was off. He felt like she wasn't being honest with him. It was as if she was trying to get some sort of confirmation out of him.

"I thought so..." She replied. "Well. I should be going. My dad is waiting for me." She looked over towards the exit and standing there was the man who tied Reighley's necktie.

"Matilda!" Reighley said before she left. She stopped and turned towards him completely silent. He felt bad. "It doesn't have anything to do with you, I just-"

"I know." She said, interrupting him and then walking away. Once his daughter arrived at his side, the man who Matilda said was her father looked over at Reighley and waved him goodbye. While the two were walking out of the building, Matilda's father spoke to her.

"Do you know that boy?" He asked.

"Yeah, but I wish I didn't." She answered. She saw how earnest Reighley was. She had seen how hard he was trying for Freya's sake and couldn't help but be upset. Not out of jealousy, but because she knew that she herself was the one at fault. She knew from the start that Reighley would say no to her; however, some part of her had hoped he would have said yes. To prove to herself that Freya wasn't worth all that effort.

"So that's why I thought I recognized him…" Reighley said, continuing his practice. He realized he had seen him pick up Matilda after school several times in the past.

Templeton had finally finished teaching the two masquerade girls how to perfectly pirouette. With his teachings, they had masterfully replicated his style. He was quite proud of that accomplishment and with that now being finished, he could finally keep a close eye on Reighley again. He noticed the interaction with the girl who walked by Reighley and watched as he turned her down. He found it unusual. It made no sense that the boy who was getting every girl he wanted would turn down someone's advances. It seemed, unlike the player Templeton knew Reighley was.

"Just what game are you playing kid?" he thought to himself. *"Don't tell me... You know I am watching you!?"* Templeton began to spin again, sweating profusely while watching Reighley learn how to dance. *"Foxtrot, huh?"* He growled with his eyes locked on the two. *"Wait, no that footwork is all wrong! Your tempo is off too! How could someone be so awful?"* It was infuriating for him to watch Reighley have no rhythm and eventually, Reighley tripped and fell again. He stopped, took a deep breath and stood back up once more.

"Perhaps we should stop for today?" Elise asked.

"No. Not yet... I can do this... besides, I want to make her birthday a memorable one." Reighley said determined to press on. He couldn't figure out why he kept slipping and falling.

"I have to give him props... The kid has tenacity." Elise thought.

Officer Templeton was pushed to his limit. He couldn't bear to watch the boy fail any longer. Instinctively his body moved on its own. Before he knew it, Templeton was standing in front of Reighley.

"Laissez-moi vous aider," Templeton said with a French accent. He reached out his hand helping Reighley up.

"Um... Excuse me?" Reighley was extremely confused by the words said. It sounded French but he wasn't sure.

"He offered to help you," Elise explained.

"Oh, thank you! Wait, you speak French?" Reighley questioned.

"Yes and four other languages." She answered.

"Uh… Oui oui! Let me show you how it is done." Templeton said. He offered Elise his hand. Elise hesitated for a moment but took it. The two began to dance in sync with each other as Reighley watched their example. While doing so Reighley noticed someone watching from the balcony upstairs and things made a lot more sense.

"Oh my, you are quite the dancer, Officer Templeton…" Elise whispered out of earshot.

"Uh… that is not me." He replied. *"How does she know who I am*!?" Templeton began to blush. *"I guess I'm just that unforgettable."* He thought, proud of his accomplishments. The truth was simple. Elise never lost sight of who was tailing Reighley and her when they entered the building. She could see right through his facade.

For Templeton It was odd. She felt so familiar to him. Like she was someone he knew for a long time. However, he couldn't figure out why he felt that way. After the demonstration, Reighley was able to block out all the distractions and get the basics of the dance down.

"Okay, I think I got it," Reighley said with a sigh of relief.

"That was one out of five dances you must learn before the party," Elise replied.

"Five?" He gulped.

"Yes, not to mention the foxtrot is the easiest one to learn," Elise explained.

"I have my work cut out for me, huh?" Reighley sighed, but the thought of Freya smiling while the two danced together gave him the energy to push on. The two practiced with Templeton critiquing from the side. Eventually, Reighley finished practicing several other dances to add to his arsenal and it was time to leave. Reighley stopped and looked at the masked man. Glancing into his eyes caused Reighley to feel a sense of deja vu. Using *Insight* he saw an envious green aura glowing around the masked person. It completely threw him off. It didn't make a lot of sense for Reighley to get offered help from someone of that particular personality type but nonetheless, he was grateful.

"Thank you for your help," Reighley said.

"Je t'en prie. (You're welcome.)" Templeton said quickly and awkwardly leaving the studio unsure what to say. On his way out Templeton began to question whether or not Reighley was truly committed to the role of swooning the women around him, or was just hardworking and diligent. Either way, Templeton was disappointed by the fruits of his labor. He had hoped to see a broken young man desperately clinging to any semblance of hope. Instead, he watched someone try their best for someone else's sake. Something he could get behind given his profession. Returning his costume he left and returned to report his findings to Jim Young, still wondering how the queen of motherboards recognized him immediately.

The studio had an upper floor that had a private dance room for those who were V.I.P.s. From the room, one could look down below through a glass panel at those who were too poor to experience the luxurious lifestyle one could enjoy at the top. Guinevere was doing just that.

(Moments before Reighley and Elise entered the studio.)

"Um… Madam Guinevere?"

"Yes, Donald?" Guinevere answered. She was sitting in a chair looking out towards the dance floor.

"What is the purpose of coming here?" Donald asked.

"Again, I don't pay you to ask questions, but I suppose I'll feed your curiosity." Guinevere scoffed. "We came here for Tea. It is simply sublime."

"Tea?" Donald doubted.

"Yes, and not because I need to refresh myself on how to dance because I was invited to Freya's party." Guinevere was completely and utterly lying. The Tea was acceptable at best, but the truth was that she hadn't been to many dances due to her parents secluding her at home throughout her life. She refused to be outdone by Freya, so she decided to observe dances done by others to refresh her memory.

"Ah! That makes sense." Donald replied. "*I need to improve my Tea-making skills for Madam Guinevere.*" He thought. Reading his thoughts with *Reverie*, Guinevere reminded herself why she kept Donald around.

"*Truly an exceptional servant.*" She thought. "*Perhaps I'll speak with my father and make him give Donald a raise.*" Guinevere began scanning the dancefloor below. She adored that those below her were admiring her beauty and elegance. It was only natural that she would steal the gaze of everyone. She was stunning. While basking in admiration and envy, she noticed everyone's eyes, who were once looking up at her, switched to a young man entering the studio.

"The audacity! I can't believe he followed me here. He has quite the nerve to steal my spotlight. She said, angrily. Guinevere watched as Reighley and a woman she didn't recognize began to practice the simplest of dances. She could only chuckle at how uncoordinated he was.

"*Go on, fall! Embarrass yourself in front of all the women here.*" Guinevere maliciously thought. Suddenly Reighley tripped over his own two feet and fell over. It was everything she wanted and then some. "HAH! Serves you right for calling me Karen!" She boasted. "*Now, what are you thinking?*" She used her pair of opera binoculars and looked over Reighley's thoughts that were floating above his head.

"*Ugh! I have to get this right.*" Reighley thought frustrated.

"Why aren't you embarrassed!? You just fell in front of everyone. I would die if that happened to me." Guinevere thought to herself.

Soon a young teenager walked past Reighley and the two conversed for a brief moment. Reighley's thoughts were the only thing Guinevere cared about knowing.

"Man... I feel bad about rejecting her like that, but I'm not going to lie or cheat on Freya." He thought.

"*Hmm...*" Guinevere was conflicted. She wanted misfortune to fall upon Reighley, but couldn't help but feel a slight attraction towards him after he turned the girl down. She knew that if she was the one who asked then it would have been a different story.

For two whole hours, Guinevere kept hoping Reighley would fall and incidentally, he did. Time after time, Reighley would trip over his own two feet. Guinevere watched from a distance as Reighley tried to figure out how to get his footing.

"It doesn't make any sense he's fallen over forty times... Just give up and go home already!" Guinevere stood up from her chair and used *Reverie,* to read Reighley's thoughts once again.

"*I can't give up! I have to make Freya's birthday a perfect one.*" He thought. Something clicked in Guinevere's head. It was such a beautiful form of devotion she had never seen before. Her parents, nor any of her servants ever displayed such loyalty. She wanted that. She needed it all for herself. That level of dedication was only worthy of her. The fact that Freya is the one who had something that special infuriated her. She needed to steal away Freya's man. That was the way she would gain the upper hand over her. Guinevere watched as a strange man in a mask offered to help Reighley learn. To her surprise, Reighley noticed Guinevere up above. He looked at her and the sense of distress on his face vanished. Like he had an epiphany.

"Hah… I guess that makes sense." He thought, giving Guinevere a fake smile.

"What makes sense!?" This struck a nerve in Guinevere. From that point onward Reighley no longer tripped during his practice. It was as if the ice under his feet broke loose.

"Donald. Find out everything you can about Ray!" She commanded.

"Yes, Madam." He answered. As Reighley and Elise left the building, Guinevere vowed to make Reighley hers, or at the very least terminate his and Freya's relationship.

As Reighley and Elise left, the two headed towards Herald who was currently teaching Ulysses how to dance at Gilford High School's gymnasium. Freya was sitting on a metal chair with her legs and arms crossed. She called Herald in because she insisted that her slow dance must remain unclaimed for "reasons".

"Very good, Ulysses," Herald commented as the two had finished their practice. Ulysses got the hang of dancing fairly quickly. He was taught from a young age to dance, specifically for the rare occasion he and his family went to formal events. This lesson unearthed the muscle memory that was stored deep within him.

"I'm impressed… For someone so bashful you've got the moves. What made you so worried?" Freya asked.

"It's not the dancing part I'm worried about... I'm afraid that things are going to move too quickly." Ulysses explained. "Like, what if Lily only liked what she initially saw? Then what? What happens if we dance, and she figures out I'm not all that I am talked up to be?"

"I believe you're overthinking it," Freya suggested. "I haven't known you for that long, but I think you are sleeping on your potential."

"I am going to agree with Lady Freya on this one, sir Ulysses. When Freya informed me you wished to become more manly, I was very confused by that statement. One simply does not become more manly. You must prove to yourself your own worth. That's what being a man is. Even if you don't feel up to the task, you must rise to the occasion anyway. That is how you win as a man; by not losing to yourself."

Ulysses and Freya stopped in their tracks and stared at Herald. They were shocked he said something so profound.

"Yo Freya, why is your butler dropping ultimate truth bombs on me," Ulysses said.

"Herald was never one to beat around the bush..." She answered.

"Ulysses, can I give you some advice?" Herald asked.

"Yes, sensei," Ulysses said as he placed both his palms together and politely bowed.

"From personal experience, I once asked my late wife Molly what caused her to be attracted to me in the first place. She told me what she saw in me. She didn't tell me that I was perfect but instead said I was the best possible version of myself. That was the type of man she was looking for." Herald lectured. "I am well aware you are aiming towards winning Lily's heart. As someone who has watched Lily grow from a young age, I know very well that she is an incredibly hard-working young woman, who would give up anything for the ones she loves. Any man would be lucky to have her attention, let alone her interest. If what Freya's told me about you is true, then perhaps Lily sees the potential in you as well. All you can do is strive to be the best version of yourself."

"My potential, huh?" Ulysses muttered to himself. *"That is a lot of pressure considering I can't even quit smoking..."* He thought.

"Ulysses, might I suggest that the next time you feel like not doing something, either because it's too hard, or scary, just do it anyway," Herald advised.

"All right... I'll try. Thank you, Herald, and you too Freya. I don't think I completely understand what to do next but I'll give it my best shot."

Ulysses waved off the two and headed home towards the subway system, leaving both Herald and Freya behind. Freya and Herald worked their way towards the school entrance.

"Lady Freya, might I ask, what is going on with your attire?" Herald asked with judgeful eyes.

"It's because Jim moved me to a new class, separating me from both Reighley and Destiny. He even used Lily to do so." She explained, obviously still upset from just thinking about the events that occurred.

"Jim, huh?" Herald questioned. "I see you're serious then…"

"Do I have your support?" Freya questioned, with puppy dog eyes. This was the same face she would use to convince Herald to let her go on all her crazy extreme sports stunts. This time around things were no different. He couldn't say no to her. It would be like saying no to his daughter if he had one.

"You always have and always will, Lady Freya," Herald said with a smile. Freya was ecstatic. She hugged Herald, catching him off guard. She had never hugged him before. She knew Herald would always have her back no matter what. It was something she wished her father would have done.

"Thank you. Really, I mean it." Freya said with genuine gratitude.

"You're welcome." Herald hugged back. Suddenly Freya received a text. She let go of Herald and checked her messages.

Reighley: ("Thanks.")

"Is he serious? I basically confessed my LOVE to him with my 'I miss you' text, and all he says is 'Thanks!'" She thought. Freya went from ecstatic to flustered in mere

seconds. It was very embarrassing for her to send that text. "Ugh!" Freya grunted. "What am I going to do with him?"

Reighley: ("How are you doing?")

"Aww... he's checking up on me. Okay, I'm less mad now." Freya thought.

Freya: ("I'm doing okay. I think I have a rough week ahead of me.")

Reighley: ("Yeah. Me too. By the way, sorry I dipped out on you today. I had somewhere I needed to be. With midterms, everything is so hectic.")

Freya: ("It's okay. You'll just have to make it up to me at my party.")

Reighley: ("Great... No pressure or anything.")

Freya: ("I'm kidding. Besides, what matters the most is that you're there.")

Suddenly Freya had a confused look on her face as a black limousine pulled up in front of her. "Elise? What is she doing here?"

Freya asked Herald. Herald seemed to be reading a text message the entire time Freya was texting Reighley. He was quite slow at using his smartphone but got the gist of the text. The plan was simple. Elise was going to take Freya out for a bit, while Herald picked up Reighley at a nearby gas station so the two could discuss.

"I have some things to attend to so Elise is going to be taking you," Herald answered.

"Oh. I see. Well alright, I suppose. Take care of yourself, Herald." Freya commanded.

"Of course, Lady Freya."

Freya entered Elise's vehicle and the two left the school grounds.

Chapter 17

The Storm

Herald pulled into a gas station where he saw Reighley leaning against the wall of the building. He pulled his vehicle up in front of him and gestured for Reighley to enter. Reighley was nervous, but he knew exactly why. The path that was laid before him was not an easy one to follow. Opening the passenger side door, Reighley sat inside the vehicle.

"I wasn't expecting you to reach out to me, Master Summers," Herald stated. Reighley braved himself and looked into Herald's eyes. Seeing his ice-cold aura, sent a chill down his spine.

"I... have something I must do and I need your help," Reighley said, his voice becoming involuntarily shaky. There was silence. Herald didn't say a word. *"No amount of time can get me used to the chills this guy gives me. Is he like an ex-assassin or something? Well, now that I mention it, that would explain his insane tracking skills,"* Reighley thought.

"Your conviction seems to be built upon a poor foundation Master Summers," Herald claimed. Reighley recognized that Herald was right yet again.

"He's right... If I can't even handle his butler, then don't have a shot at Jim himself. If I am serious about this, then I can't be scared of him or Jim won't take me seriously." He encouraged himself and took a deep breath to calm his nerves.

"Very good. Now, what is it that you want?" Herald asked.

"I must speak with Jim Young," Reighley said. Herald showed concern from that answer.

"What will you say when you do?" Herald questioned.

"I'm going to tell him to be there for his daughter on her birthday," Reighley explained. Herald frowned, he was conflicted by this. At first glance, it seemed like a noble cause, but he was almost positive it would backfire on Reighley.

"I do not believe that that is a wise choice. As someone who has worked for the Young family for a long time, I know better than anyone that he does not like being told what to do." Herald suggested.

"I kind of figured that one out already," Reighley said sarcastically.

"Then why go through with it?" Herald asked.

"Because not trying anything is even worse," Reighley said. These words moved Herald's heart. There were plenty of times he wished he would have advised Jim to spend more time with his daughter, but chose not to, for everyone's best interest.

"Very well. I will get you an audience with Jim Young but on one condition." Herald said.

"And what's that?" Reighley asked.

"You promise to make Freya's birthday a memorable one, regardless of whether or not her father is there," Herald said.

"Heh. I planned on doing that anyway." Reighley stated. The two left the gas station and headed toward the Young family's estate.

Meanwhile, Officer Templeton was in Jim's office giving his report. When he entered, Jim turned in his chair and clapped several times to Templeton. Behind Jim, on his computer, were monitoring cameras of class 2-B. It was zoomed in on Reighley's distraught face.

"Well, well, well. Congratulations Templeton. Did you see the look on Reighley's face? Your suggestion of separating the two went just as you said. Look forward to a promotion in the near future." Jim praised.

Thank you, sir! Templeton saluted. *"Yes!"* Templeton pumped his fist. *"Finally! After all my hard work it finally paid off. My future as Mr. Young's right-hand man is just within arms reach.*

"Now that that punk is no longer classmates with my daughter, Freya should return to normal. Well. You can leave now. I'm a busy man."

"Of course sir!" Templeton answered and left as told. While walking away he had a flood of emotions rush through him.

"I'm only a few moments away from winning it all. It's so close… and yet… why don't I feel happy about it?" He thought.

("Perhaps we should stop for today..." Elise said.

"No. Not yet... I can do this... besides, I want to make her birthday a memorable one.")

Templeton recalled what he had heard prior. If Reighley was truly just using Freya, it didn't make sense for him to try so hard for her sake. Templeton began to doubt whether or not he was in the right in all of this. Would getting a promotion matter if it meant trampling on the innocent? His entire worldview was shaken to its core. It was so easy for him to despise Reighley because he thought he was a bad person, but no one would trip and fall, over and over again simply for someone else's happiness. Eventually, Templeton headed towards the exit of the mansion, and standing by the door drinking from a glass of wine was Prismarine. Once she had finished she lowered her glass and glared at Templeton.

"Just so you know, whatever you two are planning is affecting real people. Real lives. That is not something to mess around with." She said, "Also, Reighley is allowed at the party just so you're aware." She said scornfully.

"Understood," Templeton said as he walked past her and out the door towards his vehicle. As he began driving away he felt guilty. He had seen Reighley's criminal record and knew exactly what had happened to him during middle school and yet he couldn't call the boy he had seen today a violent criminal. Unsure what to do, he went home for the day.

Shortly after, Herald and Reighley arrived at Freya's home. Reighley was in awe to see such a place. It was magnificent beyond anything he had seen before.

"It's a bit weird to come over to Freya's house without her being here, especially since it's to speak with her father. Isn't that something you normally do when you ask for a marriage blessing?" A sudden thought stumbled into Reighley's head. *"What if he thinks I want to get married to Freya!? I'm not ready for that. I have too many women in my life to take care of right now anyway!?"* Reighley began to appear very worried and impulsively started to freak out a bit.

"Master Summers, calm yourself. There is no turning back now." Herald said. Reighley looked at Herald and nodded, taking a big gulp. He steeled his nerves as the vehicle pulled up to the entrance. The entrance was like a hotel. It had several pillars holding up an awning. With a built-in carport. The surrounding area was filled with hedge trees, neatly snipped, and flowers in full bloom. The mansion was massive. Reighley couldn't believe that it was all for one family. Finally, both Reighley and Herald exited the vehicle. Reighley looked down at his school uniform and began to wonder if even that was presentable enough for this household. He felt underdressed.

"Follow me," Herald said. Once inside Reighley could see that the interior was something out of a movie set. He felt like he was in a castle due to how fancy things were. Maids were scattered about, dusting and tidying things that already seemed spotless. In the foyer, the floor had a red carpet that led towards two spiral staircases, and the areas without a rug were clean to the point where you could see your reflection. Leaning on the wall next to the entrance doorway was a woman in a red gown who was drinking Moscato wine. Herald walked over to the mistress and whispered something to her. Suddenly, the mistress spit out her wine, losing what was left of her composure.

"Oh my, so you're Reighley. Freya sure knows how to pick'em, doesn't she? I'm Prismarine, but you can call me Mom, or Mother. It's nice to meet you, young man. I've heard all about you!" Prismarine said excitedly.

"It's a pleasure to meet you," Reighley said. *"Ahh! What should I say? What has Freya told her about? How should I conduct myself in front of someone of this status? Do I shake her hand, or should I kiss it? Never mind that's stupid. I'll go with a bow."* Reighley was like a robot in how he conducted his mannerisms but politely bowed.

"Relax, young man. There is no pressure here. Like I said. I've only heard good things about you from my daughter." Prismarine insisted. Reighley attempted to loosen up but it was difficult for him.

"Thank you," Reighley said.

"You know, you are the first boy my sweet Freya is serious about. She tells me all the time how sweet you are." Prismarine explained. Reighley could only turn red from embarrassment. Despite talking himself up, nothing could have prepared him for this. He looked towards Herald for help, but the butler ignored his glance.

"Thank you," Reighley said, again unsure what to say. He was simply as red as could be. Reighley was reminded of advice his mother gave him when looking for a future spouse.

"If you want to know what the girl you like will look like in twenty years, just look at their mother and that's what they'll turn into." He was surprised to see how true that was. Freya's mom looked exactly like Freya, just more mature. Reighley tried to picture in his head a life ten years down the road of what life would look like if he and Freya were together, but couldn't. The only image that went through his mind was the look on Freya's face when the two would inevitably call off their deal. It saddened him slightly, but also reminded him why he was here. To let Jim know what was going on.

"I would love to chat, really, but I need to speak with your husband about something important," Reighley stated. Prismarine's playful demeanor changed to a sober one. It was as if the comment burnt the alcohol that was in her bloodstream.

"You're going to ask for my daughter's hand in marriage!?" Prismarine asked.

"No, no, no! I was going to-" Reighley was interrupted.

"So you *don't* want to marry my daughter!?" Prismarine accused.

"No that-" Reighley tried to explain himself but it was like he was caught in a web of misfortune. He watched as

Prismarine let out a smile as if she got all the information she needed from him.

"Good. I expect you to treat her well and take good care of her for the rest of her life." Prismarine said.

"We aren't getting married!" Reighley covered his face in embarrassment and Herald could only hold back a laugh off in the distance.

"Oh whatever you say son-in-law" Prismarine teased. Reighley immediately understood where Freya got her teasing from and couldn't help but just accept the consequences of coming here. However, accepting it didn't make it any less unbearable. "Now in all seriousness. Be very careful what you say to my husband. He is, well... a very serious individual. I'll be cheering you on from a distance for sure," she advised.

Reighley lifted his head and nodded. "Thank you for the warning." Then he followed Herald upstairs. When he reached the top he saw a giant portrait of the Young Family hanging on the wall. Its frame had many grooves and etchings. In the photo was Freya who looked several years younger. She had a big smile on her face when it was taken and standing behind her was Jim who had a fake smile. Reighley had finally seen what Freya's father had looked like. He was only slightly taller than Prismarine in the photo and had black hair. He appeared to be a mix of Asian and caucasian, with a chin-strap beard. Seeing him beforehand didn't make any of this process less nerve-wracking. Eventually, the two made their way down an incredibly long hallway and Herald advised Reighley to wait outside of the door.

Jim was working inside his office. He was currently on the phone with an assistant preparing a flight for his next business trip. It was scheduled to last the rest of the work week.

"Yes. That should work just fine." Jim said. When Herald knocked on the door, Jim finished up his phone call quickly and hung up. "Yes?" Jim asked.

"It's me, Herald, Master Jim," Herald stated.

"Come in," Jim said. Herald entered and Jim got straight to the point. "What is it?" he asked with an annoyed tone.

"You have a guest wishing to speak with you," Herald informed.

"If it's Templeton, let him know I have nothing more to say to him." Jim turned away from the door. He assumed it was the officer returning to butter him up for a bigger promotion.

"It's someone you've never met before sir. It's Reighley Summers. He wishes to speak with you."

He turned back to Herald giving him his undivided attention. "Bring him in. Now." Jim snarled as he commanded.

"Yes sir," Herald said.

Meanwhile, Freya was riding along with Elise. The two had been driving around for quite some time. "Um...

Where are we going? We just missed our turn to go home."
Freya asked. Her woman intuition was tingling. She could
just tell that something was off as the two had been driving
for some time now.

"Oh, did we? My mistake..." Elise lied. She could
only stall for so long. The truth was that she was driving in a
large circle. Freya was usually on her phone during the rides
home so it was easy enough to distract her until now.

"Elise... What is going on?" Freya had a bad feeling.

"I was told to keep you out of the house for some
time. That is all I know." Elise lied again. She was convincing
though. These words left Freya feeling awful in the pit of her
stomach.

"Take me home, now!" She commanded.

"I'm afraid I cannot do that, Lady Freya," Elise said.
"This is all for your sake."

"What do you mean!? Is it about my outfit? Did
Herald tell you to make sure Jim left before I got home so he
couldn't see me dressed like this?" Freya said frustrated.

"No, it's-" Elise couldn't get a word out.

"I'm sick and tired of people doing stuff for my sake.
I can take care of myself! Now take me home." Elise paused
and let out a sigh.

"Alright... Very well, but don't say I didn't warn
you," Elise said.

"I'll be fine. He can't hurt me anymore." Freya
claimed. However, Elise knew that wasn't the truth. Freya
wasn't entirely broken by her father's actions. Elise truly

believed there was still hope to salvage things between the two.

Reighley walked into the office and stopped only after a few steps. The pressure in the room was immense. It was beyond anything he had ever felt before. He froze like a deer in headlights when he looked at Jim. There was a grim atmosphere in the room and it all stemmed from the aura that appeared before him. It was blood red. It felt like Reighley had a knife to his throat.

"Is this the type of person you need to be to be on top of the world? Does power make you cutthroat to an almost literal degree?" Reighley asked himself.

"You. Sit down." Jim ordered.

"That isn't necessary. I won't be staying for very long." Reighley answered. He stood in front of Jim's desk and couldn't help but think of the dream he had recently that was similar to this situation. The office was almost the same as the one he had dreamt about. The thought of Isebelle and Herald coming out of the corners of the room actually lightened the scenario for him.

"You have some nerves. Do you have any idea the amount of strife you have caused in my household? Don't think for one second that I don't know all about your little rampage in middle school. You spent an entire year in a juvenile detention center for what you did." Jim scorned. It was as if the knife held to his throat was pressing into his skin right out of the gate. "Let me make myself clear. I want you out of my daughter's life, is that understood?"

Reighley calmed himself, taking a quick breath. The thought of Freya being happy gave him courage. "Sir, that's what I'm here to talk to you about," Reighley said.

"What?" Jim asked, confused.

"I came here to tell you I planned on ending things with Freya after the birthday party," Reighley explained. "You're right. I am the cause of the problems that have been happening as of late, but I'm not the reason Freya has changed. You are." Reighley claimed.

"Excuse me…" Jim's face was expressionless.

"Freya just wants to spend a single day with you. Just one and yet you haven't made any time for her since before I met her. No one should go that long without their father showing they care! I know that better than anyone. You weren't there to see her face after you separated her and Destiny. Did you even consider that? Ripping her best friend away from her? I bet the thought didn't even cross your mind, did it?" The accumulation of his nerves over the situation, combined with the desire to protect Freya from going through the same ordeal as his sister, helped push back Jim's oppressive aura.

"This isn't about me! It's about her, and her happiness. It's about her father being there for her on her birthday. I don't want her to go through what my sister does each year, so do your job, but put your family first before you lose everything you hold dear." Reighley scorned. Every accusation directed at Jim had the conviction of a knife. Stabbing at the hurts that only a neglected child could know.

These words came unbidden to his lips as it was his own father that he saw before him.

After his outburst, there was silence in the room. Jim looked at Reighley with daggers for eyes and pointed towards the door.

"Get out," Jim said. His aura was stagnant. Like a silent wrath was about to unfold.

"Just because you ignored how she felt before, doesn't mean her feelings have stayed the same. That's why I am taking myself out of the picture. So there is no one else to blame but yourself. " Reighley said. "I'll see you this weekend," Reighley lifted a hand while walking to the door signaling he was heading out.

Reighley stepped out of the room and Herald was waiting for him with his fingertips placed on his forehead.

"Master Summers, that may have been the least tactful way to have approached that. I think you may have started a war." Herald said. He looked like he had a headache.

"Yeah, but we have to fight for those we care about, right?" Reighley asked.

"Well, said, but did I hear you correctly? You plan on ending things with Freya?" Herald questioned with concern.

"Yes. I think if I'm out of the picture, Jim will see that some of the problem is his fault." Reighley confided.

"I see..." Herald realized that being in the picture himself may have been part of the problem. He encouraged Freya's independence, only lessening her need for a father over the years. He considered Freya as a surrogate granddaughter, and let his personal feelings get in the way of the objective right decision.

"I think this is for the best…" Reighley said.

"It will be awkward at school you know?" Herald said.

"I'm aware," Reighley said.

"You've grown quite a bit over the past month young man." Herald commended him and turned to lead Reighley back down the hallway to the staircase. On their way out, Prismarine was still at the door waiting with a fresh glass of wine.

"So how did it go?" She asked.

"Not favorably. I wouldn't be surprised if I was never allowed to step foot in here again." Reighley answered.

"Reighley sweetheart, you are welcome here anytime you'd like. I don't care what Jim says." Prismarine encouraged.

"Thanks for having me." Reighley waved goodbye and he and Herald departed from the manor. By the time Freya had returned home, Jim was en route to the airport. Freya stormed into the house with her punk outfit on and looked around the lobby, paranoid.

"Oh, hi dear," Prismarine said. At this point, she was sitting on the floor leaning up against the wall. She had mascara running down her face. She was wrapped in a blanket so she stayed warm.

"Mom!" Freya said, rushing towards her side. "What happened? Are you okay?"

"Oh, it's nothing. Your father just left again. What about you? What's with your outfit? You could poke someone's eyes out with those things." Prismarine said while poking the tipped spikes on Freya's jacket.

"Let's put the wine away," Freya said, taking her glass and setting it aside.

"Aww is my baby going through a phase," Prismarine said while pinching Freya's cheek.

"It's not a phase Mom..." Freya claimed while picking Prismarine up off of the floor. "I'm rebelling. There's a difference"

"Oh yeah. Your boyfriend came over today." Prismarine said. Freya, out of pure shock, dropped Prismarine on the floor.

"He what!?" Freya shouted. "Oh... uh here sorry mom." Freya picked her mom up one more time. "Elise, can you help me?"

"Of course Lady Freya," Elise replied.

"Did you know about this?" Freya interrogated.

"Yes," Elise answered. She had no more reason to lie.

"He was so sweet. He told me he wished for my blessing to marry you!" Prismarine said.

"There is no way... He wouldn't do that, right? Marriage? I'm too young." Freya placed both her hands on her cheeks blushing. Elise caught the weight of Prismarine and offered her a shoulder.

"No. Reighley wished to speak with your father." Elise explained.

"With Jim? But why?" Freya asked.

"He came here to convince him to stay at your party," Elise said. Freya froze. No one had ever stood up to her father for her before. She had completely given up on him being there for her.

"*He did that for me?*" Freya asked herself. "*Why? I don't deserve that. He saw a problem and tried to fix it and didn't care about what would happen to him.*" Something stirred in Freya's heart. She couldn't believe someone would try to do something she thought was impossible. "*He really is a keeper, isn't he? We must be able to work things out between us right? I don't want to lose him after the deadline. He must feel the same way. Why else would he try this hard?*" Freya was halfway up the staircase when she slapped the cheeks on her face, strengthening her resolve. "*Alright. I've decided. I'll try to talk him out of the contract and remove the clock from expiring us.*"

Once in her room, Freya walked straight toward her bed and flopped down on it, lying on her stomach. She couldn't help but miss Reighley from not seeing him the entire day. "Ugh. I miss you." She said, looking at the photo of Reighley she stored on her phone. "Does that make me clingy?" Freya asked herself.

"Yes, but that is not a bad thing," Lily answered. She was cleaning Freya's room off in the corner before Freya had entered.

"Lily! Uh... how much did you hear?" Freya frantically asked.

"Oh my darling Reighley, how I've missed you," Lily said, imitating Freya.

"Hey, don't forget who you work for," Freya said with a grumpy expression.

"I see how it is." Lily pretended to scoff.

"I'm kidding. I would be miserable without you around Lily. Who else would do everything I need for me." Freya explained. Lily didn't answer. Instead, she became much more serious.

"Freya, I'm sorry. I wanted to apologize for not telling you in advance about Master Jim's plan."

"I'm not mad at you. It's not like you could have said no anyway." Freya sympathized.

"I know, but still." Lily frowned.

"Hey, just forget about it. Instead, how about you help me study for the midterms? I've been trying to teach class 2-D. Ulysses is in there you know."

"I... knew that already," Lily claimed.

"Don't break his heart, okay? He's a good guy and is trying his best to impress you." Freya suggested.

"I wouldn't plan on it," Lily confirmed.

Once Templeton arrived home, he fixed himself a TV dinner and imagined it was prepared by Ch@mberMade. However, while eating, something didn't sit right with him. The fact Jim was boasting about Reighley's face during the event in class 2-B bugged him. Templeton wanted to see for himself the look on Reighley's face when things went down. He was fairly lazy after a long workday so he kept his laptop he had on the couch. He picked it up and put it on his lap. Once he logged in, Templeton pulled up a video feed of class 2-B. He searched through the footage and quickly found the moment he was looking for. When he viewed the recording he zoomed in on both Freya and Destiny's faces when the event happened. Their faces looked horrified. Like someone had ripped the joy straight out of them.

"Wait… This isn't right… It… just hurt these girls… We just hurt these girls…" Templeton thought to himself. Templeton then zoomed in on Reighley's face and realized what he believed was a lie. The distraught on his face wasn't from being separated from Freya but came from him seeing the girls in pain. *"And yet, Jim only cared about what happened to Reighley."* Templeton was troubled. He couldn't let things stand as they were. So he sent himself the footage he had witnessed and logged out of the security feed.

The rest of the week went by and not a single student nor teacher had time to spend together due to a tremendous workload. When midterms finally ended. Lily was called into the teacher's office for questioning. She knew exactly why she was brought there. It was to see if she had caught Reighley cheating.

"Welcome Lily. Please, have a seat." Mr. Rugborn gestured towards a chair in the center of the room. Lily sat down and found herself surrounded by a multitude of staff and faculty members. Many seemed to be anticipating Lily's observations, with a few exceptions of course. Lily specifically noticed both the school's nurse and math teacher were displeased by the meeting. Behind the teachers was her boss, Jim Young up on a screen. He was watching in silence.

"Ms. Monet. Thank you for coming." Mr. Rugborn said. "We have some questions for you regarding your assignment. Are you ready to answer?"

"Yes," Lily replied.

"Well. Let's start with the first question. Did you notice any unusual behavior from Mr. Summers?"

"No," Lily said. She was straightforward and honest. She had fulfilled her job and took it very seriously.

"I see. Are you sure?" Rugborn pressed.

"Yes," Lily answered.

"What about during the tests? Did you perhaps see him with answers written up his sleeve, or with an extra piece of paper that no one else had?" Rugborn interrogated.

"No. He didn't have anything of the sort." Lily responded. She looked over towards Jim Young up on the screen and she noticed a dismayed look on his face. She found it unusual as Jim was a stoic individual, who rarely showed signs of worry.

"What about his phone? Did he check his cellular device, before, during, or after the test?" Mr. Rugborn was beginning to show passion behind the questions.

"No," Lily answered. After this, many of the adults in the room began to chatter with one another about the validity of this test.

"I think she's hiding something." Teacher A whispered.

"How do we know she isn't lying." Teacher B asked.

"What is up with these guys? It's like they can't accept 'no,' for an answer." Lily thought, attempting to hide her look of annoyance.

"Quiet!" Jim said. Immediately everyone hushed to the sound of his commanding voice. "Lily is a reliable source of information and for you to doubt her, is for you to doubt me."

"Of course, of course, Mr. Young, but let's be reasonable. The boy is a violent criminal, who just got lucky enough to be picked for this school."

"That isn't true!" Kaede exclaimed. "He earned his scores in this school and has maintained them since."

"It's true. Reighley hasn't dropped a single score point from the top spot in any curriculum." Cynthia announced.

"Oh, come on now. None of us were able to hold perfect scores above the board. It's simply not possible for someone like *him* to manage that. So, Ms. Monet, let me ask you a different question. Reighley, hasn't by chance, threatened to harm you if you spoke out about him, did he? You can be honest with us. You're in a safe environment. That's why you can't tell us right? Reighley said he would do terrible things if you exposed him." Mr. Rugborn questioned.

"Hey!-" Kaede shouted angrily.

"Mr. Rugborn!-" Cynthia was heavily upset by the claim. However, both Cynthia and Kaede were interrupted.

"No he did not, Mr. Rugborn." Lily corrected. The teachers were astonished. Everyone began to look around the room, hoping for someone to step in and say something that could prove Lily wrong, but none did.

"Tch! That can't be right. Ms. Monet, you can't be serious. Just be honest with us." Mr. Rugborn uproared.

"I think I've heard enough. Mr. Rugborn, the behavior you displayed this evening is beyond childish. That goes for all of you... Miss Clevens, Nurse Kaede, you did well to believe in our students. The boy in question, despite how you all feel about him, is not a cheater. End of discussion. That is all." Jim said, ending his transmission.

The teachers were left with a bad taste in their mouths as that wasn't what they had expected. They began to gossip to each other about the truth. Instead of chatting, Cynthia and Kaede walked to Lily.

"Thank you, Ms. Monet. You can go now." Cynthia bowed.

"No need to thank me. I only did as I was told. If Reighley was cheating, then I would have said he was."

"But you don't believe that he would, do you?" Kaede questioned.

"No... I do not." Lily replied.

"Then thank you for believing in him." Kaede bowed as well. Lily nodded and walked out of the room with new understanding.

"Geez, Reighley. It must be tough to have everyone against you. Well… not everyone I guess." Lily thought.

Jim was sitting in a hotel room highly irritated by the meeting that had happened. The conduct of his teachers was highly unprofessional. This bothered him because these were Freya's teachers. He had hand-selected them himself, and despite his better judgment, he chose poorly. Beyond that, Reighley's words looped again and again in his head. He kept thinking about all the times he picked up the extra shifts, extended business trips by another week, and pushed himself beyond limits all for his little girl. But one day, he had come home, and Freya wasn't little anymore. She was a teenager, and he had completely and utterly missed her childhood. Still, he blamed Reighley since he was the reason she was growing up so fast. Jim was on his laptop in the back of a personal taxi and looked through Freya's official social media posts on SocialLight. While scrolling, he found the one that advertised Freya's upcoming birthday. He looked at what time it started and calculated that he had less time than he thought. He would only be able to stop by for a brief thirty minutes before heading back to work.

"She'll understand when she's older," Jim reassured himself. He continued to scroll through the event page and noticed some of the attractions that would be available to those who attended.

(Sixteen Michelin Star: Gordan Romsly)

(Ballroom Dance: Formal Attire)

(Core Temperatures: Laser Tag)

(Ice Sculpture: Freya-Two)

(The One Hundred Zombie Run!)

The event that caught Jim's eye was the Zombie Run. It was said to have one hundred paid actors in professional makeup that would chase you down as you went from point A to point B. The winner of the race would get a single dance with Freya Young as she was the prize. This was an eye-opener for Jim.

"This is what she's spending all my money on? More importantly, what is that prize!? No one is allowed to dance with my daughter. Period." The thought of Reighley slow dancing with Freya ignited a burning fire inside Jim's soul. *"He mustn't make it to the end. How do I make sure that doesn't happen?"* Jim asked himself. He looked back at the details and had an idea come to mind. *"One hundred paid actors, huh?"* Jim pulled out his cell phone and made a quick phone call.

("Hello, this is One Hundred Armed Security. How may I help you?")

("This is Jim. I have a request to make to my security team.")

After the phone call, Jim noticed he had an email in his inbox that he had yet to open. A brief glance at the sender reminded him why he didn't bother to open it.

(From: Templeton.)

(Subject: Video Attachment.)

"That's odd... I thought this would be about his promotion." Jim thought. He clicked on the attachment and a video pulled up on his screen. It was footage of Freya. He

watched as his daughter became mortified by what was said to her and the camera tracked Freya as she screamed and exited the room. After, it showed Destiny and her reaction. The girl was almost in tears by the end. It was hard to watch. Jim remembered what Reighley had told him.

("You weren't there to see her face after you separated her and Destiny. Did you even consider that?")

"Tch!" Jim scoffed while closing his laptop.

Chapter 18

Her Birthday

Friday night came to a close, and it was time for the weekend. Freya's birthday party had been the talk of the net. Chat rooms were bursting with theories and talks about what was going to happen at the party. There was a small community of individuals pining over not being able to attend. The event was getting global recognition on the scale of the Velvet Carpet during their award ceremonies. This was of course due to Freya's announcement that she would reveal who her boyfriend was at the party. Everyone waited with bated breath barely able to conceal their anticipation for the stream to start.

(Stream Starts in: 01:59:99)

There were less than two hours before the party and Freya couldn't help but be nervous. Today she turned sixteen. It was her birthday and yet the only thing on her mind was what was coming after the party. She had never felt anxious like this before. Freya, Destiny, and the multitude of staff were at Fiore Gemello. The five-star restaurant the Young family had rented out for the evening. However, the building was more than just a restaurant. That was the first of the many events planned out for the evening.

"The countdown begins!" Destiny dramatically exclaimed. She looked over towards Freya, who appeared down and tapped her on the shoulder. "You okay?."

"Yeah… I'll manage," Freya replied. Her thoughts were elsewhere. *"Will I really be able to convince Reighley to stay? I can't just ask him without giving him a reason. I… have to tell him how I feel before the night ends."* Freya looked at the time and wondered what Reighley was doing at the moment. She had barely seen him all week thanks to midterms. The two would have an occasional lunch every so often, but Freya was too busy helping class 2-D with studying. She requested that Herald pick out a nice suit for Reighley to wear for her party. She wanted to be sure that he didn't spend the money that she had given him at the start of their relationship.

(Stream Starts in: 01:34:29)

Reighley was at home, currently in a black suit and tie. He was looking at himself in front of a mirror in the bathroom, mindful to avoid eye contact. He thought he looked quite nice, but still couldn't get his tie right. He tried to replicate what he had seen earlier in the week but it was no use.

"Need some help, sweetheart?" Jericho asked. She noticed Reighley in the restroom while passing by. He had left the door open. Jericho walked over to her son and turned him towards her to help him.

"Look how handsome my boy has become," Jericho said with a smile, tying the tie.

"Thanks, Mom." Reighley smiled back.

"You better watch out at this party. Those girls will be all over you. Don't forget to beat them off with a stick." Jericho laughed.

"As if. Most people at school are scared of me already." Reighley played along.

"Well, they shouldn't be. Also, be sure to take care of your sister. I'm counting on you." Jericho asked.

"I will," Reighley promised.

"Isabelle, are you ready?" Jericho shouted across the hall.

"I've been ready all week long! I can't wait for this thing." Isabelle said. Reighley sighed, he was coerced into bringing his younger sister to the party the moment she found out about it. She progressed very quickly from begging to blackmail. She began by saying things like "I'll never be able to live on if I don't go!" or "I have to know what fancy food tastes like. I'll stop waking you in the mornings unless you take me!" Reighley couldn't say no. Her happiness was the reason he had been working so hard. He knew that if things went according to plan, then this may be Isabelle's only chance to experience something like this. Normally he wouldn't blatantly spoil his younger sister but today was an exception. Freya was gracious enough to loan Isabelle one of her dresses that she had stored away, free of charge. Reighley suspected it was for some extra brownie points from his little sister but he couldn't help but be a cheapskate when the time called for it.

"Mow!" Morgana meowed, as he pounced on Reighley's shoe. Reighley looked down towards his feline friend and picked him up, being mindful not to get any shedding fur on his suit.

"Hey, little buddy. Sorry, I can't bring you today. I'll be sure to introduce you to Freya next time for sure." Reighley reassured. "Mom, take good care of Morgana while I'm gone." He said handing the cat to his mother.

"I will. Now go eat your dinner." Jericho said.

"And watch out for his claws," Reighley warned.

"Right…" Jericho said semi concerned by the advice. Reighley and Isabelle ate their meal together while Jericho kept Morgana away from the two.

"Not bad sis. Looks like I'll have to beat up some guys tonight." Reighley said while taking a bite. He was only partially kidding with her. He had come to realize that his sister was growing up fairly quickly and he needed to be wary of guys with bad intentions.

"Please don't go to jail again," Isabelle said.

"I won't," Reighley replied.

(Stream Starts in: 00:34:29)

Herald arrived at the Summers' family household and sent Reighley a text, notifying them that he had arrived. Freya made it clear that Reighley and his sister Isabelle were to be privately escorted to the party before others arrived. Freya planned on introducing him to the rest of the world but wanted to keep Reighley a secret as long as possible. It was to have him all to herself. She knew that if the world knew about him then girls were bound to covet him and competition was the last thing Freya wanted.

"Isabelle, come on, let's go. Our ride is here." Reighley ordered.

"Ahh!" Isabelle screamed.

"What's wrong?" Reighley looked as if his sister was struggling to pass through the hallway.

"I don't understand how girls wear high heels all day. It's like I'm walking on a tightrope." Isabelle complained.

"I think it's a bit much. A girl your age shouldn't be wearing something like-"

"Yeah, yeah. Just let me be pretty for once, okay?" Isabelle remarked with a snarking tone. Reighley loomed over his sister and let out a sinister chuckle.

"It would be such a shame if a gentle breeze were to come and knock you over," Reighley teased. He pretended like he was going to push Isabelle on the forehead slightly and knock her over.

"Hey! Don't-" Isabelle said. Reighley instead flicked her on the forehead and moved along. "Ouch! What was that for?" Reighley had seen her aura. It was that of a princess in a gown. He didn't want her to get in over her head. Becoming prideful before the party would cause issues. He knew the type of people that would be attending and it was inevitable that they would feel the same about themselves. He figured that sort of attitude would only lead to conflict.

"Be humble today. We don't want to embarrass Freya. She went out of her way to invite us to this, so let's not make our family look any worse than it does." Reighley explained.

"Yeah, yeah, all right," Isabelle said, slightly demoralized. After saying goodbye to their mom and Morgana, the two went out towards the limousine awaiting them on the side of the road. Once the two approached, Herald got out and opened the door for them.

"Wow, special treatment today I see," Reighley said to Herald.

"It's a special day. Besides, both you and your sister are guests of honor." Herald explained.

"Reighley, he's so cool! Can we have a butler?" Isabelle asked. She admired the gentlemanly aesthetic Herald gave off. Reighley internally shrieked at the suggestion, as he could only picture the emptying of his wallet as well as his life savings as a result of such a purchase.

"Yeah, no…" Reighley said, lightly guiding his sister into the vehicle. Right after, Herald took the gift bag Reighley had in his hand and took off and the two made their way to the party.

(Stream Starts in: 00:08:29)

Eventually, the three arrived at restaurant Fiore Gemello with eight minutes left to spare. Reighley began to feel like he was on the velvet carpet as there were a multitude of press, and fans waiting outside. The building was enormous. The restaurant itself had a fortified brick wall built around it. Reighley found it a bit excessive but the venue was essentially enclosed behind the castle walls. While driving by, famous people began to exit vehicles in a line one at a time down the carpet. Herald however had an entrance point where the limousine could enter without anyone spotting them. Reighley noticed that the paparazzi became ecstatic when a young man exited a vehicle. The teen had blonde hair and blue eyes and would flip his hair and pose every few steps forward like he was a runway model at a photo shoot.

"I've never seen this guy before. I wonder if he's a big deal or something?" Reighley asked.

"That is Deven Stallik. Freya's ex." Herald said.

"That guy?" Reighley got a glance at his aura while driving by. His aura was a burnt orange color and as enormous as his ego. Orange auras usually meant the person in question was very charismatic or good with words. The lighter the color the more altruistic the person was. The darker the colors the more narcissistic they would typically be.

"He looks obnoxious," Isabelle said.

"You would be correct. Freya only stayed with the boy for twenty-four hours before she lost all respect for him." Herald replied.

Reighley let out a laugh from the comment. *"I guess you don't need eyes like mine to see that, huh?"* Reighley thought. He still felt a tad bit insecure. *"Wait... am I jealous?"* There was something primal in him that caused his heart to ache slightly. Like he didn't want anyone else to have her. *"If I break up with*

Freya, is there a possibility she could date someone new immediately? Come on Reighley, you have to be strong... You already decided you were going to burn that bridge, so just enjoy tonight while it lasts." No matter what he told himself. The thought of Freya being with someone else ignited something in his heart that he could not extinguish.

The limousine pulled up to a side entrance of the building. There was a sliding reinforced garage door that kept unwanted guests out. Herald spoke into a speaker to the left of the vehicle and announced he was there. Shortly after, the door opened and the three entered the building. Once parked inside Herald opened the door for the two and the group proceeded to the venue doors.

"Reighley!" A voice said. Before Herald could open the main doors, Freya burst through them and lunged into Reighley's arms. He was genuinely surprised by this. He caught her and hugged her back.

"Happy Birthday, Freya." He said. Reighley fought the urge to flirt with Freya. Normally he would have said something like, "You missed me that much?" to her, but ultimately he held back because tonight was going to be hard enough as is.

"Wow, you must really have missed my brother, huh," Isabelle said. Freya was embarrassed but nodded to Isabelle.

"Come on Isabelle. You're not making this any easier." Reighley internally sighed.

"Well, yeah. We haven't had much time together thanks to midterms." Freya explained. Freya then turned towards Reighley who had just let go of her, and began to pout.

"*Ahh man, now what?*" Reighley observed her demeanor. He now had the opportunity to take her appearance in and she quite literally took his breath away. She truly went all out for the occasion. She was wearing an aquamarine gown with curls and spirals that unfurled into flowers that poofed outwards from her gown. The dress complimented her eyes.

"You look amazing," Reighley said honestly. Freya's expression switched to a joyful one, once she got the confirmation she was looking for.

"*Thank goodness... He thinks I look good.*" Freya thought to herself. She knew that looks alone weren't going to convince him to stay, but she hoped it would work in her favor.

"Freya. I'm nervous..." Isabelle said. She looked incredibly bashful. "What if they don't like me?" Freya paused and looked at Isabelle. She saw a person too scared to come out of their shell. She knew just the fix.

"Come on Isabelle, I have someone I want you to meet," Freya said while taking her hand. The two left Reighley and Herald in the dust and rushed towards the streaming equipment.

(Stream Starts in: 00:04:11)

Destiny was hard at work. She was performing at a producer level. Multitasking and micromanaging the stream as well as the production crew. She asked Freya not to worry about the setup involved. Freya knew full well that Destiny was quite capable of whatever she set her mind to, so she trusted her best friend and left it as is.

"Destiny, this is Isabelle." Freya introduced her. Destiny peaked her head out from behind a computer screen and noticed the young girl standing next to Freya. To her, she looked similar to Reighley, but if he was a girl.

"Freya. What did you do to Reighley?" Destiny exclaimed.

"Uh. This is Reighley's younger sister. I think the two of you would get along well." Freya explained.

Destiny took one long stare into Isabelle's eyes. Her intuition told her the young girl had a mischievous look hidden behind her eyes. Destiny envisioned a future where the two would make for an unstoppable team. By a single glance, she knew that the potential in this young girl was boundless.

"Come here youngling. You have much to learn..." Destiny beckoned, appearing to sound like a wise old woman.

"Thank you for having me!" Isabelle greeted. She walked over next to Destiny at her set up and Destiny put her arm around her.

"Listen up, kid. You and I are going to run this show!" Destiny claimed.

"Huh?" Isabelle was dumbfounded.

At this point, Reighley and Herald caught up, and Reighley took a look around the venue. Looking up, he realized there was no rooftop, just a see-through glass dome above. The floor was covered in a soft astroturf. The venue itself seemed like a convention center, separated into sections depending on what one wanted to do. The west section had the restaurant with Gordan Romsly cooking in the kitchen as well as other attractions like mini golf and laser tag. At the east section, there was a specific area closed off that led outside. The area was highly guarded. It had the length of an airport runway. It stretched about a mile long and was shot far beyond the rest of the building. Above the exit that led outside was a sign that stated, One Hundred Zombie Run. This immediately caught Reighley's attention over the rest of the things to choose from.

Coming from behind Reighley and Herald were Ulysses, Elise, and Lily. Lily was clinging to Ulysses's arm, holding him closely while the two were walking. Ulysses was tapping his fingers together, completely red as could be. The two were wearing matching outfits together.

"Hey dude!" Reighley noticed his friend behind him and waved.

"Help me. She won't let go." Ulysses began to mouth words silently toward Reighley.

Reighley noticed Ulysses was struggling and gave him the signature thumbs up that Ulysses would always give him.

"Good for you man." Reighley mouthed back. He only wished his predicament could be that simple and wholesome. It had been a while since everyone had been able to meet up like this. Reighley could only smile while it lasted.

(Stream Starts in: 00:00:15)

Freya grabbed a hold of Reighley's hand to make it clear to everyone that he was her boyfriend. She then looked at the young man standing next to her. For some odd reason that she couldn't explain, Reighley was almost glowing in her eyes. He was all she could think about. His smile warmed her heart. His cheeks had a blush to it that she hadn't noticed before. She was genuinely happy. It was like the two were a real couple. She knew she had to thank Herald for picking out such a nice outfit for him to wear. She made a mental note to have pictures taken of the two together before the zombie run.

(Stream Starts in: 00:00:01)

"Attention everyone. Open the gates!" Destiny shouted as the stream started. The staff did as they were told and Destiny couldn't help but take pride in the fact she had power over the staff. Destiny pulled out a wireless microphone and began commentating. Isabelle was in awe of Destiny. "All right, stream! It's ya girl, DJ Destiny! We have a multitude of events here! I'm here with my co-star, Frizzy Izzy. Can I get some excitement in the chat!?" Destiny pulled Isabelle next to the camera, and put up a peace sign. Isabelle became incredibly shy and could only wave.

Charlie_SL: OMG! She is so cute!

Assassin_Freed: I know her! She is from my school!

Apollo_Sky: HYPE! HYPE! HYPE!

Marine_Fan: Where is R?

The chat became ecstatic as the giant doors opened up allowing those at the entrance to come inside. Reighley recognized some faces from school entering the venue, but the majority of people he didn't know. A strange phenomenon occurred to him. It was as if everyone's collective aura were floating above the room. It was as if the northern lights were indoors.

"That's... odd." Reighley thought to himself. He realized the color represented the atmosphere of the party itself. Unsurprisingly, the lights were purple.

Most of the people he didn't recognize. For each person that entered, that was on the list, Destiny announced them to the audience.

"Known for his lady killer looks, here comes the boy wonder. Deven Stallik!"

Reighley watched as Deven Stallik walked in. He glanced at Reighley and gave him a side-eyed glare as he walked past.

"What's his deal?" Reighley whispered to Freya. He already knew that he was competition but wanted to know what Freya thought of him.

"He's an actor in my movie. Don't worry about him. I only invited him here for the clout." Freya reassured him, squeezing his hand tighter.

"Our next guest is someone I know you love. Here she is. The Symmetrical Savant. The Ice Queen of the Hill.

Guinevere Pendragon!" Destiny announced. She then put her microphone up to Isabelle's face and asked her a question. "Frizzy Izzy, what's your thoughts on this guest?"

"I think she is very pretty." Isabelle quietly responded.

"You heard it here first, folks. However, there can only be one queen here tonight. Let's turn our attention to the guest of honor. The mean, red, not green, crimson darling of the screen. Freya Young!" Destiny pressed a button that switched the camera over to Freya and Reighley. "Oh, and what's this? Who is that stranger standing next to her? Is that… the mysterious R!?!?!" The chat began to overflow with responses. The viewer count had skyrocketed to over one hundred and fifty thousand.

"Freya, what's the big idea… You know I didn't want too much attention drawn towards me." Reighley whispered.

"Just smile and wave. Starting today, you're my official boyfriend." Freya quietly explained.

Guinevere walked towards Freya and Reighley and looked above their heads. She used *Reverie* to read their thoughts.

"*Now everyone can see how serious I am about you…*" Freya thought.

"*Ugh… I know what you're trying to do… You want me to stay after tonight, right?*" Reighley thought.

"Hmph!" Guinevere turned away after she read their thoughts. She then strutted towards the venue. "*Hah!*

401

Reighley's feelings are already beginning to waver. Looks like I'll have my chance to steal him tonight after all." Guinevere thought.

Once the rest of the guests entered the venue, Destiny briefed the audience on the events that were to happen tonight. First Freya had her photo taken next to her ice sculpture. She struck different poses for quite some time. Anyone who wished to have their photo taken with Freya had to wait in line.

"Not your typical birthday party is it?" Reighley asked. He stood next to Ulysses and Lily.

"No, it's not. This is the life she lives outside of school. She's always busy." Lily answered.

"You'd better start getting used to it, young man," Prismarine said sternly walking up to Reighley.

"Ah! Mrs. Young." Reighley began to panic again.

"Again, that's mom to you." She said, smiling towards Reighley. "Look at my daughter. Isn't she just the prettiest little thing?"

"Yep... She sure is..." Reighley complacently agreed.

"My husband should be arriving shortly. I'm not sure what you said to him, but his opinion of you seemed to have changed a bit." Prismarine explained. "Good work."

"Seriously?" Reighley was surprised. He half expected some sort of assassin hit to be placed on him. He figured it would be Herald who would end up putting him six feet under. As he considered he glanced nervously at the driver.

"Next thing on the menu, pun intended, is dinner!" Destiny announced. Everyone made their way to the west wing where the restaurant was located, and took their seats. Ulysses, Lily, Isabelle, Freya, and Reighley were all seated together and ordered their food.

"Could I join you?" Ash Fjord asked. She had arrived late due to work but had just got off in time.

"You came!" Freya replied. "Please have a seat." Freya was beginning to have her doubts whether or not Ash would show up or not. She felt very proud that she was able to mend the first of many friendships. Ash took a seat at the table and many people began to snarl at her for having the audacity to sit with Freya. "Don't worry about them." Freya reassured her by hugging her. She whispered in her ear, "Truly, thank you for coming. It means a lot." The group began to eat a twelve-course meal and laugh together throughout it. Isabelle got her wish and was able to try fancy food. It put a huge smile on her face.

"Freya, you are the best sister ever!" Isabelle hugged her. She then gave her a sinister glare towards her older brother. One that openly read, "If I lose this, you'll regret it."

Reighley let out a sigh and reluctantly ate his dinner. *"Isn't this a bit overkill?"* He thought. *"I don't think I could get used to this life..."*

"Ah, shoot." Destiny was in a pickle. She realized she had overscheduled the amount of things that were going to happen for tonight. She muted herself on the stream and began to brainstorm on how to fix the problem at hand.

"What's wrong?" Isabelle asked.

"There isn't enough time," Destiny said, handing the schedule over to Isabelle. "We only have the venue for a few hours tonight. Gifts are next, but just looking at them tells me that it's going to take way longer than expected." Isabelle took the pamphlet from Destiny and gave it a look. She was right. If things kept going as is, they would fall way behind schedule. She looked at the events and an idea came to mind.

"What if we combined these two into one," Isabelle asked.

"Isabelle. You're a genius." Destiny praised. Eventually, dinner came to a close and the group heard the commentator speak once again.

"I have an announcement to make!" Destiny said. "I'm sure you all have been looking forward to the Core Temperature's Laser Tag, and the Zombie Run. Our dear friend Frizzy Izzy came up with the idea to have both at the same time! What's better than running from zombies? Shooting them! Remember to keep your eye on the prize kids. Literally. For those who do not know, the winner of the zombie run gets a slow dance with Freya Young."

"What!?" Freya choked on her food. She cleared her throat and whispered, "I didn't agree to this. Destiny!"

"Why couldn't tonight just go smoothly?" Reighley thought. The thought of anyone else dancing with Freya bugged him to no end. He knew he couldn't continue to feel this way if he were to go through with his plan. In the middle

of his thoughts, Reighley felt a hand grab a hold of his shoulder.

"Hello, son." The voice said menacingly. Reighley saw Freya's reaction and looked upward, only to have his heart drop. It was Jim tightly gripped onto Reighley's shoulder and he bent down to whisper in his ear.

"You have no chance of winning, kid," Jim said maliciously. He then stood back up and waved towards his daughter.

"Happy Birthday, Freya," Jim said. Freya rolled her eyes at her dad, with no response. She then looked towards Reighley who was glaring at her. She couldn't tell if he was asking for help or genuinely wanted her to say thanks, still she reluctantly replied.

"Thanks, Jim," Freya said angrily. Immediately Jim let go of Reighley's shoulders and walked towards Herald.

"Herald, make sure the team is ready," Jim commanded.

"As you wish sir," Herald replied and quickly made his way towards the closed-off zombie run area.

Lily and Ulysses were also sitting at the table eating with the group when a concern entered Lily's mind.

"Are you going to participate in the run, Ulysses?" Lily asked

"I need to help my bro," Ulysses said. *"Let's go! I said six words to her."* Ulysses thought.

"I see... You better not win, okay?" Lily frowned while she asked.

"Why would I want to dance with Freya when I have you." Ulysses agreed. Lily was swooned by this comment even though Ulysses had no intention of being smooth when he said it.

"All right party people! It's time for gifts! We have to let your stomachs settle a bit before the Apocalypse Run!" Destiny announced. All the attendees stood around Freya handing her gifts as one by one, she opened them. She received a multitude of extravagant gifts. Some families offered her unlimited access to their establishments, while others bought her designer clothes. Now and then Freya would look over towards Reighley.

"I wonder what he got me?" Freya thought. It was the only thing on her mind. The gifts she was receiving became more over the top as the night went on. From her first vehicle from her parents to a private island resort that belongs entirely to her. Still, she couldn't help but wonder what Reighley had got her. She made the internal decision to like whatever it was that he got for her regardless of the price. She would treasure it, just like her bracelet. She knew he was thoughtful, but also knew that she didn't *need* anything. Reighley however had his present for Freya in a small box in his back pocket. He thought it would be fitting to save the best gift for last, not for the dramatics, but as a parting gift.

"There really is no end to all that wealth, huh?" Ulysses said. He had walked up next to Reighley. He was sweating profusely through his white tuxedo.

"Yeah… It seems that way." Reighley agreed.

"Would you be with her, even without all that money involved," Ulysses asked.

"To be completely honest. The money is nice and all, but it complicates things. Too much drama. Like even this suit for example. It isn't mine. I didn't pay for it. I would rather she had been poor when I met her, but none of that matters after tonight."

"What do you mean, Aniki?" Ulysses questioned.

"After tonight Freya and I won't be dating," Reighley explained.

"What? Why?" Ulysses was astonished.

"It's for the best. She and I belong to different worlds. I can't be the source of her happiness. Things need to be right in her own home before anything else. I'm just in the way." Reighley explained.

"I... don't know what to say to that," Ulysses commented.

"Well. You are the only one I've told this to. I trust you not to say anything to anyone else." Reighley said.

"Dude, as your best friend... I won't tell a soul. However, I would like to at least try and give you advice. It's okay to be a little selfish sometimes. I know we haven't been friends for long but I can tell that you always are putting others before yourself. I know it's against your nature to think of yourself first, but you should know by now that no one is going to hate you for it." Ulysses said. Reighley paused and took into consideration what Ulysses said.

"I think I am being selfish, this time at least," Reighley said.

"Well… then… I got your back no matter what." Ulysses said, placing a sweating hand on the back of Reighley's suit.

"So… what about Lily? I see she finally let go of you." Reighley questioned.

"She went to the bathroom, and it's a good thing too. I was having trouble just breathing with her that close to me. I don't know how I'm going to slow dance with her in front of everyone." Ulysses said. "And look at my armpits, I'm sweating just thinking about it!" he said, slightly raising his arms.

"Don't worry man. You'll do just fine, I'm sure." Reighley said.

"Thanks… I'm going to freshen up." Ulysses said as he scurried off to the restroom. Reighley waved his friend off and then after a moment looked back into Freya's eyes. This is the thing that had him worried all night. Her aura. It was two of her streamer-like arrows that formed a giant purple heart aloft above her head. Several other arrows pointed directly at him. He had never felt affection directed towards him at this scale before. It made him begin to worry.

Chapter 19

Apocalypse Run

Reighley felt a tap on his shoulder. He turned around and saw Ash Fjord standing behind him. Reighley could tell at first glance that Ash was happy she came to the party. She was sipping on green tea and had a grin on her face that told him everything he needed to know.

"Glad to see you made it." Reighley greeted.

"I have you to thank for that. Heaven knows that Freya is often stuck in her ways. Whatever it is that you've been doing to help Freya out, keep doing it." Ash said. Looking into her eyes and using his *Insight*, Reighley saw Ash's aura. It was a calm turquoise. Its aura itself had a shape to it for once. It had an assortment of small river-like flows that poured into her from outside of the aura. From it was tranquility. He could tell she was truly laid back and at peace with being here. It made him wish he could be as lax and worry-free as her.

"I didn't do anything," Reighley said. "Freya made those changes on her own."

"Come on. You have to take some credit. She and I were like mortal enemies before you showed up." Ash exaggerated.

"I don't think that's real." Reighley laughed. "What about the others? Hear anything about their opinion of Freya?"

"Well… to be honest. Matilda warned me not to come here. She said I would be publicly embarrassed in front of everyone." Ash said.

"Yikes," Reighley stated.

"Samira and Yula on the other hand haven't spoken poorly of her or anything. I think they will have a change of heart if Freya reaches out to them." Ash explained.

"Freya just wants to make things right, you know?" Reighley said.

"Yeah. I've seen the change in her. I believe that is thanks to you." Ash said.

Reighley was curious about something. He remembered the time when he used his *Insight* to dissect the colors from Lily's aura and wondered if he could do that on Ash's. With only a thought about doing so, it worked. Ash's aura separated into two. He already knew what the result was going to be as blue and green were the obvious answers, but his experiment worked.

Freya had an instinctive reaction to become jealous. She was watching Reighley chat with Ash, and although she was happy Ash had shown up to the party, seeing Reighley speak with any girl made her feel overprotective of what was hers. Her immediate thought was an accusatory one.

"*I can't believe after inviting her out here she goes and flirts with Reighley.*" Freya thought. However, Freya caught herself in the middle of this thought process. She remembered the last time Reighley had spoken to girls, and her reaction at that time only worsened their relationship. She knew she couldn't jump to conclusions. Freya swallowed her pride and calmed her emotions.

"*I... have to trust him.*" Freya thought. "*I know he isn't flirting or anything, but still... I can't help but want him all to myself.*" At this moment, it was as if every guy who was at the venue was invisible to Freya. Everyone except for Reighley. They couldn't have gotten her attention even if they tried. "*I can't control everything that he does and I can't just overreact like last time, otherwise that will set me back to square one with him. I want to be a girlfriend he won't be embarrassed to have around him. I have to become someone he can be proud to have around his friends.*" Freya patiently waited for Reighley and Ash to finish talking as she watched from the distance, while unwrapping gifts, with a less-than-pleased reaction from them.

Eventually, gift wrapping came to a close and Freya was at her limit. In all honesty, she could have cared less about the presents she received. She was grateful nonetheless as that would be rude not to thank those who went out of their way to do something for her, but to Freya, it was the equivalent of receiving a gift from one of her father's business partners. It was a nice gesture but they all lacked sincerity. Not to mention she would most likely never use them. All she really wanted was to be alone with Reighley and go on a second real date with just the two of them. Freya's thoughts were interrupted by the commentator. However, it was not Destiny this time around.

"Check, check… is this thing on?" Isabelle asked while tapping her hand on the microphone several times.

"Yep. It's on. You got this." Destiny said.

"Okay. It's me, Frizzy Izzy, and I'm here to announce it's time to get ready for the Apocalypse Run…" Isabelle said. She still had her coy demeanor, but she attempted to give it her best shot. The chat could not help but fawn over how cute she was. Reighley, however, could only give himself a facepalm as he knew the repercussions of becoming famous were not going to be good for his younger sister.

"*Her ego is already huge, as is…*" Reighley thought with a sigh.

"Good work, my lovely co-host. Now, all of those who are participating in the Run please make your way to the changing room. There, uniforms and equipment have been provided for you. Afterward, line up at the starting line and get ready for the fight of your life!"

"*I really, really, hate running.*" Reighley thought. He looked over at Freya who was still the center of attention and using *Insight*, saw that her aura had shifted along with her eyes. Both were moving and directing him to participate in the run. "*There is no way out of this, huh,*" Reighley asked himself. He knew this was something he must do, in order to give Freya the best night. He also couldn't justify learning how to dance just for someone else to slow dance with Freya before him. *"All right. I'll do it, but only because she wants me to."* He lied to himself to bolster his resolve.

Both men and women alike made their way backstage to the changing room. Before arriving, all participants had to sign a waiver indicating that the run was not responsible for any injuries. Freya signed and then disappeared from the crowd for the duration. She went to a disclosed area to get ready. Once their paperwork was taken care of, Reighley and Ulysses both quickly got changed.

"Freya made sure to get something in my size," Ulysses said, shedding a single tear of appreciation.

"This gear seems very... fitting," Reighley said. He and every other contestant were given a briefcase with their name on it. Inside on the bottom was an outfit, while their equipment was hooked to the top of the interior. Reighley's clothing was ripped linen and torn cloth. He strapped on knee and elbow pads as well as a vest. The vest had the letter Z spray painted on it. He then pulled his laser tag gun out. It appeared that the L for "laser" on the weapon was now a red Z. He could tell it was an impromptu switch at the last minute. He gave his outfit a good look in the mirror and couldn't help but feel cool. He used his hand to block out the reflection of his face. He had always wondered if he would do well in a Zombie Apocalypse. He was self-aware that he didn't have typical leadership qualities. He knew his strengths were his ability to come up with solutions on the fly, as well as being extra critical about survival choices. As far as speeches go, charisma was something he lacked.

"Wow, the production crew went all out," Ulysses said. He was wearing a black unbuttoned trench coat, with a black shirt and matching cargo pants. He wrapped a headband around his forehead as well. He strapped on the same equipment as the rest and walked up next to the mirror with Reighley. "Yo, Aniki. Check it out, man. I look like I'm ready for anything!"

"You look like a juggernaut." Reighley complimented. Ulysses flexed in the mirror and the fibers of his coat began to stretch to their absolute limits. Tears could be heard from the coat.

"Such filthy wretched outfits. Please, do stay out of my way. I plan on taking the prize right from under your feet Mr. R." Deven said.

"Uh... what? Are you talking to me?" Reighley asked.

"Oh. So you don't know. You must have been living under a rock. That explains why that outfit looks so fitting on you." Deven flipped his hair. He was wearing an orange track uniform that had not a single spec of dust or grime on it. "You've been the talk of the town for the past few weeks. The whole internet had been waiting to find out who Freya's boyfriend was. She called you R. I too was very interested in the person Freya Young ended up choosing. Personally, I was disappointed."

"I guess some people can look good in anything. "Reighley replied snarkily. "Have you ever met Guinevere? You guys would be perfect for each other." He couldn't care less what Deven had to say. He couldn't believe someone could exceed the self-entitlement he experienced from Guinevere.

"I have no interest in the Ice Queen," Deven answered. "Besides, if Freya knows what's good for her, she'll dump a loser like you and get back with me."

"Yeah, and hopefully your next attempt will last longer than twenty-four hours," Reighley commented. Ulysses was watching the two converse back and forth. He hadn't realized how bold Reighley had become as of late.

"Whatever. You'll regret speaking to me this way when I steal your girl." Deven threatened.

"That was pretty cringe," Reighley said. Deven stuck his nose up until he saw Jim standing nearby. His demeanor was like someone who acted like a teacher's pet. He headed towards Jim, ready to clean his boots if he needed to.

"Oh! Mr. Young! It's an absolute honor to meet you, sir." Deven said.

"Who are you?" Jim asked.

"My name is Deven Stallik. I'm just someone who admires your hard work ethic and diligence. I would love to work under you someday. Freya and I have a history you know." Deven complimented.

Jim looked the boy up and down and saw how pompous the kid was. Deven's outfit was an expensive one from a rival company. He knew his sincerity was disingenuous.

"Leave us," Jim said coldly.

"Certainly... Don't forget to contact me if you need an intern!" Deven scurried off. Despite his attempts to plead with Jim, he was terrified by the look he had just been given.

"Great... I have another punk kid I have to worry about." Jim said. He walked up to the two boys and straightened up his tie. Jim was still in his dress attire. "Hello, Ulysses. How are you doing son?"

"Oh! Hello Mr. Young. I'm doing well. Thank you for asking. And about Deven, I don't think you'll have to worry about him." Ulysses replied, abruptly ending his flexing in the mirror.

"Good. Your mother and I were just chatting the other day. She said you had grown quite a bit since the last time I saw you." Jim stated.

"You spoke with my mom?" Ulysses asked.

"Yes, and your father as well. You look a lot like him." Jim said. Reighley looked over at Jim with confusion. He noticed that Jim only put on the vest and pads for safety, but left the outfit to the side.

"You're not going to get changed?" Reighley asked.

"I have a meeting after the run. I'm just here to make sure no one else wins." Jim said as he holstered his Z-blaster in his belt buckle and walked out the door to the runway.

Reighley was hoping to use *Insight* to get a feel of what Jim was thinking, but he didn't have a chance to as Jim never once looked Reighley in the eyes.

It was finally time for the event to start. All the contenders lined up at the starting line. The track had a multitude of obstacle courses thrown in the way. Fake houses were set up for looting, as well as broken-down cars. The stop signs that were placed had additional things written on them like "STOP, TURN BACK". It was almost believable. There was an eerie feeling in the atmosphere that came from a single question in everyone's minds except for Jim.

"Where are the Zombies?" The participants thought.

Meanwhile, hidden and scattered about the runway, were the 100 security guards now dressed as zombies. They were added to the run last minute by Jim Young.

"Omega Z Squad, this is Alpha Leader with the Delta Z Squad. Do you copy? Over." The Alpha Z and Delta Z squads were crouched behind a house while performing radio talk.

"Omega leader here. We hear you loud and clear Alpha Z. We are with Epsilon Z Squadron. Over." Omega Z and Epsilon Z squads were on top of high points, like artificial trees and or buildings.

"Make sure you let your men know that *Zed said* we needed to go all out on this mission. No one gets past the finish line. Period. So no holding back, is that clear? Over."

"Copy that. Over."

Reighley noticed that everyone's attention diverted from the mile-long street back to the venue, as a group of people came from it. It was Freya and class 2-D. They all walked in unison towards the starting line. Jim's jaw could only drop from seeing what his daughter was wearing. She looked like a biker leading her gang. They all had matching black spiked gear on to match their outfits.

"Freya! What is the meaning of this?" Jim tried to stop Freya in her tracks but was completely ignored by her. Freya walked past Jim, towards Reighley and placed a hand on his shoulder.

"So… what do you think?" She asked. Reighley looked into her eyes and used *Insight* to see her aura. It looked sporadic in nature. Like electricity was flying chaotically from it. He thought the way she acted was similar to when she first asked him out at school. However, this time he didn't mind it as much. Instead, it sort of worked on him as he became flustered by her touch.

"You… look… uh… strong and independent?" Reighley said. *Insight* broke as he had trouble looking her in the eyes. *"She's too close…"* Reighley thought. He felt like the best way to describe her was like Freya had been slapped by a punk metal album. However, Reighley preferred Freya in her flowery gown.

"Freya. What on earth are you wearing and who are these people? Did you hire actors to come out on display?" Jim asked. Freya turned towards her classmates, completely ignoring her father.

"Just ignore Jim, he has a bad habit of judging people by appearance and not by their character," Freya said, looking back at Reighley.

Suddenly it all made sense to Reighley. Freya was trying to use him and her classmates as an act of rebelliousness towards her dad. He guessed it was her way of saying she wanted to be with him regardless of what her father wanted. He had to stop this. He didn't like the feeling of being used by her to get back at her dad.

"This is getting unhealthy..." Reighley thought. "That's enough," Reighley said quietly. He gently grabbed her wrist and moved it off his shoulder.

"What?- What's wrong?" Freya frantically asked.

"You shouldn't disrespect your dad in front of all these people," Reighley said as he looked at the crowd of people watching. "These are his coworkers and his friends," Reighley said quietly to her.

"But... you're supposed to be on my side-" Freya was interrupted by the speakers outside. From it, the commentators interrupted the two.

"All right, survivors! It's do-or-die time! DJ Destiny here will explain the rules." Isabelle announced. A projector screen that displayed Destiny and Isabelle was cast on a nearby wall. The two were standing parallel together and had fake blood splatters on their faces. Destiny had put on her blue biker jacket to show her support to Freya and Isabelle was wearing a similar jacket but was in her favorite shade of pink.

"Okay runners, listen and listen closely because I'm only going to tell you this once. There is a whole horde of infected people up ahead of you. The only way forward is through! You'll have your trusty Z-blaster at your side to help get you there. The infected are wearing suits that will indicate whether or not you shot them and will flash red on a hit. Each zombie has a fixed amount of bullets he or she can take, and that number is not displayed. Once a zombie has been shot past that point, their suits will display a red color indicating they are dead, locking up the body suit for the remainder of the run. Your suits are similar. If you get tagged by a zombie, your suit will light up green. Assuming you escape the zombies' grasp, you have one minute from that point to find a sterilizer to neutralize the infection. Know that the timer will not reset even after you heal up, so if it took you thirty seconds to find and administer first aid, you only have thirty more seconds to find your next for the remainder of the run. Keep in mind ammo is limited. One Z-blaster magazine carries twelve charges. The houses ahead have all sorts of loot, like other weapons, but don't take too long because there is only one winner. Last but not least, friendly fire will be disabled for the first half of the run; however, once you reach the Dead Man Zone, it's game on." Destiny said, wiping the sweat from her brow. "You got anything to add, Frizzy Izzy?"

"Yes and good work DJ Destiny. Be wary survivors. The trials ahead of you are broken into three sections."

Drones began to cover the skies giving a birds-eye view of the course. The screen showed the location the runners were starting and had a tag on it that said 'Area One'. The drones panned across the first section and showed broken down vehicles, and houses with crushed rooftops, and stopped at a roadblock. "The first zone is called Dead Residents. It is where the majority of your loot is going to be found. Keep a watchful eye as the undead can reside anywhere in and outside these houses."

The image switched to 'Area Two' showing a military base that covered the entire path. One of the drones showed a med bay area, and another showed a gun vault. "The second zone is the Risen Army Base! There won't be much loot lying around, instead, the best equipment will be located in the gun vault and med bays. Keep in mind there is no way around this structure. You'll have to navigate your way through and get to the final zone."

The drones then switched to 'Area Three'. The display showed a wasteland of scorched earth. Many of the buildings were burnt down and the area gave off an abandoned western theme. "This is the Dead Man Zone. Where player versus player is allowed. It's the last and most dangerous of obstacles between you and victory. Survivors, please heed my warning... There is one zombie you must avoid at all costs. They call him Z.E.D. You'll know him when you see him." Isabelle added. The display changed to a blackened silhouette of an incredibly muscular person briefly, only to switch back to the girls. "You all signed the waiver before coming right? We are not responsible for any injury sustained by this. Also please refrain from assaulting your other contestants as that will result in instant disqualification."

"I couldn't have said it better myself." Destiny nodded. "All right, you guys have five minutes to get in places before we start."

Right after Reighley looked back at Freya.

"Wow... she's really getting into it, isn't she?" Reighley said lightly. He tried to change the subject as Freya's expression was progressively flashing from confused, to hurt and coming to a rest on upset.

"Reighley..." Freya muttered with her head down.

Reighley looked over Freya towards Jim and noticed agitation from the man. However, it was different this time. Reighley didn't need his *Insight* to see the pain Freya inadvertently caused her father by seeking comfort from someone other than him. Reighley could see the disheartening look in Jim's eyes become more permanent. Reighley looked back at Freya and lifted her chin upward. Her eyes were vulnerable.

"Hey... keep your head up. I am on your side." Reighley replied.

"I hope you win," Freya said. Reighley realized he would have to address Freya's actions later. This one hurt him. Seeing her like that was incredibly difficult for Reighley. He realized he was failing at making tonight a good night for Freya.

"We're on your side too." Ulysses chimed in. Ash, Herald, and Ulysses walked up to the two.

"Yeah. We'll do whatever we can to make sure Reighley gets across the finish line." Ash said. She was holstering two Z-blasters and wearing a cowgirl hat and a sheriff's outfit.

"Howdy partner. Where did you get the second blaster?" Freya asked.

"Oh, I just asked some guy to give me his so I could have two. He gave it up after I sweet-talked him a bit." Ash explained.

"Smart gal," Freya said.

"Wow. Poor guy. I hope he can run fast." Ulysses said.

"Hey. Sometimes you have to take advantage of the womanly charm given to ya." Ash said. "And Reighley, you should be a little more concerned about the competition. Look around. Everyone has their eyes on you." Reighley took a look down the starting line in both directions and noticed that faces, both familiar and unfamiliar to him, were all competitively looking at him.

"Looks like I'm common enemy number one..." Reighley said. He looked over and noticed someone in particular was glaring at him. It took him a second to recognize who the stranger was but after a moment Reighley realized it was Guinevere's butler.

"Don't worry about him, Master Summers. I will handle it. From one butler to another." Herald said. "You just worry about getting to the finish line."

"Boss, Odysseus Sir, what do you want us to do?" The red headband student of class 2-D asked. Class 2-D were up and arms ready to fight. They had all come fully prepared to fight for Freya. Freya looked towards Ulysses and nudged him on.

"Go on, give them an order, 'Odysseus.'" Freya said. Ulysses stopped and looked towards his friends and knew he could do anything if it was for them.

"We'll protect Reighley with our lives!" Ulysses ordered.

"You heard the man! Let's show these zombies why they call us the misfits of Gilford High." The headband student said.

"Sir, yes sir!" Class 2-D cheers.

It was time. Five minutes had almost passed and as the contestants lined up, Destiny and Isabelle began to count down in unison.

"All right survivors, the run starts in 3... 2... 1... Go!" The two girls said. At that moment the 200 contestants who were lined up, took off down the runway. There were several houses nearby, many looked to be abandoned. Some contestants headed directly down the center of the track while others took a rather methodical method by attempting to scavenge loot in nearby houses.

"Here goes nothing… Come on guys let's go!" Reighley said as the group began to follow him. Reighley knew that he would have to come up with a plan while on the move. *"What would be the best strategy for success?"* He quickly began to attempt to calculate his odds. *"What should I do? Think Reighley, think! No precedent for the infected has been set as of yet. We don't know anything about them as of yet. Each person only has twelve bullets in their Z-Blasters and we have thirty-three members in our group. The group consists of Class 2-D, which includes Freya and Ulysses. Add on Herald, Ash, and I, and in total that is three hundred and ninety-six charges of ammunition. That combined with Ash's additional gun she managed to snag off a contestant makes a total of four hundred and eight charges. That is plenty to start, the only problem is, we don't know what the average bullet count is to take out a zombie. We don't know the effective range or accuracy of our current weapons. Also, more people we have means less loot to split between the group."* This was all happening in the span of ten seconds. Finally, Reighley decided on what to do. "All right, here's the plan. Hey headband guy?" Reighley shouted. He wasn't sure if he could lead everyone or not, but he had to try.

"Yes? Also, my name is Arend Selkie, Sir" Arend replied.

"Okay, Arend. You and the rest of class 2-D go on ahead and take out as many infected as possible, but don't get eliminated. Try to thin the herd while gathering information. Retreat if you have to. Freya and Ulysses, you come with

Herald, Ash, and I. The five of us will try to get better equipment in the houses just up ahead." He said.

"Got it! You heard the man. Charge!" Arend shouted. He and class 2-D began to take off ahead, while Reighley and the rest turned towards a nearby house.

"*You're amazing.*" Freya thought. Watching Reighley lead, made her heart flutter. "*Whether it's for me, or a stranger, you give it your all. It's my favorite thing about you.*" She thought with a smile while tailing behind Reighley. Before they could even reach the house, however, the five of them heard screams coming from the distance. Their attention turned down the street as Destiny and Isabelle began to announce what had happened.

"Uh oh! Looks like some contestants are already infected." Isabelle said.

"That's right. Now they have a minute before they are eliminated and look at those zombies! They're huge!" Destiny said. She pressed a button and on the bottom left corner of the screen displayed a number and text.

(Remaining Survivors: 200)

"Looks like we're in for a blood bath, make sure you have your umbrellas ready, kids!" Destiny shouted.

"Uh, Reighley I don't think that we are dealing with normal zombies," Ulysses mentioned. The group paused at the infected ahead. It was one undead and it wasn't acting like normal zombies like the ones in a video game or movie, instead, it was swift and tactical with its takedown tagging six people in the span of a few seconds. Doing all while preventing any injury. It was using objects to hide behind total cover and vaulting over obstacles in their way at extreme speeds. Its appearance was undesirable to look at as well. The infected looked incredibly lean and physically fit. While their makeup and effects on them made them look like undead, they were still wearing tactical suits underneath the disguise. Finally, after tagging ten people in small groups the zombie's suit locked up and it went down.

"That's all right! Let's worry about our gear first." Reighley reassured. *"Looks like I made the right choice to air on the side of caution."*

"That one took thirty-four," Herald said. He paid close attention to the amount of bullets it took to take him down and counted each time the zombie's suit flashed red. "It took thirty-four bullets to finish the zombie."

"Now how is that fair? I don't even have that many bullets in my two guns combined." Ash mentioned.

"We can't slow down. Come on let's get inside" Reighley said while opening the door to the house the group was standing in front of. The house had broken windows. Once the group entered the living room through the entrance they quickly scanned their surroundings. Inside the living room was shredded furniture. There were bloodstains on the floor, when Freya saw it she visibly became nauseous.

"Reighley, somethings not right... I hired actors to play the zombies, not super soldiers." Freya explained.

"You think your dad tampered with the run?" Reighley asked while reaching his hand towards a door knob leading to a bedroom.

"I don't think it would be past him to do something like that," Freya said. Suddenly from down the hallway, an undead came running towards the group after bursting through a different bedroom door. The noise scared Reighley causing him to trip backwards. The group turned their weapons towards it and unloaded them at it. It was mere inches from reaching Reighley before Ash was able to unload both of her Z-blasters at it.

"*Dang it!*" The zombie thought as he collapsed playing dead.

"Phew! That was close." Ash said, helping Reighley up.

"Are you okay?" Freya asked Reighley. She was concerned for him.

"I'm all right... It looks like this zombie wasn't an elite like the one we saw earlier. More importantly, look." Reighley pointed. In the room where the zombie came from he saw a care package of supplies. The group quickly cleared the rest of the house and found two supply crates. Inside one loot crate Reighley found a Z-Assault Rifle and a single infection sterilizer. Inside the other, Ulysses pulled out the Z-Buckshot, a shotgun, and four more Z-blasters.

"You should give Freya the shotgun, and me the rifle. Herald said. "Shooting is something I am rather good at.

Not to mention Freya has joined me out to the range plenty of times in the past."

"*Right, right, ex-assassin.*" Reighley thought.

"Got it." Reighley agreed, handing the weapons over to the two. He expected this. Once the team was locked and loaded they headed back outside.

"It looks like our favors to win have just exited their looting building!" Isabelle said. "You got this Reighley."

"Isabelle! You're not helping!" Reighley shouted at the screen. He noticed something worrisome. The amount of people left had dropped at an alarming rate.

(Remaining Survivors: 157)

"Forty-three down already? The game just started!" Ulysses asked.

"It's all right they potentially took down some zombies with them. It will make it a little easier for us down the road." Ash said.

"I think we should move on ahead. We are already so behind." Freya said, pumping her shotgun.

"I agree. The longer this is drawn out the more difficult it will be." Herald advised.

The group pressed onward, managing to pick up three more Z-blasters off of the floor where contestants had lost. Most weapons were empty on arrival. The team stumbled upon Lillie Two, who was completely alone and out of breath. She was hiding behind a vehicle wearing a black poncho. When she noticed the group she beckoned for them to come over toward her.

"Lillie Two? What happened to everyone else?" Freya asked with concern.

"I don't know... As far as I know, Arend and Joy went on ahead." Lillie Two explained.

"Why did they leave you?" Freya asked.

"I had to tie my shoes..." Lillie explained, "But it's too late for me, I just got infected..." She pulled her poncho aside and revealed a green light on her vest.

"Wait, we have a sterilizer!" Reighley said he pulled out the device and quickly tried to hand it to Lillie, but she stopped his advances with her hand.

"Save it. Don't waste that on me. Your life is more valuable than mine." Lillie said. Suddenly Lillie looked down at her vest and the green light turned red and a buzzing sound went off.

"I just... wish I could have been... more... useful..." Lillie said, closing her eyes and slumping her head over.

"We'll avenge you, Lillie... I promise." Ulysses said. The thought of protecting his friends filled him with a burning passion to win.

(Remaining Survivors: 156)

"Why is she playing dead?" Herald asked.

"Don't take this moment away from her!" Ash said. Freya walked over and took the time to tie Lillie's shoes which were still untied, for her.

"Thank you for your help Lillie Two. Your sacrifice will not be forgotten." Freya said with compassion.

"For goodness sake, she is not dead!" Herald complained.

Lillie then pretended to rise up as a zombie and walk back towards the starting line of the race.

"Attention all survivors... *Z.E.D.* has entered the fray." Isabelle said. "Avoid at all costs. I repeat, avoid at all costs." The group looked up at the display as it switched to a horrifying scene. A monster of a man was holding two people off the ground in separate hands. There was no mistaking it. This was him.

"Wait... is that?-" Reighley stuttered.

"Dad..." Ulysses muttered while his heart sank.

Chapter 20

You Must Live

"**W**ait... You're telling me that *that's* your dad?"
Ash commented.

"I've seen him before..." Freya said. Even under all the makeup, Freya recognized his face.

"Wait, you know my dad?" Ulysses asked.

"No, but I've seen him come over on weekends before. Him and some other lady." Freya said.

"Did she have white hair, a fur coat on, and is always wearing sunglasses indoors?"   Ulysses questioned.

"Yeah. That's the one. Who is she?" Freya asked.

"That's my mom, Kokeisha." Ulysses sighed. "I knew our fathers were friends, but I don't know why both he and my mom would be coming over to speak with your dad on the weekends..."

"Guys... I hate to stop the chatter but look!" Reighley pointed ahead down the road. Twenty-five meters away, there was a small horde of infected, about nine in total and they were sprinting directly towards the group. "Fire!" Reighley shouted. Herald hoisted his Z-Assault Rifle onto the hood of the vehicle that the group was using as cover, and he methodically began to target the incoming horde. His aim was true. Reighley underestimated how difficult it would be to take down such a small number of infected. The horde were using unreal evasive maneuvers, they were fully embracing their feral ideology by refusing to move in a coherent line. They wove in and out going between vehicles and some even dropped to all fours. The group slowly whittled away at the incoming infected. From a distance, the group managed to only bring down four of the zombies. The five remaining infected continued to bear down upon the group. They utilized anything and everything they could as cover. By that time the horde was fifteen meters away and the worst-case scenario occurred as an audible *Click* *Click* *Click* *Click* was heard.

Reighley, Ash, Ulysses, and Herald, all were out of ammunition.

"It can't end like this!" Freya said courageously. She sprinted out from behind the trunk of the car with the Z-Shotgun in hand.

"Hey! Over here!" She shouted. Freya stood out in the open acting as bait. The five undead noticed Freya and charged directly at her. Freya fired a flurry of shots at the undead. The shotgun itself displayed what appeared to be twelve lasers at once, indicating that multiple charges were sent flying. The first barrage of lasers didn't stop any undead, but after the second, Freya managed to take down a zombie. At this point, Freya had a full-on adrenaline rush from her courageous act. All she had to do was convince herself that it was life or death. The rush made her senses heightened to the limits. Freya unloaded her ammunition on the next two zombies and they too fell to the ground. When Freya went to shoot the fourth…

Click

Freya gasped when she realized she was out of ammo. *"Is this the end?"* She thought. As the last feral zombies were only a mere three meters away, she accepted her fate.

"Freya!" Reighley shouted. He felt completely powerless. Panicked, he looked around for a spare ammo clip when he glanced at the floor and noticed the Z-blaster that Lillie Two had left behind. Reighley picked it up and leaped after Freya going over the hood of the car, but before Reighley could fire a single shot, a bright and powerful red laser lit up the zombie closest to Freya. A loud bang resounded from behind the group, and the zombie went down. When the last zombie was close to Freya, it too went down after a single shot. Freya was shocked by the outcome and looked behind her. The person who finished off the last infected was Jim, and he was wielding a Z-Sniper Rifle.

"Keep moving!" Jim shouted as he slid his bolt action rifle back and forth, to ready the weapon.

"Dad?" Freya thought to herself. She didn't expect to be saved by her father right after disrespecting him. She wasn't sure what to think of it but was grateful nonetheless.

The group didn't hesitate from the order and began to press forward. They managed to scour a commodity of

434

Z-blasters from what they could only assume were competitors that lost just minutes before them. Many of the weapon's magazines were empty, but they managed to scavenge enough ammo to give each person a full magazine. At this point, Jim caught up with the rest of the group. When he did, Reighley noticed Jim was completely stacked on weaponry. He had the aforementioned Z-Sniper Rifle, the Z-Shotgun, and a better-looking version of Herald's Z-Assault Rifle, all strapped to his back.

"This guy is stacked..." Reighley thought. He wondered if Jim paid for info on where those weapons were located. The weapons had real weight to them so he guessed Jim was in incredible shape to be able to carry all three of those on his back. Freya watched her dad approach and walk up next to her.

"Are you okay?" Jim asked jogging next to Freya.

"Yeah... thanks for saving me." Freya reluctantly said while swallowing her pride. She felt torn. Her dad helping her wasn't going to magically fix the amount of times he was absent. She also was still angry at him for what he did to her at school and his opinion of Reighley. Still, she knew that the right thing to do was to at least thank him. If it wasn't for his help, the group would have already lost.

"Area Two... is just up ahead!" Ulysses said, breathing heavily.

"Are you okay Ulysses?" Ash asked.

"Yeah... I'm just... winded." He answered. Ulysses was having a hard time breathing. He knew the exact cause. It was his smoking addiction. It was holding him back. *"Geez... I'm pathetic... I haven't even been running for very long. I have to step it up. As a man!"* He thought. This issue made him seriously consider going cold turkey from cigarettes. Especially if it ended up being the reason he let his best friend down.

The group arrived at Area Two, The Risen Army Base, and they vaulted over the barricade. Reighley took a mental stock and knew that they were in a pinch. If they were attacked again by the infected they would lose.

"We have to get better weapons... If we could just make it to the gun vault then I think we could finish the run." Reighley thought. "Guys we have to get into the gun vault. It's our best shot at winning." The group nodded in agreement and headed inside.

"Master Summers... It appears that many of the contestants are inside the base. I'm afraid I think we are in last place." Herald said as he pointed towards the remaining people left.

(Remaining Survivors: 103)

"What did you call him Herald?" Jim questioned.

"I called him Master Summers, sir," Herald answered. "Is there an issue?" Jim didn't respond, instead, he silently pressed onward into the base.

Meanwhile, only slightly behind Reighley and the others, was Deven Stallik. He had been letting the others carve a pathway forward for him.

"This is perfect... That's right, just keep clearing the way for my inevitable victory. Once we reach the Dead Man Zone, you'd better watch your backs." Deven said and then laughed maniacally.

"It's time we announce our current standings in the race!" Isabelle said. "Take it away, DJ Destiny."

"It looks like the person sitting in last place is Deven Stallik!" Destiny announced.

"You're not helping!" Deven shouted towards the screen.

"Following slightly ahead of Devin we have Freya and her groupies! With Loverboy R. leading the charge! In second place we have Class 2-D. They seem to be formidable opponents. All the way in first place is Donald Fitzgerald! It appears he has already made it to the armory. Don't fall behind now!" Isabelle said.

"Thanks for the heads up D," Ulysses said, looking at the monitor.

"We don't have time to worry about those who are behind us. We'll deal with them later." Ash said. "We have to press on."

The group made their way inside the base. It was dimly lit, with small electrical lamps hanging from the ceiling every few meters apart. The base had green tarps on the wall and multitudes of graffiti with writings of things like (There is no help here) or (Only God can save us now.)

Immediately the group was given a choice. There were three paths for them to choose. To their left was the path

437

towards the med bay. To their right was the path towards the armory. The final path was directly ahead of them and had a sign on it that said (Dead Man's Path). Reighley guessed that the middle path was the quickest and easiest way through, however, he knew that there was no reward. The med bay path he assumed was a slightly more difficult path due to the rewards being far less useful than actual weapons. He knew the group needed gear so he made his decision.

"All right, guys I say we go to the-" Reighley was interrupted after being shoved aside by someone.

"OUT OF MY WAY!" Deven Stallik screamed. He pushed Reighley and ran directly down the Dead Man's Path.

"Watch it!-" Reighley said before looking back at what Deven was running from. "Oh no..." Reighley became fearful at what was headed their way. It was a horde of undead. He guessed the numbers were around fifty to sixty and they were coming in fast. Quick to react, Ash unclipped Jim's special Z-Assault Rifle off from behind him.

"Hey! What are you-" Jim shouted.

"Buying time," Ash said as she rushed back toward the horde of undead. "Now go!"

"Ash no!" Freya shouted sorrowfully. Ash hopped on top of a nearby humvee that was flipped upside down and took a deep breath.

"I'll hold them off," Ash said, glancing backward. She then looked towards the horde in front of her and began shouting crazily while unloading her weapon trying to draw the attention away from her team. The Z Assault Rifle she had stolen from Jim was suspiciously effective at taking out the undead. It only took roughly four bullets per zombie, but Ash knew that math didn't add up to her success.

"Come on! We can't let her sacrifice be in vain. Freya, and Jim, go down the med bay path and get as many sterilizers as you can hold. Ulysses, go with them so you can catch your breath. Herald and I will get the weapons we need for the rest of the run." Reighley ordered.

"But…" Freya hesitated. She was torn between going with Reighley and her father. She didn't want to go with Jim, but she also wanted to show that she trusted Reighley's leadership as a man.

"All right, bro. Don't die on me. I'll see you on the other side." Ulysses agreed and headed down the med bay path. Jim watched as Reighley led the group. Reighley reminded him of himself when he was younger. A go-getter with a lot of potential to lead. He couldn't help but be impressed by the kid's conviction.

"Keep her safe," Reighley asked Jim.

"You don't have to tell me that." Jim scoffed. He then made his way behind Ulysses.

"Reighley. Please don't do anything crazy!" Freya begged. Reighley turned towards the armory path and began running.

"I'll be okay! I'll definitely survive!" Reighley said. The groups split up into two.

"Stop raising death flags, dude!" Ulysses hollered.

"It looks like our protagonist has decided to separate the group," Destiny announced. She had a drone tailing behind Reighley and the group watching their actions.

Once out of earshot, Herald looked concerned. "Master Summers, are you sure it's wise to separate the group?" He asked.

"Yeah. Something wasn't sitting right with me. If there is a Dead Man's Zone up ahead and we can shoot each other, then there must be Medi-packs to help with the damage taken from Z weapons. We'll definitely need those if we are going to make it through. Not to mention I think the med bay path would be safer for those who don't wish to be shot by friendly fire. I'm sure the majority of people who are willing to shoot someone to win also went down this hallway." Reighley explained. The two were running down a hallway after making a sharp ninety-degree turn to the left. Suddenly Reighley's vest glowed blue and Heralds did as well. A voice prompt spoke from their vests. It sounded like Destiny's voice.

"Congratulations. You have reached the halfway mark. You're officially in the Dead Man's Zone. Friendly Fire is now activated." The vest cheerfully said. "Your vest can take three shots before turning completely red. The first shot will change your vest to yellow, while the second one will turn it a flashing red. If you get shot one more time you'll hear a buzz sound and your vest will turn a solid red color signifying your death. Only Medi-packs can repair the damage you've taken." The voice explained. "Now good luck and don't die!" After the voice finished its explanation their suit colors turned off.

"Master Summers we must be incredibly careful from this point onward," Herald said.

"Right... That's partially why we split up. I don't think anyone will dare to shoot Jim or his daughter in their own game. Me on the other hand, I would put them in danger, even if it was from stray bullets." Reighley explained.

"Ah. so it's okay for an old man like me to catch the extra bullets." Herald jested.

"No, no! You are the most experienced out of all of us. I need your expertise." Reighley explained trying to salvage the situation.

The two trod carefully as their path became more narrow. They kept up the same pace as the groans from the undead could be heard from behind them. Herald and Reighley knew the zombies were inexorable in their path to catch the living. They headed down an elongated hallway with several outcroppings strategically placed along the path. The hall had several exit signs ominously posted throughout the hall for those who lost the race.

The two were approaching the armory, but eerily, they noticed there were no zombies nearby. Instead, all they saw were several people who looked completely defeated with solid red vests walking past them towards the exits nearby. Among the defeated competitors was Arend.

"Arend what happened?" Reighley asked.

"Sorry pal. Dead men don't speak. Oooooooo." Arend said, sounding like a ghost. He then left through an exit.

"It must be *him*," Herald claimed quietly.

"Who?" Reighley asked.

"An old friend," Herald explained.

Herald and Reighley stealthily entered the armory. The room was circular in shape and had a dome rooftop. It was difficult to see inside the room as its light source was a mere three lanterns hanging atop the ceiling barely illuminating the objects on the floor. The floor had many three–foot–tall glow-in-the-dark barricades randomly scattered throughout the room. Directly in front of the duo were two barricades stretching a couple of meters from the hallway's entrance. The barricades appeared to have a small graveyard's worth of weapons left behind by the defeated competitors. The vault door was on the opposite end of the room from the hall that Reighley and Herald were walking. It appeared to be slightly cracked open, signifying they weren't alone. Someone had already entered inside before they arrived. The door leaked light through the cracks on a barricade off to the left of it. The vault's handles and center were completely smeared with glow-in-the-dark paint.

Herald was on high alert due to the weapons from those who had fallen. He held his weapon at the ready. He knew of only one man skilled enough to eliminate such an exorbitant amount of foes. Herald noticed a glimmer of light from the vault reflecting off an object elevated on top of a barricade on the other side of the room. He couldn't make out what the object was, but every instinct in him indicated that it was dangerous.

Get down!" Herald shouted, quickly shoving Reighley behind the cover. From this, Herald's vest changed to a yellow color after taking the shot that was meant for Reighley. He then immediately dropped behind the barricade and placed his back against it next to where Reighley had fallen.

"Are you alright Master Summers?" Herald asked.

"I'm fine. Thanks…" Reighley was in shock by the selfless act from Herald, but then sat up and placed his back to the barricade.

"Hello, Herald." A voice reverberated by the vault.

"Donald. Good to see nothing has changed and that you're still up to your cheap tricks yet again." Herald said. He never considered the possibility of laserless weapons. He assumed it must have been a specialty item. Something Donald must have acquired from the vault.

"I'm just here for the boy Herald. Don't make me do something I might regret." Donald threatened.

"It wouldn't be the first time that's happened, would it?" Herald pressed.

"Look. We both know who the better shot is between the two of us. Just look the other way." Donald pleaded. Herald's hand landed on the small mound of handguns and weapons that lay next to the barricade. He turned towards

Reighley and saw how desperate the boy was to win. He knew what role he had to play in order for victory to occur.

"Reighley... I have a plan to get you to the vault. When I give you the signal I want you to make a run around the right side of the room towards the exit. Do you understand?" Herald whispered. Reighley peeked out of the right side of the cover and his eyes followed the curved wall. He immediately noticed that the east side of the room was darker than the rest due to the vault shining light upon the west side.

"Okay, but what about you?" Reighley whispered back with concern.

"Do you have that little faith in me, Master Summers?" Herald said with a smile.

Reighley glanced over to his companion and replied, "No, I trust you." Herald then gave Reighley a decisive nod, waiting for the boy to get ready. Once in position, Herald quickly dashed out behind the cover to the west side of the room with four objects in hand. He picked up three Z Blasters and a single Z-Grenade from the weapon pile nearby. He hurled the three Z-Blasters one after another towards the lights above while running towards a cover on the west side of the room. His impromptu projectiles shattered the fragile lamps hanging on the ceiling, shrouding most of the room in the darkness that could rival the abyss. The only light source remaining was coming from the vault itself. Donald was ready for any movement at the entrance and began firing at Herald as soon as he dashed. Herald took a second shot from

Donald turning his suit a flashing red color before he reached his point of cover. Knowing he couldn't stop, Herald pulled the pin on the Z-Grenade and tossed it directly at the center base of the vault while diving behind a nearby barricade.

"Crap!" Donald shouted as he dove towards the west side of the room. Herald threw the Grenade to force Donald to retreat away from the vault. Herald knew the only way for Reighley to get through was to clear a path for him. Once the fuse expired, the Z-Grenade became as bright as a disco ball, reflecting lasers all around the vault door.

"Now Master Summers!" Herald shouted. During the Z-Grenades light show, Herald had run across the room and positioned himself behind a barricade. He placed himself between Donald and the vault while still remaining in the darkness. This left Reighley a clear path to run across the darker east side of the room. Reighley wasted no time, as he blindly slid his hand across the wall following its curvature towards the door.

"Herald! Stay out of this!" Donald shouted in frustration.

Herald knew exactly where Donald was. If he tried to move the light from the vault would expose him making for an easy shot. As Reighley arrived near the vault, he could hear Donald's desperation. Donald peered around the cover on the lookout for a shot at Reighley only to immediately get shot by Herald, turning his vest yellow.

"Now, now, that won't do at all. Keep your focus on me." Herald taunted.

"This is all for Madam Guinevere. I'm just doing what was commanded of me." Donald shouted.

"*Guinevere?*" Reighley thought. "*What does she have to do with any of this?*" Reighley quickly pried the vault door open and began to use the door as cover. Reighley's heart began to pound as he heard and felt the incoming horde of infected. It seemed that the horde had finally caught up with them. He looked into the darkness but Herald was nowhere to be found. Desperate, Reighley cried out.

"Herald it's time to go!" Reighley warmed.

"I'm not afraid, Master Summers. You're the one who needs to live above all else. I have complete faith in you." Herald praised. Reighley paused and took a deep breath.

"*Thanks, Herald.*" Reighley thought. He quickly dashed through the open door and went into the gun vault. He knew that closing the door would signify the end of the butler's race.

Ulysses was astonished as Jim led with complete authority. Although the three had just entered the Dead Man's Zone, no one dared to shoot Jim or those who were with him. Jim didn't know what to say to his daughter so he kept quiet. The three made it through with ease and found a spacious room that had a tent set up in its center. At the far end of the room was a singular exit that appeared to lead outside. The tent had a red cross on it and was holding a large number of Medi-packs.

"Pack them up. Reighley needs these." Ulysses said.

"Here! Take this bag." A feminine voice said.

"Joy, you made it!" Freya turned and greeted her classmate with excitement. "Where is everyone else?"

"The boys went down the armory path while the girls went down the med bay path." She explained while handing the bag to Ulysses. "We all sort of have a truce not to shoot each other while we're in here."

"I hate to break it to you, but there is a horde on its way, so we have to go," Freya explained. Slightly alarmed by the news, the remaining survivors gathered their gear and headed towards the exit, hoping that it would lead them outside the confines of the building. Upon exiting the room they closed the door behind them and sealed it shut to prevent any of the infected from getting through. Freya scanned her new surroundings. The path that lay in front of her was a vast wasteland acute to a desert. The sand around her feet made it difficult to run let alone walk. The artificial trees placed ahead were dead and bare. The majority of the structures ahead were torn-down barns or stables similar to old western movies. The center focal point that drew Freya's attention was placed where she could only assume was at the finish line. At the far end of the desert was a four-layered pagoda tower that stood ominously at the end. With Reighley nowhere in sight, she looked towards the opposite end of the base hoping to find him. To her relief, she saw him exiting the armory side. He had a large bag filled with weaponry peeking out over his shoulder.

"*I knew he could do it!*" Freya thought. She looked for Herald but realized quickly that he was gone... Freya headed towards Reighley and when she was close enough she saw a laser pointer on him.

"Freya!" Reighley said with excitement. He watched as she ran towards her. Reighley looked up at the remaining contestants and saw the number left was incredibly low.

(Remaining Survivors: 27)

"Wow. Talk about thinning the herd." Reighley said to himself. Two drones were carrying a plain white banner in the sky. A third drone was projecting Destiny and Isabelle on the banner. He looked at Freya and she didn't look happy to see him. Instead, she had a look of fear. Reighley was incredibly confused until Freya stepped in front of him. He watched as her vest turned from blue to yellow, from yellow to a flashing red, and eventually a solid red vest signifying she was eliminated with a buzz sound. It all happened so fast that Reighley couldn't even comprehend what had just occurred.

"Party foul!" Isabelle was outraged over the speakers. Destiny was irritated by who the shooter was. It was Deven Stallik, who was in first place. He was waiting around for Reighley to come out so he could take him out.

"Yeah! Everyone knows you don't shoot the birthday girl, even if it does make for some good content. That's right I'm calling you out Deven Stallik! Stop hiding like a coward behind that barn." Destiny said.

"That's completely unfair. Stop giving away my position!" Deven Stallik shouted in frustration. He was hidden behind a run-down barn just a bit further ahead of the rest but quickly fled while shouting. "I did not go through all of that suffering just to get eliminated here!" Devin had flashbacks of what had happened in the Dead Man's Path and only managed to survive thanks to a sterilizer he was lucky enough to find. In reality, he only had to face a single zombie, but that alone was enough to slightly traumatize him.

"Sucks to suck." Isabelle taunted. Deven scurried off further down the path completely infuriated by the bias towards Reighley and Freya.

"Why does everyone ship them together anyway? Freighley is an awful shipping name." Deven said before running off ahead out of sight.

"Freya…" Reighley said as she jumped into his arms.

"Oh thank goodness. I made it in time." Freya said with a smile.

"Dummy…" Reighley said with a chuckle. "You know, I'm surprised you even participated. You don't like scary stuff, right?" Reighley asked.

"I don't, but… I actually had this all made for you. I know you mentioned you enjoy horror stuff." Freya said. Reighley felt like an idiot. He didn't put two and two together.

"You… did all of this for me?" Reighley asked. He couldn't even fathom the amount of money it must have cost Jim to produce something to this scale.

"Yes. Also... It's been fun. I can see the appeal of running for your life." Freya said. Reighley could feel her pulse just from holding her.

"Sorry... I'm kind of sweaty." Reighley said.

"I don't care. I don't get to hold you very often." Freya said. Reighley used *Insight,* when he looked into her eyes her aura was gently wrapping around and enveloping him with a comforting embrace. He could feel the warmth of the aura around him. It was akin to sitting next to a campfire on a winter night. The warmth surrounded him and kept the cold isolation of winter at bay. As if being in his arms was exactly where she was meant to be.

"You've been giving it your all for me," Reighley said. It took everything in him to continue with his plan, hating himself all the while. His guilt was beginning to become unbearable. *"Is this the right thing to do?"* He thought.

Taking in Reighley's intense stare Freya became flustered. "Stop... it. You're making me blush in front of everyone." Freya whispered while she turned red with embarrassment. Freya felt Reighley's skin but it was cold to the touch, she thought it was odd, but before she could say something about it, Reighley let her go.

"Freya, we'll talk later. I have a race to win" Reighley said, letting go of Freya. Jim approached the two with Ulysses following behind them.

"Give me one good reason why I shouldn't shoot you right here and now." Jim threatened while holding the Z-shotgun pointed towards Reighley.

"Well, Freya just sacrificed herself for me so that would make you look worse... Would you rather have Deven win?" Reighley said.

"Good point." Jim lowered his gun.

"Reighley look!" Ulysses said, pointing towards the remaining survivors.

(Remaining Survivors: 11)

"That's all that's left? What's happened to everyone?" Reighley asked. He looked around, and the people who exited the med bay were leaving the race. He immediately noticed that their vests were still blue in color. *"They're walking away, but they haven't lost yet?"* he thought.

"A lot of us planned on walking out after the second half of the race was finished," Joy said.

"Why is that?" Freya asked.

"I don't think anyone wanted to deal with Z.E.D." Joy explained. "Don't worry though! As the last remaining underling of class 2-D, I am going to see this through to the very end."

"So earnest..." Ulysses praised.

"Here. I got this for you all." Reighley said. He started unloading weapons from his bag. He managed to snag some rare equipment in the vault. He thought he grabbed multiple copies of each weapon. However, they were different. "These weapons are the special version of our starting gun. Just like the rifle Ash stole off Jim from earlier."

"Well. I best get going and catch up with the rest. Good luck!" Freya said. She handed Reighley one of the

Medi-Packs she had found in the bay and then left after blowing a kiss towards him. This caused his heart to flutter a bit and caused Jim to slightly quiver in anger from it.

"Did you see that honorable sacrifice by our dear Freya? What a noble heart she has. She was willing to give it all just for R. I'm sure she'll tell you all about it when she makes her way backstage for an interview." Destiny announced.

"Truly it must be love! Is there anything more poetic than someone willing to give up their life for the sake of their loved one? It's so romantic!" Isabelle fawned. "She must have full faith that he will win in the end."

"Isabelle! Just what are you saying?!" Reighley cringed

"Chat, let's hear your thoughts," Destiny said.

FDSA_MOXIE: It reminded me of the movie trailer for *Princess Charming, Sleeping Handsome.*

Taco_Panda: That's why we love our Freya.

QueenyFishy12: I really hope R wins!

FunnyUser232: Who is this R guy? What's his name? Will he be introduced later?

Gasp_For_Air: I totally would have dodged out of the way of those shots.

"I don't have time to stand around and do nothing. I have to get moving." Reighley thought. He looked at the path ahead of him and the majority of the runway was completely covered in sand. The structures on the path were decayed and broken down only acting as a cover to hide behind instead of places to loot. It was hard to get a grasp on where the finish

line was as there were plenty of white dead trees in front blocking the view. *"It's like the wild west out here."* Reighley turned towards his remaining allies and pointed at one of the covers. "Let's make our way from cover to cover. There are still contestants out there who are potentially hiding. It's best not to take our chances, especially with Z.E.D around."

"Now that you mention it… Jim, why is my dad here?" Ulysses asked.

"I'm sorry son. I can't tell you that. I just asked a favor from an old friend. That's all. If you want to know more, you'll have to ask him yourself." Jim replied.

"Ulysses, are you going to be alright bro?" Reighley asked.

"Yeah. I don't know if I can beat him, but if I have to take on my dad in order for you to win, then I'll gladly do it." Ulysses said courageously.

"Neither of you are winning. I just need your help to make sure that rat Deven doesn't win." Jim mentioned.

"Thanks for the warning. Now let's move." Reighley replied.

The four swiftly pressed onward towards the goal. Ulysses was the frontliner and Joy walked next to him. Jim and Reighley were behind the two ready for anything. The group stumbled upon a barn that wasn't in shambles and found two survivors hunkered down behind a hay barrel. After sneaking up on them, they made quick work eliminating them from the competition.

"Nothing personal," Reighley said as he and Jim shot the competitors from behind. It didn't bother him to play dirty. He felt like that would have been the only way to survive in a real apocalypse. Survival rule number 1. "Why play by the rules, when there are no rules?" Reighley knew there was no honor at the end of the world. Just winners and losers.

(Remaining Survivors: 9)

As the four traversed through the barn, they heard a creaking noise come from above them. The sound caused their hearts to skip a beat. When they looked upward they could see red glowing eyes from a massive figure hanging from the ceiling.

"It's a trap!" Jim yelled. It was like that of a horror movie. The figure let go and fell directly between the diamond formation that the group was moving in. There was a mad scramble as the party skittered away from the infected Zombie. This involuntary reaction further dispersed the temporary allies from one another. To make matters worse, a shadow stepped from behind the massive form. This other creature could be considered slim and nimble only because he stood next to the monstrous form of Z.E.D. Ulysses reflectively dodged back as he saw a streak of white flash before his eyes.

"Hello, Brother," Sunny said. "Are you ready for your lesson?"

"Sunny!?" Ulysses yelled. When Ulysses looked at Sunny he noticed that Sunny was sheathing his blade that he had. Ulysses looked down at his vest, and it was switching between green and yellow colors. He had been slashed in that instant of dodging.

"What are you doing here? What do you mean, lesson!?" Ulysses questioned.

"Mother asked us to test you. Now prepare yourself!" Sunny threatened.

"Ulysses! I can't help you." Joy warned. Ulysses looked over at Joy and to his surprise, she had been eliminated in the blink of an eye.

"Ahhhhhh! I am Z.E.D. The Zombie Enhanced Dad!" Todoh roared as he began to charge toward Reighley and Jim.

Chapter 21

Those Who Stay Faithful

Earlier in the evening, shortly after the birthday gifts were received, Lily entered the restroom for a second time for the night. She felt as though she would pass out if she stayed any longer. Her heart was racing out of her chest.

"*I can't believe I'm back in here. Get a hold of yourself, Lily. You can't avoid him all night. Ulysses and I entered the party together for Pete's sake. I wonder if people thought we were a couple.*" Lily thought, while simultaneously placing both her hands on her blushing rosy cheeks. "*I've never been like this before. Is this love? I need to calm down. Gather your senses, Lily.*" It was unusual for Lily to get worked up by anything, except for Freya's previous brat-like behavior. Her ability to keep her emotions in check was something she was fairly proud of, but this was different. Lily took a deep breath. She looked at herself in the mirror and stared at the dress she was wearing. It was a Klein blue color made from polyester. She was crowned with a silver French net headpiece with a flower that matched the color of her dress. "Freya really helped me out this time. I owe her one." Lily said.

Earlier during the week. Freya and Lily were in Freya's bedroom. Freya was lounging around on her bed while Lily was sitting on a chair at her bedside.

"Ugh! I miss him like crazy." Freya complained.

"Why don't you just call him?" Lily asked.

"I can't because he said he was busy and I don't want to distract or bother him," Freya explained.

"Well, if you're not going to call him, could you instead help me with something?" Lily asked.

"Don't *I* pay *you* to help me?" Freya said while kicking her legs up and down.

"I'm being serious," Lily reassured.

"You need my help? Isn't there like nothing you can't do?" Freya joked around.

"There are plenty of things I can't do and I definitely can't do this alone," Lily explained.

"Oh alright... I suppose I can help you out. What is it that you need?" Freya questioned. After a brief explanation by Lily, Freya seemed to be in shock from what she had just heard.

"You don't know what to wear? You prepare all my clothing. How do you not have a good fashion sense by now?" Freya asked skeptically.

"This is different. I want to look my absolute best so I can take his breath away." Lily elaborated.

"Trust me. You do that already." Freya said. "Besides, Ulysses is one hundred and ten percent interested in you. You don't have to try that hard." Freya attempted to persuade her to give up so she wouldn't have to go shopping.

"Please?" Lily asked.

Freya let out a sigh and began taking Lily seriously. "Okay. What's your budget?" Freya questioned.

"5,000 yen. USD 36.00." Lily told her while pulling out a borderline empty wallet.

"How are you broke? Don't you get paid for working here?" Freya was astonished by the amount mentioned.

"I've been paying off my debt using my paychecks. I owed a total of 5,000,000 yen (37,500 USD) Thanks to the coffee accident last year. I'm almost done actually. I've paid off most of it with only roughly 714,285 yen (USD 5,109.85) left." Lily explained.

"You're in debt? From what?" Freya asked.

"You're joking right?" Lily questioned. This struck a nerve in her. She had been working incredibly hard for the past seven years to pay off the debt she owed for her parent's medical bills and had spent the last year using every yen she could spare to pay off the dress she spilled coffee on almost a year ago.

"Do we not pay you!?" Freya asked concerningly.

"It was the dress from last year. That thing costs more than a fortune. I've been paying it off since then. How do you not know this?" Lily asked.

"You've been paying all that off?" Freya said. "I had no idea…"

"You can't be serious." Lily was getting genuinely upset until she considered Freya's words. She truly didn't know the struggle Lily was going through just to get by. "*I can't be mad at her for being an idiot If she truly didn't know. Besides, it was my fault for spilling the coffee on her. I did it on her birthday too of all places.*" Lily thought.

"Consider it gone," Freya said.

"What?" Lily thought she had misheard Freya.

"I'll take care of the rest of your debt. You've already done enough for me. No friend of mine should live their life but be unable to enjoy the hard-earned money they've made," Freya explained. "I'll speak with my mother and have her refund all the money you spent paying off my dress."

Lily didn't know what to say. The thought of Freya erasing her debt like dust in the wind seemed like a fairy tale to her. She was speechless. Her emotions were beyond control as tears began to flow uncontrollably down her face. However, Lily did not sob instead she stood there with a static look, still processing what was just said.

"Lily!? Are you okay?" Freya asked. She had no idea why Lily began crying. Freya dropped her phone she was idling playing on and rushed over to Lily to comfort her. "Did I do something wrong?"

"You… have no idea what that means to me." Lily tried to wipe her tears but couldn't stop them from flowing.

"Hey, hey. It's okay. Let's get that taken care of now and use a bit of that refund on a beautiful dress for the party." Freya suggested.

Lily had to take a moment to regain her composure.

"Okay... but you're choosing it." Lily agreed, finally able to stop the tears.

"We'll get you something nice," Freya said. Before she knew it, Freya became someone Lily was proud to serve. From that moment onward, Lily was debt-free.

After thinking about what had happened before that week. Lily couldn't help but be incredibly grateful. She hadn't realized it but thinking about the past made her cry once more. Lily had no more financial issues and was now free to do whatever she wanted in life. Freedom was something Lily never would have thought she would reach until adulthood. She expected to live a life of indentured servitude for the remainder of her youth. The possibilities for her future were endless. She couldn't help but think about the potential of what she could accomplish after a few years.

"How filthy." A feminine voice could be heard from the bathroom entrance.

"Oh no... I'm still crying, I have to hide!" Lily thought. She rushed into a bathroom stall and hid covering her face while the sound of footsteps walked by towards the sink Lily was just at.

"This restroom is a disaster. Nothing is symmetrical at all. I suppose it makes sense since this place was rented out by Freya." The voice said.

"Phew... that was close. What on earth is this girl talking about?" Lily asked. She was standing up peeking through the

stall door's crack and immediately recognized the person entering.

"It's such a pity that she will end up exposed to the rest of the world that she had to buy herself a boyfriend," Guinevere chuckled. She was talking to herself in the mirror, or that's what it appeared at first glance until Lily noticed she seemed to have a wireless earpiece in her ear.

"What...? Isn't that Guinevere?" Lily questioned. *"She's talking to someone... but who?"*

"I'm going to need you to gather up the crew Donald. Also please don't disappoint me during the race. Your job is on the line here. Make sure you eliminate him no matter what. Understand?" Guinevere said. She was listening to a response but her expression became soured due to a long reply.

"I don't care who is involved. If you can't handle him, then I have no reason to keep you around. Now do what you were told!" Guinevere ordered. She then abruptly hung up the phone by clicking a button on the earpiece. Guinevere let out an exasperated sigh and then pulled out her phone." It's impossible to find good help these days."

"Wow..." Lily took that personally. She felt as though that was a completely unreasonable thing to say. The hardest-working people she knew were those in her line of work.

"All right, time to post," Guinevere said. She took out her phone and began to type at high speeds. In a matter of seconds, she hit the post button and posted something on what appeared to be SocialLight.

Buzzing sound.

"Ah! My phone." Lily panicked. A notification sounded off from Lily's phone. Immediately Guinevere turned towards the stall Lily was hiding in as a reaction to the sound from within.

"Who's in there!" Guinevere scornfully said while approaching.

"This is bad... I knew I shouldn't have followed Guinevere's SocialLight page!" Lily thought. Before asking Freya for help, Lily attempted to fix her problems before dumping them on someone else. She ended up following many fashion accounts on SocialLight, with Guinevere's account being one of them. However, the notification became the smoking gun for Lily. She was about to be caught listening and she didn't know what to do.

"Come out, now," Guinevere ordered. She noticed the person in the stall was standing up.

"What's with all the ruckus?" Lily replied. She attempted to fool Guinevere by sounding like an elder.

"I'm not going to fall for something that stupid. Now hurry up." Guinevere said. Reluctantly, Lily opened the door to a cross-armed Guinevere, who was tapping her foot in annoyance. Guinevere took the hat off of Lily's head and tossed it on the floor, using *Reverie* to read the script of text hovering over Lily.

"What do I do? I was told not to interact with this girl."
Lily thought.

"Tch! You don't seem pleased to see me." Guinevere
said. She recognized Lily as a maid who worked for Freya.
Guinevere had conducted some personal research in the past
in order to learn anything and everything she could about the
Young family household to get an advantage over Freya. If
Freya had fifteen maids in the household Guinevere would
have sixteen. If Freya posted on SocialLight Guinevere would
post twice. Her life was a constant living attempt to one-up
Freya in everything she did.

"I recognize you. You're Freya's handmaid. Lily, was
it? What's a commoner like you doing here out of uniform?
Your dress is rather distasteful." Guinevere said, placing Lily
under scrutiny. Although she wished to insult Lily for
working for Freya, the jab towards her carried no real weight
to it, simply because it was untrue.

"I'm here as Freya's friend," Lily explained.

"Hah! You should have tried being a comedian with
jokes like that." Guinevere closed in on Lily. "Stay in your
lane where you belong. People like you shouldn't even be
here." Lily lowered her head slightly in irritation.

"Tell me, how much does Freya pay you to keep
your mouth shut about all the terrible things she's done?
That's what she does. She pays people to get her way."
Guinevere questioned. "It must be a lot, right?"

"I don't bad mouth my friends," Lily said.

"Oh, please. You must have been miserable spending all that time with Freya." Guinevere said.

"*That's true...* Well at first it was, but now she is someone I care about. You're not getting anything out of me, so give it up." Lily said.

Guinevere was trying to get a mental response but when she used *Reverie* on Lily, there were no words above her head. "Why don't you change out of this hideous dress? Here let me help you!" Guinevere grabbed a hold of Lily's dress around the top of her thigh and began to rip the seams apart downward with her bare hands. "There we go! Much better! Wait no, no, no. There is still something missing. Oh that's right, it's not symmetrical." Guinevere said menacingly. She then proceeded to rip the dress starting at the other leg all the way down to her ankle. However, still, she got no response from Lily. There was a cold silence.

"*What is wrong with this girl?*" Guinevere thought. "Here, let's take a photo to commemorate the occasion," Guinevere said. She pulled up her phone to take a photo of Lily. She couldn't wait to see the anguish on the girl's face, but when she held up the screen, the only thing on it was Lily, looking at her with fierce determination. "*Why isn't she blowing up with anger? Is she a robot or something? Get angry, cry, do anything, but please, stop looking at me like that!*" Guinevere was terrified by the face she was being given by Lily. The expression was a sort of resolve she couldn't possibly imagine someone like her showing.

"Are you done?" Lily asked.

"Shut up!" Guinevere said, snapping a photo. "I'll post this! Don't think I won't! I'll ruin you for making a mockery of me."

"I don't care," Lily answered. "Do whatever you want, just leave Freya out of this."

Guinevere was waiting in anticipation for Lily's facade to crack under pressure, but nothing happened. No words appeared above Lily's head. Throughout all of Guinevere's years using the power of *Reverie*, she had never met someone who wore their heart on their sleeve quite like this. There were no alternative motives nor conniving plans of revenge. She was just waiting patiently for Guinevere to stop her tyranny.

"Huh, that's odd..." A sleeping memory awoke inside Guinevere. There was one other person she had met before. A person who was the same as Lily. Someone who when faced against *Reverie*, didn't have their inner thoughts revealed because there was nothing to hide. The memory was a simple image of a girl who was long dead and gone. A stranger in a casket. The face was blurred and unfamiliar and yet the only thing recognizable was the ivory hair of the individual.

"Who... is that? Why don't I remember them?" Guinevere asked herself. The sound of footsteps entering the women's restroom brought Guinevere back to her senses. She wasn't even aware that the whole time she was lost in thought she had been belittling Lily and degrading her with harsh words. Panicked, Guinevere stopped what she was

doing. "This... isn't over!" She threatened as she fled hastily out the door.

Lily was left in the stall with her head towards the ground. She looked at her torn gown and let out a sigh. She wasn't intimidated in the slightest by Guinevere.

"Sorry Freya, the dress you picked out, it's ruined..." Lily muttered. "I can't let this stop me from helping," Lily recalled that she had gotten a notification on her phone. She checked it and saw it was a post on SocialLight from Guinevere herself.

(Big DRAMA Coming Soon. Keep an eye on the next few posts for updates.)

The post had already reached the spotlight on the website, which was on the trending feed. Its growth in attention was steadily rising.

"What is she planning?" Lily questioned.

"Probably nothing good," Elise said. She was standing at the entrance with perfect posture.

"Elise!?" Lily was shocked. "How- how long were you standing there?" she asked.

"Long enough. Why didn't you fight back? We both know you're capable due to your self-defense training. " Elise asked.

"Because I would have lost," Lily said.

"Lost?" Elise questioned.

"Yes. I represent Freya, whether I like it or not. I can't go around giving her a bad name." Lily explained. Elise smiled at that answer.

"Good answer. Also Lily, about your dress… It's in shambles." Elise said.

"It's alright. It's just clothing." Lily said. "We have more important things to worry about."

Elise was amazed to hear that response come from the girl in front of her. She began to wonder who was standing in front of her. *"She's changed… I've known for a long time about the negative mentality Lily had been bearing since becoming Freya's maid. If it wasn't for the help her parents were getting thanks to all her hard work, Lily would have surely snapped by now. Yet, the girl in front of me would have given up everything to help Freya just a moment ago. You've become an S-Tier character Lily. Truly such a wonderful young lady."*

"Stay right there. I'll be right back." Elise said. Within a few minutes, Elise returned to Lily with something in hand. "Here. Take this." Elise said, handing Lily a change of clothes.

"Thank you." Lily took the clothes and in a matter of minutes was in a maid uniform. When she walked out of the stall she looked at herself in the mirror and felt like this was what she felt most comfortable in. "Hey, Elise?"

"Yes, Lily?" Elise answered.

"This is more my style don't you think?" Lily asked.

"I couldn't agree more," Elise said with a smile. "So what will you do now?"

"My grandma taught me at a young age that bullies only win if they get you to break. The only power they have over you is the power you give them. However, she also taught me that those who bully, are more than likely hurting on the inside. Far worse than you or I. That's why they hurt others. To make everyone feel just as awful as they do." Lily explained.

"Your grandmother is a wise woman," Elise said.

"Yeah, even still, I can't help but want to help Guinevere. Even despite everything that just happened, I feel like she is hurting deep down inside." Lily explained, "That being said, I still have to stop her from whatever she's planning on doing to Freya."

The two left the stall and made their way out of the restroom.

"*Oh my goodness that was awkward!*" Sarah thought while bursting out of a stall at the end of the restroom. She had overheard the entire conversation. Sarah Bellum was abnormally tall for a girl, standing at a whopping 183cm tall (6 feet). She was slim and her eyes carried bags under them from lack of sleep. The dark circles that rested there were permanently imprinted on her skin. She was average in the looks department and didn't think very highly of herself but she was aware of that fact and it didn't bother her. She had brown eyes and hair that swayed low below her waist.

"Here I thought Freya was pretty bad just a year ago. This Guinevere girl completely sucks! Still, I have to disagree with Ms. Service on this one. Guinevere is awful and some people don't deserve a second chance. It's a good thing my *Presage* told me about this, otherwise, I could have been in a really sticky situation. I'd better get out of here before things get worse." The young girl began walking towards the exit before slipping on the wet floor. The lack of resistance from her shoes combined with the liquid on the ground caused her feet to flip one hundred and eighty degrees. Before she could even process what happened, her head was where her feet were supposed to be.

"OUCH!" Sarah Bellum said as she crashed and tumbled into the wall. "Stupid power! I'm supposed to be a Visionary. Why can't I see these things in advance? What's the point of being able to see the future if it never benefits me? Stupid, stupid, stupid."

Sarah Bellum could see visions of the future using her ability *Presage*, but mostly for other people. While she was looking into the future, she entered into a trance-like state. To others, she looked like she was lost in thought. To make matters worse, it happened randomly at times which made life very inconvenient for her. She had to see the person in order to get a glimpse of what ill fate the individual in question was about to experience. She thought of it similar to the way superheroes have a sense that alerts them to danger, except it wasn't very handy for herself. *Presage* was like a sixth sense that granted her knowledge more acute to misfortune. Additionally, Sarah could use *Presage* on command and on herself but needed a mirror to be present to look at her own future. All her visions had one thing in common. None of them usually had good outcomes, but with her precognitive sight, she could attempt to avoid those outcomes. This was why she never got any sleep. She was paranoid of a bad future. Although she could see glimpses of other people's far future, the farthest she could see of her own was only a maximum of three hours. So, she arranged her sleep schedule to only sleep three hours at a time. Although it never really helped her, she did manage to save herself from getting bitten by a poisonous spider at one point in her life.

"Okay. It's time to get out of here." Sarah said. She stared at herself in the eyes using the restroom's mirror and used her *Presage* on herself. Her vision suddenly collapsed on itself like a kaleidoscope. She was shown a potential possibility if she continued her current route. Sarah discovered if she had made up her mind that she was going to do something, then *Presage* would tell her how that would end up. The vision of the near future played out in her mind in the first person. In a mere moment, she obtained the knowledge needed to do what she had come here for. Sarah walked out of the restroom and immediately walked towards the venue with condensed crowds.

She needed to waste a little more time before she went for the targeted bag she was told to grab. She thought it would be best to use the pickpocketing skills she had acquired on those more fortunate than her. Her hand mirror had a secret compartment. By pressing a button on the side of it, a razor blade would slide out.

"All right. Time to get to work." Sarah thought. She swiftly slid past a multitude of crowds. During this, she spotted high-quality bags that were being worn by some of the guests. She had done her research and knew that the bag

in question, the Yulie Futo brand bags, had a special compartment specifically designed to hold people's cell phones. Sarah was a smooth criminal. Her getting caught wasn't in the future she saw. Using her almost phantom-like movement, combined with her clumsiness, she gracefully bumped into her targets while slitting the slot with surgical precision. The cell phones would fall right into the purse she had in hand. She was grateful that she was nigh invisible to the rest of the world. She didn't have the apparent beauty that the Young family was renowned for. Her partner in crime Lai, told her it seemed like second nature to her to hide her presence. She managed to grab four cell phones.

"Like taking candy from very rich babies." Sarah thought. She didn't plan on selling the phones as a whole, since people had ways to track their devices in case they ever got lost. Instead, using a contact her partner knew, they would sell them to scalpers in parts. It was a brilliant scheme in her opinion. She was in a way, giving back to the world, even if it was a small amount. Sarah knew that the middle class to lower classes couldn't just buy a new cell phone the moment it broke, unlike the wealthy. It was a win-win. She got a decent bonus on the phone parts and less fortunate people like her could get their phones fixed instead of being forced to buy a new one. Parts for new phones were few and far between. Those who could afford a new phone would simply throw the old ones in the trash and dispose of them. "Okay, it's time for a snack before the real prize," Sarah said quietly. During her escapade, she noticed that food was being

set up in the ballroom. She made her way inside and decided to watch the rest of the Apocalypse run on a screen nearby while snacking on hors d'oeuvres.

"Tasty…" Sarah thought. She was starving. It didn't help that she was flat-out broke thanks to her rent being paid only recently. She had been living from paycheck to paycheck, so buying groceries wasn't exactly something she could afford. *"You certainly have it easy, don't you Freya?"*

Lily found herself standing with Elise in the foyer outside of the Apocalypse run. The area was set up with TVs all around to show different angles for contestants. It had already begun. Lily wished she could have been there to see Ulysses off, but knew that she had more important things to deal with. She needed to figure out Guinevere's plan. She began looking around the crowd of people who were spectating the race, but Guinevere was nowhere to be seen.

"Where did you go?" Lily asked herself. With no luck Lily eventually stood back and watched the race with Elise, all while keeping a watchful eye on those around. One by one her friends were eliminated from the game. Until finally Reighley and company were up against Z.E.D. and an unfamiliar face.

("Hello, Brother." Sunny said. "Are you ready for your lesson?")

"Brother!? I didn't know Ulysses had a brother. What on earth is going on in this race? Now that I think about it… I don't know anything about him." Lily thought. It made her feel disheartened. She hardly knew Ulysses at all.

Buzzing sound.

"Again?" Lily said. Another notification went off on her phone. She went and checked what it was and noticed Guinevere had posted a second time. The post was conspicuous yet odd. It was a blank post that had a linked attachment to a website domain. It felt incredibly sketchy. Part of her believed that if she clicked the link, malware and viruses galore would infect her phone.

"I'll get a new phone later if I need to," Lily reassured herself. She clicked on the link and was taken to a site.

(BOUNTY TO ELIMINATE REIGHLEY SUMMERS FROM THE RACE: 5,000,000 Yen.)

(35,902.00 USD.)

(Place Your Bets)

(12 WIN | LOSE 120)

"What on earth is this!?" Lily asked. She showed Elise the website and Elise placed a finger under her chin. The number of votes for Reighley to lose began to skyrocket in a matter of seconds. The total went past four thousand in an instant.

"Hmm. Interesting. It seems that Guinevere set out a bounty to take out Reighley from the race." Elise explained. "Not very honorable if you ask me."

Suddenly the TV's image began to statically flicker back and forth until it changed to all black. The drones' projections outside began to as well. Then from the darkness, a woman in a dragon mask emerged.

"Testing, testing… Is this thing on?" The voice said. "Ah. Yes. Hello. I am the wise Dragon of Wind Valley. I have come to inform you all that Ray Summers has a bounty on him. Anyone brave enough to eliminate him from the game will receive 5,000,000 yen in prize money." The voice said.

"That's not even a remotely clever disguise." Lily cringed.

"Who knew she was a closet weeb?" Elise said.

"That is all." The Dragon of Wind Valley said before flickering back to Destiny and Isabelle.

In a vehicle parked just east of the runway, Guinevere had taken off her mask.

"How'd I do? With acting as good as that, perhaps they will offer me the next big movie role instead of Freya." Guinevere said jokingly.

"Marvelous, Madam Guinevere. I'm sure no one had a single clue it was you." Donald said.

"What the heck Guinevere!?" Freya shouted at the top of her lungs.

"How did she know it was me!?" Guinevere shivered in fear. "I was flawless."

Chapter 22

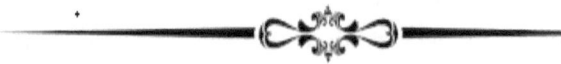

A Minute to Win it.

"Hey! Who do you think you are, stealing the spotlight away from us show hosts?" Destiny shouted into the microphone.

"Yeah, my brother is definitely worth at least 6,000,000 yen, and stop ganging up against him! He's very sensitive." Isabelle said.

"Isabelle! Geez, I'm going to become the laughingstock of school. Never mind that. I don't have time for this." Reighley thought.

The situation immediately became dire. Reighley was at odds against the behemoth of a man that separated him and his best friend. The arrival of Sunny who was now fighting Ulysses tilted the scale towards defeat. The announcement made about his bounty was just another brick of weight added to that pile and despair began to set in.

"A 5,000,000 yen bounty? How is that even fair?" Reighley looked over at Jim and noticed a look of genuine fear. A man Reighley thought was stoic and unshakeable, quivered at the threat that opposed him.

"Come on now, Todoh! This isn't what we agreed upon." Jim attempted to reason with the man.

"A true chef does not discriminate against who they serve!" Todoh yelled.

"Well said, Dad." Sunny agreed. Todoh's arms swept at both Jim and Reighley. It was like two large logs were being crushed together and Reighley and Jim were trapped between.

"They're Fast!" Reighley thought, tracking the incoming attacks. The two ducked underneath the incoming arms narrowly avoiding becoming infected. "You brought him here!?" he shouted at Jim. Reighley took a moment and stared into the eyes of Todoh the tyrant. His aura was as fierce as fire. It almost scorched the earth around him with his blazing battle spirit.

"Why is everyone always against me!?" Reighley desperately rolled away and stood back on his feet. He had no choice but to run away out the end of the barn as Todoh took pursuit. He looked back and noticed that a bunch of weapons spilled out of the bag he acquired from the armory.

"No!" Reighley shouted.

"It looks like our survivors are making a break for it. Go, Reighley! Go!" Isabelle cheered.

"That's right Frizzy Izzy. Come on chat! Let's hear it for Reighley!" Destiny attempted to get some hype generated for her friend. Unintentionally, the rest of the world now knew the name of the mysterious *R*.

"Reighley!" Ulysses shouted. He attempted to charge toward his friend with reckless abandon but stopped.

"Nuh-uh. Not so fast. You'll have to get through me." Sunny said, holding his hand on his weapon blocking the path. Ulysses knew that if he stepped into Sunny's range it would be over in an instant. Sunny was wearing a traditional sports kimono. It was pure white, without a single stain. On it were the characters Shiro, (白) which means white, and shi, (死) meaning death. White Death, was a homage to a famous sniper with over five-hundred-and-five confirmed kills.

"Get out of my way!" Ulysses said, firing his Z-blaster at his brother. It was ineffective as Sunny drew his sword and parried all the blows. He did so with a glowing wooden bamboo sword, labeled Z-Saber.

"You blocked those!?" Ulysses was shocked.

"Did you expect anything less?" Sunny taunted.

"Well... I guess I'm not too surprised. Sunny has always been amazing." Ulysses thought as he began to lower his head along with his guard, accepting the inevitable. *"It's... no use. I can't beat my brother."*

"Don't give up! Do you hear me? You can't stop now. She's... watching. She's watching you!" A loud voice echoed through the barn. Ulysses glanced backward and on the display was Freya, who had taken over the microphone.

"Freya?" Ulysses said.

"There's no way you can just quit now. Everyone is counting on you!" She shouted into the microphone.

"Freya... I... No, you're right. I can't just quit now." Ulysses bolstered himself.

"Do you think you have the luxury to look away!?" Sunny said. Instantly a slash came at Ulysses. He attempted to guard the attack with his Z-blaster while jumping backwards to dodge but his brother was too quick. The end of the blade phased through the weapon as if it was a phantom glazing Ulysses on the jawline leaving a cut up his cheek. That was all that was necessary for his vest to turn from green to yellow.

"Dude! Watch the face!" Ulysses shouted. He placed his hand on his cheek and saw the small amount of blood on his hand.

"Don't get distracted in a duel between men. It's disrespectful." Sunny said.

"It's just a zombie game. It's not that serious man." Ulysses tried to reason with Sunny.

"You're wrong. That friend of yours, she's not the only lady who's watching right now. We need to know if you're ready."

"What? Mom's watching? Ulysses thought, "Ready for what, bro? What does Mom have to do with any of this?" Ulysses questioned.

"I can't tell you that," Sunny explained.

"You've always kept things from me," Ulysses said. "I'm not a little kid anymore!"

Isabelle and Destiny's jaws were dropped from the tension.

"Is that allowed?" Isabelle pointed out Sunny's direct slash at Ulysses.

"I don't know but it sure looked cool! drone guys, get a focus on this battle! This will be great for views." Destiny was ecstatic by the content that could be made from this fight.

Four years ago... during Sunny's senior Kendo tournament. Ulysses was watching his older brother face off against the previous year's winner of the San Fran Kyoto Regional Kendo Championship. Both contestants sat on their knees and took a bow to each other at their respective starting lines that separated the two a short distance. This was required before the start of each round. The objective of the match was to score points by striking your opponent. However, one could not simply strike at a random spot on the body. There were four areas that, if hit, would score you a point in combat. Because of this, a round could end in a matter of seconds. These four are the MEN (the head), KOTE (the wrists), DO (the body), and TSUKI (thrust to the throat). Once any one of those four points was touched by an enemy blade, the swordsmen would score, reset, and start again. The matches would usually be decided by three points.

"*Come on Sunny. Show him who's boss!*" Ulysses thought. The arena was in complete silence. Sunny had his Shinai (Bamboo Sword) at the hip. Readying his Iaijutsu style for combat. It was a completely unconventional fighting style, especially for Kendo. Sunny chose that style for the extra challenge and that it balked in the face of tradition. When he fought back against his opponents it was as if a beast sprang towards its prey with serene grace. Taking advantage of momentary weakness with undiluted ferocity.

The round started and Sunny's eyes tracked his opponent's movements with perfect precision. With each step his opponent took, Sunny would adjust his distance and dodge strikes accordingly and when the moment arrived, Sunny struck his opponent in a single blow scoring him a point.

"Wow! He's so cool." Ulysses' eyes lit up with excitement.

"He sure is." Kokeisha agreed. She was lighting a cigarette in the arena next to her son.

"Umm... Ma'am, you can't smoke in here." A tournament organizer said as he approached her.

"Huh?" Kokeisha scowled.

The second round started as quickly as the first and the competitor came down swiftly with an overhead strike. Sunny's movements seemed inhuman. It almost appeared as if Sunny was experiencing reality in slow motion as he effortlessly dodged the flurry of strikes.

"It's over!" Sunny thought as he drew his sword, slashing his foe. The strike was like that of a phantom. It seemed to pass through the opponent's attempts to guard it and with that, Sunny won the second round.

"So that's the famous phantom strike, huh? Isn't that like cheating or something? Pretty dangerous stuff if you ask me." The tournament organizer said.

"You're wrong. There's more to it than that." Ulysses said. The sound of someone calling his brother a cheater upset him. "Just watch!"

Ulysses' eyes were focused on the movement of Sunny. What others may have called a phantom strike, Ulysses noticed the slight shift in Sunny's wrist which changed the direction of the attack causing it to glide by the defending weapon.

"See! What he does isn't cheating. It takes real skill!" Ulysses defended his brother's honor.

"Looks like cheating to me, but oh well. A wins a win." The tournament organizer announced that Sunny won. He then went on to win that championship and qualify for nationals.

After the fights, Ulysses approached his brother.

"Bro. They are calling you a cheater!" Ulysses said.

"Don't mind them. They aren't exactly wrong…"

"That's because you're just that good, right Sunny?" Ulysses asked.

"Right…" Sunny reluctantly agreed.

"Hey, how did you do that thing where your sword went right through his defense?" Ulysses asked.

"I'll tell you when you're older buddy." Sunny smiled.

"Hey, that's not fair. No keeping secrets from me!" Ulysses pouted.

"You'll know one day. I promise." Sunny patted his younger brother on the head and walked away.

(Back in the present.)

"No matter how hard I tried, I was never able to replicate what you can do, but… I've watched you. For years, I've watched you. I know just how dangerous you are with a blade," Ulysses thought while stepping into the striking zone.

Sunny was surprised by Ulysses' choice, and ecstatic that he chose to face him in close quarters.

"Show me what you can do!" Sunny drew his blade as fast as the wind, ready to end it all in a single motion. Ulysses went to guard the strike coming at his side using the end of his Z Blaster. He watched carefully as Sunny's wrist began to shift ever so slightly to bypass his weapon. However, this was what Ulysses was waiting for. At the moment of impact when the weapon clashed against Ulysses' rib cage, Ulysses lunged towards his brother effectively absorbing the blow and closing the distance between the two. In doing so, his vest began flashing red as he simultaneously wrapped his arm around the blade. He managed to grab a hold of it with his free hand. In a battle of strength versus skill, Ulysses had Sunny beat one hundredfold. Sunny desperately tried to pull free, but when he realized he had lost he couldn't help but grin with pride.

"I know you better than anyone. With a sword, you're a monster, but… without one, you're just my amazing normal older brother." Ulysses thought as he snapped the sword in two holding his Z-blaster a mere inches away from his brother's head.

The audience was in silence. No one said a word as Ulysses stared down his brother. Sunny let go of the weapon and then untied his vest and tossed it on the ground lifting both hands in the air.

"Congrats bro. You win." Sunny said. "Now go and save your friend from Dad."

"He did it!" Isabelle, Destiny, and Freya all screamed into their respective microphones as the chat went wild.

FunnyUser232: Bro, popped off!

Definitely_not_lover_boy: Rigged.

JIMnasium: YO! He had no right going that hard.

DHARC_Blade: One fell swoop.

Lily had to stop her search to look for Guinevere. She couldn't help but cheer on Ulysses far more than the people around her. Many viewers in the crowd knew that she was who was watching. The girl Freya mentioned before.

"You don't look surprised that he won that," Elise said.

"I never doubted for a second that he would win," Lily explained with a smile.

"Where exactly does that faith come from? You would make an excellent Cleric." Elise asked.

"Love... probably," Lily whispered embarrassingly.

"Atta boy, Ulysses!" Reighley cheered.

Reighley and Jim were in a full sprint, shooting their weapons at Todoh. It appeared that weapons did not affect him. Todoh, who was in pursuit of the two, was falling behind at a steady pace. Luckily for the two, Todoh's enormous frame was more of a hindrance as it prevented him from being an effective sprinter. Reighley knew that he couldn't just run out in the open either. That would make him an easy target for those wanting his bounty. Looking over his shoulder at Todoh as he ran, Reighley almost felt like he had better odds facing hunters than he did against Ulysses's dad.

"The finish line is straight ahead." Reighley pointed towards the pagoda tower that marked the end of the race. It was just past one more landmark. Just ahead was a town pulled straight out of a Flint Wastewood movie. He noticed that the path up ahead was strangely absent of competitors. *"Something's wrong."* He thought. *"I'm certain that besides Ulysses, we're in last place."* He looked up at the remaining survivors and to his surprise, the number hadn't decreased since they took out the two people in the barn and lost Joy as an ally.

(Remaining Survivors: 8)

"Jim… I think there is a trap set up ahead." Reighley panted heavily.

"What makes you think that?" Jim said.

"Look how many survivors are left, yet there's no one up ahead. They must be hiding somewhere." Reighley claimed.

"Hmm, you're probably right." Jim agreed.

The path ahead was riddled with artificial tumbleweed and sand. There appeared to be a few structures before the end of the race. This made the pagoda tower at the end feel more like a mirage as the setting sun reflected off its multiple rooftops. Reighley had lost some deadweight thanks to him spilling the weapons he worked so hard for, but he still had some firepower to spare. He had two Special Grade-Z Blasters, four Z-grenades, and a Special Grade-Z Rifle left over in his bag. He knew he would need every last piece of ammunition to reach the end.

Finally, Reighley and Jim arrived at an outpost. The area up until now had been marginally open, but now it was as if they arrived in a small western town. The town itself was only a mere crossroad that had a saloon, inn, and other commodities.

"It looks like our main survivors have arrived at Deadwood Outpost. This original town was imported from Spain." Destiny said.

"It's a ghost town. This is the place where dreams go to die! Your ambitions, hopes, and aspirations all mean nothing when looking at the barrel end of a gun." Isabelle said with a country accent.

"You mean a muzzle right? Also, you do know those words basically mean the same thing." Freya explained.

"Don't steal her thunder, Freya. It's the narration that keeps the spectacle alive." Destiny said.

"Imported? Glad to see all my hard-earned money go to good use." Jim groaned.

"Really? That's it? That's what caught your attention and not the entire zombie run itself?" Reighley asked.

"Well. Fair point." Jim agreed as the two approached an old wagon tipped over on its side.

"How much did those Elite Zombies cost?" Reighley interrogated.

"What Elite Zombies...?" Jim began sweating nervously.

"Right..." Reighley rolled his eyes.

Their conversation was suddenly interrupted by the sound of glass being stepped on coming from the saloon.

"Hold it right there!" a voice came from inside the saloon to the right of them.

"Who's there?" Reighley sighed.

"It's me Deven Stallik. The dashing gunmen here to win the race." Deven growled.

"Who?" Reighley asked.

"Ugh! You're so annoying! You very well know who I am. I'd quit acting so smug if I were you. You're not in the position to bad mouth me. You're completely surrounded."

"Is that so, then why don't you stop hiding then Deven?" Reighley was feeling brave; he then noticed the red lasers all pointing at his chest. There were people set up on the balconies of the buildings. Each with their own Z Rifle pointed at Reighley.

"Crap. I didn't think he would get everyone to work together." Reighley whispered.

"Is he one of Freya's fans from SocialLight or something?" Jim asked.

"Stop mocking me!" Deven yelled. "I'm Freya's ex-boyfriend."

"Oh, you mean Todd! I remember you now. Why are you going by your last name?"

Deven could only scream in annoyance. His rage was deafening to the ears.

"Go on, Mr. Young. We have no business with you. You can go on ahead." Gunman B shouted on top of the Inn.

Reighley was up in arms ready to draw his weapon at his enemies like a good old fashion standoff. He noticed something was odd. There were only four enemies including Deven and no infected. Ulysses was not far behind them.

"But if there are eight remaining survivors, who's the last one?" He thought. His attention was immediately drawn towards Jim, who he expected to abandon him altogether.

"What's the hold-up, Mr. Young?" Gunman A questioned from on top of the Saloon's balcony.

"Don't make us shoot you." Deven threatened.

"Oh? Go on, try me." Jim scowled. Deven, who was peeking out of the saloon's double doors aiming his weapon at Reighley, had a shiver sent down his spine.

"Looking cool," Reighley said.

"That bravado of yours ain't so bad either kid. You've sure got guts." Jim smirked.

Before they knew it the two enemies were back to back in a standoff against four gunmen.

"So that's it huh? You guys are going to kill me and split the bounty?" Reighley asked.

"Yeah! What of it?" Gunmen C asked on top of the General Stores balcony.

487

"What exactly makes you all think that the one who finishes me off is going to share that 5,000,000 yen prize with the rest of ya?" Reighley asked.

Reighley's eyes were dead set on victory. He knew that question alone was all it took for their alliance to waiver even just for a second. He carefully watched as three of the four lasers swayed off his body momentarily. He seized the opportunity, quickly drew his special grade Z-Blaster, and fired directly at Deven, who was the only remaining one targeting him. Reighley's aim was true. He hit Deven and watched as a single shot turned his vest to a flashing red. This caused Deven to retreat into the Saloon in panic.

The moment Jim saw Reighley act he capitalized on Deven's dismayed reaction. He took his Heavy Z-Sniper Rifle and aimed down his sights towards the survivor on top of the General Store. The weapon immediately turned the vest on the gunmen from blue to a solid red, eliminating him in one shot. A person's weapon functionality was directly tied to their vest. If their vest signified them dead, then their weapons would not fire. This gave both Reighley and Jim enough time to find cover to hide behind. They both dove toward the knocked-over wagon. It was positioned with just enough room for the two to survive the onslaught of shots from the gunmen.

"Man, Mr. Young, that gun sure is overpowered," Reighley complained. He couldn't help but talk with an old-fashioned southern drawl the longer he stayed in this place.

"Well it's technically a cheat weapon, but I've got some bad news. It's out of ammo." Jim said.

"Cheat weapon? What type of cheat weapon runs out of ammo?" Reighley didn't hesitate in giving Jim his spare Special Grade Z Assault Rifle.

"Yeah. I had it especially made to be used on you to eliminate you in a single shot and I was going to do it too." Jim said.

"Then why didn't you?" Reighley questioned.

Jim paused. The sound of incoming fire was present during their conversation but that didn't stop the two from conversing, it only drowned out the drone's ability to pick up their voices.

"Because... shooting you would make me look like the bad guy. I couldn't just shoot you after you dove out and tried to protect my little girl. You know, I had a realization during all this. I thought to myself, 'Just when did my daughter get so many friends and why didn't I notice it before? When I looked at those surrounding Freya, they genuinely cared and supported her. I came here ready for war, but I couldn't find an enemy amongst them. Even you, who was someone I didn't approve of. I could no longer deny the efforts you made to make my daughter happy. It was just so frustrating for me. When Freya chose to run over to you rather than her own father. That hurt me more than you could ever know. I tried to control her, but I only ended up pushing her further away. Instead of being a businessman, I should have just been her father. I'm so used to getting what I want because of my profession so when she rebelled I was irrationally angry. I let those emotions of anger consume me and I blamed you. I wasn't sure what to do. All the money in the world would mean nothing to me if my family wasn't my legacy. And now, because of my actions, my only child refuses to look me in the eyes. But with you, I had never seen Freya so happy before." Jim confessed everything that had been on his mind as of late.

Reighley thought the man before him was stone-cold and borderline heartless, but that changed when he looked into his eyes. Reighley saw his aura. It was simple in shape and brown in color. There was no spectacular image, no knife held to Reighley's throat, instead just a normal man with a normal brown aura.

"I'm... sorry I made you feel that way. You won't have to worry about me after tonight." Reighley replied.

"You were serious about leaving her?" Jim asked.

"Yeah," Reighley said.

"Then why are you trying to win?" Jim asked.

Reighley didn't have an immediate answer. There could have been a multitude of reasons why he tried so hard. Part of it was due to the sacrifices others made for him to get to this point. Another reason was that he wanted to give Freya a memorable birthday. However, he knew the truth.

"I just really want to dance with the girl I like," Reighley answered honestly.

"Would you look at the two! These two opposing forces have continually been put under pressure and seem to have formed an unlikely alliance. What could possibly be more inspiring than the bond of a man with his future inlaw?" Isabelle asked.

"Yeah sound crew, what's the big idea? How come we missed out on all that spicy content." Destiny was outraged.

"It appears the sound of the gunfire is distorting our microphones." Sound Guy A answered.

Freya had stepped outside of the display and was watching the run from a setup. She looked at the onslaught of incoming fire at the two most important men in her life. *"What… are they talking about?"* Freya wondered. *"I've never seen my Dad look as vulnerable as that. Reighley… even now, you're trying to help us aren't you?"*

"That's some man you brought here. I'm not sure what those two are talking about but I've never seen Jim look like that before." Prismarine said.

"Mom…" Freya said.

Reighley was feeling the pressure from the incoming fire and knew something had to change.

"Here. Can you cover me? I want to get into the Saloon." Reighley asked.

"I can't. There isn't an opportunity to fire back. Don't these guys ever run out of ammo?" Jim scoffed.

"This is getting bad… It looks like Todoh has caught up with us.' Reighley said, pointing towards the entrance of town at Todoh. He looked winded but managed to catch up being forty meters away.

"We have to make a move now!" Jim said assertively.

"No. Not yet." Reighley said.

"What? Why? We're screwed if he makes it to us." Jim explained.

"He won't! My friend was behind us. He'll stop him.

"How can you be sure?" Jim asked.

"Because that's the type of man he is. He'll definitely show up for sure." Reighley said.

The two waited in anticipation as Todoh gradually grew closer to them until suddenly he fell to the ground straining to move.

"Sorry to keep you waiting!" Ulysses shouted over the incoming fire. He wrapped Todoh from behind and put him in a Full-Nelson knocking him to the ground. It took every ounce of strength out of him to hold his father in place. "Go! I can't hold him forever." Todoh touched Ulysses' arm, turning his vest green, starting the timer to his demise.

"Took you long enough dude!" Reighley said with a wholehearted laugh.

"Sorry to burst your bubble, kid, but that doesn't change that we're boxed in and under fire. Once his vest times out we're done for." Jim worried.

"Don't be so sure. Isn't that right Herald!?" Reighley shouted with a smile.

"Herald?" Jim was astonished. Immediately, one of the gunmen stopped firing, and then the next. Herald, the eighth and last remaining survivor, strolled out of the shadows after shooting both armed men on the two balconies.

"Glad to see you still believed in me, Master Summers," Herald said with a smile.

"Look how the tables have turned. The last remaining contestants were eliminated leaving Deven in first place, with Jim, Herald, and Reighley just behind him, with Ulysses in last." Isabelle said.

"Somebody please don't let Deven win! We can see that he snuck out the back of the saloon and is headed towards the finish line," Destiny shouted.

"I'm calling my lawyers after this! This game is completely rigged!" Deven hollers from a distance.

"Oh, would you look at that? Breaking News! It's been rumored that apparently Devin Stalik and Freya Young kissed during their recent movie recording session." Destiny said.

"*What?!*" Both Jim and Reighley both jumped up simultaneously.

"DESTINY!" Freya shouted.

"Alright, we have to cut the commentating momentary-" Destiny was immediately shut off from the screen as the monitors now displayed Deven who was en route to the pagoda tower.

"Come on, let's go!" Reighley said.

"You go on ahead... This old man has had enough adventure for one day." Herald said completely out of breath. "I'll cover you in case the undead show up."

"Well done." Jim praised his butler.

"Yeah. Thanks again, Herald, and thank you, Ulysses!" Reighley waved off his comrades and rushed towards the pagoda tower. He couldn't waste another second. However, some part of him knew that reaching the tower wasn't the end. He had a sneaking suspicion that once there, you would have to climb the tower.

When the two arrived, Reighley half expected the undead to start rising up from beneath the earth. When he entered the building, a quick look at the interior showed the structure was built like a giant spiral staircase. The floor was made of a sleek dark wood and hanging on the walls were Japanese black ink paintings of ancient warriors of the past fighting Oni. Up above, the sound of a weapon was being fired only a floor above.

"Come on Jim, Let's go!" Reighley beckoned. "You still have some fight left in you? If you slow me down I'll leave you behind."

"Heh... Plenty. Don't underestimate me, kid." Jim replied, gasping for air.

Suddenly both ankles of the survivors were latched onto by hands below the wooden floors. This caused both Reighley and Jim's vest to turn green, initiating the countdown towards infection, afterward the hands broke their hold on Jim and Reighley.

Time Remaining: 58 Seconds

"You've got to be kidding me," Jim complained.

"It's alright! I have a sterilizer! One of us can still make it-" Reighley said, pulling out the temporary cure for his infection.

"We're sorry. Healing and curing items are temporarily disabled for dramatic effect." Destiny's voice said from within Reighley's vest.

"Now that's just cruel." Reighley groaned as he was given no choice but to scale the tower in a minute's time.

Deven was ahead, but not by much. He too was infected, now racing against the clock. As Reighley ran up the staircase Deven spotted him from above.

"Come on man! Let me have this!" Deven shouted, he was half a floor up and was firing down across the interceding space. He had no luck hitting Reighley, as the railings on the staircase had subsequent wooden pillars in between, making for a hard shot.

"Fat chance!" Reighley said, aiming his weapon to return fire at Deven. *"He's hard to hit!"*

"You don't understand!" Deven screamed while taking out the undead that lay before him. "I need to win this!"

"Dude. All you do is win! You're basically blessed." Reighley argued.

"Me? Blessed? As if! My blessing is a curse! Because of my father and his career, no one will ever attribute anything to me. No matter what I do, people will always say that I only got the opportunities I was given because of my Dad! I'm always living in his shadow."

"His dad is a famous actor from the eighties." Jim nodded.

"Ugh... Come on heart, don't make me sympathize with this guy!" Reighley thought. *"He's a scumbag, who kissed your girlfriend and he doesn't deserve to win."* Reighley couldn't help but reflect on himself at this moment. *"Then again... neither do I."*

Reighley knew what he had to do. He took his pistol and aimed a shot at Deven Stallik directly in the back. The shot connected right before Deven made it to the second floor staircase eliminating him from the competition.

"Sorry man, but tonight isn't about you. Nothing personal, but I can't let you win." Reighley shouted. Eventually, Jim and Reighley passed Deven, who was looking grim. His head was down and his weapon was dropped.

Time Remaining: 25 Seconds

Reighley and Jim were on the third floor. They could see the finish line from the top of the stairs. With their Special Grade Weapons and leftover grenades, They made swift work with the undead that appeared out of nowhere like ninja. They would be hidden behind paintings or underneath floor mats. When the two made it to the final staircase to the top floor, Jim was falling behind. Reighley was halfway up when he noticed Jim had stopped running.

"Go on kid... You earned it." Jim praised, while exhausted. He bent over, putting both hands on his knees. Reighley completely understood what Jim was feeling as his legs felt like he had lead weights strapped to each of them.

Behind Jim was an undead ready to pounce on the now exacerbated-looking man.

Time Remaining: 12 Seconds

"Ahhhhhh!" Reighley yelled with determination. He turned around and went back down the staircase, shooting the undead and hoisting Jim up, lending him his shoulder.

"What are you doing?-" Jim was confused.

"We started this together, and we're finishing it together!" Reighley said, exerting all the energy he had left in him to help move Jim.

"*This kid…*" Jim couldn't help but chuckle at the thought.

With that Jim and Reighley made it to the top floor, and awaiting them were two flags and a red ribbon to cross.

Time Remaining: 3… 2… 1…

Before the countdown could finish, Reighley shoved Jim across the finish line, ending the race. Reighley's vest turned a solid red, eliminating him from the race. The sound of fireworks went off, signaling the end of the competition, bringing back the commentators' feed, as confetti rained down around the victor.

"But… why…?" Jim asked with shock.

"Like I told Deven, tonight isn't about us. It's about what Freya needs." Reighley explained. "And right now, she needs her dad to be here for her birthday."

The fact Reighley was willing to give up his earned victory, so Jim could have a father-daughter slow dance, seemed like lunacy to him, but even so, Jim couldn't deny the boy's feelings.

As the feed returned to normal, it showed Freya who held Destiny in a headlock while Isabelle was smiling and waving at the cameras.

"And the winner is… Jim?" Isabelle announced.

"What?" Destiny and Freya said together.

"Dad won?" Freya let go of Destiny, completely stumped by the results of the race, along with the millions of viewers, who were also shocked by the result.

Chapter 23

The End of Everything: Part 1

"**I**n a shocking turn of events, it appears that Reighley, better known as, Loverboy R, pushed Jim Young across the finish line!" Destiny announced.

"It's better this way." Reighley thought. He was completely and utterly exhausted. Every muscle in his body was telling him to collapse.

"I thought you wanted to slow dance with the girl you liked?" Jim questioned.

"I do," Reighley said. He then walked towards the stairs and made his way down the pagoda tower. Jim was blown away at what had just happened. He didn't know people like Reighley still existed. The world Jim was used to was cutthroat. It had to be since everything was business-oriented. Even though he had won the race, Jim felt like he had lost as he watched the back of Reighley slowly disappear down the stairs. With no choice, he pulled out his cell phone and called his assistant.

"Susan, it's Jim. I need you to push the meeting to tomorrow. I'm spending tonight with my family." Jim said and hung up the phone on his assistant before she could respond. He knew that it was bad for business to reschedule things, but tonight was different. It was his daughter's sixteenth birthday and after everything he had just gone through, he wouldn't miss it for the world. Knowing that the situation was still rocky between him and his daughter, Jim did the only thing that he could think of to get her to talk to him. He got out his phone and texted her.

Meanwhile, Sarah Bellum was captivated by the zombie run, it had made her lose track of time. She looked at the watch on her left wrist and knew it was time to make her move. She immediately walked towards the area with all of Freya's gifts. Her vision told her that she could take one without any major issues. She walked past the table with many of the gift bags and nonchalantly grabbed one while passing by. She then quickly made her way towards the exit.

"Okay Sarah, remember what you saw." Sarah encouraged herself. On her way, she was stopped in her tracks.

"Hi, Sarah! Long time, no see. How are you dear?" Prismarine asked.

"Hello, Aunty Prim Prim. I'm doing fine." Sarah greeted with a fake smile. She knew this was coming, but she still didn't enjoy speaking to any of the Young Family.

"What do you have there? Is that your gift for Freya?" Prismarine asked.

"Oh, this? Yeah, but I forgot the card for it in my car. I have to go run and grab that real quick." Sarah explained.

"Oh well, you can leave the gift on the table. I'll make sure Freya doesn't open it beforehand." Prismarine suggested.

"No, that's fine really. I would rather I give it to her in private." Sarah was trying desperately to flee. She knew if she was caught stealing from her cousin her life would be over as she knew it.

"Alright, and you need to start taking better care of yourself young woman. I don't wish for you to end up like my sister." Prismarine said with concern.

"Yeah. Will do." Sarah nodded. Like a punch to the gut, those words cut into Sarah's soul. *"Like you actually care,"* she thought to herself. Sarah proceeded to head toward the door so she could escape in her vehicle. She drove herself here in her early 2000's Chevi. Now was the perfect time to leave as most of the crowd seemed to have gathered at the runway. Okay, just one more obstacle. I can't be spotted by Freya. Sarah while walking outside knew that Freya was leaving the property for one reason or another. She saw the girl exiting the side entrance and heading towards the streaming setup. Curious, she decided to use *Presage* on the birthday girl. The vision showed Sarah, Freya's up-and-coming bad future.

"I see you've changed a lot." Sarah thought. Finally, she arrived outside and she knew this was where the misfortune was going to occur. Her vision warned her that she was going to trip and fall and break the items stolen in the bag she had just stolen while going down the steps of the

entrance. So she gently placed the bag on the ground and then turned towards the two security guards at the entrance.

"Hey, don't mind me," Sarah said as she hurled herself down the steps as if she had jumped off a cliff. This was the trick to her thievery. As long as something bad happened to her that was similar to what she had seen by the end of the vision, she could circumvent the ending. Sarah tumbled down the steps until she reached the bottom and caught herself.

"Hey! Are you okay?" The guards asked with heavy concern.

"Yep! Perfectly fine." She gave a thumbs-up while still on the floor. She was exhausted, bruised, and scraped, but she did it. She had survived the future she had seen. She walked all the way back up the stairs, grabbed the gift she placed down, and walked toward her car without any further issues. Once at her car door, she looked back at the entrance of Fiore Gemello, and with one final thought, she departed.

"Sorry Freya, but tonight isn't going to end well for you." Sarah thought while leaving the party.

Freya didn't know how to feel. Part of her was angry, while the other half was scared. She knew deep down that she didn't have to slow dance with her dad, but also knew that if she didn't then she would end up making Reighley upset with her after he tried so hard to get the two together. Freya, in desperate need of guidance, grabbed her best friend Destiny and pulled her away from the stream setup.

"Destiny, what- what do I do?" Freya asked.

"Well, he did win, so...." Destiny shrugged.

"I'm serious. I don't think I want to be anywhere near him right now." Freya said.

"Do you really hate him that much?" Destiny questioned.

The question caught Freya off guard. She was at a loss for words. Although he hurt her deeply, she couldn't call her feelings towards her dad hate. She was just upset that he had been gone for so long. For the entirety of his absence, she had missed him. Then, when he finally came home, instead of giving her the attention she needed, he threatened everything Freya had been working towards up until now.

"Of course, I don't hate him. He's my Dad." Freya answered quietly.

"Then dance with him. I get that you were mad at him for separating you from everyone, but I think it's time you stopped running away from your problems. Whatever you decide, I'll stand by your decision." Destiny advised.

Freya stopped and considered everything. She still didn't completely know why Reighley pushed her dad over the finish line after working so hard. She wanted him to dance with her first. To show the whole world just how serious she was about Reighley. She was torn on the decision to make until she received a sudden text from her father.

Jim: I canceled my meeting.

"Canceled? Does that mean he's staying? Well to be honest.... I'm surprised he stayed for as long as he did." She wondered if it was Reighley's doing.

Meanwhile, Donald and Guinevere were hiding away inside a van that was parked nearby. She had been watching the race from inside and was enraged at the fact Reighley threw the race.

"What on earth does he think he's doing? The finish line was right there. Why'd you have to go and lose on your own terms? Don't tell me... you wanted the bounty all for yourself?" Since she assumed Reighley was greedy, Guinevere guessed Reighley must have thought eliminating himself from the game would make him the prize winner. She couldn't feel anything other than cheated. She had gotten what she wanted, but not the way she wanted it. She was supposed to be reveling in the fact that Freya had completely lost, but the look on her face when Reighley got eliminated was all wrong. She had paid a fair amount of pocket change for the bounty on his head, yet no one managed to take him out except for himself.

"Why, why, why? Why her!?" Outraged, Guinevere began to knock equipment around in the small van. "What makes her so special? Is it her hair? I can change my hair to red. Why go so far for her? It doesn't make any sense. She's the worst!"

"Madam Guinevere?" Donald said before being interrupted.

"Don't get me started with you! You were supposed to eliminate him! Why do I even keep you around? You're useless! Get out of my sight! You're fired!" Guinevere yelled at Donald.

"I... I understand. I'm sorry... I wish I could have been of more use to you Madam." Donald nodded and exited the vehicle. Before he closed the door behind him he wished to give Guinevere one more piece of advice. "Might I suggest you tell the boy how you feel?" Donald advised and then took his leave.

She hadn't even processed what she had just done. She looked at the only remaining ally she thought she had and watched as he turned his back to her, both physically and emotionally.

Guinevere used *Reverie* on the butler, reading the thoughts above his head. It read, "*And after everything I've done for you...*" Donald thought. Soon, he was out of earshot and Guinevere was left alone.

"Fine, leave! I'll do this myself! It's not like that will work anyway! I already know how he feels. Anyone could tell that by now." Guinevere's tone began to settle down. Her shouts reverberated in the van causing even the silence after to seem loud in comparison. The rush of anger inside her turned into overwhelming loneliness. "Besides, he can see right through me... He would know that I wasn't being genuine." Guinevere answered as if someone was listening to her, but no one was. She was alone just as she always had been. What Guinevere wanted more than anything was for someone to put up a fight for her. To stay, even if she told them to leave. To accept her as a whole and show unconditional love. Not even her parents did that for her. She had hoped that Donald was that someone, but she was wrong. Frustrated, she looked down at her phone and checked the results of the voting.

(BOUNTY TO ELIMINATE REIGHLEY SUMMERS FROM THE RACE: 5,000,000 Yen.)

(35,902.00 USD.)

(Place Your Bets)

(34,231 WIN | LOSE 15,456)

Somewhere along the race, even the audience started believing in Reighley. At the end of the race, the people who won the voting were awarded a free subscription to Guinevere's SocialLight page for a month. As a subscriber, they would get access to exclusive streams that wouldn't be posted on her main account, as well as custom stickers they could use in her chat. She had hoped that this event would increase her growth on social media, allowing her to surpass Freya. She quickly checked her analytics and to some degree, it worked. She had a spike of five thousand followers, but that still brought her nowhere near the amount of followers Freya had.

"I'm always losing to you. Everyone always caters to you." Guinevere said with resentment. She was looking at the livestream of Freya's party. It had a camera just switched over to Freya before Destiny began to announce the next event.

"Ladies and Gentlemen! I am happy to announce that we are moving on! That's right. It's time for the Ballroom Dance! I'm sure I don't need to tell you where to head next. The dance will commence in twenty minutes, please use that time to freshen up. We have showers prepared for those who competed." Destiny said. Not all hope was lost for Guinevere. She still could continue her plan. She just needed to get a chance to talk with Reighley alone.

Ulysses had been waiting for Reighley inside the locker rooms. He had already finished showering and instead stayed because he needed advice from his best friend. Reighley walked through the doors looking like a corpse.

"Dude, did you get turned by the zombies? You look terrible." Ulysses said.

"I feel even worse." Reighley groaned like an undead and nodded. His movement was sluggish. He was given a ride back to the locker in a golf cart, but even the walk from the cart to the locker room felt like an extra mile to him. The locker was filled with plenty of people who ended up losing the race alongside Reighley. Ulysses didn't want people to overhear him so he got close to Reighley and whispered to him.

"I want to ask Lily out. What should I do? I'm nervous." Ulysses asked.

"What? Why are you nervous? She'll say yes for sure. You have a guarantee." Reighley encouraged. He used *Insight* on his best friend and noticed that the flaming aura he was so used to seeing was but an ember in comparison.

"That's the part I'm nervous about. What if she says yes? What do I do after that? How do I have a girlfriend?" Ulysses was starting to get flustered.

"To be honest, I'm not sure I'm qualified to answer you, but still, I think you're overthinking it dude," Reighley said.

"Funny... Freya told me the same thing" Ulysses mentioned. "Still I want to do it, but I'm just not ready."

"Here, I'll go do it," Reighley said, as he began walking past Ulysses towards the exit of the locker room. It was as if the objective gave Reighley newfound strength. Ulysses began to realize that Reighley was serious when he had almost reached the door.

"No! Wait!" Ulysses began panicking as he stepped in front of Reighley, blocking his path. "You can't do that. I'll look like a loser. I would die of embarrassment." Ulysses pleaded.

"Then man up. If you don't, I'll do it for you." Reighley threatened.

"Fine! I'll- I'll do it. Just please don't ask her out for me." Ulysses said.

"Good. Now excuse me while I go to recover in the shower." Reighley gave Ulysses a thumbs up. "You got this bud. Tell me how it goes." Soon after, Reighley walked into a shower room and began to sulk. "*At least one of us gets a happy ending.*" He thought as he crouched down with a bittersweet smile.

Lily was waiting for Ulysses and Reighley just outside the entrance to the locker rooms. She figured she could tackle two things at once. She wanted to congratulate Ulysses, and also speak with Reighley to inform him that

Guinevere was up to no good. Eventually, Ulysses walked out of the locker room and Lily caught his attention.

"You were amazing!" Lily rushed over to Ulysses embracing him with a hug.

"Lily!?" Ulysses didn't know where to place his hands. *"Is it okay if I hug her?"* Ulysses thought to himself.

"I knew you wouldn't lose," Lily said. "And even if you did, that wouldn't change a thing."

"Hah… thanks." Ulysses awkwardly scratched his head until he realized that Lily had changed out of her clothes. "What happened to your dress?"

"Umm… it got ripped. Don't worry about it." Lily lied. She noticed Ulysses' arms were hovering dormant as if lost in space. She knew he needed the small push, to let him know it was okay. She whispered teasingly, "If you can't hug me back then our dance later on tonight is going to be a bit awkward." She grabbed onto both arms and wrapped them around herself. Ulysses began blushing as red as the sun.

"I thought it looked great on you." Ulysses complimented.

"Your apocalypse outfit was pretty neat too." Lily smiled.

"I was trying to look cool for you…" Ulysses replied.

"Dummy… you don't need to change a thing." Lily squeezed Ulysses.

"Someone told me recently that I need to live up to my potential." Ulysses hugged Lily back. For a moment he began to wonder where the two stood and what type of relationship he and Lily had. *"Is this alright? A girl like this wouldn't wait outside to hug me if she didn't like me. I feel like, if I asked her out, things would work out, but that's scarier than being rejected. Should I do it? Reighley said if I don't he'll do it. I couldn't live with myself if that happened... Both Freya and Reighley told me I had been overthinking things. Okay Ulysses, tell her how you feel."* Ulysses was feeling abnormally courageous. He attributed it to the fact that he had defeated his brother and put his father in a Full-Nelson. Briefly, after the race was over his father told him he was proud of him as soon as he had been let go. It had been the first real praise he had received from his father since he picked up cooking.

"If not now, then when?" Ulysses encouraged himself. The thought of confessing caused Ulysses' heart rate to accelerate to new heights. He opened his mouth to ask the question and he could feel his adrenaline spike as fear and hope seeped through him simultaneously.

"Ulysses, are you okay?" Lily said, looking upward deep into his eyes. She could feel his heart racing. He had his mouth slightly opened but had yet to say a word causing Lily to become embarrassed by how long she was being held.

"Lily. I like you." Ulysses confessed. Words began pouring out of him in a rush. "I like everything about you. The way you're beyond thoughtful, and how you like my cooking so much. I like how you know exactly what I mean even when I can't get the words out the right way. I like the way your blue eyes remind me of the sky and the way your hair reflects the light of the sun right off of it. I like how beautiful and kind you are, and how you see the best in me, even when I don't. I know that this isn't an ideal place or time, but I need to know… Lily Monet, will you go out with me, just us, like on a real date?" Ulysses asked.

"You sure mentioned my looks a lot." Lily teased.

"I- uhh…" Ulysses was stumped.

"I was waiting for you to ask," Lily mentioned. "Yes. I will go out with you. On a real date." Lily chuckled. She thought the way Ulysses stumbled upon his words was cute. Although she was remaining calm on the outside, feeling butterflies was the only way Lily could describe how she was feeling. Her heart had skipped a beat when he spoke.

"Congrats you two!" Freya said with excitement. Her sudden appearance caused Lily and Ulysses to let go of each other due to the surprise. They couldn't look Freya in the eyes and were stunned with embarrassment. The embarrassed silence between the two of them was nearly palpable as both Ulysses and Lily refused to look at one another. "Now we can go on a double date."

"Yeah…" Ulysses nodded uncomfortably. For once, he was grateful for his social awkwardness since he knew that there weren't any double dates after tonight. He was determined to be the best friend that he could be. It was his duty to keep the secrets of his brothers.

"Have you guys seen Reighley? I feel like I haven't got to see him much tonight." Freya said.

"He's freshening up," Ulysses replied.

"Well… if you see him, tell him I need to talk to him. It's important." Freya explained. She had been getting antsy at this point. She didn't know why but she could feel Reighley slipping away from her with each passing second. She wanted to talk with him about their future more than anything. Freya knew how she felt about Reighley and how he felt about her, or at least she hoped she knew how he felt. Some part of her had a sneaking suspicion that Reighley had been avoiding her all evening, but she wouldn't let him run away. They need to have an honest talk about where their relationship stands after tonight. Deciding to push it off until the two danced together, she walked away from the new couple with a nervous look in her eyes.

Eventually, Destiny announced that it was time for the Ballroom Dance, and all the attendees made their way to the ballroom that was located in the northwest section of Fiore Gemello. She surveyed the crowd looking for the headliners that would be making the biggest splash of the night. She first noticed Freya, who was waiting on the dais next to a booth that had DJ_Destiny icons all over it. She appeared to be looking for Reighley to show up amongst the crowd. Destiny then spotted Elise and Lily talking to Herald, and after a brief discussion, the three split up while on high alert for someone. She found Jim waiting off in the corner rehearsing words to himself, and then saw Ulysses towering awkwardly on his phone while by the punch bowl. He was looking for someone while using his cell phone to text. Isabelle was still commenting about how awesome the race went, going over highlights. She was so involved with the role of commentator that she took the lead as host. Destiny's surveillance had to come to an end as she needed to leave the streaming booth to rescue Ash from being hit on by a now romance-hungry Deven Stallik.

During all of this, almost everyone had the same question on their mind.

"*Where is Reighley?*" They thought.

Meanwhile, Reighley had just put his suit back on. He was looking at himself in the mirror, still unable to look himself directly in the eyes.

"Things haven't changed one bit..." He muttered to himself. He heard a buzzing sound from his phone. He had received a text from Ulysses.

Ulysses: Hey. Freya wants to talk to you. She said it's important.

Reighley: Thanks.

He closed his phone, placed it in his pocket, and made his way out of the locker room. Waiting there for him was Guinevere, who ambushed him. She had managed to sneak back into the party and found Reighley out of coincidence. She pulled him the furthest away from the ballroom against his will.

"What in the!" Reighley yelped.

"Shut up and come with me!" Guinevere threatened.

When the two were finally alone Guinevere realized she was holding Reighley's hand and became flustered, letting go immediately. She used *Reverie* to read Reighley's thoughts.

"*I don't have time for this.*" Reighley thought.

"*So, I'm not even worth your time.*" Guinevere thought.

"What do you want?" Reighley asked. He was on edge. "*Please, I've already worked so hard. I just want the day to end already.*" It had been the first time in a long time that Reighley had complained out of frustration.

"Just be quiet, will you? I just need to talk with you for a minute." Guinevere explained.

"Make it quick," Reighley ordered. "*I'm sick of this girl.*" He thought. Those thoughts cut a deep wound in Guinevere's already gaping heart.

"This... is for you." Guinevere held a card towards Reighley.

"What is this?" Reighley was puzzled.

"5,000,000 yen. You won it since you eliminated yourself. This is what you wanted right? That's why you dated Freya. It was for the money, wasn't it? Now you don't have to be with her anymore." Guinevere was shaking. The anxiety she was feeling sank to the pits of her stomach, making her almost want to throw up.

"I... don't know what to say," Reighley said. For once he actually didn't feel gross by receiving money from someone. He did go out on his own terms, so it made sense that he won the prize for his bounty. "*I guess she's not all that bad...*" He thought. "*It's true that I started dating Freya because she paid me, but that isn't why I stayed.*"

"Please just take it." Guinevere extended her arms outward. "It's not a trick or a trap. I'm not deceiving you. You earned it."

Reighley finally looked Guinevere in the eyes using *Insight* on her while accepting the card and pocketing it. He braced for the cold wasteland he had known her for. Yet instead, he was greeted with the feeling of cold isolation. Something he knew far too well. Guinevere's aura appeared to be a silhouette of someone desperately holding onto dear life as a vicious blizzard was actively killing them. He had never experienced loneliness to that degree, despite his escapades in Juvy. Guinevere looked at Reighley as if he was the only source of heat in one hundred miles.

"Now that you're basically single... would you go out with me?" Guinevere asked. Deep down she knew what the answer was going to be, but part of her wanted to try asking anyway because Donald had suggested it.

"Guinevere... I'm flattered really, but you don't want me." Reighley said.

"But... why?" She asked

Reighley didn't have to search very far inside his heart to find the answer he was looking for.

"Sometimes... We fall in love with the wrong people. I'm not that person for you or anyone." Reighley said with saddened eyes.

"But you have to! Otherwise, I'll tell everyone that Freya paid for you to date her. I'll ruin her whole career!" Guinevere threatened.

"Guinevere. Don't do this." Reighley said.

"I'm out of options." She replied. "My parents, they don't speak to me unless they have to. Even my butler left me. I have no one." The sheer isolation caused Guinevere to break out in a cold sweat. She was getting desperate. The shock to her body stimulated a feeling of anxiety she had only felt one other time in her life. "She's always taking things from me. Even... back then." She finally remembered what had happened.

"Back then?" Reighley questioned.

"She died. My one and only friend. The only one who didn't leave me by choice. Ivory" Guinevere answered. The memory of the girl in the casket became clear as day. It had been so devastating to her, that she attempted to block all memory of it as a sort of self-defense mechanism to maintain sanity. "The first time I met Freya was at the funeral of my first and last friend."

This was a time before Guinevere's family was filthy rich. The Pendragons were by no means poor, by any standard, but they were always looking for opportunities for their big break. They often jumped through hoops and kissed the behinds of anyone they needed to in order to network. The opposite was true with Ivory's family as they were incredibly wealthy due to owning a lucrative mining company that specialized in rare gemstones. The family also ran and owned a famous jewelry company. However, Ivory was very ill and couldn't leave the house often due to her sickness. The Pendragon family found out about this and contacted the family setting up a playdate between their children. From the onset the two children became inseparable.

Nine years ago… The two girls were in Ivory's parent's jewelry room. The family sometimes took a personal interest in an exceptional stone. They had a small stone-cutting polishing station built on their property. They also had a vault of such stones kept in reserve in case of an emergency. Seven-year-old Ivory was climbing on a ladder to retrieve the family's latest acquisition. She had opened a case containing a necklace and pulled it out.

"Isn't it pretty, Guin?" Ivory asked while holding up a chain with a neon blue gemstone on it.

"I don't think we should be in here. We are going to get in huge trouble if we are caught." Guinevere said.

"This necklace has a gem on it. It's called a Paraiba Tourmaline! It's super rare!" Ivory said excitedly. She then held it out to Guinevere.

The light from a nearby window refracted off the gemstone into Guinevere's eyes. It was the most beautiful thing she had ever set her eyes on. It was a radiant cut gem. Symmetrical and without flaw. It was as if she was looking into the ocean and all of its beauty.

"It's… perfect." Guinevere gazed upon the stone in awe of its wonder.

"No, something's not right. I think it needs to be worn by someone." Ivory said. She began placing the necklace over Guinevere. The gemstone rested gently around her neck.

"There! The perfect stone next to the perfect friend." Ivory said with a smile.

"Hey! What are you two doing in here!" Ivory's mother shouted after bursting through the door.

The sudden startle caused Ivory to jump, slipping off the ladder she was on. She fell and landed on her ankle. A quick snap was heard as the girl let out a scream.

"Ivory!" Her mother yelled, dashing towards her daughter. When she got near Guinevere, she recognized that she was wearing the necklace. "Take that off, you two shouldn't even be in here!"

After a quick rush to the emergency room, Ivory was told she had broken her ankle. Guinevere felt to blame. She riddled herself with guilt for her friend getting hurt. A week had passed and Ivory was still in the hospital. Guinevere thought it was weird that they didn't discharge Ivory after putting a cast on her leg. It wasn't until three weeks later that she finally saw Ivory again, still in the hospital and completely bedridden. Before she went inside to speak with Ivory, Ivory's parents sat her down outside. They needed to explain something important to her.

"Cancer?" Guinevere asked.

"Yes... You see, Ivory is very ill. She has been for a long time. That's why she can't go outside very often. But don't worry, we have the best doctors in the world helping her right now." Ivory's dad said. *"But... it's not looking good."* he thought. Guinevere read the thoughts that appeared above his head and began to worry. She didn't exactly know what cancer meant at the time and how devastating it can be to someone and their family. Soon after Guinevere went inside the room where Ivory stayed.

"Hey, Guin." Ivory greeted with a smile. Her beautiful ivory hair was completely gone. She was being treated with chemotherapy.

Several months had gone by with no change in her recovery. Things had only gotten worse. Guinevere wanted to celebrate her birthday with Ivory so she visited her in the hospital. The two were left alone in the room, by request of Ivory.

"Happy Birthday Guin!" Ivory greeted.

"Thank you... I wish we could go spend it together somewhere. I want to take you to Distracto Land and all sorts of other places! When can you get out of here?" Guinevere asked.

"The doctors say they don't know," Ivory answered. "But it's okay since I have my best friend here with me. That makes it all better." She smiled.

"Ivory..." Guinevere had been visiting weekly. Ivory was the only person Guinevere could find comfort with.

"I have a gift for you," Ivory said. She pulled out a small bag and handed it to Guinevere. "I asked my parents if you could have it since you liked it so much." Guinevere opened the bag up and looked inside. There was a small keepsake box with a note saying, "To my perfect friend." The handwriting was barely legible, but Guinevere appreciated that Ivory wrote it herself. When Guinevere opened the box, inside was the Paraiba Tourmaline necklace. It made Guinevere speechless.

"Are you sure this is alright?" Guinevere asked.

"Yeah. Whenever you put it on, think of me, okay?" Ivory said.

"Okay!" Guinevere hugged Ivory and the two enjoyed the evening together. A week later, Ivory died. Guinevere screamed in agony when told about the loss of her best friend.

When the funeral finally came, Guinevere broke down in tears in front of the lifeless corpse of her former friend. She looked over at Ivory's parents who were sobbing beyond belief and they glared back at Guinevere with contempt staring at the gift their daughter gave her. Using *Reverie* she read their thoughts.

"I can't believe I let you near our daughter. You were just using her!" Ivory's mom thought.

"How dare you cry fake tears over her! You weren't even her real friend." Ivory's dad thought.

"What? I... don't understand. How could they think that? Ivory was my best friend!" Guinevere thought to herself. *"Why would they think that about me?"* She looked at Ivory one last time before her parents guided her back to her seat while she was still crying. Off in the distance, another child was sobbing hysterically. So loud that it caused Guinevere to stop crying.

"Mother... who is that?" Guinevere asked about the child.

"That is Freya Young, the girl who gets anything she wants." Guinevere's mother explained.

She was friends with Ivory as well. However, Guinevere noticed something was different about this girl and the way others treated her. When Freya began sobbing, Ivory's parents, as well as other families began surrounding her in order to comfort her. Including Guinevere's parents, leaving Guinevere sitting all alone.

Guinevere's parents knew who the child was and used this opportunity to meet Jim and Prismarine Young. They had been networking instead of mourning, getting terrible glances from Ivory's parents.

Finally, when the funeral was nearly finished, Freya went over to Guinevere, who was devastated. She attempted to start a conversation with Guinevere since she was the only girl around the same age as her.

"That's a pretty necklace," Freya said.

"**YOU CAN'T HAVE IT!**" Guinevere screamed. The fear that Freya would take what was hers caused her to instinctively hold on to the necklace.

"Guinevere! Be nice to the girl, she was only complimenting it." Guinevere's mom reprimanded. Freya began crying, as up until that moment, no one had ever yelled at her like that before. The commotion caused Jim and Prismarine to approach and see what had happened and Guinevere's father used this chance as an opportunity to introduce himself.

"We're so sorry about our daughter. As you can see she is quite distraught over Ivory." Guinevere's dad apologized, bowing over and over to Jim and Prismarine. He shook Jim's hand and then turned over to his daughter and grabbed her wrist, hurting her while pulling her aside. "Guinevere!" He whispered harshly, "That girl is the daughter of a very important person. Don't ruin this for us! Just play nice with the girl." He then turned back to Jim and shook his hand once more.

"Again, we're sorry about our daughter's behavior. She's an odd one." Guinevere's dad said. *"More like a freak."* he thought, as he reflected on his daughter's uncanny ability.

"It's quite alright. Everyone seems to be on edge." Looking to change the subject, Jim pointed out the necklace on Guinevere. "Say, how much was the necklace? That's quite the piece there." Jim asked.

"Oh Jim, is now really the time to be talking business? We're at a funeral for goodness sake." Prismarine reprimanded.

"Yeah, I suppose you're right," Jim responded.

"You have quite the eye there Mr. Young. Are you perhaps interested by chance? It was a recent acquisition. A very rare and exceptional piece. I'm sure it's nothing out of your pockets." Guinevere's dad said as if he were a salesman. It was as if he was possessed by a spirit of greed.

"I see. Well, I was just curious so I could buy one for my daughter." Jim said.

"Here, take my card. I'm sure we could work something out." He offered with an unpleasant grin.

A week later Guinevere's necklace went missing.

"Dad! Mom! Do you know where my necklace is!?" Guinevere asked. The moment she saw it was missing she rushed over towards where her parents were sitting at the dinner table. They both had smug self-satisfied expressions on their faces.

"Oh, you must have misplaced it. Here... we'll help you look for it." Her dad reasoned. With no thoughts of thievery above them, Guinevere took his word at face value not thinking about the conversation that transpired at the funeral. No matter how long and hard she searched, they never ended up finding her necklace.

As the years went by the necklace remained lost. Guinevere never got over her guilt and shame for losing it. During this time the Pendragon family continued to accumulate wealth with the now found help. They ended up starting their own jewelry business with the help of connections through Jim Young and eventually bought out Ivory's parents' company. Their new brand was called The Pendragon's Hoard. Due to her family's success, Guinevere reentered Freya Young's social circle. The Young family had invited the local stockholders to a dinner banquet. It was a celebratory dinner to the continued success of Slowsoft's partnership with neighboring companies.

Guinevere was heading towards her dinner table when Freya walked past her. While she grudgingly admired the girl's outfit she came to an abrupt halt. Her body went rigid as the plate she was holding slipped through numb fingers, causing it to shatter on the ground. Freya was wearing Ivory's necklace.

The sound of shattered glass hitting the floor snapped Guinevere out of her shock.

"You stole it!" Guinevere attacked Freya, attempting to take the necklace off of her, and violently pushing her to the ground.

"Guinevere! Stop! That's her necklace." Guinevere's mom said.

While having Freya pinned on the ground Guinevere stopped after hearing what her mother had said.

"Huh? What did you say?" Guinevere's heart almost stopped. She couldn't believe what she had heard. That was most definitely her necklace. There was no way she wouldn't recognize it. She collapsed on her lap still straddling Freya. While her father pulled her off of Freya, her mind shattered into a million pieces. The last remaining reminder she had of Ivory was gone. "How could you?" She looked at her father. As she recalled the smug self-satisfied smile he had on his face when she originally lost the necklace. Hatred filled Guinevere's heart. "How could you!" She screamed.

Guinevere glared at Freya with violent intent. Freya had a confused horrified expression on her face and Guinevere couldn't help but feel completely disgusted by her.

What was worse was that the necklace matched Freya's aquamarine eyes. Like it was made for her. It looked truly immaculate on the girl. It was as if fate approved of the transgression against her. This was the worst-case scenario for Guinevere. The anxiety in her created a fight-or-flight response. In order to not have a mental breakdown right then and there, Guinevere blocked the memory of Ivory in her mind. She began to withdraw into herself as a blank expression came over her. She had to, or else she would have done something irreversible.

After her outburst, her parents took Guinevere and left the banquet early. The entire time she was kicking and screaming until finally, something snapped. She went limp in her parent's arms as she was hauled away from the dining hall. She had begun to withdraw into herself as her rage slowly curdled up inside.

"You lied to me." A cold voice pronounced. Guinever's parents gave an involuntary shudder as they turned to look at their daughter. The look she gave her parents made them feel unsettled.

Guinevere's mom "Are you hearing yourself right now?" she stated, "You're the one who lost their mind in front of some of the most prominent business people in our country! You are being very selfish right now. Complaining as if some rock were more important than our livelihood. I'm sure that poor girl that you attacked doesn't go out of her way and try to put her whimsical wants over the betterment of her family.

"I agree. That girl never caused any problems for her parents and she always does what she's told. You need to start acting more like her! Besides, You should thank me! I'm doing this for your future. We can always get you a new necklace when we're rich." Guinevere's dad said.

That was the last straw for Guinevere. The amount of emotional turmoil she was faced with, caused her to mentally age several years in an instant. Never again would she take someone for their word. She needed revenge. She needed her parents to feel as bad as she was, and she knew how. She had the secrets her parents had been hiding from each other. The ones she had been reading above their heads for years. The bad things she had been told to keep quiet about. That was how she would control them.

"Betterment of the family!?", Guinevere sneered." Do you know what would be *better* for the family? If you weren't cheating on mom with your business partners' wives, or if mom wasn't spending all her time stealing things actually went to work. Wouldn't it be *better* if someone found out about that? Hey Dad, wouldn't all of our lives be *better* if I went ahead and told your coworkers what you've been doing? Oh, and Mom, wouldn't it be *better* for our family image if I contacted the police and showed them where you keep all the things you've stolen?" Guinevere threatened.

Their daughter was unrecognizable with the crazed look she now had in her eyes. Both parents were horrified by the monster they had created. Terrified, they knew they had to tread very carefully if they wished to keep their volatile daughter in check.

Back in the present... Guinevere finished explaining the past details of her life to Reighley, leaving out the part about her being able to read minds.

"I've been alone ever since. After that, no one cared long enough to stick around. People rotated in and out of my life. I can't even remember their faces." Guinevere said.

"I can't imagine living with such terrible parents. It must have been awful being alone for that long without having someone to trust. If there was ever someone who was in need of a hug, it would be this girl." Reighley thought. After reading his thoughts with *Reverie*, Guinevere leaped into Reighley's arms.

"I knew you would understand," Guinevere said, hugging Reighley.

"Hey! Hold on," Reighley said, trying to extricate himself from her desperate clutches.

"Reighley, I want to understand you as well... please, would you tell me? Tell me what *Insight* is?" Guinevere begged.

Chapter 24

The End of Everything: Part 2

"**W**hat did you just say?" Reighley was blown away by the term he had just heard. "How do you know about that-?" He was abruptly interrupted by the scorn of a redhead.

"Hey! What do you think you're doing? Get off of him" Freya shouted in the distance. Feeling that she had waited long enough for Reighley, Freya went to find him herself. She didn't expect Guinevere to be all over him. An exorbitant amount of jealousy surged through Freya's heart. "Stay away from Reighley, you homewrecker!" Freya shoved Guinevere off him, knocking her to the floor.

"Freya wait!" Reighley shouted.

"Reighley, stay away from this girl. She's nothing but bad news. She's the one who put that bounty on you during the race. She even had the nerve to have people place bets on you losing." Freya explained.

"*What should I do?*" Reighley asked himself. He was stuck between both girls unable to pick a side. "*This is just a big misunderstanding,*" he thought. "*These girls are two sides of the same coin. Can they really not get along? Not to mention...*

How did Guinevere know about Insight?" He looked at Guinevere, whose head was down, and then back at Freya. Freya's aura was like a roaring lion. He could tell she was ready to fight if it came down to it as her fists were clenched.

"Reighley... Who is this harlot to you?" Freya asked.

"She's..." Reighley's heart was being torn in two. Guinevere needed someone to help her more than anything and yet Reighley felt like if he took her side it would make things worse. Guinevere looked up at Reighley, anticipating what his next words were as if her life depended on it.

Insight showed Reighley Guinevere's aura. It was fickle. Ever changing and without shape, yet still cold, retaining the opacity of black ice.

"She's... my friend," Reighley said. He couldn't justify shutting her out. Not after seeing Guinevere's aura and hearing about her past. Reighley knew she needed help like plants need sunlight.

Upon hearing this, as if the summer had finally arrived after nine years of winter, all of Guinevere's icy aura melted away in an instant. Her opaque black ice disappeared, and in its place was a mixture of green on the ground below, and a light blue above. The aura showed Sunflowers beginning to sprout around her as an open sky appeared with the light of the sun beaming through it. For once, someone stood up for her and took her side even when it was risky. Even if it would benefit them not to. Guinevere knew that this was the perfect opportunity to abandon her and yet Reighley didn't.

"How did I not realize it before?" Reighley couldn't believe what Guinevere's aura had become. This was the first time *Insight* allowed him to witness hope be born. It was as if a breath of life had been breathed into it. It was beautiful. He didn't consider the possibility that Guinevere's aura wasn't always cold.

"It was just frozen over," he thought. It was a hidden prairie; a lost summer. He never thought to ask what led to her becoming such a mean-spirited and cold person. *"Just how many people's auras have I seen that I didn't think twice about before tossing them all into the same basket? How many terrible people weren't always terrible people?"* Reighley asked himself.

Guinevere was in awe as she read the words above Reighley and began to have an understanding of what *Insight* truly was. She wished to see the world through his eyes. She felt like she finally had obtained something of value that Freya could never have. Relatability. They were in the same metaphorical boat together. They both had something only the two of them could ever truly understand. She and Reighley were different from the rest of the world, and due to this, she knew that she could trust him with the knowledge of *Reverie*.

"Well sorry, I don't care if she's your friend or not, but she's uninvited from this party," Freya said to Reighley. She then pointed towards Guinevere and glared harshly at her. "Guinevere, leave, now, before I have you thrown out." Freya threatened.

"Fine. I'll go." Guinevere said. She stood up and dusted herself off. Freya watched her and was shocked she didn't put up a fight.

"You'll be hearing from my lawyers by the way," Freya said, trying to provoke Guinevere.

"Freya, stop. That's enough." Reighley said halting Freya. He could see the aggressiveness in her that she took after her father, as at that moment she reminded him of Jim.

"No, you stop! Stop defending her like… like she's your girlfriend! You shouldn't even be talking to her. What if she stole your first kiss or something?" Freya said. She was genuinely worried that had happened while she wasn't there. Guinevere was always doing crazy things to her whenever she was given the chance.

"Who knows? Maybe I did…" Guinevere deviously taunted, putting her fingers on her lips.

"Ugh! Just get out of here!" Freya yelled. Finally, Guinevere headed to the door, but before leaving she looked back one more time.

"Freya. You don't deserve him." Guinevere said. The look on her face was completely serious. After that Guinevere left.

"Oh yeah? Well, your haircut looks stupid! Fishbowl!" Freya needed to get the last word in. Even if the insult was lame. "*Still, why do I feel like I lost?*" Freya thought with her fists still clenched. "*Where does she get off at, telling me I don't deserve Reighley? I've worked very hard on myself lately. She doesn't get to decide that.*"

"She didn't kiss me," Reighley reassured. He could see the strain the dispute caused her and hoped to put her at ease.

"Don't talk to me right now…" Freya was beyond upset. She grabbed ahold of Reighley's wrist and began pulling him towards the Ballroom. Not many people were out in the venue, but the commotion that the three were in, had the attention of those lounging around. *"Why is he acting so different? When did it start? Was it back then?"* Freya felt like everything was falling apart. Brick by brick, her world began tumbling down. *"Was it at the start of finals? Did I do something wrong? Was it because I told him I missed him? Why won't he stay by my side?"* She thought. The questions in her mind clouded her head and misty eyes clouded her vision as she walked, putting her on autopilot. Without any answers, those questions lingered and continued to roam like an endless mist narrowly avoiding the ground. The seeds of insecurities that had been sowed in her mind began to sprout. Suddenly, Freya felt a jolt in her shoulder just before the two were about to reach the door to the Ballroom. Reighley had pulled away from her, deftly slipping from her grasp.

"Freya, listen to me," Reighley said abruptly. When Freya turned to look at him, she saw steady determination in his eyes. "Whatever happens after tonight. I need you to know that-"

"Stop! Just… stop. Please." Freya shouted with her head down and eyes shut. She thought she was prepared for the conversation the two needed to have, but she couldn't bear it at the moment. "Can we just go back to the Ballroom? You and I are supposed to dance together. Can this wait until after?" Freya pleaded.

"Yeah." Reighley conceded. Freya grabbed ahold of Reighley's hand but it was one-sided. His grip on her hand was loose. She tightened her fingers, to convey that she would never lose hold of him again.

The two arrived in the Ballroom, hand-in-hand, and a spotlight shone upon Freya, leaving Reighley in the shadows.

"What the..." Freya said shocked squinting her eyes, unable to see a thing.

"There she is! The lady we have all been waiting for." Isabelle announced. Freya covered her brow with her hand to block out the spotlight to see what was ahead. She was surprised by a spark that flickered in the center of the room. The crowd around her parted creating a walkway for her to reach the center.

"Happy Birthday!" Everyone shouted in celebration. Destiny appeared behind Freya as if out of thin air. She shot off party poppers and confetti in succession. Afterward, the rest of the crowd did the same. Freya's heart skipped a beat. Not just from the surprise, but the jostling she got from Destiny, as she gently pushed her toward the center. This caused her to let go of Reighley. She glanced backward into the crowd but couldn't see him anymore. The blinding spotlight that followed her made it all but impossible to recognize anyone's face at a distance.

Before she knew it, the spotlight faded away. The only remaining light was that of candles. The red and orange of the flames cast a ruddy glow upon her. She was in front of an extravagant birthday cake. Standing slightly apart from the crowd was her family. She looked over at those who helped raise her. Herald met her eyes with a warm smile. Like a proud grandfather. He was standing with arms behind his back in his usual professional manner in his butler attire. Elise was standing next to Herald, looking as serious as could be. She curtsied when Freya looked at her. Lily, however, waved at Freya, finally acting more casual with her, even in uniform. Destiny, who was in a snow-white dress, placed her hand on Freya's shoulder getting her attention. She whispered that she helped make the cake. Lastly, her parents looked at her with separate expressions. Prismarine had the face of a proud mother. She had the look of someone who was teary-eyed at the thought of their little girl becoming all grown up. Jim appeared stoic, but on his face was a grin. A simple smile stating loud and clear he was happy to be here. The two wore matching color-coordinated outfits that likely cost more than most people's mortgages.

"*No, no, no…*" Freya had a terrible sinking feeling in the pit of her stomach. As if she knew deep down inside that was the last time she would ever hold Reighley's hand. Desperately, she searched deep across the crowd for him.

"Freya. What's wrong? Are you okay dear?" Prismarine asked. "Are you feeling alright? You look unwell." Her maternal instincts told her something was wrong with Freya. She knew her daughter well enough to distinguish a worried look from a surprised one.

"Where's Reighley? He was just here." Freya said loud enough for the crowd to hear.

Jim, being one of the tallest persons present, was the first to spot Reighley in the crowd. Reighley returned Jim's inquiring gaze with steady determination. Jim shifted his head back in a beckoning jester, silently inviting the young man to come up and join the family. Reighley lightly shook his head "no", subtly signifying to him that this was how things needed to be.

"*Is this what you really want?*" Jim thought. His eyes furrowed slightly in bemusement. He didn't understand why Reighley still wished to leave Freya. He even succeeded in giving Jim a fighting chance to fix things. Because of this, Reighley had earned his respect over the course of the night. "*Fine. I'll keep your secret. From one man to another.*" Jim gave Reighley a slight tilt of the head confirming to him that he wasn't going to say a word.

Moments later, Isabelle changed the screen to Reighley, putting a spotlight on him.

"Don't worry! Reighley's over here by me." Isabelle said. Freya's heart began to settle when she saw him standing over by his sister. He idly stood by the streaming setup. When he realized he was spotted, he waved at her as he leaned back against a wall.

"Come over here dummy!" Freya shouted. The rest of the crowd laughed at the remark. However, Reighley, before heading over, whispered something into Isabelle's ear and then placed one arm over the back of his head, laughing it off as he approached.

"Happy Birthday, Freya," Reighley said when he arrived.

"Hey, kid." Jim nodded as Reighley waved back. Freya felt it odd that there was no animosity between the two. She attributed it to the 100 Zombie Run. The hardships they had faced together and overcame, squashed the quarrel the two shared. Freya felt envious about how easily they could settle their differences. She could have never imagined that happening between her and any of her female friends while they were fighting. She knew just how vicious girls who did not like each other could become. She was in fact one of them. If the roles were switched, she knew the zombies would have been the least terrifying thing for her to keep a lookout for.

"Geez... don't scare me like that. Well... perhaps I was worried over nothing." Freya thought. She took a deep breath, letting out all the anxiety that had built up, and turned back towards her family. The cake that awaited her was white, red, brown, and orange. A five-tier cake with separate stacks each with a different flavor. The bottom tier was a Lemon Meringue Cake. The ever-swirling frosting covered the entire section, making a beautiful brown-tinted pattern. The second

tier was a Red Velvet Cake. It was sprinkled with thousands of tiny broken chocolate bits. The third tier was a Fudge-filled Chocolate Cake. Surrounding the cake was a bowl of pure milk chocolate around it. It was designed to catch any fudge filling from leaking onto the other layers. The fourth tier was a ridiculous, Pineapple Upside Down Cake. Written sloppily around it were letters that spelled, "made by Destiny." causing Freya to let out a hearty chuckle upon reading. Finally, the fifth tier was a strawberry shortcake. It was perfectly assorted with strawberries on the edges of it. On it were sixteen candles and the words, "Happy Sixteenth Birthday, to the best daughter parents could ask for."

It dawned on Freya. The realization that she had just obtained everything she could have ever wanted in one day. *Almost Everything...* Her family was able to spend an evening together without the quick departure of her father. All of her friends and loved ones are nearby to celebrate and appreciate her. Being loved and cherished by them caused most of her worries to escape her mind. All except two. Although She wouldn't admit to the first one, she didn't exactly know how to talk to her dad. There was a level of respect and mannerisms that Freya needed to uphold in his presence. The fact that most of their conversations happened monthly and only during meals, didn't leave much time for practice. This made their upcoming dance seem rather terrifying in retrospect. The second worry was with the boy she loved. Although close, recently he seemed so distant. Like someone itching to leave the space they were in. He appeared uncomfortable, with a fake smile, like he didn't belong here. She had to figure out a way to show Reighley that this was where he was meant to be. She and her family welcomed him with open arms.

"Alright party people. It's time to start singing!" Isabelle announced. "DJ! Take it away!"

Destiny cleared her throat and led the song, Happy Birthday in an octave just a tiny pitch too high. She did so, in the hopes that during the singing, the voices of the choir would crack from being unable to reach their notes. She was successful in her attempt as well. The voices of several guys cracked during the final Happy Birthday verse in the song. One of those poor souls was Deven Stalik. The singing was like nails on a chalkboard, and Deven immediately played it off like it was someone else. Destiny acted as if she was a mastermind who had it all figured out since the start. She struck a pose while letting out a small chuckle.

After the singing came to an end, the chat went wild over the voice cracks and several people failed to hold back laughter causing Deven to flee the scene. Freya took one last good look at the cake that awaited her and engraved its design in her heart. After taking a moment to contemplate what to wish for, she blew out her sixteen candles with one deep puff of breath. Celebration and cheer erupted from the crowd. The loud clapping of hands drowned out every noise. Freya walked over to Reighley and grasped his hand with a gentle touch. When he looked back at her with agency, she mouthed the words *"I love you"* to him. Reighley's eyes widened as he read her lips. He was too late. The worst had occurred. Freya leaned in on Reighley and spoke into his ear.

"You don't have to say it back. I just… wanted you to know." Freya said blushing. She let go of his hand and backed away. She told him how she felt. It wasn't a last-ditch effort to get him to stay with her or a desperate attempt to win his heart. She felt like, at that moment, she had to say it. So, while the attendees of the party and those who were watching over the internet were celebrating and would remember this day as the sixteenth birthday of Freya, only the two of them would share a different memory than the rest of the world.

The cheering subsided and Isabelle began to announce, yet again.

"Alright, people. It's time for the lady of the hour's first dance of the night. DJ! Get over here." Isabelle beckoned for Destiny to approach the DJ stand that was set up center stage. Once she stood behind the table, she pulled out a microphone and began speaking.

"Freya. As your best friend and as someone who loves and cherishes you, I would like to make the first song out to you and your father. Enjoy." Destiny said. She began playing a slow dance song.

Freya was static. The nerves were getting the better of her. Jim walked over to her and held out his hand giving a courtly bow.

"May I have this dance?" Jim asked. Freya replied with a nod, taking his hand the two made their way from the crowd and began to waltz.

"Hello, Father," Freya said, unable to make eye contact. She instead watched as their feet moved together.

"Hi, kiddo." Jim awkwardly answered. The two's movements were slightly off-beat from each other.

"Have you been well?" Freya asked. She didn't know what to talk about or to say. She couldn't help but speak formally to him, even after all this time.

"Honestly? Pretty terrible. Work has been keeping me busy." Jim answered with a chuckle.

"Yeah… it has." Freya agreed. They were both in the center of the dance floor, and all eyes were on them, but no one could hear the conversation they were having. The two had a silence between them for a brief second until Jim spoke.

"Freya," Jim asked, "Would you please just look at me?" From the start of the song, Freya wouldn't meet his gaze. Hesitantly she looked up at her father. When she finally looked into her father's eyes, she saw it. On his face, he had the look she had hoped to have gotten out of him when she tried to get back at him. He looked exactly how she pictured it in her mind, but… it wasn't everything she thought it was cut out to be. To her, he looked old and deeply saddened. The look on his face caused her heart to ache.

"Father, I…" Freya couldn't help but feel awful.

"Freya, I want you to take a good look at everything around you," Jim asked. Freya was confused but listened. As the two spun, her eyes began to wander. She looked from the DJ table, to the streaming setup, then to the birthday cake which was now being eaten, and then all the way over to the tables with refreshments on it until her Jim spoke again. "Every object and possession you see in this room I own or very well could own, but... I don't own you. You've become your own person, and I am so proud of you. When I came here tonight I thought I would still see my rash little redhead. Now look at you. You're already sixteen years old. It felt like it was just yesterday when I came home and saw my little girl just learning how to walk. Today felt like it was so far away, but here we are.... You're all grown up now, and you're free to make your own decisions and choices. And I just wanted you to know that I would give it *all* up, just so I could be your dad for one more day."

The rigid movement of their dance slowly softened. The structure and formalities of the waltz fell apart along with the barrier between the two of them.

"Dad. I'm sorry. I love you so much." Freya began to cry slightly. "I am grateful for how hard you work. Because of you, Mom and I live an easy life while you work endlessly. I know that, but I just wanted you to see me again. You were gone for so long. I felt like I didn't matter to you anymore. When I finally accepted you were out of my life, you started getting in the way of everything." Freya let it all out. She held nothing back. "You started problems between Reighley and me. From the start, you were against him, and for no reason! He's an incredible guy and he doesn't deserve to be treated

541

that way. And then... you made Mom cry. I started hating you for that, but all I really wanted was to see you and to live life as a normal happy family. That's so hard when you're never around."

"I know... and I knew about your mother too.... The staff at home told me about it. I just chose to ignore it, because it was out of my control. But nothing is ever really out of our control. I just didn't make the time, that's all. I put my job before my family, but no more. That's going to change from here on out. I'm going to spend more time at home and see you and your mother more often. I promise." Jim answered, hugging his daughter tightly.

"And Reighley?" Freya asked.

"You're right about him. He's a good kid. I misjudged him from the beginning because of his criminal record. I thought I was protecting you from him but look at me. I am in his debt. Turns out I was just trying to protect myself from realizing my daughter had grown up. I won't treat you like a kid anymore. I'll start trusting your judgment from here on out. So tell me why you are serious about him. I've never seen you fight so hard for anything or anyone before." Jim's opinion of Reighley had improved a lot over his interactions with him, but he wanted to know what Freya saw in him.

"He's incredibly selfless. Like way too selfless. He puts everyone else around him first, even to his own detriment. He's hard to impress. I'm pretty sure I annoyed him when we first started dating. Well, I probably still do sometimes. Oh yeah… the allowance you gave me, I sort of used some of it to persuade Reighley to be my boyfriend," Freya confessed awkwardly, "so thanks for that. Reighley was the first person I had ever met who wasn't star-struck just by seeing me, and the only guy who's ever treated me like a normal girl."

"I'll choose to ignore the part where you said you used my money to pay him because it's your birthday, but… It sounds to me like you have it all figured out." Jim began to question just how different the world had become since he dated. *"Just how crazy have things become that something like this could be considered okay?"*

After a tearful apology from the both of them, the two began to dance perfectly in sync with each other, and with smiles on their faces. Prismarine was off to the side and began to cry with a smile as well. She didn't know what was said between the two of them, but knew what had been left unsaid, was now spoken. Eventually, the slow dance came to an end. Freya hugged her dad and then both Jim and Freya took a bow towards each other and stepped aside as the rest of the party applauded.

"Isn't that just beautiful?" Isabelle said, wiping a fake tear from her eye. "Okay, now we dance!" She shouted. "DJ hit it!" On her signal, upbeat music more fitting for the rest of the crowd kicked in and everyone there began dancing. Freya gave her dad one more hug and then left to go find Reighley on the dance floor. She didn't have to look far, as he had been watching the interaction nearby. Freya approached him with a bashful look. The last thing she told him was that she loved him and her heart began to beat rapidly and she had butterflies in her stomach.

"Good for you," Reighley said. "I'm glad things are better between you and your dad."

"I know you did something." Freya pulled Reighley in close and kissed him on the cheek. "Thank you." She said in his ear.

"I didn't do anything." Reighley blushed.

"Our dance is next, so I hope you practiced," Freya said.

"Right. Hey, I'm going to go get a drink real quick." Reighley lied.

"Okay!" Freya said with a smile. *"I can never tell what he's thinking. I wish I could read minds just so I could hear his thoughts."* Freya thought. Reighley headed towards the drink table and waited until Freya turned away from him and began talking to some of her friends. Then he snuck out of the ballroom and back into the venue heading to the table where the guest placed their gifts. He reached into his back pocket and pulled out a small keepsake box and placed it on the table. He then subtly snuck out of the building.

Reighley wasn't looking forward to walking home. He factored in how long a fifteen-minute drive would take as a walk home. When he reached halfway down the stairs he had begun to lose the resolve to finish what he started.

"Where do you think you're going?" Officer Templeton asked. Reighley had completely missed him. Officer Templeton was standing next to the entrance at the top of the staircase.

"Oh, you're here? Look, man... I'm not having a good night tonight. I just want to go home." Reighley explained. He had a lifetime's worth of trouble with the law, so he tried to be polite. Reighley knew that Officer Templeton, at the end of the day, was a public servant. Still, he didn't want to waste time talking to him.

"Where's your mom?" Templeton asked.

"She's at home," Reighley explained. The fact that Templeton didn't ask about his parents and instead only about his mother, told Reighley just how much Templeton knew about him.

"I can give you a ride. I'm not stationed here." Templeton offered. Reighley watched as Templeton made quick work of the stairs and pointed towards his patrol vehicle which was parked right off to the side of the lot.

"Um... my mom told me to never get into white vehicles with strangers." Reighley jested.

"Yeah, and I bet she also told you not to walk home alone at night." Templeton sternly lectured.

"Fair point." Reighley acknowledged. He then hustled to catch up with Templeton and walked with him towards his car.

"Where were you headed?" Templeton asked.

"I live near San Fran Kyoto Peak, but you probably already knew that, didn't you? You can just drop me off at the station." Reighley elaborated.

"Not happening. I'll take you home, don't worry." Templeton said.

Reighley looked at Templeton's aura using *Insight*. It was slightly different compared to the last time he had seen it. He was shrouded in a normal green aura in the shape of a trench coat, almost like an honest hard-working detective. *Almost*. Reighley was sure he recalled Templeton's aura being much darker in color.

"Come on. Get in." Templeton said.

"My mom will flip if she sees me in a cop car," Reighley said, entering the vehicle. He took a moment and silenced his cell phone, preparing to ignore the incoming spam calls and texts Freya was bound to send him. The two began heading towards San Fran Kyoto Peak. Reighley was sitting in the front passenger seat and couldn't help but feel awkward. After all, Templeton was the first of many who ended up giving Reighley such a hard time.

"So how's school going?" Templeton asked.

"Uh... good I think." Reighley was boggled by the question. He wasn't sure if Templeton was baiting him into admitting something he didn't do, like cheating.

"Yeah, that's good. I wanted to apologize for the way I treated you before. That put a stain on my badge." Templeton said.

"Oh. Well, thanks I guess. You won't have to worry about seeing me anymore anyhow." Reighley explained.

"What, why's that?" Templeton asked.

"I'm switching schools after today," Reighley said.

"Was that because of me?" Templeton questioned. He sounded genuinely concerned that he was the cause of Reighley's sudden departure.

"No. There are a lot of reasons, but surprisingly, the way I was treated at school was not one of them." Reighley said.

"Ah… Well, I see that's a relief. Oh! Not you leaving Gilford High, just the fact that it wasn't because of me." Templeton corrected himself. Reighley let out a slight laugh causing the tension to dwindle. The two began to chat for the remainder of the ride, no longer at odds with one another. Eventually, the two arrived at Reighley's place. Jericho, hearing a car pull up, looked outside and saw her son in a police vehicle.

"Oh no… not this again," Jericho said worriedly. Once the vehicle was parked, Templeton awkwardly began twiddling his fingers.

"Umm say. Mind if I ask you something before you go?" Templeton said.

"Shoot. Not actually though." Reighley said with a chuckle.

"That lady at Motherboards. The one who's like a genius at gaming. What's she like?" Templeton asked.

"Oh, Elise? She's a tough cookie, but she's a nice lady." Reighley explained.

"Elise? Why does that name sound so familiar?" Templeton asked.

"What? You don't remember her name even though the both of you work for the Young Family?" Reighley asked bewilderedly. It was like a bomb went off inside Templeton's brain. All the dots finally connected.

"What!? Elise, is *that* Elise?" Templeton freaked out.

"Yep," Reighley confirmed.

"How did I not know?" Templeton asked himself.

"You should probably get to know the people you work with for good rapport and all," Reighley suggested. Templeton started contemplating his work relationships.

"Do you... think I would have a shot with her?" Templeton asked.

"I don't know, your badge looks pretty polished to me," Reighley said, exiting the vehicle. When he did, Jericho rushed towards the car.

"What did he do this time?" She asked while pulling Reighley close, ready to discipline him.

"Oh, nothing Ma'am. I was just giving him a ride home, that's all." Templeton said.

"Oh thank goodness. I was worried. He has gotten into trouble in the past. Thank you very much for bringing him home, sir." Jericho thanked.

"Oh, it was no problem at all. You've got a good kid. He's a smart one. Well, I'll get out of your hair now, you two have a good night and make sure you stay out of trouble, kid. You have a bright future ahead of you." Templeton said while driving off.

Reighley and Jericho walked towards their doorstep until Jericho began probing how the night went for her son.

"So, Reighley, how did the dance go? Did you and your girlfriend have a good time?" Jericho asked. "Also, where's Isabelle?"

"Isabelle is getting a ride home from a staff member," Reighley explained. He had asked a favor of Elise, to give Isabelle a ride home at nine o clock. "And no Mom, we... broke up," Reighley said with a sad expression.

"Oh... buddy, I'm sorry. Well, don't be too down on yourself. I'm sure you can do better next time.

"It was me Mom. I ended it." Reighley confessed. "*I was the problem,*" Reighley thought.

"Oh. Well. I trust that you knew what you were doing. Let's go inside now. I'll cook you some dinner and get you some ice cream, okay?" Jericho said. She knew just how hard breakups could be, especially for teenagers. "*The last thing I want my son to be is bitter towards the world and at himself. Come on, Jericho! Cheer him up. For the first time in his life, your little boy needs you. I've been waiting so long for an opportunity to act like a real parent.*" Afterward, the two went inside.

Freya spent some time socializing and thanking attendees for their gifts and realized Reighley had yet to come back from getting his drink. She looked around toward the fruit punch bowl wondering where Reighley had gone. Another slow dance song started and she was ready to hear him out. However, she was looking all over but couldn't find him anywhere. Eventually, her search led outside of the ballroom and as she passed the gift table, something caught her eye. Although it was small, it stood out from the rest of the gifts. She walked up towards it and had a gut feeling that this was Reighley's gift for her due to what it said.

To: A good person.

The card didn't have the name of the donor on it and yet that phrase could only have come from Reighley. When she opened it she saw a necklace. It was a beautiful lavender flower. It looked like it had been removed from something and soldered onto a hoop to rest on its chain. Underneath the necklace, however, was a card. When she opened it, she felt her heart break into a million pieces as she read what it said. "I don't love you."

She dropped the keepsake box and the necklace. Her hands began to shake, and then the rest of her body involuntarily convulsed for a moment. She was about to fall to her knees, but the thought of Reighley still being near, gave her the strength to stand.

"I... I have to find him! Before it's too late." Freya seeks the help of her friends and family. She decided to ask everyone she could to see if they knew where Reighley was. Freya didn't care if people saw her crying. She felt like she didn't have much time to explain everything. She started with Ulysses, who, when asked, couldn't look her in the eyes.

"Do you know where Reighley went?" Freya said with tears in her eyes.

"Uh… I have no idea. I was dancing with Lily, so I've been pretty distracted." Ulysses answered honestly. He didn't know how to handle the delicate situation.

"Okay… I thought you would know." Freya replied with disappointment and hurried on to the next. She met with Isabelle and pulled her aside.

"Izzy. Where's your brother? Did he say something to you earlier?" Freya asked.

"Uh. I don't know. He just said that Elise would be taking me home soon. Is everything alright?" Isabelle asked worriedly.

"I can't find him anywhere." Freya panicked. She felt her hope had begun to fade away, but she wouldn't let that stop her. She had to find him and she knew the perfect person to track him down.

Herald watched Freya approach him with tears in her eyes. *"So the young master went through with it after all."* Herald thought. He knew exactly what had happened.

"Herald. I need your help. I can't find Reighley. Tracking people is your specialty right?" Freya begged.

"Of course Milady. I'm no Mr. Templeton, but I can manage just fine. Follow me." Herald answered modestly. After he agreed, the two immediately left to head towards the exit of the venue.

Jim stepped in front of Freya, halting her from leaving the venue.

"You have to respect his decision," Jim said placatingly.

"You knew? What did you tell him? Is he leaving because you told him to?" Freya became completely hysterical. She made the immediate assumption that Jim was the reason Reighley was acting this way.

"No. He told me about it earlier this week." Jim explained.

"So you are still trying to control my life! Didn't you just tell me you'd trust my judgment?" Freya asked, her voice filled with scorn. "My life isn't one of your business transactions! !" Freya said while stomping past her dad.

"No, I was just trying to…" Jim quietly answered.

Freya rushed out the front door, hoping he hadn't been picked up yet or had walked home. *"I should've known something was wrong!"* Freya blamed herself. She was balling her eyes out, but she was still determined to find Reighley. Looking towards the stairs at the entrance, it revealed she was too late. He was gone. There was no sign of him.

On their way there Freya tried to rationalize why Reighley abandoned her.

"Okay let's think this through… What exactly do I know about Reighley." Freya pondered the question, but after a long thought, she realized that she didn't know all that much about him, other than the vague rumors she had heard before he arrived at school.

"Think, Freya... think! There has to be some reason he left." Freya finally thought of where to start. She reflected on her first date with Reighley. It was all going smoothly until the two went to the Hall of Shadows. *"When we entered the Hall of Shadows together everything was still fine. That all changed once we entered the mirror maze. That's when Reighley had a mental breakdown. Gosh! Why didn't I bring that up again before now? Clearly, he was not okay."* She then thought about the first dinner she had at his house. *"It wasn't just then either. There wasn't any mention of Reighley's dad being absent from the family. The only mention of him happened the first time I picked him up."* She remembered the single photo that Reighley had with his dad. The one she saw after dinner. *"Everyone went quiet when that photo came up. And his criminal record... I don't even know what he did, except for the fact it exists. No, that's not right. I've always known, haven't I? Everything about him. I just chose to ignore it all and be infatuated with him."* It dawned on Freya that she had been a self-absorbed terrible girlfriend.

"Wow... There is so much about him that I don't know. I never even tried to learn anything about him. I'm not sure what he likes, what he does in his free time, his favorite foods, nothing... I only projected what I liked on him." She thought.

When they arrived, Freya could see the light seep through the crack in the garage door. She had been texting and calling him the entire ride over, but he never answered or replied. Before Herald had even placed the vehicle in park, Freya rushed out the door and stood outside on the doorstep. She knocked on the door.

"He has to answer!" She thought. *"There is so much more I still need to say to him!"* She waited and then knocked again. Finally, Jericho opened the door. Freya's heart was aching but she knew she only had one shot to fix things.

"Hello Freya." Jericho greeted.

"Hello, Mrs. Summers. Is Reighley home?" Freya asked, wiping the stained mascara off her face. "I'd like to talk to him," Freya said.

"Yes. Let me go grab him." Jericho said. She went back inside and the moments between her entering and returning felt like an eternity. Freya knew her feelings would reach him. To her, they had to. Otherwise, nothing else mattered. Finally, after a minute had passed, Jericho pried open the door and said.

"I'm sorry, but he said he doesn't want to talk to you," Jericho informed. Freya fell silent. She couldn't process what had just happened to her.

"Oh… Okay." Freya cried. The tears wouldn't stop pouring out of her eyes. She walked over to the garage door and looked down at the floor. She could see the shadow of someone standing on the other side. "Reighley. I liked your gift. It was really thoughtful. I know you can hear me. I don't know what's going on with you, but I need you to know that I chased after you, because you're someone worth chasing after." Freya waited for a response, and after a few seconds, the shadow disappeared. That's when her heart truly broke. Time had frozen over from how cold he was. It was as if he was someone completely different. He wasn't acting the way she knew him to. It didn't make sense to her why he would just up and leave. She felt he was forcing himself to be the bad guy, but it didn't matter to Freya either way.

Later on, Freya never returned to the party. Instead, she went home and cried herself to sleep. After that, Monday came and Reighley was nowhere to be found at Gilford High School. All that remained was an empty desk. Even Kaede didn't know where he had gone. Reighley ended up switching schools. He also moved away to a different house. He used the money he won from the very race she had made for him to do so. No matter how often she texted him or called him, he never answered. Several months went by and she still believed deep down that one day, Reighley would realize how much he loved her and the two would make up, but that never happened. It hurt, more than any physical wound she had ever suffered. Her heart hardened and became more and more jaded each time she contacted him with no reply. Eventually Freya Young became bitter. She felt like she was talking to a brick wall. A year later, she stopped trying to contact him when he blocked her number...

JAIDEN WINTERS

"..."

"Is that it?" You thought to yourself. *"After all that. That can't be how it ends… right? I thought this was book 1?"* Normally, this is where the story would come to an end. We don't always end up with those we cherish the most, do we? Did you forget the name of the series? Not all of us get the happy endings we desire. Most of us are lucky enough just to experience the precious times we've had throughout life with the ones we love. But you, you're different, aren't you? You kept searching. Page after page you never gave up hope. You didn't stop at the end. You kept reading despite being told the story was over. Maybe for the hope that things could turn out just a little bit differently. For the small chance that someone, anyone could undo and change what had just happened.

Well… sorry to disappoint, but what you read *is* the true ending. I am running short on the gifts I have left to give. I have but one more. Which I have chosen you to take. If you were satisfied with the ending, then stop reading.

However, if you're still unsatisfied…
Then turn the page. After all… you too have an ability. The power to change how this book ends. All you have to do is keep reading…

So, will you turn the page…?

(Very well. It has been unwritten...)

(Someone turned back the clock)

SSSSSSSSSSSSSSSSSSSSSSSSSSSSSSSSSSSSSSSSSS
SSSSSSSSSSSSSSSSSSSSSSSSSSSSSSSSSSSSSSSSSS
SSSSSSSSSSSSSSSSSSSSSSSSSSSSSSSSSSSSSSSSSS
SSSSSSSSSSSSSSSSSSSSSSSSSSSSSSSSSSSSSSSSSS
SSSSSSSSSSSSSSSSSSSSSSSSSSSSSSSSSSSSSSSSSS
SSSSSSSSSSSSSSSSSSSSSSSSSSSSSSSSSSSSSSSSSS
SSSSSSSSSSSSSSSSSSSSSSSSSSSSSSSSSSSSSSSSSS
SSSSSSSSSSSSSSSSSSSSSSSSSSSSSSSSSSSSSSSSSS
SSSSSSSSSSSSSSSSSSSSSSSSSSSSSSSSSSSSSSSSSS
SSSSSSSSSSSSSSSSSSSSSSSSSSSSSSSSSSSSSSSSSS
SSSSSSSSSSSSSSSSSSSSSSSSSSSSSSSSSSSSSSSSSS
SSSSSSSSSSSSSSSSSSSSSSSSSSSSSSSSSSSSSSSSSS
SSSSSSSSSSSSSSSSSSSSSSSSSSSSSSSSSSSSSSSSSS
SSSSSSSSSSSSSSSSSSSSSSSSSSSSSSSSSSSSSSSSSS
SSSSSSSSSSSSSSSSSSSSSSSSSSSSSSSSSSSSSSSSSS
SSSSSSSSSSSSSSSSSSSSSSSSSSSSSSSSSSSSSSSSSS
SSSSSSSSSSSSSSSSSSSSSSSSSSSSSSSSSSSSSSSSSS
SSSSSSSSSSSSSSSSSSSSSSSSSSSSSSSSSSSSSSSSSS
SSSSSSSSSSSSSSSSSSSSSSSSSSSSSSSSSSSSSSSSSS
SSSSSSSSSSSSSSSSSSSSSSSSSSSSSSSSSSSSSSSSSS
SSSSSSSSSSSSSSSSSSSSSSSSSSSSSSSSSSSSSSSSSS
SSSSSSSSSSSSSSSSSSSSSSSSSSSSSSSSSSSSSSSSSS
SSSSSSSSSSSSSSSSSSSSSSSSSSSSSSSSSSSSSSSSSS
SSSSSSSSSSSSSSSSSSSSSSSSSSSSSSSSSSSSSSSSSS
SSSSSSSSSSSSSSSSSSSSSSSSSSSSSSSSSSSSSSSSSS
SSSSSSSSSSSSSSSSSSSSSSSSSSSSSSSSSSSSSSSSSS
SSSSSSSSSSSSSSSSSSSSSSSSSSSSSSSSSSSSSSSSSS
SSSSSSSSSSSSSSSSSSSSSSSSSSSSSSSSSSSSSSSSSS

"I... can't bear to see her like that."

"It... hurts too much to watch."

"Is there really no other way...?"

RE: Chapter 24

~~The End of Everything: Part 2~~

Changing Everything

It was bugging her to no end. The future she had seen. The one that awaited her cousin, Freya. What bothered Sarah Bellum the most about it all was that there was something she could do to prevent it from happening, assuming she cared of course. The visions of the near future played like a sequence in her head over and over again. It started with Reighley leaving the party early without saying goodbye, then Freya finding the gift he had left her, and finally Freya crying alone in the venue. No matter how she looked at it, it was a bad end.

"Lai, it's Sarah, are you there?" Sarah asked over her earpiece.

"Yeah. What's up?" The voice replied.

"I got the bag you said to grab," Sarah explained.

"Sweet. I'll be seeing you shortly." Lai confirmed.

Sarah was driving, already halfway to her destination, when she looked over at the blue gift bag she had stolen from Freya's party. Curiosity was getting the better of her. Her partner Lai was a reliable source. The two had been working together for over five years at this point. Lai always managed to know where a decently valued item to take was whenever the two had a theft job together. His ability was called *Voyager*, but that's all she was ever told about it. Somehow, by using it, he always knew where to find things. They often stole things that the rightful owner wouldn't even notice had gone missing. Sarah never did look inside the bag. All she was told was that she needed to snag the blue bag hanging off the corner of the table.

"Say... Lai?" Sarah asked.

"What is it?" Lai questioned.

"What's in this bag anyway?" Sarah said while rummaging her hand through the bag. Her hand felt what seemed like chalk through a fishnet sack.

"Oh, just some luxury bath bombs. Each one is worth 5,000 yen. There should be at least thirty of them in there." Lai answered.

"What!?" Sarah jumped out of her seat. "I hurled myself down a flight of stairs for some bath bombs!?"

"Woah, woah, woah. Take it easy, will ya? Trust the process. That's at least 150,000 yen (1,061.66 USD). It should get us by for the month, and besides, I know the perfect group of sorority girls who will buy this stuff right off of us." Lai elaborated.

Sarah let out a sigh and looked at her bruised body. "Alright… but you better let me use one of them," she said seriously.

"It's coming directly out of your cut." Lai compromised.

"Fine… but you're buying dinner." Sarah reluctantly agreed.

"Deal," Lai answered.

While Sarah was driving down the road, ahead of her was a billboard sign. It had a video ad on it for SocialLight. On the ad was Freya herself. She was taking a selfie of herself and posting it directly on the site. A second after she posted the photo, it gained millions of likes, which Sarah found hard to believe.

"This could be you. It's time for your spotlight!" The closed captions on the ad said.

"Tacky," Sarah commented. A moment later she was past the billboard. That feeling was eating away at her. At first, she felt bad, but it proceeded to change into guilt. She had no real reason to help Freya, after all, Freya and her family didn't help in her time of need. Sarah's father passed away at a young age. When she turned sixteen, her mother, who was Prismarine's sister, died. This left Sarah to fend for herself. When Sarah came looking for help from the only other family she had beside her grandmother, no one was home to answer her. It seemed their life of stardom placed the Young family in what felt like a different plane of existence.

They didn't even come to her mother's funeral due to them being across the world at the time of her death, and yet....

"Lai... I'm going to need a rain check for dinner?" Sarah asked.

"Huh...? What's going on?" Lai questioned.

"I- I have to take care of something real quick," Sarah said. She looked across the road, making sure traffic was clear, and made a U-turn back the way she came.

"*I just had to look, didn't I? I can't let things end this way. If I do, I won't be able to sleep at night.*" Sarah thought to herself, determined to change fate.

She had sped fast back to the party. If it hadn't been for Lai, taking her in, she would have been living out on the streets. He didn't have to do that for someone like her, but he did anyway. She wanted to be more like him.

"Please let me make it in time!" Sarah prayed.

She arrived back at the parking lot and opened her car door. A guard in the distance saw her and called her out.

"Hey! You can't just park there!" Guard A, said.

"Sorry, but this is an emergency!" Sarah claimed as she rushed past him.

"What? What's wrong?" Guard B, asked.

"It's a crisis of the heart!" Sarah said. Both guards watched her clumsily stumble past them and gave her an odd look. They knew who she was however and didn't stop her from entering as the Bellum family was listed as a V.I.P. guest.

After running into the venue, she sprinted past Reighley who had just placed his gift down on Freya's gift table.

"Thank goodness. There's still time!" Sarah said. She ran into the ballroom and thanks to her foreknowledge she knew where Freya would end up. Hastily she grabbed her on the shoulder.

"Sarah!?! H-how have you been? I haven't seen you in ages, I honestly didn't expect you to show up." Freya said.

"Yeah, don't get used to it. I came to tell you that I saw your boyfriend sneaking out the front entrance." Sarah warned.

"What?" Freya's heart sank.

"Don't waste any time! You can still catch him." Sarah encouraged with a shove on the back. She led Freya towards the exit.

"Ah! Right!" Freya was very confused about why Sarah told her this but was thankful nonetheless. The two sprinted towards the ballroom exit and when she passed through the doors she saw the back of Reighley who was walking out of the entrance.

"He was just going to leave?" Freya thought. *"Oh no you don't. You're not getting away that easily."* Freya rushed out the door and by the time Reighley was down the steps Freya shouted from the top of her lungs.

"Reighley, I love you!" She screamed. "Didn't you hear me the first time?" Reighley was sure he wasn't followed, yet Freya somehow showed up.

"*I don't understand. Why are you here?*" Reighley thought to himself. He then looked into Freya's eyes and replied to her. "No, you don't."

"Alright. I'll be taking my leave now." Sarah said awkwardly. "*There... the rest is up to you. You have your chance now.*"

Sarah, who was right behind Freya, walked past the two and raced her way back into her car. However, she was seen by Officer Templeton, who was sitting in his police vehicle eating a burrito. He noticed the bruises on the girl and when she took off, he followed her.

Freya couldn't believe how frustrating it could be to hear someone tell her how she was feeling.

"Yes, I do. You don't know how I feel inside!" Freya yelled.

"*Yeah, I do, and that's the problem.*" Reighley thought, clenching his fist. He could see her aura. "That doesn't matter. It's only been a month. There's no way that you've fallen in love with me in that short amount of time. Besides, our deal was based on whether or not I love you, not the other way around." He said. Both guards A and B were standing between Freya. They felt awkward so the two side-stepped their way inside.

"Then tell me. How do you feel about me?" Freya asked desperately.

"I... You are someone I *could* fall in love with, but I can't." Reighley stopped looking Freya in the eyes as he lowered his head.

"Why not!?" Freya questioned.

"I just can't, okay?" Reighley shouted. It was the first time he had ever raised his voice at her, but it wouldn't stop Freya.

"BUT I LOVE YOU! I don't care who knows it!" Freya shouted even louder than before.

"Stop lying! You can't love me. How could anyone love me…? All I do is push the people I care about further away. I'm a terrible person…" Reighley tried to hide the anger on his face.

"That's not true!" Freya claimed. She hated seeing him hurting. She wanted more than anything to help him.

"It is, and I'll prove it to you…" Reighley said softly.

"Reighley stop this!" Freya pleaded.

"Do you want to know the real reason why I even dated you?" Reighley asked.

"Please! Don't do this!" Freya begged.

"It wasn't for the money. I only entertained the thought of us being together, because I thought you were *awful*. I thought that I deserved someone like you, but I was wrong. You're too good for someone like me. You're completely out of my league in every way. I'm just a hypocrite. I told you this entire time to be a good person, but that's impossible for me." Reighley looked back up at Freya. The look in his eye told Freya just how long he had been feeling this way. There wasn't self-pity, or pain, just acceptance.

"Reighley, you know that's-" Freya tried to get a word in but was abruptly interrupted.

"So our deal is off. I haven't fallen in love with you in the month we spent together. So that's that. We're breaking up." Reighley said as he turned to walk away. Freya watched the back of Reighley and noticed he hesitated with his decision.

For some unexplained reason, the phrase, "*You chase after those worth chasing,*" echoed into Freya's heart. She had never heard anyone say those words before, yet it was the green light that signaled her body to move.

"*You can't fool me.*" Freya thought. "*I won't let it end this way!*" Freya rushed after Reighley down the steps and hugged him from behind.

"Hey!? What are you doing-" Reighley felt the embrace of Freya and began to struggle slightly.

Freya ignored Reighley and pulled him close, squeezing him and refusing to let go.

"I don't care if you're a flawed person! I don't care what my dad thinks of you or if everyone else detests me. I had to chase after you because you're someone worth chasing. It doesn't matter if you love me or not. I need you in my life, and I don't want to lose you!" Freya confessed.

"To: a good person," Reighley said.

"Huh?" Freya muttered.

"Did you see my gift box?" Reighley asked.

"No," Freya answered.

"It said, 'I don't love you' on it," Reighley said. "I was trying to get you to hate me."

"That doesn't matter. Whatever it is that's eating you up inside, we'll work through it together, I promise!" Freya reassured him. "So, please... Don't leave me..." Reighley quit struggling. He knew he had to tell her. It was the only way she would let go of him.

"Freya, I... ruined someone's life," Reighley explained. He recalled the first time he deliberately hurt someone. The image of a boy clenching his knee, completely helpless on the ground was static in his mind. Freya stood there clinging on to Reighley. She didn't respond since this was the first time he opened up to her. Instead, she listened to what he had to say. "Back in middle school. There was this kid. He was a prodigy or something on the track team, but to me that was irrelevant. I only saw him as a bully. Someone who picked on other kids... One day, he and his friends were harassing a boy in my class. So I stepped in."

"That doesn't make you a bad person. You defended someone." Freya said.

"I broke one of his legs," Reighley admitted.

"But, you didn't do it on purpose though," Freya argued.

"I did. He was already on the ground after I punched him in the face, and you want to know what's even worse? I enjoyed it. After I beat up his lackeys I went straight for his leg. There was something so satisfying about snapping his kneecap in two. Knowing that the damage I had done would never truly heal. The thought that I ruined his entire running career invigorated me. Turned out that was the case. He couldn't run track any more thanks to me. His future was cut short. They had the entire confrontation on camera. I'm incredibly lucky I only got one year in Juvy." Freya didn't know what to think of Reighley's story. She knew that in his heart he was a good person, even back then. "Do you know what it's like to live with that? Do you have any idea how much I hate that part of myself? I have to wake up and live with that, every day. I can't even look myself in the eyes!" Reighley yelled. Afterward, he lowered his guard and relaxed the tension in his muscles. He knew that was it. The secret was out. He was now too scared to turn around and face the girl he loved. He couldn't bear to see the face of disgust she must have been unable to hide. He expected her to run away and yet still she didn't let go of him.

"Freya, let go. The last thing I want to do is ruin your life. That's why I need to go. Go and get as far away from you as possible. That's why you need to let go." Reighley said. There was no response for a short time. The two stood there in silence until Freya finally had the words she wanted to say.

"Reighley... leaving me would ruin my life," Freya said. He didn't have a response to that. It sounded dramatic, but he could tell by the tone of her voice how serious she was. He couldn't understand someone caring about him so much that if he disappeared, their life would be ruined. He couldn't fathom deserving someone like that in his life.

"Forget the deal we made." Freya acknowledged. "That doesn't matter. You have been nothing but good to me. Everything good that's happened to me was because you entered my life. My friends reconnecting, my friendship with Lily and Ulysses, fixing my relationship with my dad. It was all because of you. You're so selfless that it's selfish. You try to put everyone first but then forget that they want you to be happy too! The way you act is self-destructive! Nobody hates you! I can't watch you throw it all away. I love you too much for that."

Reighley turned around to see the girl he had spent the month with. She looked at him with a comforting and loving smile. Her aquamarine eyes shimmered with admiration. He couldn't get it. He told her about how he felt about himself, but she didn't seem to care.

"But... I was going to leave you, without even saying goodbye..." Reighley said.

"And I would have followed you no matter where you ended up, even if you never accepted me. I would wait forever for you to come around." Freya promised.

"Is this really alright?" Reighley asked himself. The aura he had seen when he looked into Freya's eyes remained unchanged, even after he told her his secrets. How he was a freak and a cynical monster. The aura showed him a light royal purple color without a hint of darkness in it. Her eyes had heart-shaped pupils and that was it. There was no more arrow pointing to whatever she wanted because she had what

she wanted. She simply felt love. Reighley stopped fighting it and let out a deep sigh.

"Alright... You win. I just can't get rid of you, can I?" Reighley conceded with a small laugh.

"Nope." Freya giggled. "I'm like super glue."

"You better not tell people that, I hear weirdos sniff that stuff." Reighley joked with her.

Freya finally loosened her grasp but didn't fully let go. She was smiling due to Reighley finally starting to act like himself again.

"Haven't I caught you sniffing my hair?" Freya accused.

"So, you noticed that huh? Guess I'm a weirdo." Reighley blushed.

"You're my weirdo." Freya hugged again. This time Reighley hugged her back.

"I love you... too," Reighley said. "I'm sorry. I won't ever leave you again. I promise."

"You mean it?" Freya asked.

"Yeah. I mean it." Reighley reassured.

"Good. Now, no more side chicks, capiche?" Freya snarled.

"What... Since when did you become a member of the Italian mafia?" Reighley played along.

"Since I ate pasta made by Gordan Romsly." Freya grinned.

"Goofball," Reighley commented.

"Dummy." Freya jested. "Can we go back inside now?" Freya asked.

"Yeah," Reighley answered.

To Be Continued...

Epilogue: B

During their conversation outside, Freya didn't learn until after the party that she wasn't the only one who was willing to confess their love in front of the whole world.

"I, Guinevere Pendragon, confess my undying love to Reighley Summers!" Guinevere shouted.

Shortly before... Guinevere had walked outside after being kicked out of the party. Waiting there for her was Donald who was driving the van the two had rode together in.

"Care for a ride Madam Guinevere?" Donald asked. To his surprise, this was the first time he had ever seen Guinevere smile.

"Yeah... but before we go I need your help getting something set up," Guinevere asked.

"As you wish Madam Guinevere." Donald nodded.

Back to the present... Guinevere had Donald help her salvage the remains of their equipment in the van so she could broadcast to the whole world her feelings for Reighley. She hijacked the stream once again and as The Wise Dragon of Wind Valley, she revealed herself to be Guinevere all along in dramatic fashion.

Epilogue: C

Jericho had just gotten home from work. She turned on the TV, to the Social Light channel and sat down on the couch. Morgana hopped onto her lap. She was grateful that she could still make it to see valuable moments in her children's lives, even if it wasn't in person. As the screen turned on, it showed Reighley and Freya slowly dancing together. The two were as close as could be. It looked like to them, the rest of the world didn't exist.

"Good for you." Jericho smiled. The mother who was worried about her child having his youth stolen away, was finally put to rest. Her son was, for the first time in his life, just being a teenager and enjoying himself like one. She couldn't have been more happy with the result. It reminded her of the first time she met the father of her children.

She then saw the stream show Isabelle who was hosting alongside Destiny.

"Alright, you two love birds get a room!" Isabelle yelled.

"Yeah, Loverboy. Don't you know this stream is rated TV-14!?" Destiny shouted.

Jericho let out a laugh and made a mental note to punish Reighley for letting Isabelle have exposure to the world when he got home.

Epilogue: D

Matilda Key watched the entire stream of the party and she was envious. She was staying over with Yula at Samira's house and the three stayed up and watched the whole thing. Ash Fjord inevitably showed up on the stream during the dance and the Zombie run. They watched her sacrifice herself for Reighley and Freya. Later she was dancing with Freya, Destiny, and Isabelle who they didn't recognize. They appeared to be having the time of their lives.

"Wow. Ash looks like she's having a good time...." Yula said.

"Yeah, she sure does...." Samira agreed.

"I don't see what's all that great about the party," Matilda remarked snarkily. "But... we should see if we can go next time."

"Then we need to apologize to Freya about how we've been treating her lately. She's obviously changed for the better thanks to him." Samira said. The three girls looked at Reighley who was on screen and nodded in unison and individually sent unprompted "Happy Birthday" messages to Freya.

Epilogue: E

After the party began to die down Lily and Ulysses sat outside on a bench. The two were holding hands while Lily was resting her head on Ulysses's arm.

"Where do you want to go?" Lily asked.

"You mean on our date?" Ulysses answered flustered.

"Yeah," Lily replied.

"How about I cook you ramen for dinner?" Ulysses answered.

"Yes please!" Lily acted as if she was entranced by the thought of eating Ramen.

"By all means, you're more than welcome to stick around afterward," Kokeisha said. She walked up to the two of them smoking a cigarette. She was wearing a fur coat, a wool felt dress, a party hat, and sunglasses.

"Mom!?" Ulysses flipped out.

"Oh, hush now dear. You act like you haven't seen me in ages. Is that any way to treat your mother after being apart for half a year?" Kokeisha asked.

"Umm... Hello, Mrs. Cinder." Lily greeted. "It's a pleasure to meet you."

"Oh, aren't you a proper one?" Kokeisha leaned in close on Lily. "I know where you're coming from. I married my husband because he can cook. Make sure you treat my boy well."

Epilogue: F

Standing by the refreshment table, Jim and Prismarine were snacking on hors d'oeuvres.

"Marine?" Jim asked.

"Yes, my darling husband?" Prismarine answered.

"I'm sorry love. I once promised you the world, but while I was out to get it, I didn't bring you with me." Jim apologized.

"I forgive you," Prismarine replied. "But now you have to go and get me two worlds since you messed up."

"Anything for you Marine," Jim replied. "Speaking of work, I've decided to change my schedule around so I have two days off a month that I can spend with you and Freya. I also plan to be home by dinner time during the evenings when I'm still in town."

"It's about time." Prismarine scorned.

"You seemed pleased. How about a toast to celebrate then?" Jim suggested.

"Heh, I would, but I think I should cut back on the drinking from now on," Prismarine said.

"Oh, one little glass won't hurt, will it?" Jim attempted to persuade her, by pouring wine in her cup.

"If I recall... You said that exact thing the night we had Freya."

"You're enabling me!" Prismarine laughed as she took the glass and the two indulged in liquor.

Epilogue: G

Sarah Bellum was on her way home. Because she altered the course of fate she was overly cautious during her commute. She knew that something bad was bound to happen to equalize the misfortune she altered. Using *Presage*, she peered into the nearby future, and to her surprise, it was only ten seconds ahead at the traffic lights she was approaching. The sound of sirens went off behind her as a police vehicle pulled out of an alleyway.

"Gosh dang it Lai! I can't afford another ticket." Sarah sobbed. Soon after Sarah pulled over and was approached by a police officer.

"Ma'am, do you have any idea how slow you were driving back there?" Officer Templeton asked.

"Uh, yes of course sir, I was just making sure to be safe." Sarah awkwardly replied.

"License and registration please. You do realize that you have a tail light out right?" Templeton asked.

"Yeah. I just found out about it." Sarah explained. After getting everything situated, Templeton handed her paperwork back to Sarah.

"Is everything okay at home?" Templeton asked with concern.

"Yeah, I just fell down the stairs," Sarah said.

"Wow… things must be rough back at home," Templeton thought. Concerned, he handed her a detective card. "Well if you ever want to talk about it, feel free to call this number." Templeton got a closer look at the bruises on the nervous-looking Sarah and realized she probably had a tough night.

"I'll let you off with a warning Ma'am. Drive safe, but not that safe okay? Holding up traffic could cause an accident. Oh, and make sure to get that light fixed alright?" He decided to let her off easy.

End of Epilogues...

Thank you so much for reading! I know this book is rough around the edges, but if you made it to this point, I just wanted to say I hope you enjoyed this book. I spent eleven months writing it and even longer editing it. I plan on releasing more things in the future. Including a sequel to this book. I had a lot to learn as a writer and I've grown a tremendous amount since I began. I wonder if you can see that too. It was a genuine endeavor, but to anyone who reads this, know that you can make it. There is a light at the end of the tunnel. Don't quit. No matter how hard things get, I've learned you can do anything you set your mind to if you take things one step at a time.

Don't forget to ask for help either. I couldn't have done anything without my friend and editor R.J.T. as well as my family's support. Without R.J.T.'s help, I definitely would have given up a long time ago. If you enjoyed this book, feel free to support me. However, I plan on continuing to write regardless, because it's something I love. I hope that whoever reads this may one day also be encouraged to chase after their dreams.

If you are curious about my plans for the future, well let me tell you. Almost Everything is only one of many series I wish to write. In fact, it was at the bottom of the list of stories I wanted to tell. So I hope you look forward to future book releases! I also wanted to give a special thanks to my friend J. Cooper, who was the first person to read my book through its entirety. Having someone read your work and wanting more chapters each week, really pushed me towards the final stretch of finishing this book. You're a true friend.

That all being said... Thanks again!